ENTROPY

Entropy

A novel

by

Shelby Guinn

This book is a work of fiction. The names, characters, places, and incidents are products of the writer's imagination or have been used fictitiously and are not to be construed as real. Any resemblance to persons, living or dead, actual events, locales or organizations is entirely coincidental.

Cover Photograph by David Ritter

Cover design by Blythe Dugdinson

This novel has been a long time in the making, and under no (and I repeat) no circumstances would it have been possible without my wife Kim. You are the beat of my heart and the kick in my pants. I love you a googleplex. This book in every way is dedicated to you.

Table of Contents

Entropy

Chapter One

Welcome Back, Opossums

Monday, August 27

Ponca City sat in a bubble of stench belched up from the oil refinery in the northern Oklahoma town, a potent bouquet of rotten eggs and burnt petroleum, branding the town far deeper into its visitors' memories than anything else the city had to offer. Most residents no longer noticed the reek, but Earnest Graves, as he entered the city's reeking bubble, wrinkled his nose, releasing a series of sneezes and spattering his windshield.

"Gross," his younger brother Eddie groaned from the rider's seat. "That 'snot very polite... get it...' snot polite... snot... hahahahah."

Earnest pulled an already damp handkerchief from his back pocket and blew his nose into it.

"Shut up," he said to his brother, the late summer cold and the first day of his senior year stifling his sense of humor.

"Look, Earnie, the Pioneer Man."

"Huh? What are you talking about?" he asked, agitated and confused. Earnest sniffed, seeing only the Pioneer Woman statue, the bronze symbol to the city's greatness, at least according to the city's forefathers who had had it built.

"Oh nothing, Earnie," Eddie howled in riotous laughter, slapping his leg.

After dropping Eddie off at the junior high, Earnest backtracked to the high school, pondering his new place in the world as a high school senior, and in spite of all the hype and glory bestowed upon the graduating class, Earnest found it an uncertain place. He stood at the precipice of his future, waiting to be pushed.

Earnest followed a line of cars into the parking lot, passing Hershel, the guard who quietly stood at the door of his brick hut puffing a cigarette and waving cars in to park. Earnest moved on, indifferent to Hershel and his wishes, and parked by a tall cyclone fence beside the football team's practice field. As he stepped from his rusting old Ford Fairlane, he heard the marching band practicing in the distance.

The world seemed a little smaller as a senior. He thought about the authority that the twelfth grade gave to him—if only within the confines of the building—and he grew a little larger.

Earnest heaved his chest, deeply inhaling the scent of his shrinking world.

And he sneezed again as the stinking Ponca City air burst from his lungs, inciting his nostrils into a flurry of rapid-fire sneezes, gagging the inflated airs out of him; a rush of air pushed through his lips, causing them to flap together like a horse. He blew his nose into his handkerchief, closing his nostrils with several quick pinches to ward off any more sneezes. Earnest watched as a pair of underclassmen walked past him, shooting him condescending glances. *Screw you, I'm a senior.* He sniffed his irritated nose and followed them into the building.

Three months had passed since Earnest had been in the

building, but upon entering, his senses were inundated with such familiar things he felt as if summer had never happened: tennis shoes slapping against polished wax floors; locker doors squeaking open and slamming closed; florescent lights flickering and buzzing; and conversations rumbling from wall to wall. Things as constant as time, drawing him back.

A growing menagerie of students filled the hallways, and Earnest weaved through the crowd of strange and familiar faces, holding his collection of virgin notebooks tightly to his side. Ahead, he noticed the students, dividing like the Red Sea to the side walls, sweeping him along with them.

An older, red-faced man, round bellied, round nosed, the Moses of this parting, pushed through the crowd, a dust mop as his staff. Earnest's friend, Ian, walked at the old man's side while the old fellow swept.

And they were singing.

De Camptown ladies sing this song,
Doo-da, Doo-da
De Camptown racetrack's two miles long
Oh, de doo-da day.

"Come on Earnie, you know the words! It's Earl's favorite song!" Ian baited. Then he and Earl began the chorus.

Earnest shook his head, noticing a few students staring who were not familiar with Earl or his singing.

The duo swept past him with waves of students rushing back together filling the hall. The pair had not walked far when Earnest heard Mr. Riggins's voice thunder, ending Ian's songs.

"Why didn't you sing with Crazy Earl and me?" Ian asked seconds later, scurrying up to his friend.

"Right…and get my butt chewed out along with yours."

"Riggins never even saw me." Ian grinned as he gave his hair an arrogant flick. "In Indianapolis, they never would have hired a retard to work in school. He would've been even crazier when we finished with him."

Earnest glanced at a slip of paper with his locker number and combination while fumbling with his notebooks.

"Earnie, it's the first day of school, and you already have your supplies. Hmmm, forgot your pocket protector and slide ruler?"

"There's worse things than being a nerd, you know, like an asshole for example…" Earnest snapped back.

While they walked, following the locker numbers toward his own, Earnest listened as Ian began soloing Earl's song, sustaining the 'do-dah-days' of the chorus with an odd pleasure.

"You're in a good mood today," Earnest remarked as they stopped.

"Yeah, sophomore girls," he uttered with a smile and a nod.

Looking at the paper, Earnest went through the combination and pulled on the locker's handle, but the lock did not give, so he went through the combination again.

"What about sophomore girls?" Earnest asked, trying the handle, but still not releasing.

"We're seniors now. They'll go out with us. How'd I look? Good, huh?" Ian said offering a pose.

Earnest had had the same thought about sophomore girls during the summer, but hearing it from Ian, he realized it sounded pathetic.

"Uh-oh," Ian chimed.

"What?"

Ian began singing Miss America's song.

Earnest turned to see RaLF approaching, her entourage orbiting like satellites about her.

"Mmmm, she's still beautiful," Earnest thought aloud.

"She's a bitch," Ian replied, "They all are."

Earnest ignored Ian's comments, taking in the width, breadth, and height of that, since even before suffering the ravages of puberty, he had held as nearly holy, cultivating what he saw as a unique form of lust in its most pure state.

Since kindergarten, Rachael L. Fletcher had been a distant yet distinct part of Earnest's life. At five years of age, with long hair flowing in waves of brown, with eyes so large, so dark they were better suited to a cartoon character than a living, breathing girl, she charmed him. And after growing into a woman, molded in his mind to the greatest point of perfection he was able to imagine, she still charmed him.

As the entourage walked, Earnest's heart pitter-pattered, flip-flopped, and continued on in a whole string of impossible verbs. The group of girls moved toward him. She drew closer and closer, every face blurring but hers. Time slowed, as inevitably the miles between them shrank to yards, to feet, to inches, to...

"Hello, RaLF," he blurted standing an arm's length away.

To which she smiled, more from reflex than a genuine response, nodded like a pageant queen on a parade float, and moved on, adding to the large chasm between them.

"What a Geek!" Earnest heard as the herd of RaLF's friends passed, stinging like a sudden slap.

"Bitch!" Ian quickly barked back, surprising Earnest. Then he turned back to Earnest shaking his head. "Told ya."

Feeling hollow, Earnest silently turned away and leaned his forehead against the cold metal of the locker door, feeling a painful rumble inside. Mindlessly, he began the combination another time, distracting his injured senior ego.

The bell then rang, signaling the new school year beginning in five minutes.

"See you later. Oh-dee-do-da-dayyyy!" Ian barked, punctuating it with a small howl.

Earnest forced a laugh as Ian walked away.

"Excuse me, Earnest."

Earnest turned around and faced Anne Endo. Graced with a hint of her Japanese father in her olive face, she stood thin and small. He moved aside, and she went to the locker that he had tried to open. She turned the dial, and the locker door swung open. Earnest felt struck by a weird embarrassment as she set her notebooks inside.

"I'm running a little late…already starting work on the paper… What hour do you have Journalism?" she asked, each word precise in her gentle voice.

"Fourth hour," Earnest answered still awed.

"Have you seen Daniel yet today?"

"Not yet, why?"

"You know. He had his surgery this summer. I was wondering how he looked. Anyway, have a nice day, Earnest. See you, fourth hour," she said, sharing her gentle smile, then walking away.

He watched her, scratching his head. Then he looked again at the slip of paper. He had locker number 1089. Anne had just opened 1098.

Idiot. He shuffled through the frenzied crowd, taking the few steps to the right locker. And, when he opened it after one turn of the combination, the final bell rang. Earnest cringed, tardy his first day as a senior.

* * *

She heard the ringing, and Mary Christmas punched the snooze button a third time, rolling away from the clock and sticking her face into the crack between the mattress and wall.

Then the knock, the Deacon's knock, a shave-and-a-haircut-two-bits knock, sounded at the door.

"Mary, let's get up, now." Even through the pillow stuffed over her head to muffle the sounds of life's unpleasantness, that voice—though deep and rich, even pleasant by most standards—remained the most displeasing sound she knew, assaulting her like a hand drill slowly gnawing into her skull. How often had she heard that knock, that voice, pushing her into a brand new day? She had to endure it only one more year, not even a year, ten months, and then no more.

After she showered and dressed, putting on a faded pair of denim overalls, a baggy, cotton, pastel blouse, and old tennis shoes over ankle socks, Mary went to the kitchen. Her parents waited at the table. The Deacon, as always wearing a pressed suit, and her mother, a dainty, pretty lady in her sixties with thick short, white hair and light, smooth skin, lightly wrinkled from age but not exposure to mother nature's elements, welcomed Mary to her place. She sat, taking a bite from the piece of toast that set upon her plate.

"Mary," her mother began, "a little make-up wouldn't hurt."

She took another bite, refusing to answer the all too familiar comment and just curled her lip.

"The hardest thing I've had to accept in my life," The Deacon said pointing his fork at Mary, "mind you, I've not accepted it, I've merely put it in the Lord's hands, is the fact that you have not yet embraced your mother's and my faith."

Lord, he likes to hear himself. Mary put the last bit of toast into her mouth.

For guidance and assurance, that voice was the perfect tool for leading a flock to righteousness. It was the same voice with which he'd wrestled the church away from its pastor and even its denomination years before Mary had been born. He still led the church, yet kept his title of Deacon. But she had grown tired of his holy rumble—where every insignificant statement—"Mary, let's get up now"—carried eternal weight.

"But all the same, you are our last daughter, the last to leave the nest, and while you are not leaving, yet, your mother and I just wanted you to know that we are proud of you, the things that you have done, and what you are going to do."

Mary jiggled her foot under the table, irritated, as if he could even guess what she was going to do. If she had been hearing these words from that voice for the first time, the rhetorical sincerity oozing from him might have moved her, but instead, she gagged and choked on them; every school year, every event in her life, he spoke those words.

So, she ignored him, taking a bite of her breakfast, Mary interrupted, "I really need to leave…"

The Deacon took his napkin and wiped a tiny line of sweat perched from his upper lip. "Well then…, let's pray."

Mary watched her parents bow their heads as she took a sip of milk.

"Father, thank you for this day and all the blessings within it," the Deacon began.

Mary's fork scraped her plate as she cut the cooling omelet.

"We ask that You watch over Mary as she begins her senior year of high school."

Her lips lightly smacked together as she chewed, and Mary made no attempt to hide it. By the time the Deacon completed his prayer, Mary had finished her breakfast. And when her parents raised their heads, Mary was leaning back in her chair, a smirk covering her face as she ran her butter knife down her tongue. Then gently placing the utensil upon her plate, she said, "I'm ready."

Mary stood and walked to the front door, grabbing her book bag from the Deacon's recliner. She flung it over her shoulder, left the house, not waiting for the Deacon to follow, and stood at his car.

Mary did not drive though she badly wanted to. She had set the curve in her Driver's Ed. class just like in so many of her other classes. But the Deacon had not yet willed it to be; it was penance for her faithlessness. Mary remained forever a passenger, so she made sure she often had a need for transport. It was penance for their faithfulness.

"It's a beautiful day," the Deacon said stepping outside. He momentarily stopped and stood on the top step of the concrete porch, brushing his suit coat.

Mary glanced at him, and she noticed that he was looking past her. He had not spoken to her particularly, she realized, but she saw he was correct in what he had said. The sun shone through a cloudless sky, and the morning felt comfortable, not humid nor overly hot as usual for August.

Mary climbed into the car and waited.

"Are you going to be ready to try the driving test soon?" the Deacon made a kind of invitation to salvation, taking his place behind the steering wheel and starting the car.

"I've been ready," she said, but he ignored her.

"There are just two things that make a person truly feel free,..." he continued as he looked out of the back window and pulled onto the street. Then shifting into drive, he said with a chuckle, "Christ and a new car."

She sat back; her jaw clinched tightly together. "I'm free enough." She growled.

The car finally turned into a lane leading to a U at the west side of the school. Before the car had reached the loading zone, Mary said she could get out and opened her door, setting off the buzzer as the car inched forward.

"Whoa," the Deacon spouted, the car jerking to a stop with a short screech of the tires. The car behind him honked.

"Mary, don't do that. Wait until the car stops."

She smiled at the Deacon, the door ajar, the buzzer ringing.

"Have a good day..." the Deacon said as his irritation ebbed, reaching to pat his daughter's hand, but she pulled away, so he felt only the faint touch of her escaping hand beneath his fingertips.

Mary noticed that he paused before saying whatever was on his mind. Then, with an unusual quiver in his voice, he said, "God bless you, Mary."

"I'll be home late tonight. I have work at the library to do, and I'll probably be doing some stuff for the paper, too. Don't worry;

Deacon, I'll get a ride." She hurried out of the car, gripping her book bag so tightly that her fingers hurt, never glancing back to see him drive away before she entered the school building.

Mary headed for her locker to dispose of the load in her bag. As she moved through the crowd, she stifled the disdain she held for most of the people about her. They seemed so happy and content in their mediocrity, it drove her crazy. She wanted away from these people—these stupid, redneck people.

"Crap," she grumbled after opening her locker. Bumper stickers covered the back of the door, proclaiming some god-awful rock and roll bands: Led Zeppelin, Aerosmith, Ted Nugent, OX. She began picking at one and tore loose a small strip. "Crap," she mumbled aloud.

"Hewwo Mawy," Mary heard from behind, as she tore another long strip loose.

She turned around, flicking a sticky strip of plastic from her finger. "Daniel?" she asked, almost unsure. The lisping voice belonged to her co-editor of the school paper, and the clothes: the permanent press slacks, the clean but wrinkled white dress shirt, and the wide clip-on tie were certainly his. But the face looked different.

"Yeth, i'th me."

"You did it? You had the surgery? You,... you almost look normal."

"Yeth, I do."

"Should you be back so soon? Plastic surgery takes time to heal...so I've heard."

"Wea, the doctow towed me to west a little longew, but, we've got the papew to do," Daniel said, his lisp still as strong as ever and his speech slightly staccatoed as he struggled to choose the correct word.

Shitshitshitshitshit, Mary thought.

"But I'm fine, weawwy. The thwewwing ith about gone, and the bwuitheth awe fading."

After a few seconds of deciphering Daniel's words, a skill at which she had not improved greatly since first meeting him two years before, she studied his face, not noticing any swelling; like her, Daniel was overweight and always exhibiting some roundness, but the yellow and blue bruises running down both sides of his face and around his mouth were obvious. Mary thought it ironic that the surgery Daniel had to lessen his Mongol appearance resulted in a bruise looking like Fu Manchu's mustache.

"Awe you going to the Jouwnawilithm woom?"

"Not yet."

"I will thee you thewe." He grinned proudly, and then he said as if nearly bursting, "Pwaith God, aww things become new." His arms swung in long arcs, his round body bobbing, as he walked away.

Growling, she took some paperback books from her book bag and threw them onto the top shelf of her locker. Then she grabbed a bag of Oreos that she had packed and angrily threw the book bag into the locker. Gracelessly ripping the Oreos open, Mary stuffed two cookies into her mouth. The cookies broke apart in violent bites. She had hoped the hope of all hopes: that Daniel would miss at least the first week of school, but her hopes were dashed—punctuated out of existence—by his diseased and swollen enthusiasm.

Although she respected what Daniel had accomplished in his life, working hundreds and thousands of hours with his mother in order to do the impossible—to become a B-average student in spite of having Down's syndrome, a one in a trillion achievement (Mary reasoned the chromosomal screw-up in Daniel's case was more physical than mental), he still could not help but drive her crazy. Just like her parents, she saw Daniel as one of the fruit loops that held the Bible belt in its place, as he seemed certain and assured that he had been touched by the hand of God. He called it his witness; she called it his witlessness.

Eating another cookie, her aggravation began to fade. She looked up and down the hallway among the groups and the stray lonesome walkers and did not see a single soul she liked. Then she noticed Earnest, the so-called "art-coordinator" for the paper. To Mary, he personified completely the half-assed nature of Ponca City, having a title for only pasting headlines and page numbers for the school paper. While she watched him go through the combination to his locker a third time, she could not stop the urge to mock him and his friend who stood beside him like a trained monkey. Mary watched him become distracted by a hoard of the feminine elite. And after they ignored him, Mary could not contain herself.

"What a geek!" she bellowed, tossing the cookies into her locker.

When she heard Ian's reply, Mary looked back over her shoulder to see Earnest back at his locker, working the combination again, and his friend angrily spouting off at the group of girls walking away. *Morons.* Then Mary grabbed her books, slammed the door shut, and walked away as the first bell rang.

* * *

Jamie Messereli popped open the hood of his rusty, '69 Chevy, unfastened the lid to the air filter, and stuck a screwdriver into the carburetor to hold open the choke. As he stood up, pushing the long strings of hair from his face, he heard the screen door of his house open with a long, painful squeak. He turned to see a strange man walk out.

A cigarette hung from the man's mouth while an old discolored, misshapen straw cowboy hat sat at an odd angle at the back of his head. He walked down the porch steps, carrying a can of beer with one hand, tucking his unbuttoned shirt into his dirty jeans with his other hand, and hacking a deep scratchy cough which he did not cover with either hand. He did not acknowledge Jamie as he walked around him and climbed into the pick-up truck parked next to Jamie's car.

"Tell your mama I said g'bye, and if she wants to see me, I'll be at K.C.'s tonight," the man smiled, deepening the wrinkles in his sun-baked face. Then he started the truck and drove away.

"Screw you," Jamie spat, climbing behind the steering wheel. He pumped the gas pedal three times, and then turned the key. The motor roared to life and continued to scream until he removed the screwdriver from the choke and readjusted the throttle with it. Then he slammed the hood shut, muting the clanky growl of the engine.

While the car idled, he went back into the house. His mother had left for work an hour earlier, so an unnatural silence filled the house. He walked through the cluttered living room and entered the kitchen. Somewhere in the pile of crap upon the kitchen table lurked a carton of cigarettes. Jamie scattered and dug and repiled until he found it and took a pack, rolling it up in the sleeve of his

OX '79 World Tour concert t-shirt. He then walked to the refrigerator, opened it and took a can of Coke from inside it. He noticed that the man had taken his mother's last can of beer, and he laughed.

That'll piss her off.

When he went back outside, he slammed the door behind him without locking it. The car continued running while he lazily walked down the porch steps, his boots landing hard upon the wooden steps with loud, sharp thuds. As he stepped into the grassless, tire-rutted yard, he took the pack of cigarettes from his sleeve and opened it, letting the breeze carry away the cellophane wrapper. He patted the top against his other hand until a few cigarettes popped out. He slid out one with his mouth and held it unlit as he rolled the pack back into his sleeve.

After he got into his car, he took a book of matches advertising one of the bars his mother frequented from the dash and lit his cigarette. He chased the smoke with a gulp of the Coke, holding it in his mouth until the acid burned his tongue and then swallowed. As he backed out of the drive, he had the same thought that had put him to sleep the night before: *why go back*. Everyone else in his family had either dropped out or had been kicked out before they had even reached their senior year.

Jamie could not think of any possible answer other than he had been there so long, he might as well finish. But deep down, he knew there was more. Never able to say it and barely able to think it, Jamie knew that he did not want to be like his mother or her friends, their whole lives contained within the open hours of the various bars and clubs and taverns in and around Ponca City. He felt that he was above it; he wanted desperately to be above it.

As he drove, he pushed an 8-track of Deep Purple, a two dollar price tag from a pawn shop sticking to it, into the tape player, but his thoughts consumed him so deeply that the music did little more than mix with the noise of the wind blowing in the open windows. The closer he got to the school, the more anxious he became. Memories of Jefferson Elementary flashed through his mind like a slide show. Always tall for his age and dark, the other kids thought that he was an Indian, though as far as he knew he had no trace of Indian blood, so they feared and dreaded him, alienating him from their play, while at other times giving him money or candy from the fear that they had angered him and the dread he would beat them up. Now, taking another drag from his cigarette and another drink from his Coke, Jamie was aware of his own fear and dread, aware he was the only one who knew and probably cared.

When he finally reached the school, Jamie could not let himself turn into the parking lot, so he began circling the high school complex. People were everywhere, moving in droves toward the buildings. And he continued to circle until the place turned nearly desolate.

Finally, he stopped his car in the street at the front of the school. He eyed the large lawn that rolled out between him and the building and looked blankly at the large banner posted in the ground that read, "The Class of '80 Sez 'Welcome Back, Opossums.'" Then he looked at the three-story, cold, brick, structure atop the small hill, the same building his mother attended and quit some twenty years before. He took a final drag and flipped the butt of his cigarette out of the window onto the brick street as his car sputtered in place. A car sped past him and turned left at the intersection ahead. "Another slacker," Jamie muttered, and followed it into the parking lot. Hershel walked to Jamie's car and peered into window.

"Yer' late," Hershel said.

"Hey, I'm a senior."

"Well, get to class, Mr. Seenyer'," and he waved Jamie by.

Jamie parked his car at the far north end of the parking lot away from the school. He slowly walked toward the building, wondering how late he was. Then he took his class schedule from his back pocket. Although it was damp and smeared with sweat, he glanced over 'American Government' to see 'Room 9.' And still, he slowly walked.

* * *

"Room 9," Earnest repeated, standing at its entrance; then, he walked inside and froze after three short steps. An assortment of outcasts and troublemakers followed behind him, adding to those already in the room, the smell of cigarettes wafting from their clothes as they passed him. The realization then came to Earnest, if he in fact had an element, he was definitely out of it.

Earnest rechecked his schedule and all was as it should be—as far as the schedule was concerned. He had requested college prep classes, but it looked as if they were equipping him for prison, instead. And while the rest of the procession of tardy students took their seats, Earnest remained motionless at the front of the class, almost as if he was on display.

"Sit down, Geek!"

Earnest angrily turned to the source and was quickly humbled by the sight of Angus Bray, a large fellow whose face was darkened with a day's growth of beard. He wore a tank top, revealing a forest of hair. Earnest shrank away and cowered to place in the nearest empty desk; his manhood not just squashed but put into question by comparison.

"There is no name calling in my class," the teacher and former soldier, Mr. Riggins, spoke and rose from behind his desk. That Ian had laughed off this man's reproach amazed Earnest. Mr. Riggins, a huge man with a buzzed-top hair cut, had the reputation as the loudest and angriest teacher in the school.

"God gives grace to sinners," Mr. Riggins rumbled, scanning the class, "I won't after today. You will not be tardy to my class again. My name is Mr. Riggins..." He paused long enough to write his name on the chalkboard, the chalk crumbling into pieces as he wrote.

Earnest nodded silently, not wanting to be here.

"Hey, Buzz, cool your engines." Angus smirked from the back of the class.

Mr. Riggins's face changed as he turned back towards the students. The wrinkles in Mr. Riggins's forehead deepened into canyons. His dark complexion turned crimson, and his face bubbled like lava. The frown covering his face melted to a violent grimace while his eyes fired to two small suns.

Earnest slid into his desk, hiding behind his notebooks, and prepared himself for the battle of the colossus.

Mr. Riggins opened his mouth and out burst an earthquake.

"YOU ARE A STUDENT, UNDERSTAND?!!!" With every room-shaking syllable, the teacher walked closer to Angus until his face stopped inches away from Angus's. "I AM YOUR TEACHER!!!

YOU WILL UNDERSTAND OR I WILL BE CLEANING YOU OUT OF THE SOLES OF MY SHOES!!! NOW TELL ME, YOU UNDERSTAND!!!"

Earnest certainly understood.

The crimson hue of Mr. Riggins's face spread to Angus. Mr. Riggins's thundering voice and Angus's embarrassment pushed the mute giant deeper into his desk than had his sloth, making Angus look as if he had shrunk to half of his original size.

"DO YOU UNDERSTAND?!!!"

"Yeah," Angus answered, taking his place among the Earnests of the world.

"WHAT?!!!"

"Yes, sir!" Angus answered more loudly, readjusting his slouch while a heavy silence dipped over the classroom.

Mr. Riggins backed away. The anger and the bright color of his face drained with each step away from the humbled student, and when he spoke again from behind the podium beside his desk, his tone returned to the one he had used at the beginning of class. "Okay, let's begin."

After Mr. Riggins finished the roll call and his diatribe on classroom rules a tall, slender, dark young man with long dark brown hair pulled into a ponytail, entered the room.

"You're tardy," Mr. Riggins said to the young man.

"I couldn't get my car started. Here's my admit slip."

Mr. Riggins took the pink piece of paper and glanced over it.

"Take a seat, Jamie," Mr. Riggins directed. "Try not to let it happen again."

Blow it out your ass, Jamie thought as he took the desk next to Earnest.

Earnest smelled the thick aroma of smoke from Jamie, too. *Another loser.* Earnest leaned forward, resting his chin in his hands.

Jamie looked at Earnest, then turned away to stare out of the window while Mr. Riggins droned on. A bird fluttered past the window, its wings flapping wildly as if it had momentarily lost it rhythm, and, for an instant, its ability to fly. Jamie wondered if he should have skipped school after all. In the distance, beyond the horizon, Jamie saw a line of smoke drift away from the oil refinery, dissipating in the cloudless blue sky.

Chapter Two

A Long Day's End

The line of smoke billowing in the distance caught Mary's eye but did not hold her attention as she stared out the journalism room's third story window. The 4th hour newspaper staff filled the room, some in chairs, some at desks, some leaning against walls and some just standing, and she stood before them set to take her place as the power upon the throne. This was her time. So, the more Mr. Addison endlessly spoke, the more she felt the need to assert herself. Her fingers found their way into her mouth, and she began gnawing loose pieces of flesh and tattered nail.

"I'm excited about the newspaper this year. I don't believe that I've ever had such a…an interesting pair as co-editors. Daniel, it's great to have you back. I was a little worried after visiting you in the hospital, but you look great."

Daniel smiled, rubbing his eyes, as a spattering of applause among the staff greeted him. He was more tired than he had expected to be. He looked over at Mary. And she looked back at him, her eyes distant and steely, harboring not a hint of camaraderie in return. "Yeth, thir, I'm happy to be hewe," he replied, turning his eyes back to the teacher.

"The first issue's theme is Welcome Back." Mary suddenly

interjected, interrupting Daniel's move to the forefront, "I talked to some of you last week about getting pictures this morning and talking to students. You did that, right?"

Some in the group nodded while Daniel looked confused.

"Sophomores, too? Some of you like to do random surveys by randomly talking to your friends."

"Yes, Mary, sophomores too." Anne Endo spoke up. "I did the interviews myself."

"Great. Our first paper is out in three weeks. That gives us all one week to fall in love and one week to get it put together. So, unless Mr. Addison has anything else to say, break up into your departments. I've already given your department editors directions." She looked over to Mr. Addison who shook his head.

As the meeting ended, Daniel turned to Mary, whispering, "When did *we* dethide on a theme?"

Mary smiled, "I decided, since you were mending. Is there something wrong with it? It made sense to me....but if you have a better idea...."

"No, that'th not what I mean..." He shook his head, tripping over his words, "It'th a pawtnewthip...."

"I'm sorry, Daniel. I thought I was doing you a favor."

Daniel rubbed his face with his hands. Somewhere between his brain and his mouth, his thoughts, his sentences collided into a mishmash of stifled words. "Oh, God," he silently prayed, but he couldn't even form a prayer in his frustration, so he just stopped and mumbled, "Thank you."

Mary's smile grew. She thought about what she had said earlier, about falling in love, and remembering a passage that she had read over the summer, something about it being better for a leader to be feared than loved. And she was getting there.

“I should show you some other things that I’ve come up with.”

Daniel, sullen and acquiescent, nodded. His tongue slightly protruded, his lower lip sticking out, emphasizing his pout. Mary turned away from him and walked to their desk, Daniel quietly behind.

Earnest jumped up from his small group and moved towards them. “Hey, Mary, I’ve been working on something over the summer. I have this cartoon idea.” He handed her his drawing, a four panel strip that he called *Earnie*. Suspiciously, Mary took the page and began reading. It began with Earnie, the main character, asking his best friend, Zeke, "What do you call Bambi with both his eyes gouged out?" Zeke drawled, "No idear," shrugging his shoulders. In the third panel Earnie asked, "What do you call Bambi with both eyes gouged out and all four legs hacked off?" Finally, Zeke cleverly continued, “Still no idear," as drawn sinister laughter surrounded their heads.

Mary looked back up at Earnest. “Are you serious?”

Earnest smiled, “Yeah!”

Daniel stuck out his hand to Mary to look at it. But Mary’s hand kept navigating the sheet so he couldn’t grasp it. Then slowly her hand closed in around the paper. Earnest’s eyes grew to large globes darting between Mary and Daniel as she turned his work into a wrinkled mess.

“I’ll get back to you when we do our mutilated animal issue.” Then she snapped, “You want something in the paper? Stick to the theme,” announcing just loudly enough to be heard over the rumble, drawing everyone’s attention; then she turned to Daniel and ordered, “Come on.”

Earnest, dumbfounded and embarrassed as they walked away, plopped back down into his chair, cursing Mary and pulling a sheet of paper from his notebook. *Fine, she wants me to stay with the theme. No problem.* He divided the page into four panels. Then he started drumming the table with his pencil. His eyes drifted about the room, landing upon RaLF. She flicked her head, sending her thick wavy hair out of her eyes, as she wrote in her notebook. He sighed and looked back at his paper, leaning his jaw upon his hand. *We're seniors and she still thinks I'm a geek. Crap.*

He started sketching out a couple of stick figures. The words 'great summer' floated to him from somewhere, and he filled a word balloon with them. Once again Earnie and Zeke were talking. And quickly an idea unfolded. In the first panel Zeke said, "Wasn't it a great summer?" Earnie countered harshly, "What do you mean?!" He continued, mouth opened wide into the second and third panels bellowing, "I was broke and sunburned. I had poison ivy and swelled up to the size of Orson Wells. I was allergic from insect bites! I was miserable!" Finally in the last panel, Zeke said with emphatic lines shooting from his head, "Now, back to school." Earnie then retorted, more glumly, "I miss summer."

Earnest sat back. "That ought'a fit her damn theme..." he mumbled under his breath.

Soon the upperclassmen began filtering out of the room, having cultivated a habit of not waiting on the lunch bell to leave. When the bell finally did ring, Mary was left alone with Daniel who at sometime had fallen asleep at his desk, sitting up and snoring in an amazingly consistent cadence. Gathering her things to leave, Mary found her own breathing slipping into the same rhythm. She held her breath, trying to counter it with another meter, but as her mind floated to another thought, her breathing slipped back into unison with Daniel's. She growled at the lisping little jerk and walked toward him, but when she faced him and watched a string of spittle drip from his mouth to his lap, she could stand no more.

"Daniel," she barked, "wake up!"

He jerked abruptly, disoriented and confused.

"What...what.....what..whatwhat?" he sputtered as the string of spittle popped like a rubber band.

"It's time for lunch." Mary moaned.

Daniel wiped the sleep from his eyes, and then, taking his tie, he wiped away the spittle that glistened across his lower lip and chin.

"Oh, for Pete's sake Daniel, get some manners," Mary snarled and walked away.

"Hmm, hath the beww wang yet?" he asked still slightly dizzy from sleep.

"Yes. You notice anyone else here?"

"Man, I'm tiud." Daniel said as he rubbed his hands gracelessly over his face.

"Maybe you should stay home until you're stronger," Mary hinted.

"I'u be okay," Daniel insisted to both Mary and himself. Sore from Mary walking all over him, he rose to his feet and stretched his arms high over his head. A moan slipped out his mouth as he wrapped himself with his arms, stretching his limbs as far as they would go. Then as he relaxed he grabbed the arm of the chair in which he sat and made a quick twist. A series of pops ran up his spine, and he sighed again and smiled, his large round lips wrapping around his full, red, bubbly face.

He sat slumped until Mary left the room. And then he took a paper bag from his desk drawer, pulled his lunch out of it and quietly ate, enjoying the room's rare peace.

* * *

The lunch line extended far away from the counter, but Earnest gladly waited. He loved whatever it was that they called a hamburger, drenched with mustard and piled with potato chips: a $1.25 gourmet feast.

"Hey Buddy," Ian grabbed Earnest's shoulder, "let's get a table close to your Midnight Lust."

"What are you talking about?

"RaLF, dumbass." He turned from Earnest and his eyes shot across the cafeteria looking for his prey. "You won't believe this but she is in every one of my morning classes. I sat right beside her, every time… She is one fine smelling woman. That perfume of hers is potent."

"Were you sniffing at her the whole time?"

"As much as I could," Ian answered. "I couldn't help it. The air was saturated with the scent of Midnight Lust. I'd recognize that smell anywhere. She must bathe in the stuff. I felt like a dog in heat."

Ian laughed at his remark. Earnest couldn't muster one, barely giving a smile, percolating with envy as he longed for his own encounter with RaLF's Midnight Lust.

"Ooh, look, and Mr. Studly isn't with her. He must have first lunch," Ian said ever so slyly, bouncing on the balls of his feet.

Earnest glanced at his friend. He had yet to figure out Ian's fascination with RaLF. It was certainly different from the infatuation he himself harbored for her. What Ian had hidden behind his smile, Earnest couldn't say. What lurked in Ian's mind, Earnest couldn't even guess.

Irritated, Earnest remained subdued while Ian's words rang in his head. *That RaLF is a fine smelling woman*. Sure, Earnest knew that RaLF smelled fine. Everything about her was fine; the thick wavy strands of cinnamon hair cascading to her shoulders and beyond, framing a face that looked better bare than painted in make up; the curvature of her—not too small—not too large—but just right—body. Everything about her *was* fine; the least of which was her smell.

And who the hell was Ian to be sniffing at her anyway, the miserable bastard?

Many years before the encroachment of Ian's nose, RaLF had been Earnest's first held hand, and that—along with a distant week in third grade when he and RaLF had actually been a couple—still lingered upon his mind like a sorrowful, blurred tattoo. On a Monday afternoon, summoning up some reservoir of strength, Earnest had sent his friend Brian to ask Suzie if RaLF would be his girlfriend. Traveling back down the chain, the answer returned as yes. He was ecstatic and over the next few days carried on in childlike amour. At school when they were lucky enough to sit together, they secretly held hands beneath the table. During the evenings when they were apart, Earnest called her and spoke with her about nothing in particular. He did everything that he could think to do. And by Friday, it was over.

RaLF sent Suzie directly to Earnest, avoiding the middleman altogether.

"RaLF doesn't want to be your girlfriend. She wants to go with Bill again."

Expressionless, Earnest looked at Suzie and said okay, taking his place at the pencil sharpener and grinding the utensil down to its eraser. The breakup had come without any warning, but so had RaLF's acceptance days before. Besides, what else could be said? Bill was every third (forth, fifth, sixth...twelfth) grade girl's Mr. Right. And Earnest was anybody's Mr. Yougottabekidding.

"Let's go see the queen!" Ian grinned, taking his tray and hurrying to find a place near RaLF. Earnest scurried to keep up.

"Earnie, it's the bearer of Midnight Lust!" Ian exclaimed upon seeing her at her table.

"Dammit," RaLF mumbled, "What are you doing in here, you freak? Isn't there enough cafeteria for you to stay away?" she asked, aggravation coloring every word.

"I brought my buddy to smell you," Ian answered with a smile and a deep, deep sniff. "He couldn't believe how good …."

"If you don't stop that..." she growled, her glare tearing Earnest to shreds.

"What...? My nose can't help but admire you."

"I'd like to rip that nose off your freaking face."

"Go away, you jerk! Bill'll kick your ass, so leave her alone." A girl piped in.

"Oooh, I guess I better go away, then." Ian feigned fear then he laughed, sitting at the table behind them.

"Did you have to do that?" Earnest asked taking his seat across from Ian. He could see the back of RaLF's head from where he sat.

"Get over it. You're not impressing her." Ian smirked, "She thinks we're nothin'. So what if I give her a hard time?"

Earnest shrugged his shoulders, mute, stinging from the truth in Ian's words.

Ian leaned back and said loudly, "She dooo smell sweet." He was enraptured by his rudeness as he stuffed his mouth.

Earnest secretly inhaled, the fragrance of dismay blended with the sweetness of longing. It was her scent, and he blushed.

"Say, are you still looking for a job?" Ian asked between bites, his cheeks stuffed full like a squirrel.

"Yeah," Earnest answered solemnly not having turned up anything for a month.

"Here," Ian said pulling a paper from his back pocket, "how about this? It's a placemat. I saw it last night and thought of you. Aren't I sweet?"

Earnest unfolded a job application for Harvey's Fine Fried Burgers. Across the top it read *Join The Happy Harvey Crew,* picturing a drawing of a handsome, racially diverse adolescent group smiling widely, dressed in their Harvey's Fine Fried Burger garb. And glinting in their finely sketched eyes, Earnest saw their invitation to join them.

"Well, I could fill it out..." Earnest said then asked, "Hey, have you ever seen the Pioneer Man?" remembering something his brother had said that morning.

"That stupid thing, my uncle showed it to me a couple of years ago after I moved here."

"Really? What is it?"

"It's so stupid. He loves it, stupid redneck." Ian's attention turned again from Earnest, "Look at her..." he muttered.

"Who? RaLF?" Earnest looked over as she and her friends were leaving.

Ian loaded his tray with trash. "Man, I hate her...." he muttered under his breath. "C'mon." he ordered.

Earnest had barely started eating, so he jumped up shoving the application into his back pocket and stuffing the remnants of his lunch into his mouth.

Quickly hurrying behind RaLF, Ian managed to stay a couple of yards behind. Suddenly, a hand reached out from a table and slapped RaLF's backside. She stopped, and when she turned, seeing Ian's twisted grin, a rage triggered inside her. He had pushed her all morning. Now, he had pushed too far. Without thinking, she swung her tray with her left hand, sending garbage flying while catching Ian in his face. Then her right fist rocketed to Ian's nose.

Blood exploded from Ian's face and followed him, arcing in the air like a comet's tail, as Ian fell backwards into Earnest's arms, sending Earnest and his food to the floor with him.

RaLF screamed in pain, grabbing her hand, as a cheer erupted from the students.

"Hey!" Earl stood at the conveyer belt for dirty dishes, so overwhelmed by the punch that all he could do was run in place.

"Let's get out of here!" One of RaLF's friends yelled as she pulled the aching pugilist behind her, RaLF rubbing her hand in horrid throbbing pain.

Earnest dragged himself from underneath Ian. As Earnest looked around, students were screaming and yelling, some stood on their chairs, looking and laughing. He turned his eyes back to his friend, and Ian lay still upon the floor, his eyes rolled white behind the tiny slits of his quivering eyelids, blood spilling from the open gash across his nose and cheek.

"Damn," He muttered, not feeling well at the sight of Ian's blood.

Nor was Earl, continuing his stationary jog.

A lady dressed in white hurried to the fallen pair and stuck out her hand holding a damp rag.

Earnest took it, and noticing a funny taste in his mouth and a weakness in his legs, he wiped his own face with the rag.

"Not you. Him!" the lady barked.

Earnest looked at her, saying "Oh..." placing the rag upon Ian's nose just as the boy's eyes were refocusing and the assistant principal walked up.

"What's going on here?"

Earnest looked at him, "I think RaLF ripped his freaking nose off…"

* * *

Earnest heard Mr. Small's secretary shuffling paper in the next room as he sulked, elbows on his knees and chin in his hands. He looked up at RaLF sitting on the other side of the room, her right hand covered with an ice pack as they waited to see the principal. He searched his mind for something to say, but every comment that came to him seemed wrong.

"I…I guess that really hurts…," he finally said, his voice saturated in uncertainty.

RaLF had intentionally been ignoring Earnest. Not that their sitting in the office was Earnest's fault, but he was Ian's friend… and that was enough. It wasn't fair that she was there, anyway. That freak had been bothering her all day. He had it coming. Mr. Small had to see it that way, too.

Her hand throbbed, so while the ice numbed the flesh, the flashes of pain continued. She wished that Bill was sitting with her, or maybe

Polly, but Polly was talking to Mr. Small. Her eyes kept moving up to the door wishing that someone would come, someone to put between her and Earnest.

"I…I guess that really hurts….," Earnest repeated, so she turned to him, and with her good hand, gave him the finger. "Yeah, I thought so…" he retorted, feeling like a gutted fish.

"Your friend is an asshole." She snapped at Earnest.

"He's not my friend," Earnest lied. "He's just someone I know."

"Well, if I get suspended because of that asshole…"

"I didn't do anything. He was just kiddin' you about me sayin' that stuff…"

"Geez Louise, RaLF, what have you got yourself into this time?" RaLF's mother walked into the office, and Earnest immediately recognized her. She was big boned like RaLF but a few inches taller, wearing a sleeveless blouse and carrying a large bowling ball bag of a purse, and like RaLF, she was very pretty, giving Earnest the notion that he was seeing RaLF's future.

"Mom, it's not my fault. That jerkface was in every one of my morning classes. He was sniffing at me like a dog, so at lunch when he grabbed my butt, I hit him. He had it coming. Ask him, he's his best friend." And she pointed at Earnest with her good hand.

Earnest eyes widened. "No. He isn't my best friend. I was just eating lunch with him. That's all."

RaLF's mother looked at Earnest oddly, and was about to say something as Bill walked in. "Are you okay, baby? How's your hand?"

"Your hand? Oh my goodness, Hon, is that the hand you hit him with?"

"Yes, Mom, and it hurts like hell." She raised the ice pack to show her hand, red and swollen. Earnest glanced at it and grimaced.

"Well, it doesn't look as bad as your friend," Bill scowled at Earnest, then turning back to RaLF and her mother, "Janet said that Ian looked like crap."

"He's not my friend...."

"How'd she see him?"

"She's an aide in the health office. She said his nose looked squished over and he had a big gash on his face."

"RaLF, what did you do?"

"I don't know. It happened so fast. I told you he grabbed my butt."

"First, you hit him in the face with your tray." Earnest interjected. "Then, you pounded him in the face again with your other hand. And that was all it took."

"Oh, Earnest," RaLF chided.

"Earnest?" RaLF's mother chimed in. "Are you Earnest Graves? From Fillmore Elementary?"

Earnest nodded.

"I thought I recognized you. You guys all know each other, and you've all grown up into such handsome people. Earnest, did you know you were the first boyfriend that RaLF ever had that called her on the telephone all those years ago. I thought it was so cute."

"When were you RaLF's boyfriend?" Bill choked.

"It doesn't matter. His friend broke my hand!"

"Your hand's broke?"

Earnest jerked to his feet, "Dammit! He's not...."

"Earnest, watch your mouth." Mr. Small now stood at his open door as RaLF's friend Polly walked out. She looked at RaLF, scrunching her face, uncertain about her time with the principal.

Earnest sat back down, embarrassed.

"Mrs. Fletcher, it's good to see you. After I talk to Earnest, you and RaLF can come into my office. Bill, get back to class, we don't need our quarterback ineligible. Earnest, step inside."

Both young men stood at the same time. Bill bent over and gave RaLF a hug, promising to see RaLF later. Then, slyly, he looked over at Polly. As their eyes met, he gave her a wink, a wink just outside the realm of innocent. As he walked away, Earnest nodded with a weak, uncertain smile at RaLF's mother while RaLF continued to avoid him altogether. He stood up and began what, oddly enough, felt like a death march. Inside, Earnest took a seat before the principal's desk.

"Earnest, why don't you start at the beginning?"

To which, Earnest confessed all the indiscretions of the damaged boy who wasn't his friend.

* * *

Mary met the green LTD in the U, near the same spot the Deacon had left her that morning. She climbed into the car, and the driver, a man older than her with thinning hair combed back behind his ears and touching his collar, leaned to kiss her softly on her cheek.

"Don't do that here!" Mary said, pushing him away.

He sighed, driving the car onto the street while Mary began reading through a paperback copy of Machiavelli's *The Prince*.

"I saw Faith," John said matter-of-factly, looking over his shoulder to change lanes. "She drove past me when I was coming here. I doubt if she even saw me."

"Of course she saw you," Mary snapped, looking at John and closing her book. "Why are you telling me this?"

"I don't know, but..."

"Should the first thing you say to me be that you saw your wife?"

"I guess not. It's just...."

"You can be so stupid."

"Dammit, Mary, don't say that," John boomed, then calming himself, "I love you, Mary." His words were short and sharp as he gritted his jaw. "Sometimes I just want you to know what's going on in my life."

Then he grew silent, wrapped in his anger, looking ahead as if he wore blinders.

Why does he have to say love, Mary wondered, staring at him, studying the wrinkles forming around John's eyes. *You're thirty years old, John. Don't act more childish than the jerks I'm in school with.*

"I don't really care to hear about Faith, okay." Mary directed, trying to remove any edge from her voice but with only minor success.

She could see John's mind working, having grown accustomed to his pouting since meeting nine months ago.

"How was your day?" he finally asked coldly.

"Daniel's back and still driving me crazy," she groaned.

John continued asking one innocuous question after another, and she continued to answer, each word acting as salve to his wounded ego as they drove to his trailer in a park outside the southeastern city limits.

"I told my parents I would be working late at the library again."

"Are you ever going to say you love me?"
Ignoring the question, Mary opened her door, sliding out, holding the index finger of John's right hand. "Come on," she said, tugging it. "Let's go."

He slid across the seat, and she led him from the car and into the trailer, never letting go until they reached the bedroom.

* * *

Jamie bounced in the bus as he returned to the school from the vocational school, sweating as a hot breeze blew in the open windows. He took the cigarette behind his ear and held it in his hand for fear of losing it to the wind.

"Hey, Messey!" Angus brayed from the back of the bus, "Gimme' a smoke." His large, hairy arm draped around his girlfriend, Fiona.

Jamie ran his fingers along the sides of the cigarette then tapped his fingertip upon the filtered end. He had loaned a few to Angus already today.

"This is my last one," Jamie replied, holding it like a trophy.

"Which one of you a-holes around here can give me a smoke?" Angus bellowed.

Jamie turned back around still fondling the cigarette. On his first day as a senior, he had no homework, which meant no reading, which meant that he was content. But he knew with certainty that assignments he was destined not to do would begin to come.

When the bus arrived at school, it emptied quickly. Jamie stepped off, moving to the side to wait for Angus, bearing a strange sense of courtesy because he didn't have a cigarette to loan.

"I heard Riggins had a fit before I got to class this morning," he said as Angus's hulking frame stepped off the bus behind Fiona's short, bosomy figure.

"He's a dick," Angus grunted, walking off with Fiona in tow, his hand resting upon her wide, round butt.

Jamie stared at the odd-looking pair, the exaggerated swing of the girl's hips, and Angus's groping fingers. The couple appeared comic, yet he could never think of them as a couple. He could imagine no romance between them.

He wondered what Fiona would say if she knew the things that Angus boasted about when she wasn't around. Hell, he wasn't even one of Angus's friends, and he had heard all about the way she wriggled and giggled. And he wondered if she said the same things to her friends.

Jamie lit his cigarette and took a deep drag. Unconsciously, as he walked to his car, he struck a pose of cool, one eyebrow arching higher than the other.

No rest for the wicked. Again his mother's words haunted him, and he could believe it, certain himself to be among them. So he slowly walked to his car, thinking about his job, loading fifty pound bags of feed—dog feed, cow feed, horse feed, goat feed, rabbit feed, ostrich feed, and every other kind of feed that he could tote and they could sell at the Ponca City Feed and Tack.

He slid out of the black t-shirt he had gotten at a concert the year before in Oklahoma City, threw it into the car and climbed in. He shuffled through a pile of 8-track tapes on the floor of the passenger's side and picked up one by OX, shoving it in the tape player. A heavy sound buzzed through tinny, popping speakers as his car roared to life.

Jamie drove Grand Street to work, meeting a red light at every intersection and parking his car in the alley behind the store. When he stepped from his car, he pulled an old flannel shirt from the passenger's seat. Dust exploded from the shirt as he shook it, and then he put it on along with a cap from the back seat. Bending over, all of his hair flew around and hung down. Jamie clumped it together and stuffed it under the hat as he put it on his head.

Then stepping into the building, he found work already waiting for him.

"Jamie, help Mr. Graves. He needs three bags of dog food, eight bags of sweet feed and cattle cubes and five bags of chicken feed."

Jamie grabbed his dolly and ventured into the dusty depths of the Ponca Feed and Tack, fulfilling his place among life's wicked.

* * *

Earl pushed the grocery cart down the last aisle. He had gotten everything his mother had listed in a notebook made up of pictures and labels of the items she wanted. As he walked by the candy bars along the last aisle, he stopped and contemplated the selection. After much consideration and little caution, he took one, slipping it into his pocket, and headed for the register.

"Find everything, honey?" the checker asked, her smile outlined in bright orange lipstick matching her hair.

Earl smiled back. "I'm good. I worked today. So many new people at school," he sighed as the checker rang up the items from his cart. "I shouldn't sing at school. Too many people."

"Honey, I didn't know you sang. Sing for me."

His face grew red as a large smile cut across it. His eyes

darted from side to side, and he lightly serenaded the checker, “Camptown ladies sing a song. Aww dee doo daw day…”

“Oh Earl, you’re a doll.” She said and gave him his total.

He dug a handful of bills from his front pocket and handed them to her. She sorted through it, took the money she needed and gave the rest back along with his change.

“See you later, hon.”

Still flushed, he turned and pushed his cart out of the store. Earl mounted his adult tricycle after placing the bags of groceries snugly in the basket behind the seat. He took off his cap and wiped the sweat from his closely cropped scalp with a blue paisley kerchief. "Purdy sky," he said aloud as he put his cap back onto his head, the sky beginning to darken as the sun touched the horizon, shooting rays of light through the clouds.

As he began pedaling, he switched on the headlight attached to the handlebars so that people could see him just like his father had told him to do.

By the time he arrived home, sweat spotted the gray jumpsuit he wore, and his eyes stung from perspiration. Worn from the weight of the heat, he panted and wiped his face again with his paisley kerchief. Then from underneath the sacks of groceries, he pulled out a long chain and wove it between the spokes of the front wheel and around a support beam of the breezeway he parked under.

As he carried the groceries to the house, his father, a stooped and shrunken man sporting a slick and shiny head, stood at the screen door waiting for him, gnawing on his gaunt, sunken cheeks with his nearly toothless gums.

"The aminal show is coming on TV, boy," the old man said, spitting a loose piece of skin off of the tip of his tongue.

"About monkeys? I love them monkeys," Earl asked, smiling and followed his father with the same stooped saunter—nearly a reflection except that he was a head taller.

"Don't aks me. I just turned it on," his father replied, his back to his son as he hobbled to their living room. "Your momma'll put up them gro'crees."

Earl's mother, also stooped and shrunken, resembling the old man except for the sparse strands of white hair decorating her head, nodded as she stood at the cabinet making sandwiches.

"Just set 'em down, and I'll put 'em up after I finish making you an yer daddy's dinner."

Earl put the sack on the cabinet beside his mother and went to the living room. He sat in an old worn recliner next to his father's. Both of the chairs, draped with threadbare dishtowels to cover the even more threadbare arms and headrests, faced the television

"The world of the spider is an amazing thing," the narrator announced as the two men sat trance-like before the glowing tube. A twenty-inch world was about all that Earl could grasp: watching, enjoying, and then moving along.

"See that spider there, boy, with the thing on its back, a black widder. I oncet got bit by one uv'em. That's how I got that hole rotted in my leg," Earl's father said while pointing at the television.

Smiling, Earl replied, "Me too."

"You did?" His father asked, wrinkling his brow. "I don't recollect..." his words trailed off, fading into an oblivion of distracted thoughts and forgotten memories.

Earl's mother brought their meals on TV trays, returning to the kitchen to eat hers.

Earl ate while the spiders enthralled him to silence.

After the ten o'clock news, he rose from his chair to prepare for bed, his father asleep in the other chair, and shuffled to the bathroom. As he brushed his teeth, he faced his reflection but looked through it as if unaware it was him, humming while he brushed, spitting out the paste that filled his mouth and hacking up phlegm from deep down his throat.

From the corner of his eye, with the toothbrush sticking from his mouth, Earl watched a spider crawl across the ceiling behind him in the reflection as the images of the television show faded in his mind. Before the spider made its way across the entire room, Earl climbed onto the toilet and stuck his hand in the spider's path. It climbed upon his hand, weaving its path around his fingers as he stepped back down, moving his hand around to keep the spider in his sight.

"Are you ready for bed?" his mother called.

"In a minute," he answered, raising the toilet lid. "Bye-bye," he said and shook the spider into the toilet bowl. He peed and watched as the spider fought the spray, and then surrendered to the swirling current and disappeared into the plumbing after he flushed.

Shuffling to his bedroom, a smile swept across his face as something in his front pocket slapped his thigh. He shut the door behind him, excited. Like a mischievous child, he hurried and sat upon his bed; then reaching down into his pocket, he pulled the chocolate bar from his pocket and stared at it like a holy relic.

Slowly, as his hands peeled away the wrapper, saliva filled his mouth. Mushy in his grasp, he eagerly devoured the bar, smearing chocolate across his hands and face. After stuffing the wrapper under his mattress among a multitude of others, he wiped the chocolate onto his gray coverall jumpsuit and undressed.

Wearing a tank top undershirt, boxer shorts, and a pair of black socks reaching his calves, Earl climbed under his blanket.

"I'm ready, Momma!" he yelled, sitting against the headboard and licking the chocolate and caramel and nuts that stuck between his teeth.

His mother opened the door, wearing a pink, flowery, flannel nightgown worn thin and sheer. She turned off the light. Like a shadow, she moved to her son's bed and sat upon the edge. He leaned forward, and she kissed his forehead and stroked his prickly hair.

"Tired?" she asked with a sigh, herself weary with life but somehow knowing that God wasn't going to take her as long as Earl needed her care.

"There was a fight today. It was bad. Blood, blood, blood. But I worked hard."Earl answered.

"I know." she said with no doubt in her weak voice.

She began humming softly. Earl slid down, resting his head upon his pillow. She pulled the blanket to his chin, humming as she did it. Then stroking his head again, words replaced her humming. "De Camptown ladies sing this song..." She sang until her son's snores over-powered her lullaby.

Chapter Three

Sinners and Saints, Princes and Papers

Monday, September 10

Through the wind and the sand, Mary could see Daniel's half-naked body spread out upon the desert. "Mawy," he called to her, his words echoing in the barren desert. "I'm tewwinging you God loves you. He gave hith thon for you!"

She walked closer to him, hearing the sound of steel upon steel as faceless men pounded spikes through Daniel's feet and hands. Then they lifted the bleeding body, nailed to a large wooden cross.

Daniel looked at Mary with pained eyes saying, "Jethuth loveth you," as his cross dropped into a hole in the desert floor. Daniel's body jerked and Mary winced as his life flowed out in red streams. Finally, the last bit of strength dripping from his wounds, Daniel lifted his head and said, "Take cawe of my papew." Then his eyes closed, and his head drooped.

Mary's stomach cramped, startling her awake. Nausea followed, and although disoriented Mary hurried to the bathroom, her stomach heaving. Falling to the floor, panting, Mary fumed at Daniel for intruding upon her sleep and rested her head upon the cold toilet, feeling too weak to raise her arm and flush.

"Mary, are you alright?" Her mother unexpectedly knocked at the door.

"I'm fine." Mary snapped.

"Let me get you something..." Her mother's delicate voice rang with concern.

"No!"

"I'll wait for you out here, honey."

"Go away."

Then after a pause, "I love you, Mary," and the floor creaked as her mother slowly walked away.

The huddled girl fell silent. Her mother's final remark angered her because she knew her mother meant it, while she, on the other hand, felt little more than tolerance for her mother. Pulling herself from the floor, she leaned against the sink, taking the washcloth draped across a seashell shaped holder, a part of the ocean motif that decorated the room. Mary sneered at the shells and dried starfish upon the counter top as her breathing became heavy, so she soaked the washcloth with cool water, and wiped it over her face and neck.

She dropped the toilet seat with a loud thud. "Sorry, Mom," she chided and sat upon it, running her fingers through her short, messy hair. A wave of depression hit her so suddenly and unexpectedly she began crying, having no other way to vent it. Then just as suddenly, it faded and the gushing tears turned to dry sniffles.

"Dammit," she sniffed, wiping her face again with the washcloth.

"Dammit," she said louder, hoping her parents heard her.

And inevitably, thoughts of her parents turned to thoughts of Daniel. For days, for weeks, she had tried to work with him. *Pwaithe God this. Pwaithe God that.* She didn't think she could take much more of him or his God. That evening they would be assembling their first issue of the newspaper, The Poncan, and she wanted to quit. With a sigh she rested her head in her hands, overwhelmed by her subsiding nausea and her increasing weariness. Her body suddenly jerked erect as she righted herself before falling from the toilet seat, asleep where she sat. In a slight delirium, she left the bathroom, returned to her bedroom, and fell to her bed. She jerked awake again, this time to the sound of the Deacon's knock, surprised she had been asleep at all. As he continued to knock, she laid there, cursing the day.

* * *

Not a minute had passed since the teacher dismissed the class, leaving only her and Jamie. And it had only taken that long for his face to blaze in aggravation, heat rising from his neck and surrounding his face so that the bright crimson hue of his ears glowed like hazard lights on a stalled car.

The teacher had said, "Jamie, I asked you to read."

"I don't wanna' read." Jamie had replied, the muscles in his shoulders taut.

"Everyone gets a chance in here." Ms. Irving had stood at her podium; a smile poised in benevolence followed her words like an exclamation mark.

I don't want a chance, Jamie thought. *I want to be left alone.*

"The beginning of section two..." She had continued, her voice never rising.

Jamie had looked at the teacher. It didn't matter to her how red he grew or how irritated he became, her smile deflected every arrow his eyes fired at her.

"As soon as the night was come..." Ms. Irving had prompted.

"As soon as the night was come..." Jamie had repeated, word for word, inflection for inflection, never looking at the book before him.

"Go on," she had prodded.

Flushed, Jamie had looked down at the book. "This is stupid," he had muttered, slamming his book shut, years of slipping by closing with it. *Get your ass up and leave; it's over. Everyone knows you're an idiot*. But he didn't rise from the chair, not even after the bell rang and he sat alone.

Jamie angrily stroked the edge of the textbook, uncertain what would happen next as the silence in the classroom intensified. He stared uneasily at the abstract painting decorating the book's cover; the bold colors burning images into his retina until all he saw was tainted and blurred. A bead of sweat rolled from his hairline and dropped to the desk, spotting the cover.

"DAMN YOU!" he roared, shoving the book from the desk into the next row.

Still not raising her voice, Ms. Irving scolded Jamie, "Don't talk to me that way."

Her calmness struck him harder than any other thing she could have done. Clutching the edge of his desk, he shook, his anger and rage ebbing into suffocating fear. "Why....?" The only word he could muster, his voice quivering and cracking along with his crumbling facade.

"Jamie, you're a senior. There was no reason for me to think that you couldn't read. You're wrong thinking I wanted to humiliate you."

Before Ms. Irving finished her statement, fear began choking him. Tears blurred his vision. *Help me.* His mind cried in fruitless silent whispers, but the words stuck behind his choking fear before ever reaching the throat.

"Jamie...?" Ms. Irving questioned.

Less than a classroom apart, Jamie felt worlds separated them. Never had he asked for anyone's help, yet he understood he could not help himself.

Years ago there had been a cowboy who had tried to help. And, as Jamie sat at the desk, his hands growing warm from nervously rubbing his thighs, he remembered him. "Your mother's no good." The cowboy whispered in a gravelly, tired drawl. Words then too complicated to comprehend. But now he was alone, and under the weight of his isolation, he broke.

"Don'cha see? I'm screwed...I'm no good at reading.... and I... I... don't... know... what... to... do...." He paused between each word, gasping for air as he let loose of everything inside of him. A collage of images from his past swirled about his head mocking his future: his mother, her boyfriends, the cowboy, even the headboard banging against the wall. His chest knotted, feeling as if someone had battered him with a ten-pound hammer, and he could barely breathe.

Looking to her, he spit and coughed, "I don't wanna' be a bum."

"No, no, you don't."

"I got no future. If I graduate, I got nowhere to go." He slumped back in his desk, drained, his voice fading to a whisper.

"Hasn't anyone tried to help before?"

Jamie shrugged; the mask was gone. He stood before her, naked. She knew his secret...passed from one grade to another... "Too lazy to learn, I guess...," he muttered.

"No, no, no. That's not it, Jamie. It's never that easy," the teacher said with sadness, wishing that it really were. Then, she looked at the clock. The bell had rung but neither of them had heard it. "Where are you supposed to be?"

He paused, afraid of what she would think when he answered, "Vo-tech." *Yeah, I know, I'm in vo-tech because I'm too damn stupid to do anything else.* "I missed the bus," he mumbled.

She stroked her chin, her mind away in deep thought.

He looked to his teacher, but her eyes seemed distant, almost as if she were avoiding him. This struck him as odd and hurtful. *I spilled my guts and she's pushing me out of her room.* He stood up from the desk. "I'll get there," he sneered, disgust venting from each word.

"Where are you going?" The teacher asked, her mind coming back to the present.

Screw you; I'm outa' here. Jamie walked toward the door, "I'm going."

"No! Not now," Ms. Irving suddenly took an angry tone. "You owe me..."

"What do I owe you?" Jamie smoldered, stepping closer to the door, never turning toward her.

"When you opened your mouth, you obligated me. You owe me the chance to help..."

Jamie stopped at the door, his hand wrapped around the doorknob, his palm covered in sweat.

"Be here tomorrow morning, before school, and we'll see what we can do."

Jamie remained silent, finding it difficult to turn toward her, his eyes staring through the door.

"What do you really want, Jamie, sympathy…pity?"

"I...don't know..."

"Make a choice, Jamie. What do you want? I can feel sorry for you. I can pity you, but I can't help you if you don't want it."

"I want more than I have now," Jamie replied, slowly turning and looking her in the eyes.

"Good. Be here tomorrow morning." She quickly filled out a slip of paper. "This will get you a parking lot pass. You'll have to drive yourself to the vo-tech." Ms. Irving quickly walked to Jamie and handed it to him.

"Thank you," he said quietly.

"Thank me tomorrow by showing up."

Jamie needed to say more, but found himself mute, so he opened the door instead.

In the hallway Earl jumped, startled by Jamie, and he dropped his dust mop. Jamie picked it up and handed it back.

"Here you go."

Earl smiled at Jamie, his head bobbing from his stooped shoulders, and he took the handle.

"Oh, de do dah day," Earl sang softly as Jamie walked away.

* * *

"Pwaith God," Daniel said, reading a list of article ideas someone had given him.

Pwaith God, Mary heard across the room, cringing even in the midst of her tongue-lashing of a photographer. *Was that the only expression he knew? If Jesus was that annoying, it was no wonder they crucified him*, she thought.

"Mawy," Daniel said, walking to her, "I think we should dwop the wecowd weview and put thith awticle in it'th plathe."

"What?!" Mary scowled. "We discussed this already, Danny-boy. It is not in keeping with this issue's theme." Her words slithered between gritted teeth.

"Yeth, it ith." Daniel rebutted.

"Dammit, Daniel," Mary barked, "I can't understand a thing you're saying."

Daniel paused in frustration, his tongue large enough to trip over.

"Yeth...it...ith." He spoke slowly, carefully enunciating every syllable. "Ouw theme ith welcoming back the thtudents. Julio ith a thtudent and mowe intewesting than thome wock and woll wecowd weview."

Mary's irritation erupted. Of course Daniel was right. She didn't care about the stupid record review either. But if she even once let the bastard have his way, she had lost everything. She scratched at her head furiously. "Are you doing this to me on purpose? Tonight we're supposed to put it all together and you're…"

"What?" Daniel questioned.

"…trying to change everything!" Mary shouted, flinging her arms.

"No, not at aww," Daniel defended, but second guessing his own judgment. "It'th a good thtory; that'th all. It meanth thomething."

Mary sensed his retreat.

"Some people think rock and roll means something." She poked Daniel in his chest with her stubby, nail-gnawed, index finger. " And it fits *my* theme." *It's better to be feared than loved*. She stood firm watching Daniel, first taken aback, then shrink away, defeated. Her smile only grew as he left the room, the door shutting behind him. She held the visage of Daniel upon a cross in her mind. With eyes closed, she held onto it ignoring the interruption of the bell. Then relishing it a bit longer as people left room, she muttered an almost celebratory, "Perfect."

"You okay?"

Mary opened her eyes, and Earnest stood before her.

"What?"

"You were just standing there. I didn't know if something was wrong."

To which she smiled and repeated, "Perfect," and strolled out the door.

Earnest meandered about the room, almost stalling when he heard the door open and saw Ian walk into the room.

"Hey," Earnest said, pasting an artificial smile to his face, as he had been unable to assuage the guilt of his aloofness that clung to him like a bloating tick.

"Where the hell've you been?" Ian's words came out angrily, his face scowling behind the bandages covering his face.

"Around..." Earnest's voice oozed the same saccharine sincerity his face expressed.

"Dammit, Earnest, I've turned into a joke in this building. I thought my best friend would at least stick around."

"I said I've been around..."

"Not around me."

Earnest knew it, avoiding Ian as if he had the plague, smallpox, and leprosy combined—as if he were the biggest joke in school.

"Did you get stitches?" Earnest diverted.

"Like you care. If you'd bother calling or maybe answering your phone now and then you'd freakin' know I had stitches and the damn cut isn't healing right."

"It's just…I've had a lot to do…with the paper and all. You know…." Earnest words were a waltz of excuses, dancing around any truth one might find.

"No, I don't know. I haven't talked to you since I was your girlfriend's punching bag…remember?"

"I'm sorry…" Earnest countered, "but you shouldn't have been pestering RaLF. You shouldn't've grabbed her ass."

Behind the white of the tape and gauze, Ian's face grew crimson, his eyes glistening. "Screw her, and screw you! I didn't touch RaLF's ass!"

From across the room, their eyes locked onto one another while a choking in Earnest's throat exacerbated the silence. Ian was a jerk, an arrogant asshole at times, but it was neither of those things that were distancing him from Ian. What strangled Earnest was his fear of being paired with Ian, becoming his equal as a school joke, and it was the same fear that wrapped his shame in a blanket of rationalization and justification. As Earnest tried to give voice to another self-acquittal, he was interrupted by the rattle of the door opening again behind Ian.

Ian's anger morphed into a fearful rage as RaLF walked into the room followed by Bill and Polly, RaLF's conversation coming to an abrupt halt at the first sight of Ian.

Yet in spite of the condescending remarks, the piercing teasing raining upon him from all corners of the school, he couldn't help himself. "Miss me?" He baited as a sly grin came upon his face. Then he turned to Earnest. "I missed my buddy, too." His grin held nothing but contempt.

"You piece of…" Bill growled moving toward him.

RaLF grabbed Bill's arm, stopping him.

"He's not worth it…" she insisted.

"Damn, you're right there," Ian snapped, and then he turned to Earnest, "Ain't that a fact, Earnie?"

Earnest held fast to his silence.

Slowly, Ian began stepping past the trio, but he still couldn't help himself. Even as he drowned in an ocean of mockery, the only life preserver available to him was his own defiance. His eyes seared RaLF's as he moved around her, but he couldn't help himself, so he slowed in his steps, taking a deep sniff behind his bandage. Then wearing a mask of total sincerity, he said, "I'll bet your shit doesn't even stink."

RaLF drew back her hand, and at that Ian flinched.

Ian flinched, and he couldn't help himself.

A loud laugh burst from Polly's mouth, and within seconds, she was joined by RaLF and Bill.

Ian hadn't meant to flinch, reducing his pretence of defiance to self-deprecation. So he moved to the door and pushed it slightly open. He turned, and through the laughter, he glared at Earnest, who stood silently stoic.

Earnest had never seen eyes so broken, yet he remained oblivious to any action he could take.

Ian turned his back to them all, and stepped out.

As the laughter faded, Bill turned to Earnest still smiling. "What's wrong? You faggots break up?"

Earnest cleared his throat, "I told you. We're not friends."

* * *

Surrounded by empty seats, Daniel sighed as he stabbed at the over-cooked burrito on his lunch tray with his fork. Mary had rendered him impotent, and he had simply acquiesced. From the other end of the table, Daniel heard a grunt and turned to see a girl in a wheelchair, her body writhing as a person beside her tried to feed her.

Daniel shuddered and turned his back. Again, he jabbed at his food, hating his place. He knew people walked by him, thinking this was the table for the special ones, and he belonged there.

Don't they notice my surgery? I look normal now.

Another grunt sounded down the table. He tried to ignore it, but spying from the corner of his eye, he could see that the girl in the wheelchair had become restless, wildly bobbing up and down. The grunts became more intense; her movement more excited. Finally Daniel looked at her. And her grunting stopped. When the girl saw Daniel looking at her, if only for a few seconds, she took control of her squirming. Then with no provocation or prodding, she pulled up her blouse and covered her gaunt face. In an instant Daniel was staring at the first bare breasts he had ever seen, and they looked back at him in some crazy cock-eyed stare.

"Ali!" the girl's assistant bellowed, scrambling to pull the blouse down and cover her. The assistant jumped up and quickly pushed the wheelchair out of the cafeteria, accompanied by a spattering of laughter.

Dumbstruck, Daniel could not join in the laughter he heard. As he looked around, all of the laughing eyes focused on him. *Oh, God,* he prayed silently, *now this*. Heap upon humiliating heap, Daniel could bear no more. While no one had noticed his entrance, everyone would watch him leave; so ignoring the laughter and the stares, he carried his restraint and his tray to the conveyer belt and walked out.

But as the cafeteria door shut behind him, he bolted as quickly as his pudgy body and stumpy legs would carry him down the hall to the sidewalk, headed for a restroom in the other building, distancing himself from the laughter and the lop-sided breasts. He crashed through the restroom's wooden door, panting.

"Thecond Timothy, fouw: eighteen," Daniel exhorted, standing with his eyes closed, every word reverberating, bouncing from the concrete walls and the tiled floor, building in its importance. "And the Lowd will delivew me fwom evwy evil wowk and pwethewve me fow hith heavenly kingdom."

He repeated the scripture as he paced, each echoing shoe-slap resonating under Daniel's words. He tried to give the scripture all his attention, but the barrage of humiliations distracted. And with the humiliation came the anger. Why couldn't he feel the anger when Mary was there? Why was her intimidation so much greater? He tried to pray for peace in his heart, but because he wanted his anger, because he felt he was due his anger, he knew no peace would come.

At the sink Daniel turned on the water and stared at the reflection of his new face. The Mongol eyes had been rounded from their squints, his wide pug nose brought to a finer point. The dark bruise that had run down his face had lightened to a nearly indiscernible yellow hue. He had felt reborn, yet nothing else around him had changed. He cupped his hands under the cool running water, pushed his face into the waiting pool and hoped to wash away his anger, his confusion, his humiliation.

Only weeks before he had felt confident, but now Mary's rebuke sent him cowering in the restroom. *I did nothing wrong. I made a suggestion. That's what I'm supposed to do. I'm the editor. Mary's taking my paper away.*

Daniel thought of the thousands of hours he and his mother had spent working together, learning his vowels, his consonants, his numbers and all of their functions. He remembered his joy when clouds would part, and he found understanding, and he remembered his mother's sad expression the day that he had asked her what "a retard" was because some kid had said he was one. He remembered the disappointment he felt realizing being special was not always a good thing.

Daniel searched his new face, looking for resolve, or strength, yet he found none looking back. In disgust he raised a wet hand and wiped it across the mirror, leaving a trail of smears and water drops, distorting and blurring his reflection. The gnarled image just seemed to mock him more, so, battered and beaten, he did the only sensible thing he knew to do: he prayed.

"Oh Fathew God," Daniel began, closing his eyes and raising his hands to heaven. "In youw wood it thath to put my buwdon on you becauth it ith heavy and to take youw yoke upon myself becauth it ith light. Tho God, I athk you to act on youw wood. Take my pain and my angew away and fill me with youw joy: the joy that thuwpatheth undewthtanding. And give me wisdom, oh Lowd, withdom to deal with Mawy. Fogive me my angew, and in Jethuth' name I pray fow Mawy'th thalvation. Thank you for heawing my pwayew. Amen."

"Amen," a voice followed from behind.

Daniel turned to see a tiny, blonde boy, shifting awkwardly from foot to foot, his hands knitted together in uncomfortable reverence while he stood beside the wall of urinals, uncertain of his next move. "I need to pee," the boy squeaked.

"Amen." Daniel repeated and left the restroom feeling better. The humiliating breasts had escaped his mind. Mary didn't seem so bad, and rightly or wrongly, he would apologize to her that evening. *That was what Jesus would do*. So much had been taken from him; he was grateful for his Father's faithfulness.

As he returned to the journalism room, Earl pushed his dust mop down the aisle toward him. Irritated, Daniel moved to the other side of the hall. But at the same time, Earl moved. So, Daniel moved again, and again Earl followed, finally facing one another separated only by the length of Earl's dust mop handle.

Earl grew frustrated, breathing heavily out his nose, accentuating each breath.

"Wiww you get out of my way," Daniel scolded and shoved the custodian.

Earl leaned nervously against the lockers, letting Daniel stomp around him. Daniel's irritation quickly faded as Earl passed out of sight, and as he entered the journalism room seconds later, he was again basking in the Lord's joy.

Chapter Four

Bit by Bit, Putting it Together

"Spot me, Danny," Reverend Green cajoled, looking up from the bench. His tanned face red, spotted with sweat.

Daniel did not like sweat, not the feel or the smell of sweat. Nor did he like the grunting, nor the clanging of weights, nor anything else about the gym, but this was where the pastor liked to bring him.

He stood behind the Reverend's head, ready to grasp the barbell if the Reverend needed it. While his pastor pumped the barbell, Daniel mentally fine-tuned the paper, praying to meet Mary's specifications and avoid another run-in with the princess of darkness. Then he caught himself. This was not what God called him to do; the name-calling had to stop.

He prayed for patience and perseverance, but then reconsidered. If he didn't already have these, he wouldn't be where he was this day. Unsure of what he needed, he felt adrift, his mind swimming with so many unclear thoughts and ideas, that he wished his brain would stop for a while.

"Danny," the pastor grunted.

He looked down to see his pastor's face now almost purple, veins bulging from his forehead. Daniel quickly grabbed the bar that rested on the man's chest and helped him lift it back on the rack.

The Reverend sat up and wiped his face with a towel. "Goodness boy, where's your mind?"

"Thowwy," Daniel said.

"Your turn."

Daniel crawled under the barbell. The surgery had saved him from this grueling chore during the summer, but the Reverend Green seemed certain that it was now time Daniel got back into the program.

"C'mon, Hoss, we got a hundred l-b-s right here for you to start with," the pastor said pulling off several large plates. "Give the devil his due."

Daniel gripped the bar and pushed, already feeling fatigued from the curls, the flies, and the extensions he had already done. The barbell lifted from the rack. Daniel moved quickly and began pumping the weights and finished his first set of ten before the pastor could prepare. All around him he could hear others swearing and screaming for motivation. He didn't need it or particularly like it. Then after the pastor loaded the bar with ten more pounds, he did another set of ten, feeling shaky and weak as the barbell fought back. With the third set and ten more pounds, he began to surrender to the weight of the barbell, himself grunting as he extended his arms as far as they could go.

"C'mon, Danny, don't quit on me now. This is that lost soul crying out to you, Danny. This is that person who thinks they're an island and can live without Christ. C'mon, Danny, show 'em they need Christ."

Daniel's arms trembled as he held the weights above himself.

That's what he was called to do. Bring people into the kingdom of God. Go out into the world and preach the gospel. Reach the lost for Christ. And when Daniel took an inventory of what he had done, the count came to a big fat zero. He was a freak of nature; not any kind of Billy Graham. So every time he lifted the barbell, he said a prayer to himself. "If you don't let me drop this on my head, God, I'll try to save a person for each lift." Faith could move a mountain, but all he wanted was to raise the barbell another time.

"Fiiiive..." the Reverend Green counted, elongating the word with Daniel's lift.

The boy's teeth gritted as he lifted the weights, his nostrils flared, his body quaked, but he wouldn't give up. All he saw in his mind's eye was a lost soul—a poor lost soul who he pictured a lot like Mary. And all he could do was sweat for her, pump a barbell, say a prayer for her, and he hoped she would answer.

"Siiiix...." the Reverend grunted for him.

Of all the lost souls in his school, why Mary? Then again, it was obvious.

"Seeveen..."

Sweat stung his eyes, and his muscles felt as if they were ripping apart.

"Eeeeiiight." Daniel chimed in with the preacher, looking at a spot on the ceiling, drilling a hole through it with his stare.

"Niiiiine."

Daniel strained and pushed in constipated fury. Mary hated his guts. She thought he was a naive fool. But his vision was clear.

"Teeen!"

He dropped the barbell with a great clang in the rack above him.

"Impressive," the Reverend Green said. "So, how many souls do you owe the Kingdom of God?"

"Thix," Daniel answered, still reclined on the bench. The preacher dropped Daniel's towel on the boy's face.

"What's your total, now?"

"Hundwedth," Daniel panted, the number already on his mind.

"Let's hit the shower. I've got something I want you to think about."

Daniel waddled behind his pastor, exhausted, wondering what he had in store for him. It had been months since the Reverend Green had put him through this torture. At least if they were showering, he wasn't going to get dragged outside to hobble for five miles—which did not negate the humiliation of the shower. The Reverend's flesh was bone-tight like Michelangelo's David. Daniel's bones, on the other hand, hid under layers of meat, tissue, and fat, so if he resembled a work of art, it might be a pear from a watercolor still life. So Daniel huddled under the cold stream of water, with his back to the pastor, soaping himself.

"Okay, Danny, I want you to think about this before you answer," the Reverend said over the sound of running water.

Daniel sheepishly looked over his hunched shoulder. The preacher's face was covered in lather, but he continued talking and spitting soap.

"We have a revival coming up. Now, it's the same week as homecoming, but it's..." the pastor paused to spit, "it's the only time we could have Ben Dunn. Now, I know they'll be people who love football, but this is Ben Dunn, the Vice President of the Southern Baptist Convention," he stood, his head covered in lather, holding his hands out like a balance weighing the alternatives. "You have football in this hand, and God in the other hand, I mean, what's it gonna' be? There isn't really a choice, is there?"

Daniel wiped soap from his eyes. "No," he answered.

"I want you to give your testimony before Mr. Dunn gives his sermon."

Daniel froze.

"No, I can't do that. Not with my lithp and thtuff."

The pastor looked intently. "Wait a minute Danny. I've prayed long and hard about this. You could at least do the same. You are our church's greatest miracle, our greatest testimony to God's might. Besides, this is as good a time as any to start on those hundred souls."

Daniel didn't want to pray about it. He didn't want to do it—that simple. Sure, he wanted those souls. More than the pastor could know, he wanted those souls. Nothing would bring him more joy than to give his testimony, and have one hundred and thirty-nine people come forward and receive Jesus as their personal Lord and Savior. But what if no one came? What if they just sat in the pews and looked at him, *their miracle*, expecting a miracle from him?

"No, I can't, Pathtor."

"Well, Danny, if you won't pray about it..." he said turning off the water, grabbing his towel, and wrapping it around his waist. "Arm wrestle me for it. If I win, you do it. If you win, well, I guess I heard God wrong." He walked to the sink and crouched down, placing his elbow on the corner. "C'mon, Hoss, we're talkin' God's will, here."

Daniel turned off the water, sensing defeat as the Reverend

Green waited for him. After toweling himself off and putting on his underwear, he walked towards the stooped preacher. Reverend Green was flexing his bulging bicep, making it jump.

"Hey, Danny, there's a frog in my arm." He chuckled.

Daniel stooped down on his knees and faced the preacher, sticking out his hand.

"Think, Hoss," the preacher said, and the game began. Immediately, Daniel's whole body tensed, and he held the preacher in place. He stared at his shaking hand and concentrated. *Be still.* But his arm gave a centimeter, weakened from the work out. His eyebrows arched, and he began to sweat in the bathroom's humidity. The pastor remained expressionless. Daniel studied him trying to read his face, but he could not. Then that first centimeter gave way to another. He held as long as he could, but he realized it was over no matter how much he strained.

"God's will be done," Reverend Green smiled, pushing Daniel's hand to the sink.

* * *

When Mary awoke, covered in sweat, she turned and looked at John's clock and read the glowing numbers: 6:59. She leaned back again and rested her head upon the pillow, feeling she needed to do something. After turning on her side, she smelled the pillow; it reeked of John.

"Ohmygod!" she screamed, “The paper!"

"What?” John asked, shaking the sleep from his head.

"You jerk! You let me fall asleep!" Mary growled and hit him in the chest, knocking his breath away.

"You said you were tired!" John wheezed, as Mary jumped out of bed, grabbing her clothes. "What's the big deal?"

"You would know if you'd done more in high school than drink and get your girlfriend pregnant. Now, get up! You've got to take me to school." Mary snapped, buttoning her blouse.

After Mary finished dressing, she violently brushed her hair, coldly demanding to go, her words slithering through the trailer like an angry serpent.

Mary sat quietly as the car headed toward the school. She could feel the adrenaline rush with which she awoke fade while her exhaustion and irritation grew. She wanted to pin her crappy attitude wholly upon Daniel, but that wasn't fair because everything set her off. Of course, fairness didn't matter, so she cursed Daniel in spite.

"John," she said, rubbing her forehead, a headache making its home in the middle of her brain.

He answered quietly, not sure if he would be stoking her anger.

"I know I've been in a bad mood lately...sorry," she said, still rubbing her head. Her eyes were closed while her throbbing head rested in her hand.

"No problem." John reached over and patted her hand upon her leg, but she pulled it away.

When they were five blocks away from school, Mary told John to pull onto a side street.

"I'll walk from here," she said as he came to a stop.

"I can drive you."

"I know you can drive me, but I want to walk! Don't be a jerk."

"I'm sorry," John said passively, leaning toward her to give her a kiss.

"Not now."

"I love you."

Mary shook her head. "Not now. We'll talk later. And don't pick me up. I'll get a ride home."

John began to say something, but Mary backed away from the car and shut the door.

As John drove away, Mary's thoughts were on her headache. Putting the finishing touches on the paper didn't seem as consequential as before, and as all she really wanted was to be at home in bed, nothing seemed consequential except sleep. Remembering it's better to be feared than loved, she sighed, thinking it was a lot of work, and quickened her pace, not wanting to be any later than she already was.

* * *

The door squeaked open and Daniel stepped into the room.

"Daniel," Mr. Addison said, "we've got a serious problem."

A thought came crashing into Daniel's mind like a car barreling through a storefront window: Mr. Addison had heard about his and Mary's fight (or at least Mary's fight—he had attended but meekly).

"I'm thowwy about the fight."

"Fight? I don't know about any fight, but this can't stand."

He held a sheet of the layout toward Daniel. It hung limply in his grasp like a lifeless kitten. Daniel took the page, and the blue marks sprang out at him as if the kitten had suddenly resurrected. He studied the marks and immediately saw the page marred by errors.

"The typetht thould've...." Daniel dodged, looking squarely at Mr. Addison, but the words faded into the abyss of Daniel's compunction. Sure he could blame the typist, or the writer, or the news editor, but ultimately he was at fault. "I'm thowwy," he mumbled, wondering if he could do anything right.

"Well, it's great that you're sorry, but that doesn't change the situation. I gave you this position because I thought you could handle it. You two are qualified, but looking at these pages, I wonder if I made a mistake. I know you two are honey and vinegar…make it work for you and not against you. Conflict doesn't always have to be bad," Mr. Addison chided. Then he patted Daniel on the shoulder. "Daniel, I'll lay this out for you. This is the kind of thing that will kill me in the Teacher's Lounge. Believe me; it doesn't take a lot for some of these English teachers to rip me a new one. Back up, take a breath, and let's get this right."

"We can pathte ovew the mithpelled wowdth," Daniel said hoping that the suggestion would appease the teacher.

"That doesn't fix the punctuation and spacing errors."

Daniel's shoulders drooped along with his hope. He sighed, "I'll thtart typing." Daniel took the pages Mr. Addison had marked and walked into the journalism room. He sat the pages up so he could read them while he typed and prepared the typewriter. Once he loaded the paper, he began. Sitting at the typewriter, Daniel had not only found his niche, he had created one. A virtuoso, having spent most of his life on a keyboard, his fingers did pirouette after pirouette, dancing to a minuet in pica.

A parade of juniors and seniors soon followed, and the room was again alive with the familiar symphony of activity as the clock neared seven.

"Good evening, Mr. Addison," Anne Endo greeted the teacher.

Mr. Addison smiled and nodded, "Ready to work?"

"Ready to finish," Casey Stephens, the advertising manager replied and hurried off to the other room where Daniel was typing.

* * *

The time soon rolled on to 7:30, and Daniel had yet to notice the caustic and abrasive atmosphere usually permeating the room was absent, much as a person doesn't notice when he or she is feeling well. Nor had he noticed how quickly the work was moving along, quietly enraptured with the rhythm of his typing, when he heard....

"Where the hell is Mary?"

"Who the hell cares?" Another declared.

Daniel turned, looking sternly about the room, not appreciating the language, but guiltily realizing the same sentiments. He found that there was peace, and it was good.

Then as if on cue, Mary entered the room, crossing the squeaking threshold from the hall. She knew that she was late and resented the staring faces telling her so. It burned her because she had been so adamant about everyone else being on time. The frown she wore became a sarcastic grin when she noticed Daniel looking back at her, and she said aloud, "Blessed are the late..." but unable to find a sufficiently sarcastic reason why the late should be blessed, she frowned again.

She wouldn't have been this late, but along her walk she sat down on the curb to cry again. An elderly woman stepped out of her house and asked if she was all right. Mary looked at the lady's wrinkled face, her old cotton paisley dress that hung from her shoulder like drapery, shaking her head, saying, "I'm swell," and she walked away. Her moods had been so flighty lately, fluctuating between anger and despair, she was forgetting how a good mood felt.

Daniel rose from the typewriter and approached her. His arms, weak from weightlifting, arm wrestling, and typing, hung limp to his waist. "I'm thowwy about today. You wewe wight. We had dithcuthed evewything and I wath twying to change thingth."

Mary stood silent, hoping her eyes were not red or swollen, not wanting Daniel witnessing any point of weakness. There was no fear of the weak, but before she could utter a reply, Daniel began talking again.

"Mithtew Addithon ith upthet with uth. The layout wath full of mithtakes. I've been wetyping evwything. He pwobabwy wanth to thee you too."

Under her breath she groaned, "Of course he does," and she walked towards Mr. Addison's classroom.

* * *

With Mary's appearance Earnest closed the psychology text book he had been reading, holding his place with his finger, and stared at her along with everyone else. Then, when she left the room, he looked back over the busy room. During his junior year, he never attended the evening layout of the paper. He was well into the first semester of his junior year before he was even aware they were taking place, and by then he reasoned they were doing fine without him. Outside of his own world, Earnest was little aware of anything else going on around him. So for him, the journalism room was filled with strangers, a number for whom he lusted, and a number with whom he thought he might like to be friends. But by now, it was too late, he sensed. Everything seemed set in stone. Besides, most of them were popular kids, the ones Ian called "the beautiful people." And to his dismay, he wondered if he couldn't be Ian's friend, whose friend could he be?

* * *

Three long tables brought together in the shape of a 'U' filled the center of the journalism room and desks outlined the room's walls. Almost every chair had someone sitting in it, working. Paper and scraps littered the floor, the desks, and the tables.

Daniel stopped typing and looked over the article he had been working on. Each page of the paper was laid out with either two or three columns of print. Daniel scanned slowly. When he noticed an error, he rolled the paper back into the typewriter, and eliminated the error by typing over it with correcting paper and then typed the word again correctly. He then continued reading over the article. When he did not find any more mistakes, he took the sheet from the typewriter and cut the article from the typing paper. He compared it to the erroneous article. After making sure that the new version would take the same amount of column space as the old, he ripped the old article from the layout page, strings of rubber cement stretching between them like umbilical cords. Daniel cut them with a sweep of his hand and then rubbed all the old glue into a little ball and flicked it with his finger. The sticky ball stuck to his fingernail, so he flicked it a second time, sending it across the room.

Daniel felt a pat on his shoulder. Earnest stood behind him and said, "Daniel, picking your nose is so unbecoming."

Defensively Daniel said, "It wath jutht glue."

A few people around him quietly laughed. Daniel, realizing that Earnest was joking, smiled. Seldom did others joke with him instead of at him because his difference made him unapproachable to many. Earnest walked on around as Daniel slapped rubber cement on the back of the freshly-typed column of print and pressed it to the blank space on the layout sheet. He stopped in the doorway separating the journalism room from the classroom and saw that Mary and Mr. Addison were in deep conversation. Hoping she was getting torn apart, he turned back around, and Daniel had already returned to the typewriter, tap, tap, tapping away.

* * *

Mary walked up to Mr. Addison's desk, feeling the onslaught of another headache adding to the one she already had.

Mr. Addison looked up. "Good evening, Mary," he said, putting down the last page of the layout.

"Before you say anything, I've already talked to Daniel. We'll do better. I won't let our differences interfere with the paper. We'll cooperate more."

Why am I saying this crap, she wondered, so sick and tired of feeling sick and tired. She could quit—be free and clear of all this hassle—this Daniel. But if she did, that would mean Daniel would win, even if by default. It would be a cold day in hell before she would let that happen.

* * *

After the sun had disappeared, leaving room for the streetlights to spot the view outside the classroom windows, people began to filter out into the darkness as they completed their work. Earnest decided if he was ever going to finish with his homework, he had better leave too and followed Axle Marx out.

Axle ranked high among the high school hierarchy, popular, an athlete, an actor, and now the next in a long line of class clowns, presenting their rants and raves to the school in the form of a humor column for the newspaper. His column was entitled 'Axle Marx the Spot.'

As they went down a flight of stairs, Axle said, "I read your cartoon. Funny. Better than anything they had last year."

"Thanks," Earnest said, surprised by the compliment, "Mary threw out my first one, said it was in bad taste."

"No kidding. If Mary didn't like it, it had to be funny. She has no sense of humor."

Earnest described the censored cartoon, and Axle laughed.

"I didn't have a chance to see your column." Earnest felt obliged to reciprocate but could not.

"Don't bother. It's crap. I put it off for too long. Did it at the last minute and it shows. Guess I'm lucky. Mary read it and put it in anyways. See you later." Axle jogged off to his car.

Earnest stood in place, somewhat surprised. Axle and he had shared a conversation, Earnest and one of the beautiful people. He shook his head in disbelief, and then hurried to his own car; his homework was waiting.

* * *

Time dragged until ten-thirty when Daniel ripped the final sheet from the typewriter saying, "Finithed." He quickly pasted it down and popped his knuckles. Typing non-stop for hours, he ached and rubbed his tired eyes.

"Well, let's see what we have," Mr. Addison commented as they cleared off one of the tables, setting each page down individually:

The cover,

Page two—editorial,

Page three—letters,

Pages four and five—ads,

Pages six and seven—news,

Pages eight and nine—ads,

Pages ten and eleven—the centerfold photo spread,

Pages twelve and thirteen—feature articles...

"Fourteen? Where's page fourteen?" Mary asked, her voice growing anxious.

Daniel shuffled through the other pages he held. Then he looked back at the table of contents.

"It wath thuppothed to be a featuwe page," he said.

They all looked at Anne across the room.

"You didn't give me fourteen. You must've changed it and not told me," Anne answered quietly.

"It was on the chalkboard," Mary gritted her teeth, her voice slowly rising.

"You didn't give me page fourteen." Anne replied, her voice still calm.

"What awe we going to do?" Daniel asked, his mind edging toward panic.

Mary's head pounded in different rhythms. She stared blankly out of the window for a minute. "Do you still have that story on the kid from Mexico?"

Daniel wracked his brain, "Oh, you mean Julio?"

"Yeah, do you still have it?"

Daniel opened a drawer in the desk that he shared with Mary, and took the story from a notebook that he kept. It was already typed.

"Hewe it ith," he said as he read over it looking for errors. Mary found a page of layout paper and drew the lines that were Earnest's responsibility, silently belittling him as she did.

Daniel, after correcting a few errors, cut it out and pasted it down when Mary finished with the lines.

"White thpathe," Daniel remarked, the article not filling the page.

"Give it a headline; I'll figure out the rest."

Mr. Addison remained quiet, watching them work as if he and Anne weren't there.

"Julio cometh to thchoolio?" Daniel said thinking out loud.

Mary looked up at Daniel, her expression confused. She didn't know what was wrong, but Daniel's words struck her as funny. She laughed, "That's the most ridiculous thing I've ever heard. Let's use it."

Surprised by Mary's laughter, Daniel joined in and started writing it out.

After Daniel pasted down the headline, he looked to Mary. "What'th going here," he asked pointing to the blank space.

"As much as I hate to do this..." she muttered and placed down a wrinkled piece of paper, ironing it out with her hand. It was Earnest's first cartoon, and it fit.

After page fourteen was put together, they put the paper to bed.

"Well, kiddos, I think we're through." Mr. Addison said.

Mary sat down, relieved. For the first time this evening she thought about John, but didn't know what to think. Regardless, the day was over, and she could finally go home. She would lie to her parents again about the library. Then she remembered that she had no ride home. It was a time for last resorts. "Daniel, can I get a lift home?"

"Uh-huh," he answered, surprised that she had even asked him.

"Goodnight. See you guys in the morning," Mr. Addison said as Daniel and Mary stepped into the hall.

Anne suddenly appeared beside him. "I'm sorry about page fourteen. But no one..."

"Don't worry. Accidents happen. The key word here is flexibility. Besides, it worked out and showed Mary and Daniel they could work together." He patted her on the shoulder. As they left, Mr. Addison turned out the lights. The door shut behind them, leaving the room to the faint glare of the street lights shining through the windows.

* * *

There was no moon as Jamie lay in his bed, looking out his open window. He sat in the dark, the glowing ash of his cigarette and the ghost-like shadow of the smoke rising from his exhale. Outside his window, through the naked branches of a dead tree in their back yard, he could see the golden orange glow of a large flame at the oil refinery.

He wondered if Mrs. Irving would really help him. Was he stupid to believe reading would help him out of this hell-hole? His mother's drunken laughs from her bedroom seeped through the wall, spilling over him, and he wished he could wash it away. He took a final drag from his cigarette and crushed the butt in an ashtray on the nightstand beside his bed. Jamie pulled his blanket up to his chest and closed his eyes. Within minutes crickets lulled him to sleep, his soft snore answering them back.

Chapter Five

Rivals and Departures

Tuesday, October 2

In a world he found devoid of heroes, blind to any conceit, Bill Wright found one in himself. Yet, this confidence failed to help keep him afloat as he sank into an ocean of consternation. Watching RaLF sitting with that Messereli fellow slapped him like a tsunami.

Bill knew and discerned the complexities of football, baseball, and wrestling. Their art and science were an intrinsic part of his make-up, but for people, he never understood the companionable elements of society. People were mysteries he could not solve—then again, it had never really been necessary. Others always made the effort to build acquaintanceships with him. Bill was the guy with whom everyone wanted to be a friend, so they catered to him, molding themselves to him.

So as he watched his RaLF and that jerk, he grew angry and concerned—so concerned, assuming Jamie planned to violate her in ways she had withheld from him, that Bill had given up his morning bull sessions with friends in the hallways to protect his RaLF's virtue.

RaLF, her own pride in tow, did not think her virtue in jeopardy. The cast around her hand and forearm and the bandage Ian still wore on his nose advertised that much. But if Bill needed to think he had to protect her, she would let him. Bill had never before shown his protective nature to her, but now her vanity enjoyed the attention, so she accepted it with minor yet insincere protest.

Jamie paused his reading and glanced across the library as Bill shuffled through the magazines. He slowly closed the book and sat back.

"I think we can stop, now."

"We've still got more time," RaLF said, confused.

"If we spend any more time on this, your boyfriend's gonna have a stroke. These books are stupid and your boyfriend is watching me like I'm a pervert."

RaLF sat silently embarrassed. "I didn't think you noticed him."

"I'm not an idiot."

"He doesn't mean anything by it."

"Yeah, I'm sure of it." Jamie replied, annoyed with RaLF, unintentionally drawing close to her as he leaned forward on his elbows.

"Anything wrong?" Bill asked, suddenly standing at the table. For days he had been waiting to approach, so when Jamie raised his voice ever so slightly, drawing close to RaLF, Bill flew to action.

"Nothing's wrong," RaLF insisted.

"No, I think there is," Bill replied, glaring at Jamie.

"You're right, Bill, but the problem is you." A voice sounded behind him.

The anger inside Bill rose. He turned around and Mrs. Irving stood facing him.

"Leave. Let these two go about their business," she continued.

"But he..."

"But he *what*, Bill?"

Jamie turned away from the conversation and stood. "Don't worry about it. We're finished, anyway,"

"Jamie," Mrs. Irving interrupted, "we made a deal. Sit down, please. Bill, leave, and if you cause any more trouble..."

Huffing, red with anger and embarrassment, Bill stomped away.

Then Mrs. Irving pushed Jamie back into the chair, and staring at him just as hard as she had Bill, she commanded, "You're going to learn this."

"I'm sick of these books," Jamie snapped back.

"Why?"

"They're stupid and boring," Jamie snapped, looking for an excuse to quit.

"Sounds like you're making progress. We'll get you different books. Look around; you're in a library."

Her words surprised Jamie. The idea of progress had never crossed his mind. The thought that he was improving overwhelmed his anger towards Bill. He listened to himself as he started to read again. The embarrassing pauses between words were shrinking. He turned to Mrs. Irving, who was still standing behind him.

"Can I take a book home?" he asked.

"Certainly," Mrs. Irving smiled.

Then the warning bell rang, so Jamie rose from his seat.

"I'll get something after school," he said to both the teacher and RaLF, trudging away.

When he stepped into the hall, Bill stood across from him, leaning against some lockers. Jamie looked directly at him, startled by Bill's glare.

"You ignorant asshole," Bill slowly spoke.

Jamie stood silent in the doorway while other students tried to filter out around him. Jamie's fist clenched.

"C'mon," Bill taunted, smiling at the thought.

"Excuse me, Jamie," RaLF said as she walked around him unaware of what she interrupted. "Let's go, Bill."

While they walked down the hall she took Bill's hand. "You're going to have to stop coming to the library. Mrs. Irving was pissed at you."

Bill gave a disgusted look.

"Sorry," she said, no happier than Bill, hoping that he would worry even more with her out of sight.

They stopped outside of her class. She looked directly into his green eyes, stroking his cheek once slowly. He had shaved this morning, so it was soft and smooth to her touch.

"I love you... you dumb jock," she said and quickly kissed him on his smooth cologned cheek.

Bill left her and made his way to the algebra class he had to pass to graduate.

Why was he suddenly so possessed by RaLF—no, possessive of her? Yes, that was right; he didn't feel that he wanted her more. He just didn't want anyone else to have any part of her. He had seen too many movies where the jock boyfriend was a jerk and lost the girl to the geek.

“I'm no jerk,” he muttered aloud to himself.

Bill entered the classroom as the final bell rang, the only senior among a roomful of freshmen and sophomores. He sat at his desk at the back of the room without book, paper, or pencil, but surrounded by girls.

"Can I borrow a pencil?" he whispered to a sophomore cheerleader at his right.

"Sure, Bill," she said, smiling and handed him the one she was holding. "Keep it."

Bill winked at her, not giving RaLF another thought.

* * *

Mary reclined herself upon the couch in the girl's restroom, with a cold, water-soaked paper towel on her neck and one on her forehead. Although her eyes were tightly shut, tears seeped from underneath her eyelids, listening to the words swimming through her mind: "I hate...." Her thoughts never continued with an object because at that moment, at that second, the objects were too plentiful to be specific. She felt hate towards everything.

"How do you feel?” Mary heard as a paper towel dabbed her forehead. When she opened her eyes, the school nurse stood above her.

Mary felt too heavy to move and too bothered to want to. A moan slowly escaped from her mouth as she remembered the bell ringing hours ago, or was it, and vomiting.

"You are a mess,” The nurse assured, wiping Mary's face.

The cool towel soothed Mary, but she grew uncomfortable succumbing to the gentle strokes. So fighting her hapless submission, she pushed away the nurse's hand.

"I gotta' get up," Mary said, pushing herself up from the couch.

"Can you tell me what's the matter?" the nurse asked.

What was the matter? Physically, she was a wreck; emotionally, she was worse. Then she said aloud, "I need to get up..." Mary asserted, pushing against the nurse.

"You're not a well young lady."

"Like I need you to tell me that." Mary exerted herself a final time and sat up. "I want to go home." *No I don't.*

"Come to the health office and rest. Then we'll call your parents."

Mary had heard about students such as herself before. The pressure builds and builds and builds until finally, they're either picking people off with a rifle from some window or falling apart. Yet, it was so early in the school year and her classes and the newspaper were going smoothly. Yes, two issues of The Poncan were down, the second issue coming off so much better than the first. She and Daniel weren't by any means a team, but they were cooperating, so why breakdown?

"I want to go!" Mary repeated a final time more forcefully, her jaw tight.

"Well, let's get your blouse wiped up," the nurse said as she began cleaning the spatter from Mary's blouse.

"Are you listening to me?" Mary sobbed, "Why won't you listen?"

"It'll be all right," the nurse whispered, stroking Mary's short hair to reassure her.

I don't even know what's all wrong. Mary heard her sobs and sniffing.

The restroom door swung open again with the clattering of a bucket and mop.

"Mr. B. said there was an accident," a custodian said, entering the room.

Mary looked past the nurse hovering over her and saw the stream that ran up to the toilet. She shook: a bundle of nerves and little else. Mary tried to stand, but her legs wobbled. "Will you at least help me up?" Mary asked, wondering if the nurse was good for anything.

She took Mary's hand and pulled her from the couch. Once Mary was steady, she walked to a sink, but refused to look into the mirror. Since nearly the beginning of school, she had felt out of sorts—as if the entire world was spinning out of control. Mary was sick and tired—literally—of her parents, of Daniel, and their God.

And then came the joke.

You can do things Yahweh, and I'll do things my way.

Mary's laughter spilled and rumbled from her. She laughed until her side hurt and then she laughed some more. It felt good to her, and with the laugher, she felt free.

I'll do things my way…

The nurse, surprised at Mary's laughter, went to the sink. "Are you all right?"

"I'm fine; I'm finally fine." Mary answered, her voice soft and gentle, as she felt a hot flash but chose to ignore it.

"Let's go so you can lie down, and I'll call your parents."

"Yes, call my parents, and when you talk to them, tell them to take all of their crap and shove it. Then tell them I quit."

Mary walked out of the bathroom.

The nurse, trotting behind Mary's swift gate, asked, "What are you quitting?"

Without turning around, Mary proclaimed, "Everything!"

She felt light as she went to her locker. Looking inside, she grabbed her book bag and shook all of the textbooks onto the floor. She put the things she wanted from the locker into the book bag and pushed everything else onto the floor.

When she stepped out of the building, the sun hovered high in the sky among a scattering of thick clouds, but the cool morning air still smelled sweet, and the grass still glistened with dew. A breeze blew from the north, pushing the odor of the refinery away from the city. So Mary started walking with no particular place to go.

* * *

The sun had moved directly overhead, hiding occasionally behind a cloud, when Mary finally plopped herself down upon the wooden porch to John's trailer. She felt exhausted, walking what seemed hundreds of miles but in fact closer to ten to the trailer park southeast of Ponca City. Old cars and rusty dogs littered small yards. And, where greenery was found, it was merely weeds choking out any grass.

As Mary sat, she noticed for the first time how well John's trailer house matched the rest. She hadn't spent any time noticing the surroundings before. They usually just went from the car, to the bedroom, and away. But seeing the deteriorating condition of everything bothered her. She stood up from the porch and saw that most of the white paint that had at one time coated the porch now speckled the ground in chips. As she tried the front door, knowing it would be locked, she saw the nylon screen covering the window was ripping away from the frame in the door. She sighed.

With sweat running from her hairline down her face and the back of her neck, she realized staying stationary made her feel more hot. She also caught her stomach growling and wished she had brought the soggy cookies from her locker.

As far as she had already walked, she decided to head back to a convenience store a half-mile down the main road that lead to the trailer park entrance. Digging through her wallet, Mary found a five-dollar bill and was satisfied that she could feed herself with that. She put the money in her pant's pocket. Flinging the book bag back over her shoulder, she left the porch and started toward the store.

As she passed the first trailer, a dog began barking at her from its small fenced yard, beginning a whole cacophony of howls from every other dog in the park. Looking around to see if anyone would see her, Mary picked up a rock from the gravel road and threw it at a spotted, thin bird dog in the closest yard. The rock went through the webbing of the fence, hitting the dog on its nose. The dog yelped and ran beneath the trailer through a hole in the metal skirting. Surprised at her aim, Mary smiled and walked on, but after she moved several yards away, the dog ran out from underneath the trailer and began barking again.

Mary's breath tasted like dirt in her pasty mouth. An old pickup spotted with paint primer drove past her, bringing a cloud of dust behind it. Mary covered her eyes and cussed the driver as she ate more dust.

When she reached the main road, the humid autumn heat no longer bothered her. The fact that summer was not loosening its grip to fall ceased to bother her. The long walk to John's trailer had given her much time to wonder, but her thoughts never seemed to stray far. *Am I really doing this?* The reality of quitting school, the actuality that she divorced herself from the only life she had ever known, anchored Mary's thoughts well. But still, she had no intention of becoming a pathetic teenage runaway either.

She was hoping for a safety net, but during the last few weeks she had been pushing John away; now she was pushing herself into the middle of the muck and mire of John's life.

When Mary stepped inside the store, the frigid air from the air conditioning felt as close to a heaven as she could imagine. She grabbed two cans of Coke, a packaged pimento cheese sandwich, and a large bag of Guy's potato chips. Her feast took the biggest part of her five-dollar bill, leaving her only a little change. Looking around, Mary took a place at a table sitting beside a rack of plastic covered magazines.

After she finished her first can of Coke in a few quick gulps, she quietly let out a belch in her hand. The quick burst vented into her nose and tickled it, giving her a quick and abrupt shiver. The pimento cheese spread on the sandwich tasted dry, but it filled her. She slowly picked through the potato chips, noticing the cashier, an older, skinny man looking at her. He smiled at her. She smiled back and got up to leave, stuffing the bag of chips into the sack.

"Thanks fer comin' by. Come back and see me, honey," the man said and winked at her as she stepped out of the store.

The clouds that had speckled the sky all morning had thickened to a deeper overcast sky. The temperature had dropped a little as well, but Mary was too preoccupied. Preoccupied to the point that it took her a second glance at the pay phone outside of the store to remember the one particular thought she had been dodging since taking her first step towards emancipation.

Fishing through her pant's pocket, she pulled out the change from her lunch. She had enough to get the call out of the way so she could get on with the rest of her life. She dropped the quarter into the phone, listening as it landed with a clink at the bottom of an empty chamber. After the dial tone sounded, she dialed her home phone number. She barely heard a single ring when the phone was answered.

"Mary?" her mother questioned, immediately.

"Yes, it's me."

"Oh, thank God; we've been so worried. I..."

"Edna, enough. I don't want to hear anything. I just called to say you're choking me."

"Please don't..."

"Please don't treat me like a child. I'm tired of school. I'm sick and tired of you and the Deacon and all your theocratic horse-shit mumbo-jumbo that you've been force feeding me all my life." *That should give her a stroke.* "I can't stand it anymore. I'll end up in a loony bin if I don't go."

"Mary, your language..."

"...is just fine. I'll be by sometime when you're not home to get my things."

"Where are you going to stay?"

"Don't worry about it."

"You're my baby. Of course I'm worried." Mary could hear her mother's voice crack. "I love you very much."

Mary waited several long seconds after her mother had finished speaking before saying anything, then finally she muttered a simple, "Whatever," and hung up the phone.

Mary leaned against the pay phone, putting her forehead on

the receiver and feeling the dizziness and nausea return. As she tasted her saliva grow thick and salty, she ran around the side of the store to a fifty-gallon drum full of trash and puked, which was followed by a few dry heaves as the mixed fumes of vomit and garbage left little room for any other reaction. After her stomach calmed, she spit a few remnants from her mouth and backed away to breathe fresh air. Her face felt hot and beaded in sweat. A water hose rested against the side of the building, so Mary walked to it and opened the valve. After emptying the hose of hot water, she rinsed her mouth and cooled her face, hoping the exorcism was over.

Panting and her side throbbing, she headed back to John's trailer. As she walked, she began to think about John, wondering for the first time what he might say about his part in all of this—wondering herself what exactly his part was.

Chapter Six

Lonely Metamorphosis

There had been little talk or grinding of the rumor mill. That Mary Christmas left the school in a sick, angry, vomitous frenzy concerned no one, save for one teacher and one student. When Mr. Addison shared the news with Daniel, the troubling consequences consternated Daniel's thoughts, constipated his speech, and led him into a flurry of lisps, stutters, and generally unintelligible gibberish.

"Slow down, Daniel," Mr. Addison said, wiping spatter from his face. "I haven't talked to her parents, so we really don't know anything."

Again Daniel tried to speak, but his frustration only multiplied the awkwardness of his uncooperative tongue, so each vowel and consonant collided into a barrage of meaningless sounds. Mr. Addison looked at him, confused and annoyed, finally taking a sheet of paper from his desk and handing it to Daniel.

"Write it," he ordered.

Daniel took the piece of paper, and as he wrote, he repeated it aloud. "Tho...do...we...go...on...ath...if...nothing...hath... happened?"

"Yes, until we get the whole story, we go on as before. I'll take up Mary's slack for now, and hopefully, she'll be back tomorrow.

The Homecoming issue is going to the printer in four days, and I don't want a whole paper of Earnest's cartoons. And then, if she's not back...." Mr. Addison ended the sentence with a shrug.

Opposed to Mr. Addison's resigned acceptance, tumult reigned through Daniel's soul, Mary's departure causing him such extraordinary and contrasting feelings, feelings that ebbed between mortification and mollification, that he could have cursed her. But, of course, that would have only cursed him instead.

Now, all roads led to him. As much as he felt Mary had taken the paper from him, as much as he had prayed Mary would loose her grip, Daniel had never anticipated—nor prepared—for the whole load. The scripture stating the Lord would never give him more than he could bear came to his mind (that would be the first thing from Reverend Green's mouth), yet Mary's departure weighed heavier upon him than the truth of the scripture, so he lingered in his tribulation like Job, prayerfully dismayed. Slouching, he walked to the newspaper room. "Thomebody, gibe me thomthing to type," he grunted with Mary-like finesse.

Anne Endo handed Daniel an article someone had just given to her. Daniel took it to the typewriter. Here, he had control, so Daniel went to work, his fingers gliding with absolute authority.

* * *

Earnest sat in the cafeteria divorced of his surroundings, estranged of his peers, eating french fries along with a burger, both appetizingly greasy in complementary shades of gray, wishing he could move on to other friendlier pastures.

Earnest would have been surprised and even amazed to find that he and Bill Wright shared the very same ineptitude in acquiring relationships beyond mere acquaintances, so ignorantly he envied Bill from afar. How they had made such divergent treks from the same grade school, Bill landing upon the high road of popularity and Earnest drudging through the low road of anonymity, agitated him to distraction. Over the years he had watched Bill and RaLF sparkle like stars on a clear, moonless night while he faded into the darkness. He was neither handsome nor ugly; neither rich nor poor; neither genius nor fool. Earnest carried the greatest burden of all: being average, and nearly grew insane with his commonness.

"Mind if I thit hew?"

Earnest looked at Daniel's round face staring back, a lunch tray in his grasp.

"Sure," Earnest said with the odd notion of superiority.

Daniel bowed his head quietly for a brief second then sniffed at his food and took a bite of his hamburger, pausing only for a few chews of his food and then said with his mouth full, "Have you heawd about Mawy?"

"No," Earnest said, remaining aloof after deciphering Daniel's words.

"The'th gone."

"Gone where?" Earnest asked, indifferently.

Daniel shrugged his shoulders, taking another bite of his burger and a finger's grasp of fries, and then he said, "Jutht gone," carefully maneuvering the food in his stuffed cheeks like a rodent.

The sounds of the cafeteria rumbled around them, and Earnest sat quietly while the sound of his chewing, the sound of his plastic utensils, and the sound of his scooting chair joined the others. He thought of Daniel's words about Mary: just gone, and stood up, stacking his trash upon his tray.

"Good," Earnest finally said, "she's a bitch."

When he dumped the trash and sat the tray onto the conveyer belt, Earnest wondered why Daniel made him so uncomfortable. Then he wondered why he had been rude to Daniel, and the answer came back simply because he could. Daniel wore his religion on his sleeve and a target on his chest.

But as Earnest left the cafeteria, walking under a large red banner reminding everyone of the Homecoming Queen election that day, he felt badly for what he had said to Daniel, for being a kind of bully to him. He turned around to look at Daniel and saw Daniel's head appeared to be bowed again. *For Christ's sake,* Earnest thought, riled at Daniel's displays and interjections: thank God, pwaithe God, and the verb "bweth" in any of its conjugations. So Earnest walked out, his regret erased by bitter rationalization.

Outside of the cafeteria, Earnest went to a table the student senate set up for Homecoming Queen voting. A small crowd surrounded the table, so he had to reach between two people to get a ballot. It struck him that all the names were those of RaLF's friends, but not hers. Then he was struck by another thought.

Earnest hadn't needed RaLF while Ian was around; it was okay for her to be a dream, so Earnest let her go like a mist from the sea. But while he looked at the names on the ballot, they reminded him that Ian had deprived Earnest, not only of their friendship, but Ian had also taken RaLF away from him in more than a figurative sense. Her indifference had evolved to outright dislike of him.

Yet, in spite of that, Earnest wrote RaLF's name on the ballot and stuffed it into the ballot box.

Working around the crowded table, Earnest headed for the exit thinking he would spend the rest of his lunch time in his Psychology classroom reading because he always had Psychology to read. When Earnest stepped outside toward the Howell Building, Ian was leaning against a walk rail, his nose still wrapped and bandaged.

Earnest looked at Ian, and in that instant he could see a haggard darkness behind Ian's eyes. Over the last few weeks he had grown to see beyond Ian's distorted skewed view of friendship—Ian liked Ian first; Ian liked Ian best. So, not from spite, but from the small amount of wisdom he had garnered, he turned his gaze away and quickened his pace.

"If that's what you want…" Earnest heard from behind, but he didn't stop. It was exactly what he wanted. A cold breeze blew past him, as he continued to his class, realizing he was no longer furious at Ian; his own indifference intruding—pushing Ian into a fading shadow of his past.

* * *

As Jamie boarded the bus at the vo-tech, he again felt the odd nervousness that he had carried with him all day. If Bill wanted to play some kind of hero for RaLF, that was fine; Jamie could shrug that off. But it was what lurked deeper in his mind that teased him. What if he was bored with the kiddie books for no other reason than they were boring? Jamie felt hampered by the burden of improvement upon him yet ridiculous hoping life could hold more for him than grease, liquor, and other such crap.

The ride back to the school did not seem long. Although he

was looking out of the bus window, he didn't see anything other than passing swatches of color. Nor did he hear anything more specific than a raucous mumble from the people around him. And when the bus finally stopped, Jamie was so apprehensive that he didn't think he could climb off. All because a lady had said he was reading better.

"You gonna' take all day?"

Jamie turned around, standing on the bus steps, and realized his mind had been wandering. He had thought he was the last one off the bus and had overlooked Angus and Fiona.

"Sorry," Jamie replied, quickly abandoning the bus.

He watched as Angus and Fiona walked away. Angus, as usual, had his arm tightly around Fiona. But Jamie was uncertain whether Angus was protecting her from the world or he was protecting himself by keeping her from slipping away. It struck Jamie as a strange parallel to Bill and RaLF. He thought about Angus, the king of the hoods, loud, boisterous, obnoxious, the man everyone feared but no one particularly liked. On the other hand, Bill seemed to be liked by nearly everyone, in spite of his obnoxiousness.

When he entered the library, he was greeted by an odd revelation. Instead of being a place to screw around, the library was changing for him just as he was changing, and in all the many volumes surrounding him, there were possibilities—for what, he wasn't clear. So he began looking, but within a few shelves of where he started, he felt lost and depressed.

"Jamie."

He turned around to see Mrs. Irving looking at him. She was very good about showing up at the right time.

"Here," she said, holding out an obviously old and tattered paperback.

Jamie took it and read the cover. "Huckleberry Finn?"

"Yes, it was the first piece of literature I ever read when I was young. After I finished it, I was shocked to find how much I enjoyed it. I've been reading ever since. Maybe I'm overly enthusiastic, but I think you can handle it. Just don't be in a hurry."

"It's thick."

"Jamie, the number of pages doesn't matter. It's all in the words, the ideas that the writer is expressing," she conceded. "This book is easy enough to read, but the ideas are...are..." She paused, looking for the right word, "the ideas are…grand."

"You're the first teacher who's ever given a damn about me."

Mrs. Irving shook her head. "No, I'm not. I'm just the first teacher you've shown you give a damn about yourself."

The weight of those words crashed around Jamie like an avalanche.

"Jamie, your problem isn't that you can't read. You read as well as many of your peers. What you lack is confidence. Your mind needs exercise. You can read this book. It might take you awhile, but you'll do fine."

Jamie was hearing words that he had never heard before, and consequently he felt something that he had never felt before.

"Keep meeting RaLF in the mornings and bring your book. Ask her questions. She's got a copy, too."

Jamie was silent for awhile. Then he finally uttered, "Thanks."

"Huck's younger than you, but I think you'll find you have things in common." Mrs. Irving reached over and patted Jamie on his arm. "I think you'll like the book." And then she left him.

Jamie's mind reeled until he remembered that he had to go to work. As he left the library, he glanced at the book in his hand, hoping he would like it, too.

* * *

After school ended, Ian drove directly to Ponca Discount Foods so that he could pick up his paycheck, loudly cursing Earnest and RaLF and anyone else that popped into his mind.

As his boss counted out Ian's money to him, he said, "See you at four."

"No, I'm not feeling good today." Ian replied, pocketing his money, ignoring his boss's odd glare, and leaving.

From there he drove to a convenience store outside the city limits that would sell beer to minors. He slowly pulled onto the gravel drive. He felt slightly nervous at first, but an inferno inside him burned, melting the anxiety into a shallow pool of meaningless doubt. His older brother had taught him he could always get away with something he shouldn't do by acting like there was nothing to get away with in the first place. *Act like you own the place*.

He opened the car door with focused determination, his knees quivering, softly shutting the door behind him. He stuck his clammy hand into his pockets to check that his cash hadn't unexplainably disappeared, but finding it there didn't ease him.

Entering the store, Ian walked straight to the coolers with the beer at the back of the store and studied the different labels through the glass doors. He grabbed a six pack of Coors and took it to the register. An acne-scarred man wearing thick black plastic framed glasses and a stained western-styled shirt sat on a stool behind the counter.

"Can I see som' kinda' I.D.?"

Ian momentarily felt panicked, but his mind quickly whirled, and instead of running out, he pulled out his driver's license, wrapped a ten-dollar bill around it, and slid it across the counter. Ian looked the cashier in the lenses. *Own the place.* The cashier looked back at Ian, his bloodshot eyes magnified behind the thick lenses, looking almost like two car headlights. Then he looked at the bill; then back at Ian. Ian's hands rolled up into fists and his toes curled up inside of his boots; his breath locked tightly inside his lungs. A large clock behind the counter advertising cigarettes loudly counted every stretching second.

Laughing, the man wadded the bill and pocketed it.

"The beer'll be three-fity."

Ian exhaled and took out more money.

As the cashier put the six-pack into a sack, Ian noticed the strong scent of the cashier's greasy hair tonic in the air. Ian took his spoils and thanked the cashier. As he was leaving, the cashier said, "Say, what happened to yer nose?"

Ian felt at his face, having forgotten momentarily about the bandage across his nose.

"I had an accident," he answered.

"Too bad. Thanks and come ag'in."

Ian hurried inside his car. Momentarily, he had smothered the inferno inside of himself with the distraction of his purchase, but having the beer now beside him, the fire was stoked. He opened the sack and pulled a can from the plastic rings holding the six-pack together. It was his first beer, so when he opened it and took his first gulp, the bitterness surprised him as did the burning that ran from his tongue, down his throat, deep into his stomach. He put the can down, waited a few seconds and then released a wild belch. Ian laughed and then took another deep gulp. It didn't taste good, but he liked it. After he finished the first can, he started the car and drove off, going farther away from the city. He thought getting away from the city and its fumes, getting away from Earnest and RaLF and school would calm him, ensure him that nothing mattered, but the alcohol merely fueled his anger, and his indignation grew. Ian could still picture Earnest ignoring him as he walked by him.

"Screw you, you buttwipe!" Ian yelled, swinging his fist at the windshield but pulling his punch so he barely tapped it. "Damn you," he muttered, feeling the onset of inebriation. He liked it, so he quickly downed the can in large, quick gulps and opened another. "Earnie, you're such a puss," Ian said, punctuating the thought with a drink.

A car shot by him in the passing lane, surprising Ian. He realized that he had been day dreaming instead of paying attention to the road. Looking down he saw that he was cruising fifteen miles under the speed limit. He chuckled, feeling as if he were moving at light-speed. Ahead of him Ian noticed a turn-off marked as a historical marker, so he pulled off to pee. He stumbled out of his car and walked around to the marker. It was a square rock pillar about four feet high; on top it had a bronze plaque which told about the Indian whose face was carved into the rock. Ian could not tell what the Indian's real name was as someone had removed it from the plaque in a sloppy bit of vandalism.

"Well, hello, Chief. It won't piss you off if I take a leak here, will it?" he laughed. He unbuttoned his fly and sighed. "Oh god, I'm a light-weight. Three beers and I'm trashed." He burst out laughing again.

As he turned around, buttoning his trousers, he caught a glimpse of his face reflected in the car window. It seemed as if a stranger was hiding behind the bandage. Ian's hand slowly rose to his face; lightly touching himself, slowly running his fingers across his flesh, feeling deeply like a blind man's touch. When he finally reached the bandage, he stroked it. Then, like a scab, he began picking at the edge till a small part peeled away from his face. Then he slowly tugged at the bandage, breaking the sticky bond between the adhesive and skin. When it at last pulled away, he rolled it up into a ball and dropped it to the ground.

"Do I know you?" Ian asked the reflection in the window.

RaLF had almost flattened the bridge of his nose and pushed it slightly to the left. A bright pink line ran across it, above the nostrils which were also slightly flared now.

"So, I guess you're mine, my pretty. Heh heh heh." Ian said in a high-pitched cackle, petting his nose, still staring at his ugly reflection. He laughed and laughed and laughed and then...Ian wept.

He saw RaLF in his head. He had felt the same way about her as Earnest had, but he didn't have the balls to admit it. It annoyed him that Earnest liked her. He was jealous, even though there was nothing to be jealous of, so he mocked Earnest and he mocked RaLF. And then she broke his freakin' nose.

"Oh, how I hate you now, my bronze beauty," Ian said to the girl's tanned image dancing in his head. He opened the door and grabbed another can of beer. "Ooooh," he moaned, taking a deep drink, "I'll get you for this, and your little dog, too," he added with another cackle. Then he belched again, bursting with laughter.

As he stared again at his reflection, his laughter rose.

"I'm Frankenstein, baby!" He screamed so loudly his voice

cracked and screeched. "I'm the freaking Phantom of the Opera." His cackle became angry.

When he finished his beer, he threw the can as far as he could into the field behind the Chief's marker.

Feeling dizzy, he fell back against the marble marker. The world began spinning, so he grabbed the pillar, hoping to slow it. Several minutes passed, and he did not move, trying to feel more stable. But nothing changed. The longer he stayed, the worse he felt, and then like a crack of lightning, his stomach jerked, and he retched all over the marker, foam and food oozing down the sides of the marker.

Sweat beaded Ian's forehead, but the spinning had stopped, and he felt a little better. "Hot damn," he said with a grin, and grabbed another beer from the sack. He opened it and took a drink, but getting a whiff of the beer, he just couldn't swallow, so he spit it out of his mouth and threw the can in the same direction as he had thrown the other one.

He relaxed again against the car, sliding to the ground, leaning restfully against a tire. Looking at his watch, as the sun edged its way toward the horizon; he noticed that he had lost all track of time as school had been out for hours. Ian's eyes closed and RaLF appeared again. He thought about how much he hated her and how much he wanted her. "I gotta' get out of here," he said, waving away the girl's haunting image, but unable to rise he sighed again as her ghost and the beer lulled him to sleep.

Chapter Seven

Homecoming: Prelude

Friday, October 12

When the dream began, Mary felt a kind of narcoleptic déjà' vu, so she anticipated it all: the empty desert, the blowing sand, the distant echoed cries, the wooden cross, two faceless Roman guards pounding spikes into Daniel's hands and feet. But she then realized Daniel was absent. Her interest piqued, her attention focused, she recognized differences making this dream less a rerun than a remake: the blowing sand thicker; the cries more faint, and the body spread out upon the cross rested in blurred anonymity.

How odd, she thought and watched herself approach the body, the sand flying wildly about her, yet feeling like strips of velvet drawn over her. Mary watched as she drew closer and closer to the body, her curiosity gnawing at her, and when she finally reached the body, Mary registered no shock when she saw that it was in fact her, bound and naked, upon the cross, waiting contentedly for the spikes to pierce her. Mary jarred in her sleep, but her mind echoed, "*It's only a dream,*" and she calmed again.

As the dream unfolded, Mary looked down at herself, awed and confused over her counterpart's submissive acceptance of the crucifixion. Mary, the soon to be crucified, looked up at Mary the observer and smiled, sending shivers through her.

"What's going on here?" Mary the observer bellowed through the howling wind and the flying velvet sand.

"Oh, don't worry 'bout her," one of the faceless guards smirked. "She's just feeling kinda' cross. Heh heh heh."

"Yeah," the other one piped in, "I know something's bothering her, but I can't quite nail it down. Hehehehe."

"Oh, shut up!" Mary said stifling the guards, then asked, "What are you doing?" Mary's voice was stern, but her doppelganger was not affected, her words fluttering away like a flock of small birds.

Mary, the soon to be crucified, raised her head, "I'm soooo tired."

The words were punctuated by the hard rapping of steel against steel. Mary looked down in panic and saw her twin smiling as crimson rivulets flowed from her body. A warm splash slapping her face abruptly awoke Mary, remembering only feelings of fear and resignation from her dream.

She tried to read the clock, but it blurred, so she wiped her eyes of sleep. It was almost five in the morning, so John would be rising with the alarm soon, but since she did not have to get up with him, she closed her eyes again. John rearranged his position, and his hot reeking breath shot over her nose.

John's stagnant morning smell seemed to be the hardest thing she had to get used to since moving in, and as yet, she had not, so Mary rolled onto her side away from the smell and faced the wall, but John did not stop breathing, and his every exhale felt like a welder's torch burning into her back.

With each breath, she counted another second ticking by and anticipated John waking up. But that would be no consolation because then they would begin what had already become a ritual, so she waited, counting every exhale, not daring to move and accidentally wake him. As she found herself about to doze off, the alarm sounded. Mary closed her eyes tight and feigned sleep. John soon rustled, and she heard him moan and felt the mattress jiggle as he turned the alarm off.

"You awake?" John finally whispered in a smelly, airy voice.

Mary remained still, but John drew closer, rubbing against her.

"You awake?" he repeated a little louder.

"No!" she grunted back.

"C'mon, you like it."

"No, not at five in the morning."

"Ah, baabeeee," John harped on, pushing his pelvis against her.

"I don't feel good."

He so immediately became still that Mary thought she had struck John dead. The silence troubled her, so she rolled over. The room was pitch black save a stream of light beaming between the curtains from a streetlamp outside. She was unable to see John, but his breathing revealed his expression.

Without another utterance, John rolled away and left the bed. "I'm sick of hearing that. If you feel so bad, go see a damn doctor."

The very day that she had moved in, Mary had felt a release. She had exorcised the ghosts from her past, and it had been good, very good in fact. And that afternoon, that evening, that night, she and John celebrated. Then, along with the rising of the sun beginning the grand new day, the same ol', same ol' crept back like a devoted mutt. The headaches, the nausea, her inability to sleep an entire night returned. And not since that first day had she felt good.

She hated John for doubting her. *The hell with him*. She had believed that John had loved her instead of just loving the sex. As a matter of fact, she had counted on it; how else could she think to move in with him in the manner she had. That long minute during her last day of school, avoiding the mirror, rinsing the vomit from her mouth, she had reasoned out the necessity of escape. Now she was realizing how stupid she was, not given herself room for the pie in the eye reality in which she found herself. Living with John was a far cry from sleeping with John, and as such, things were changing between the two of them. Disillusioned that John expected her to play house and depressed that her debilitations had returned, Mary wondered if she had been better off before, but she had made her bed, and for now, she was too proud not to sleep in it—even though John kept prodding her awake every morning while she tried. In what seemed the next instant, Mary lurched from the slamming of the trailer door. Twenty-five minutes had passed, and she realized that she had fallen back to sleep. She almost felt sorry for John, but, even more so, she felt sorry for herself, fearing she had begun something that would perpetuate beyond the irritation it now was. With that, her stomach knotted, and she ran out of the bedroom for her morning deposit.

* * *

'...It's lovely to live on a raft. We had the sky, up there, all speckled with stars, and we used to lay on our backs and look up at them, and discuss about whether they was made, or only just happened--Jim he allowed they was made, but I allowed they happened...'

The words read smooth as butter, and Jamie consumed them like a starving man. *'It's lovely to live on a raft.'* Jamie read and reread this sentence, pausing when he finished it to read it again. He could hear the river; he could smell it, see it with the vast blackness of the river's night sky above, perforated by pinpricks of light. Mrs. Irving had been right. Jamie considered Huck his confederate, and although Jamie had never lived on a raft, he just as easily understood Huck's love of freedom. He had experienced it himself, driving his car under Oklahoma's own night sky away from the city.

The glass in the library windows buzzed in their frames as the music of the pep band left the gymnasium, rose into the sky, and tapped less than gently upon the window panes. Jamie continued reading to himself, trying to ignore the constant reverberations, but as he read, the buzzing became a nuisance, just as the whole pep assembly was a nuisance because RaLF took the day off from her tutorial to see her best friend, Polly Perks, reign over her court, appearing for the first time as Homecoming Queen.

Jamie on the other hand did not go to assemble or to be pepped, and instead went to the library as he usually did on Friday mornings. And as Jamie trudged on along the muddy banks of the Mississippi River, he found satisfaction in that he was surviving the current of the sentences and the undertow of the words.

A detached burst of impassioned percussion from the assembly broke the library's bashful silence, pushing its way through the windows, wave by spirited wave and quickly followed by the muffled roar and rumble of several hundred screaming young adults, happily lead by the blue and gold skirted priestesses of Po-Hi.

Trying to be chivalrous and showing his appreciation in the best way he could to RaLF, Jamie had not had a smoke yet this morning. He thought that the smell on his breath bothered her by her expression when they studied, so he deferred until after the lesson. That morning he had forgotten that RaLF would not be at the library and failed to remember until after he had entered the library and the first explosion of noise from the gymnasium tapped his ear. With time to spare before school began, he stuffed the paperback into his back pocket, pulled the tail of the untucked flannel shirt he wore as a jacket over it, and headed to the smoke pit.

The 'pit,' as it was called, was a walled, open air, concreted space, nestled between the three major buildings of the school, delegated as the place for adolescent smokers to keep them out of the restrooms. Jamie took a seat on a bench next to Ned "the head," an obese fellow with long wavy hair and a beard of ambitious fuzz.

Ned "the head" reached over and yanked lightly on Jamie's hair asking, "Where's the tail?"

Jamie's hair hung loose and strait, just short of draping over his shoulder; his bangs dangled before his eyes so he intermittently and unconsciously pushed them out of his face with a quick jerk of his head. He shrugged his shoulders replying, "Had a wild hair."

Ned “the head” nodded back, dragging on his cigarette, oblivious to Jamie's joke.

Laughing, Jamie lit a cigarette, stole a quick puff, and then took it from his mouth, the filter pinched between his middle finger and thumb, cupping the ash end in his palm. Looking around the usual collection of nasty girls and bad boys, he noticed someone new.

"Who is that?” Jamie asked Ned “the head,” pointing with the filter of his cigarette.

"The guy who looks pissed off at the whole world?"

"Yeah."

"Dunno, but he has got one ugly nose on him. Guess I would be pretty pissed off too if I had to look at that schnoz first thing in the morning." Then Ned “the head” snickered.

"Yeah," Jamie agreed.

Ian, standing at the other side of the pit, caught Jamie's eye for a split-second. That instant of eye contact disquieted Jamie, so he dropped his cigarette and crushed it under his boot.

"Take it easy, Ned-head," Jamie said, and he left.

The music of the pep band and the roar of the crowd boomed in the pit, so Jamie missed Ned’s parting words, reentering the Howell Building. As he stood at his locker, getting the notebook he had recently started to carry, the five minute bell rang, and within seconds the hall filled with people. On his way to Mr. Riggins's class, someone carrying a thick stack of papers quickly shoved one into Jamie's chest, then hurriedly walked on, distributing the rest as quickly as he could. When Jamie looked at it he saw that it was a roughly drawn map with the heading !!!MAJOR KEG PARTY!!! He shoved it into his pocket without much thought.

* * *

It was finished, and Daniel smiled with the results. The Homecoming issue of the Poncan was off the presses and being assembled for distribution. Like an assembly line, the staff willing to sacrifice the pep assembly paraded single-file along a table, holding the separate pages of the paper in stacks, taking each page, putting one on top of the other in proper order and folding the whole thing in half to end up with an eight by eleven and a half inch high school news magazine.

Polly Perks made the cover along with her attendants, all dressed in gowns. She wore a tiara and held a bouquet of flowers in place of a scepter. The photograph was taken at the historic home of a former oil baron and Oklahoma governor, giving the photo, and the girls, enough regalia to suit the occasion. Behind the cover, there were news stories about the debate team's success, the unusually high number of teacher pregnancies, and plans the city was making about opening a youth center. The paper also carried a record review of the new, highly anticipated OX album, *Babies with Rabies*. There was an article on odd student pets. Earnest drew another cartoon. Polly had an article about her to accompany the cover. The sports section was filled with information about that evening's game against Blackwell as well as the highlights, few as they were, from the previous devastating loss to Tulsa Washington, a school whose marching band had more athletic prowess than the Ponca City Opossum football team.

Overall, the paper was a success, and that Daniel and staff had pulled it off without Mary's assistance made him feel so good he thought it almost sinful. Now, the sermon stood before him that night, and as God had already been showing him what to say, Daniel was confident God would answer his prayer of leading at least one to salvation. As he thought about it, Daniel smiled with the idea of giving someone a homecoming of another sort.

* * *

Kick em' in the knees!
Hit em' in the head!
We'll kill Blackwell,
Dead, dead, dead!!!

And the crowd exploded in a lustful, savage cacophony of cheers, the pep band roaring in a brassy, percussive exuberant overture. Earl stood taping his feet in a corner enjoying the festivities, his dust mop in hand, waiting to sweep up when all was finished.

Get up 'Possums!
Don't be shy!
We'll help the Pirates
Die, die, die!!!

The football team, wearing their jerseys, sat on the bleachers, taking in the crowd's idolatrous worship and loving every minute as the cheerleaders darted into the gymnasium, revealing much of their femininity in their blue and gold mini-skirts. They jumped, hollered, twirled, twisted, somersaulted, yelled, vaulted, skipped, hopped, tumbled, leaped, danced, and shimmied their way onto the center of the floor, whipping them into rapturous, ecstatic pandemonium. They had the words; they had the gyrations. Music with a heavy bass beat, boomed loudly from the intercom system, the volume so high that the sound distorted into an aural blur. But no one cared. The cheerleaders danced like slaves to the music, moving to and fro with every beat. They worked and worked, teased and teased, and just before reaching the moment, the very instant of climax—the music stopped, the motions ceased and the girls let out a thunderous war cry:

Eat em' up; spit em' out; stomp em' to the ground!
The Blackwell Pirates are goin' down!
Ain't no need to shake; ain't no need to shiver!
We'll feed the Pirate his own liver!!!

By the time the cheerleaders finished, the students salivated like Pavlov's dogs, yearning for victory. This year, though, the gods had smiled upon Blackwell's football team while Ponca City had gotten little more than an annoyed sneer. Nevertheless, with the specter of another loss looming over them like a hungry buzzard, the Ponca students boldly cheered, carried away by the excitement.

When they see our team,
They'll hold their breath!
Cause were gonna' take em'
To the Valley of Death!!!

Coach Burnside, accompanied by a rousing version of the Opossum fight song, went to the podium to speak. He was greeted by a stirring round of applause in spite of his lackluster performance as head coach. But all felt encouraged this morning and somehow hoped that Homecoming would spur the boys to accomplish a feat beyond their abilities.

Coach Burnside, modulating his voice a little louder with each word, ended with a scream. "I want to thank you all for coming out this morning and showin' my boys you believe in em'. We're gonna' do our best to make you proud and show Blackwell what us Opossums are made of!" The crowd stood in thunderous glee while the pep band roared to life. The coach smiled, raising his arms, conducting the adulation, and as his arms lowered the intensity of the praise softly fell. "C'mon boys!" he yelled, waving the team to join him, "This is for you!" And the crowd burst out again in gracious applause and music as the football team rose and surrounded their coach at the podium. "This is it! The one to remember!" The coach screamed into the microphone, the speakers ringing with feedback. The crowd screamed back. The cheerleaders jumped and tumbled. God was on this throne and all was right in the world.

Pity the Pirates,
When we're done!
Cause they're gonna' need a
Sur--ur--geon!!!

* * *

Ian sat on a bench, smoking a cigarette in the pit outside the gymnasium exit, watching the delirious student body march by. As his eyes followed, he chanted his own special cheer, his voice petering out to a lonesome whisper:

Two, four, six, eight,
Who do I appreciate?
No one, no one, noooo one."

Chapter Eight

Homecoming: Pregame

Football and alcohol reigned as the most popular topics of conversation reverberating throughout the school's halls. Although the enthusiasm of the pep assembly had seeped out of the gymnasium and onto the remainder of the morning's activities, by lunchtime it had mostly evaporated. Conversely, the optimism in regard to the MAJOR KEG PARTY remained high, and if anything, it surpassed the football game as the day's MAJOR event.

So, while the school day progressed, the anticipation grew thick and arduous for most, but for Earnest, it held little reward. Earnest had to work. So when school ended, he drove to wallow in hamburger madness.

After he arrived at Harvey's Fine Fried Burgers, Earnest checked the next week's schedule noticing the dirty work of Helmet-head's red pen—a long crimson mark eliminating some unsuspecting employee from the happy Harvey crew. He drudged downstairs to the basement, cold and damp like a dungeon. He took off his shirt and hung it on the rack that held the happy Harvey crew's uniforms, taking a pastel Harvey smock and a paper Harvey hat for himself. Then as soon as he went back upstairs, Helmet-head Smith sent him to the grill.

Earnest nervously loaded it up with frozen meat patties, landing with the sound of falling bricks, and he slapped the button that started the burger timer. Earnest always felt nervous at the grill, lacking the coordination needed to flip burgers the Harvey way—a strict, regimented method of frying burgers.

"Move it Graves; we gotta' beat *that friggin' clown*." Helmet-head Smith's arid, high pitched voice obsessed, giving Earnest the shakes.

"That friggin' clown, that friggin' clown," echoed throughout the kitchen.

Earnest hated that friggin' clown.

Then the buzzer buzzed.

Earnest slid his spatula under two patties at a time and flipped them over and restarted the timer.

"Sear the burgers, Graves!" Helmet-head belted out.

Sear the burgers? Earnest thought.

Helmet-head grabbed Earnest's hand holding the spatula and pressed the spatula down on a pair of patties on the grill. "Sear the burgers," Helmet-head grunted, the scent of stale cigarette breath floated about Earnest's face. Helmet-head then let go of Earnest's hand as his expression screamed, *"That friggin' clown."*

Earnest's mind raced to remember everything he had seen in the Happy Harvey instructional videotapes during his first day at work; so much to pack into only one brain.

Then the buzzer buzzed again. They were always right, so he scooped up the burgers in pairs, just as he had turned them, holding them to the spatula with his fingers, the grease bubbling at the top of the patties burning him as he placed them upon perfectly prepared buns.

"Hustle, Graves, hustle! *That friggin' clown*!"

With every word, Earnest grew anxious, and as were Helmet-head's wishes, Earnest moved faster. However, as he gained speed, he sacrificed the fine acumen of a professional burger maker. With a quick turn to the buns behind him, the two patties on his greasy spatula slid from underneath his fingers, flew over Helmet-head's head, knocking off the manager's paper Harvey hat, and adhered to the exhaust fan above the fries, looking like two large, tear-filled brown eyes watching the kitchen laborers below.

Everyone stood silent, returning the hamburger patties' stare, Earnest's heart beating in his temples. Slowly, one of the patties began to slide. Then followed by the other, they landed on the floor with two simple plops.

Then another buzzer buzzed.

"Fries up," someone said, and the kitchen jumped to life while Earnest waited for something dreadful.

"McCormick, take the grill," Helmet-head boomed. "Graves, clean up your mess and hit the dishes!"

Deflated, Earnest slouched his way to the hamburger patties on the floor and tossed them into a plastic barrel labeled 'waste.' Then, embarrassed by every look that came his way, he mopped up the greasy mess. Afterward, he humbly slogged his way to the back of the kitchen. The fear of the red pen swam around in his head as he watched the suds bob to the top of the sink. When the bubbles reached their peak, he dove into the dirty dishes, pleased to be away from the grill and doing something where he could prove his worth.

So he scrubbed, quickly, efficiently, the happy Harvey way, and when he finished, Helmet-head gave Earnest a broom and sent him to sweep sidewalks. Outside, Earnest was at least out of Helmet-head's laminated hair.

Earnest met Clinton Smith, Manager on his first day of work and had surprised Earnest, looking to be not much older than himself. A beard refused its place upon the manager's chin, the chin of a teenager, speckled with bright red pimples. His dark brown hair covered his ears, combed back into a pseudo-pompadour like a televangelist and saturated with a gel rendering it incapable of motion. And, if one hair did by some occurrence move, every other hair on Clinton Smith, Manager's head moved with it. Someone of the happy Harvey crew had christened him Helmet-head, and the title took its place at the top of the list of other names (most of which had an orifice of the human anatomy as their root) Clinton Smith, Manager, had been called during his reign at Harvey's Fine Fried Burgers.

Earnest quickly learned of the strong dislike for Helmet-head amongst the happy Harvey crew, and it did not take much time before Earnest's own dislike fell in league with the rest. Helmet-head, a company crony, armed with his red pen, terrorized his employees, saying the end justified his meanness. So, while Earnest swept and mopped the tiled sidewalk, while Earnest picked up the wind blown trash and discarded Harvey's food paraphernalia, he couldn't help but wonder if he too might soon be another casualty in Helmet-head's friggin' burger war.

* * *

The musty smell of man's righteousness permeated the church, floating from pew to pew and into the high ceiling's arches; weaving in and out of every nook and cranny, resting woefully and completely upon the faithful who had come to hear the absent Ben Dunn, a Vice President of the Southern Baptist Convention, fallen ill at the last minute. An organ thundered hymns of salvation, each note springing forth from pipes, bouncing from wall to wall like a chromed globe inside a pinball machine.

So, as Daniel stood behind the ornamental pulpit, the cavernous sanctuary was but speckled by a spattering of familiar smiling faces. The revival was a bust; the Reverend Green's poor planning had stalled it; the missing Vice President had incapacitated it, and the homecoming football game had finished it off.

Although not surprised at the low attendance (God had warned that few would heed the call), it irritated Daniel. He saw lives hanging in a balance, choosing their eternity with less care than they did their dinner from a Harvey's Fine Fried Burger menu, so he prayed.

When he finished the prayer, the tiny congregation joined in a weak, scattered chorus. Looking around, sadness enfolded Daniel. What before that had seemed so wonderful, now felt dull and inconsequential. These people didn't need anything he had. They were his family; some had prayed for him before he had been born. Sighing, he realized several long, silent seconds had passed since he had finished praying. Even the face of the stained glass Jesus across the church, arms outstretched welcoming all that came, waited for what was coming next from Daniel. So Daniel looked back at the stained glass, deep into the visage of his savior. *Ithn't thith what you wanted me to thay,* thinking deeply on the testimony of his miracle.

"I pwayed and pwayed and pwayed and pwayed," he said, looking down at the open Bible upon the podium, "not knowing how to anthwer Weverwend Gween." He paused and looked up, clearing his dry, scratchy throat.

Then as if a spotlight shone down from Heaven, he saw her, a stranger, and even though she sat near the back, as was the Baptist way, her eyes betrayed her. The distant dark orbs, hiding behind the flowing mantle of her dirty-blonde hair, told him much more about her than did her unfamiliar face: she was hurt.

She was his audience this night, and Daniel's anxiety sifted away.

"But I am the gweateтht miwicle I know of, and I believe God would like fow me to teww you about me." He looked directly at the young woman, hoping she would get his message and answer the call.

Daniel began with God knitting him together in his mother's womb; occasionally growing so excited, he had to slow his words to be understood. His Bible, though he had yet to quote a single scripture from it, was freckled with his raining spittle. Sweat beaded his forehead, so he pulled a handkerchief from the back pocket of his baggy black slacks and wiped his face; to be safe, he wiped his lips too, worrying they dripped with saliva.

Daniel's narrative delivered like a school girl's forbidden note, each flap interlocking, creating a solid envelope, yet as Daniel spoke, a flap would come undone; a crease would unfold and the secrets within appeared. He told of his mother's fears and tears, his father's broken pride and weighty shame because of that pride. He spoke how some always saw him as a fat retarded boy though his grades might be as good as theirs. He spoke of the weight of Down's syndrome, and the blessing of rising above the niche of which so many thought he belonged.

As much as he hoped to reach the mystery lady, Daniel found he was talking to himself even more. Getting by day to day—the mundane overtook the incredible, and Daniel would forget what he was. Now, behind the podium, in front of this woman, he remembered that he was a gift.

"Wejoithe in the Lowd, alwayth," he said and shut his Bible. Then looking at the mystery lady at the back, he continued. "I'm thpethial becauthe God made me thpethiel, but no mow than you. In Chwitht Jethuth, you can do all thingth. In Chwitht Jethuth, you can beat any thiwcumthtanthe. You have a choithe tonight. If you don't know Jethuth, let me pway with you. Have faith and thay yeth to Jethuth." The Bible said to be bold, and he was being as bold as he could. He looked at the woman, trying to welcome her. His eyes pleaded to her. "Have faith," he repeated. The organist began the opening measure to "Just as I Am." Daniel stepped from behind the podium to the front of the platform, ready for her. And she stood. The boy felt his stomach dance. *This is it.* She scooted down the pew to the aisle. He smiled, more sweat beading, his temples pulsing. He raised his arms to welcome her into the kingdom of God. Then he watched as she disappeared out of the door.

* * *

Atop flatbed trailers and pickup beds, giant papier-mâché' Opossums, standing in various poses of destruction aimed at smaller yet still larger than life papier-mâché' Pirates, were parked along the west end of the football field, near a waiting ambulance. Local radio stations' banners flew from the press box atop the bleachers. Homecoming had arrived, and Ponca City prepared for a battle.

Coach Burnside's boys huffed and puffed and cussed and beat their helmets against their lockers to pump themselves up for the game—ready to meet the devil himself and give him all the hell he could take.

The coach spoke to them of winners and losers, victory and defeat, and the boys listened while huffing and puffing and cussing and beating their heads into lockers. One player stood and prayed, so the others reverently lowered their heads, quietly huffing, puffing, cussing and tapping their heads into the lockers.

When the time finally arrived, with Bill Wright leading, the boys charged out of the locker room and onto the field, ripping through a large paper banner. The cheerleaders instigated such a roar from the crowd one would have thought they announced the Second Coming. Everything that the students had felt during the pep assembly returned. The want of blood permeated the air; a violent spirit reborn.

The Opossums won the toss and choose to receive.

It was a good start.

* * *

RaLF sat proudly in the bleachers; her best friend, the Homecoming Queen; and her boyfriend, the football star (albeit shining dimly). She smiled, gleefully, as the Blackwell Pirates kicked the ball to her Opossums. RaLF stood, shrieking "Go 'Possums," along with the rest of the people in the stands as the ball glided upwards. The Opossums waited on its slow descent while the Pirates charged. The ball thudded into a receiver's arms. *"Go 'Possums!"* The receiver ran five yards, bolting forward right into a Pirate tackle. *"Go 'Possums!"* The receiver's lungs emptied with a mighty huff, and the ball flew back up into the air. *"Go 'Possums!"* Gravity reclaimed the ball, and it tumbled toward Earth, landing in the grasp of some Blackwell Pirate who ran it into the endzone for a touchdown.

"Ooooohhhh," RaLF moaned along with the entire south bleacher.

The extra point was good, of course, and it too was followed by another anguished moan, a devastating ending to their good start. Accepting the same tinge of despair that had tickled her for the last two losing seasons, RaLF and two of her friends left for the snack bar.

Under the bleachers, parents worked the concession stands, pouring drinks, grilling wieners, bagging pickles, and popping corn. The line was long and confused as there were as many people behind the bleachers, either waiting for a place at the counter or roaming about in the darkness of the autumn evening, as there were people watching the game.

RaLF and her friends ventured into the crowd, stopping to talk to other little packs of the school's elite along the way. Finally, taking her place in line, RaLF remained silent, listening to her friend's banter. Soon the girls' words became a droning to RaLF, her mind wandering, yet interjecting enough one syllable comments that neither of her friends detected her sudden depression.

It had come upon her as they had passed Polly and her attendants, looking ever so regal as they oversaw the festivities of Homecoming. RaLF had personally seen to it that Polly received a free gown from her mother's boutique, The Perfect You. She was happy for her friend, but at the same time, she felt covetous for the attention.

The line slowly moved forward. RaLF's friend's conversation went on with much greater momentum than did the line; their droning had become like elevator music, filling the cracks in the evening's ambiance before RaLF knew the cracks were there. Every few minutes, loud roars would spill over the top of the bleachers and sprinkle upon them like a May shower, telling them not so great things were happening on the playing field. But the roars did not grab a hold of RaLF, for they merely spoke of Bill, the football hero.

The depression sank in deeply and by the time the gun signaled halftime, it had paved the way for unabashed pity. Sitting in the bleachers, holding an empty paper tray with specks of solidified nacho cheese stuff and a cup half full of diluted cola, RaLF sat oblivious that the Opossums were down by thirty-five points. And when the parade of the papier-mâché' monuments began, Polly and her court blindly waving from shiny convertibles, RaLF didn't care. But when the cars stopped, and Bill, the King of Homecoming, greeted his queen with a kiss at the fifty yard line—a kiss where lips parted, a kiss that made jaws ache, a kiss that went on to the end of the ages—RaLF began to, a ghost of the embrace burned onto her retina, blurring all within her line of vision.

* * *

Earl's father's attention was divided between the football game on the radio and the hissing police scanner, periodically squelching awake with reports of peeping toms or speeding drivers or some other minor violations. As a fan of Opossum football, the old man was avid as well as livid, wondering why the hell Coach Burnside still had a job. The old man leaned forward in his worn recliner, slowly rocking his head and shoulders back and forth. Earl listened too, but he was so enraptured by the pictures he saw flipping through National Geographic that the announcer's play-by-play remained nothing more than static.

His mother clanged about the kitchen.

"Earl," she called.

He looked up. "Maw?" He enunciated slowly and precisely, his voice pitched high and delicately.

"C'mere. I want you to go to the store."

"Can't the boy wait till half-time?" the old man called back.

"If I could wait, he could, but I can't, so he can't."

Earl stood up from his chair. "I want to go," he said smiling, as his thoughts of candy bars teased him like a shameless teenage girl who had learned the power of her breasts, butt, and lashes. His father leaned a little closer into the radio, his brow furrowed all the way up his bald head, waving his son on, saying, "Hurry."

His mother handed Earl his notebook with the pasted picture shopping list. He looked through it as the silver haired woman pointed out what each item was. Clinging tightly to the notebook, he went to the garage and pushed the large tricycle that he rode out onto the driveway. He tossed the notebook safely into the big wire basket on the back. Then he straddled the seat, turned on his headlight, and peddled away.

The trail was the same as he had been taught years ago and had since followed unwaveringly. The headlight bobbed along the bumpy streets as Earl peddled by reflex, the trip imbedded in his subconscious like a tattoo on a rock star's backside. The streets he traveled were barren, so Earl maneuvered through them easily. Looking ahead, Earl could see the glow above treetops from the football stadium lights blocks away, and hear the distant roar of the crowd.

Night set in with a near full moon casting shadows slithering upon the ground. Earl slowly peddled amongst them. His mind focused on his candy bar. In the darkness, his single thought was free from distraction, and as such, grew like a cancerous organ feeding upon itself.

The grocery store's parking lot was as deserted as the streets Earl traveled. Only the football stadium and the city's clubs and bars could boast of a busy evening this Friday night. Earl parked his trike in front of the store, walking it up over the curb of the sidewalk surrounding the store to get the trike out of harm's way. He then grabbed his shopping list from the basket and went inside.

Earl took his familiar path; just like the trek to the store, Earl's walk through the store was every bit as ingrained. He pushed the cart up or down every aisle, taking an item from the shelf whenever he saw the one that matched the picture pasted inside the notebook.

When he reached the last aisle, he looked to the other end. Eyeing the assorted boxes of candies, a wave of excitement flooded over him. His cart weaved right and jarred back left as Earl hurried to the far end. The jitters and tingles within him erupted in a maddening fury when he finally stood before the candy. He grabbed a chocolate bar and slid it into his pocket, calm sweeping over him, relieving him like a cold front sweeping across the Oklahoma plains in July.

Earl pushed his crippled cart to the only open register. The checker read the price of each item aloud as she rang it up. Her horn-rimmed glasses, her colored red hair, her bright clothes and bell-bottomed pants, her painted face and thick orange lipstick echoed her name, Kitty. When Kitty had the total, Earl gave her the money. A young man sloppily sacked the groceries for Earl, and after Earl pocketed the change, the sacker handed the bag back to him. Earl took the sack, holding it tightly in his grasp and left the store.

"S'cuse me, you need to pay for that candy bar."

Earl heard the voice behind him, but it didn't occur to him that it was directed at him, so he walked on.

"S'cuse me..." the voice spoke again.

As Earl put the sack of groceries into the basket, he felt a sharp tug at his shoulder. Earl turned to see a face hidden in dark, blotchy shadows of the night.

"I have to go home," Earl replied, his voice unassuming.

"That candy bar in your pocket needs to be paid for."

Earl pulled away, taking his seat upon the trike.

"My daddy said to hurry back."

The man from the store grabbed the basket.

"You're not going anywhere until that candy bar is paid for."

Earl began to peddle. The trike slowly inched forward, but the man was steadfast in his grip. Earl grunted, his hands shaking from his tight grip.

"I'll call the police," the man threatened.

"Uuuhhh, I've got to go home," Earl strained his stout legs, and the trike kept moving forward, but the man stayed close behind. Waving an arm behind him, Earl tried to shoo the man away like a bothersome gnat.

The trike jumped the curb, jarring Earl.

When the back wheels left the curb, the man lost his footing. So as Earl's trike shot forward, the man fell forward with it; his chin landing hard upon the concrete parking lot, splitting his chin open and biting off the very tip of his tongue.

"Ow, thit!!" he screamed as Earl sped away. "Call the polithe!!"

Earl panicked, his fear erasing the trip home that before he had never even contemplated. He looked around confused and uncertain. The trike moved quickly as Earl peddled as hard as his adrenaline pushed him, his heart beating well up into his temples. He had no idea where he was headed besides away from the store, but the direction of his tricycle took him away from his home and closer to the high school where the half-time festivities had just begun.

When he saw the school, a little of the fear abated, and he headed his trike directly to it. "No police," he cried, knowing if he saw them, he would be in trouble. Reaching the school, he pulled into the faculty parking lot on the north side of the Howell Building and parked his trike in the same place he parked every morning, huffing and puffing, his heart palpitating.

A loud siren suddenly erupted from the stadium, and terror gripped Earl. *Police.* A horrified moan escaped his lips, and he darted away from the school, peddling madly, while a sudden pain burst across the right side of his head, blurring his vision.

For as long as he could, he rode, blinded by fear and pain, but his trail had no reason. He turned right or left without discretion or thought and occasionally circled a block. When finally spent, exhaustion taking its advantage over him, he stopped in the alley behind a small strip mall. Parking his trike beside a large green dumpster, his front wheel bumped into the building's wall. Earl was unable to decipher or understand the events of the past hour. He was not even sure of the amount of time that had passed. All that he did feel was the shaking of his body, his tingling arm and his throbbing head. And with his vision remaining blurred, he began crying in his confusion and pain.

He had forgotten about the candy bar in his pocket, and the remembrance slowed the tears. Taking the candy bar from his pocket, it had lost its shape, the chocolate melting from the heat of his sweating body. He opened the wrapper, and quickly ate the candy, the sticky goo smearing across his lips like lipstick on a little girl's face. When the candy bar was gone, he wiped his hands on his coveralls, and ran his arm over his mouth, smearing chocolate from his face to his forearm. His arm smelled of sweat and tasted of salt.

Not knowing where he had stopped, Earl sat on the ground, hiding in the shadows as if behind a black velvet curtain, shaking occasionally as cool drafts of air made the dampness of his coveralls frigid. Finally, the pounding headache beat him to sleep. Sitting curled against the wall, a stream of snores floated into the air like smoke signals calling for help.

Chapter Nine

Homecoming: Postgame

The final gun sounded, and the divisiveness within the stadium was palatable. The half-time score of thirty-five to zero had been nothing in comparison with what was to come. The game ended at eighty-five to nothing, and nothing proved precise. The Opossums presented nothing in the place of defense, and even less in the way of offense. The greatest challenge the game did present, if any, was to the poor parents running the concession stands, and upon eating the food that they served, it was plain to many that the concession's offense was also stronger than the football team's.

The north side of the stadium, where the visitors sat, boasted a gleeful barrage of approval. They came to witness an ass-kicking and left appeased. The Opossums had simply rolled over to be put down as so much extra-curricular road kill. At least there would be a wake: a MAJOR KEG PARTY to drown their Homecoming sorrows; a chance for the students to come together and mourn and then puke. So the crowd trickled from the stadium, dispersing like streams from a river, glowing processions headed in two directions: north to Blackwell or west to the MAJOR KEG PARTY.

RaLF drove alone to the MAJOR KEG PARTY. Her Corvette's stereo boomed so loudly her ears rang. She pouted, her bottom lip sticking out just the way it used to do as a child, lost between exhaustion and self-pity.

Then again, perhaps it was her period. It had come upon her that morning barreling like a train jumping its tracks. She felt cramped. She felt bloated. And she felt ugly. The day had started with her staring at *the horror* in the mirror, her skin mocked by pimples. Regardless of how she fixed her hair, how she rubbed, brushed, or blotted her make-up, it remained an *ugly* day.

At the city limits, she pulled into a convenience store and bought a pack of cigarettes. She didn't normally smoke, but it seemed the thing to do while drinking—and she planned to be drinking a lot. She imagined herself as a happy drunk, and she wanted to be happy.

After pulling off Highway 60 onto a gravel road, RaLF drove slowly so not to kick up any rocks and chip the paint of the nice car her daddy was paying for. She slowly sucked on her cigarette, breathing it deep into her lungs unlike those pretentious little princesses who only puffed. When she reached the closed gate at the entrance, a guy walked up to her car.

"Hi, RaLF, where's Bill?"

She shrugged. "He'll be here sometime, I guess."

"Cool," the guy answered, his head bobbing up and down like some kind of toy. "It's five dollars to get in."

RaLF handed him a five dollar bill from her pocket.

"See ya," she said, sending him away.

"Yeah," he replied, his head still bobbing.

Another guy opened the gate, and RaLF followed a trail of

flattened grass. Up ahead a large bonfire burned high into the sky, along with several smaller fires that were scattered about like a litter of newborn flames, the temperature of the night air dropping. She parked her car next to a giant jacked-up four wheel drive truck with huge tires. When she stepped out of her car, the loud drone of rock and roll filled the air; the bass sounding like the earth's heartbeat. RaLF walked towards the big bonfire where ten kegs of beer, all iced up and tapped, waited for her, ready for a party. Someone had pulled their car up and opened their hatch, pointing two huge booming box speakers out towards the beautiful outdoors. RaLF recognized the song as one of her current favorites, so as she approached the kegs, she sang along with it, swaying her hips back and forth. She stood ambivalent and distracted among dozens of people, of whom none wanted to stray too far from the beer.

"There you are! We lost you after the game." RaLF's two friends came up to her. Both held a cup of beer in one hand, a cigarette in the other, and an extra five years of attitude. RaLF smiled, knowing that they had not lost her; she had lost them, tired of their chatting. She took a cup from one of the kegs and said, "Let's get shit-faced." They erupted in laughter. RaLF filled her cup to begin her long night.

* * *

It was near noon when Mary pulled herself out of bed, and although she had spent most of the prior fourteen hours asleep, she had still felt ragged and tired. Drowsily, she had pulled herself to the kitchen and fixed a can of bean soup for lunch. After she had eaten, she took a long shower, ending up in a recliner in front of the television, watching soap operas. While she watched, letting one program blend into the next, Mary paid little attention and as time went by unnoticed, the story lines mixed and tangled amongst one another, giving Mary in her semi-conscious state a spider's web of plots to comprehend. Her thoughts floated freely without the benefit of a current to direct them, and they bounced from the web of fiction into the stream of her own melodramatic life: *Why are these people so stupid? Why is John always upset? Should I see a doctor?* By the time six o'clock rolled around and John was late from work, Mary countered the seriousness of the problems of her own life over the silly situations of daytime drama.

Not once had she risen from the chair. For hours she had became one of the living dead, and she left it now only to pee. Wiping herself, she thought about her period and wondered if it would ever be normal. She envied women who had a perfect twenty-eight day cycle. Hers had always been incredibly irregular, and now it had been weeks since her last. Yes, yes, yes, maybe John was right; maybe she should see a doctor, and find out once and for all what was draining her, destroying the Mary who had once thought that it was better to be feared than loved. She felt empty, realizing that there was no one around to fear her even if she had been able to elicit such a response, so she returned to the recliner.

As the sun set, Mary became aware of how angry she really must have made John for him to be so late. Mary remembered when their relationship began. She had been the dominant one. John, curious and bored, followed where she led. But since moving in the scales shifted, her power usurped, and Mary found herself submitted to John. Before, he would have not dared to make her wait; now, she didn't dare tell him not to. She moved in almost daring him to refuse her. John could not, so Mary entered his house—but in doing so, she became dependent on him. Something she had not anticipated at all. Food, shelter, hope, in whatever degree, were all there because of him. She had curled up and let a little comfort, very little comfort, wear away her edge. She didn't understand this. She had been just as dependent on her parents, but she hadn't let them put her into such a submissive roll.

She felt a touch of fury rise, a touch of the old Mary, and she left the recliner for the kitchen. From a cabinet over the sink, she took a bottle of Kentucky bourbon. Mary poured some in a cup and slowly sipped it. The alcohol warmed comfortably like an old friend all the way down to her toes. As she began to pour herself another cup, she stopped. She did not want to be unsteady when John got home. So feeling calm, finding old pieces of Mary drifting into place, she returned to the recliner, continuing her vigil.

A little after eleven, she heard the familiar rumble of John's car outside of the trailer. Mary's hands squeezed the arms of the recliner till her fists were white.

"Where the hell have you been?" she spewed with all the rage she could muster as he stepped into the trailer, surprised at the anger in her voice.

John looked at her and laughed.

This was not what she had anticipated, and she hesitated.

"Where have I been?" John repeated. "I don't answer to you."

"You jerk," her voice squeaked loudly.

"Yeah, maybe...." he said coming toward her.

John seemed different, frightening her.

"What the hell are you talking about?" Mary asked rising from the chair.

John pushed her back into it, smelling of the same bourbon Mary drank earlier.

John held her in the chair, tightly grasping her neck. She struggled to breathe, even as his grip grew tighter.

"I saw a football game, got drunk, and I got some good advice," he said, breathing his fumes on her, staring her down with poisonous eyes.

"What advice?" Her voice cracked.

"Baby, if you're not gonna' give it, I'll just take it," he calmly answered and started tugging at the fly of her jeans.

"Stop it!" She shouted, trying to wriggle out from his grasp, but he only squeezed tighter, stronger than she had ever realized. He quickly had her pants open. When she felt his fingers slip into her underwear, her squirming quickened. She looked at John, beating at his arms and slapping at his face, but he aimed his wild stare down at his hand, ignoring all of her struggling.

"John, dammit. Let me go!" Then as his fingers pushed up inside of her, tugging and yanking her, she shrieked, bringing up her knee hard into his groin. The kick sent him reeling back, and he fell into the television set. With him startled, Mary jumped ran for the front door, choking for air. Before she reached it, John lunged at her. Unable to grab her, he pushed her instead, and she flew forward, her face crashing into the door.

"Shit!" she screamed and turned around, ready to fend off another attack as best as she could, her face wrapped in agony.

The instant John saw her and the blood running from a gash across the bridge of her nose, he melted, his drunken thoughts vanishing.

"My god, you're hurt," he said shocked and surprised.

Mary froze, tasting the blood, but thought little of it, intending only to protect herself. As John approached, she backed away.

"No, Mary," he said, his voice calmed, reaching his arm and pointing. "Your nose…it's bleeding."

Mary shook from fear and rage.

John darted from the room, returning with a damp cloth.

"Here, put this on your nose."

Mary did as he said. "Ow," she answered with a tinge of pain.

"I'm so sorry, Mary," John said, unable to look her in the eyes. "I don't know what to say."

"Asshole," she snapped, pressing the cloth tightly against her nose, not for a moment showing weakness, so, holding the cloth with one hand, she slapped John across the face as hard as she could with the other. He didn't move as if expecting another.

When she didn't slap him a second time, John looked up and said weakly, "I'll take you to the hospital. You might need stitches."

This was the oddest thing that Mary had ever witnessed. First, he attacked her; now, trying to help, it seemed like something from one of those soap operas.

"No." Mary growled, "I'll take myself."

"I can help."

"No…no you can't."

John handed her his car keys.

"Please let me take you."

"Back off."

John fell into the same recliner Mary had spent her day. "I know…" he moaned.

She grabbed her book bag from the kitchen counter, keeping her eyes on John, now sobbing with his face buried in his hands.

As she left the trailer, Mary felt her heart beating in her nose. And when she pulled into the emergency room's parking lot, Mary could feel every living soul's heart beating in her nose. She continued to curse John with every ounce of anger and hatred in her body. She turned off the car's engine and walked into the hospital.

Mary went to the counter, the cold room smelling antiseptic, making her a queasy.

"I've had an accident." Her voice sounded as if her nose was plugged as she held the blood-stained cloth to her nose.

The receptionist looked up and nodded. "Yes, I see." She handed Mary a clipboard with a form attached. "Fill this out."

Mary took the clipboard, but returned an aggravated glare.

"Will you be paying with insurance, check, or credit card?"

It had not occurred to Mary that she would be required to pay for this. It hadn't occurred to her at all. She just had a need that required fixing. She shrugged her shoulders. "I don't have any money…" she said, irritated, then feeling another throb, she angrily snapped, "I'm bleeding, dammit."

"Have a seat," the receptionist pointed to the waiting area, "We'll get to you as soon as we can."

It's a good thing I'm not dying, Mary thought and went to a chair and began filling out the paperwork. She had not paid much attention to the other people around her before, but now she could not help but notice them. Beside her sat a young couple with a baby. Mary noticed that one of the child's eyes was swollen shut. The mother looked sullen and concerned while the father cracked jokes, thumbing through a magazine.

"Ohhh, give me a tissue," the young mother said quickly.

He dug through the woman's purse, pulling out one and handing it to her.

When the mother raised the swollen eyelid, thick yellow pus drained from the eye, looking like a lanced boil. Mary turned away from the sight; she had not expected this either, and it only encouraged her nausea.

Across from her, an old red faced, balding man sat coughing a deep and desperate gravelly cough. His eyes were a light, transparent blue, and where they should be white, they were bloodshot and yellow, nearly the same yellow as the drainage from the baby's eye.

The odor of the room suddenly changed, and she caught a strong whiff of ammonia and alcohol. She watched as the fellow's dirty trousers darkened, urine dripping from the inside of his cuffs to the floor.

As she was about to get up and tell the receptionist about the old man, he went into a fit of coughs. He did not cover his mouth, and the top plate of his dentures flew from his mouth followed by a string of phlegm which tumbled through the air like a twirler's baton, landing half on Mary's shoe. The dentures failed to make it that far, landing on the tile floor between them with a slight slap.

For a reason Mary could not gauge, she could not rise from the chair. The sights, sounds, and smells came together too quickly with the pain in her face. The frailties of the human body sickened her, nauseated her, and when her mind told her body that it could no longer prevail, her vision faded and her body deflated like a balloon, sliding out of the chair, her face landing upon the old man's teeth.

Mary awoke still in a daze, in a bed, separated from the rest of the world by walls of white curtains—the pain in her nose spreading over her entire face, weakening her.

"Hello?" she asked.

Mary thought back to the last thing that she remembered: an old man and his teeth. But what did that have to do with her being here?

"Hello?" she repeated.

The curtain in front of her slid open, and a tall, broad Indian woman dressed all in white walked into the curtained cubicle. Mary was instantly stunned, the size of the woman leaving her silent.

The nurse wore her long, black hair in a thick braid, solid as a club. Her coffee-colored eyes poked through Mary like a toothpick in a piece of cheese. Acne had scarred her face, leaving it blotched and discolored with burgundy spots. She made Mary nervous.

"Yes?" the nurse asked, her voice deep as a man's.

"What happened?" Mary asked, her voice unusually subdued to a whisper.

"You fainted."

"When?"

"A few minutes ago."

It seemed much longer.

"My face hurts."

"You fell on it."

Mary reacted with silent surprise. "I fell?" she thought, setting up. Her head pulsed as if little gnomes were running a jackhammer into her brains. The nurse handed Mary a mirror. On her cheek, teeth marks impressed a bruise in her face, so between the bruise and the cut, she looked battered.

"Can I have a pill or something? My face is killing me."

The nurse's face wrinkled as she looked at Mary.

"Not till the doctor looks at you. But in your condition, you should be careful of medication."

"I'm in pain; that's the perfect condition for a pill."

The nurse stepped up to Mary's bed. This was the first time Mary took the opportunity to read the nurse's nametag: Lita Mankiller, RN.

"Pregnancy isn't," she finally retorted.

"Pregnant?!" Mary questioned, "What are you talking about? I'm not…" Mary noticed the nurse looking at her left hand. She had only been unconscious for five minutes, so she had been told, and there wasn't a test in the world that would say she was—(she could barely even think the word for the fear that the woman was right; but that would explain her being sick all the time…). "How can you even say that?" Mary snapped at the brawny nurse.

"I spoke out of turn."

"No," Mary sat up, scooting to the end of the bed. She looked at Lita Mankiller directly, her intimidation petering out with the sudden bizarre turn her visit had taken. "Why did you say that?"

Lita Mankiller drew her face close to Mary's. The Indian's large brown eyes swallowed Mary, and Mary could not fight or pull away from the stare. Lita Mankiller paused, sticking her nose into Mary's hair and taking a deep sniff. "You smell pregnant." She paused again, raising Mary's left arm and running her hand down it, from the elbow down to the fingers. "You feel pregnant." Then Lita Mankiller cocked her eyebrow, "And you look pregnant."

Mary sat motionless, her stomach churning.

Lita Mankiller set Mary's hand back onto her lap. "It's written all over you...you only have to read it."

Before Mary could utter some kind of response to the Indian's meta--physical, the curtain flew open again. A man wearing a white smock and a stethoscope around his neck entered.

"So," the man said, "I see we have a nose to fix here. How is she?"

"She's pregnant."

"Really?" the man smiled, "How far along?"

Mary, slowly pulling herself away from Lita Mankiller's eyes, replied, "Oh, just about one minute."

* * *

The woman's cackling persisted more than Jamie thought it had any right to. He buried his head, but still the noise burrowed its way through the pillow, into his cranium and jabbing him like a sixteen-penny nail shoved into his forehead. The men his mother brought home amazed him, never caring that he would be trying to sleep in the next room.

Jamie rolled under his sheet restlessly, angrily, and then the cackling stopped. He jumped out of bed, no longer caring to fight the war between his weary body and his mother's drunken giggles, angry because it was about to begin. As he pulled up his jeans, he heard the headboard's first bang against the wall. And while he slipped on a hooded sweatshirt, a loud explosive laugh from his mother shook the room.

You act like a damn man, he thought, leaving his room, grabbing his paperback book. As he walked through the dark house, he saw a pair of unfamiliar boots beside the couch, so he grabbed them as he went outside.

The city limits ran along the street in front of his house, and on the other side of the street was a large pasture with a few wandering cows. He walked across the street, passing a strange truck, which he figured belonged to the boots, and stopped at the bar ditch. "Ride em' cowboy!" he said aloud and sent the boots soaring through the air into the pasture, tumbling like lopsided boomerangs and landing with two distant thuds in the dark.

While contemplating where to go, the chilly night air sent Jamie's hands into his pants pocket. He felt a piece of paper, so he pulled it out and looked at it. It was the map to the MAJOR KEG PARTY. Although hours after midnight, he thought something might be going on there. But he really did not care; he just wanted to be someplace other than that house.

He turned the key in the ignition. The engine grinded, turning over, sounding uncertain if it wanted to start but then kicked in and coughed to life. With a puff of exhaust, Jamie was gone.

The street in front of his house lead to the highway heading west out of town. As Jamie raced down the highway, the chilly air gusted into his car, blowing around trash inside. As his hair whipped around, his eyes squinted from the sting of the wind. The rhythm of the engine grabbed his attention and reminded him of the banging headboard and he wondered what put her into a constant state of heat.

He then thought about the men that had walked in and out of his home, remembering when he had been eight years old and awakened for another time by weird noises from his mother's bedroom. He went to the living room and sat quietly frightened. After so much time of silence, he turned on the television, a small black and white set that filled the room with a gray glow.

He had watched for about an hour, waiting on the Frankenstein monster to fight the wolfman when a door squeaked, sending him nearly out of his skin. He turned around to see Frankenstein coming toward him. The monster turned to a man, slipping his hands under Jamie's arms and raising him off the couch. Jamie's limbs dangled loosely, and he hung like a fish on a hook, terrified.

“I had no idee…” the man said quietly.

Jamie stared into the gaunt face, the flesh gray and the eyes reflecting little images of the horror movie on the television.

"Beware your momma, son," the stranger said softly.

Jamie did not recognize the face or the voice, but his words confused him more.

The man lowered Jamie back to the floor, and he stood motionless before the stranger, his legs unable to move—or even bend, so he just looked up at the tall man's face, looming over him like the moon. The man pulled his wallet from his back pocket and took a bill from it and handed it to Jamie. The little boy took it and saw that it was a five-dollar bill. He had never been so rich before. "For me?" Jamie asked.

The man crouched down; his boots squeaked as he changed positions. He patted Jamie's cheek and then held Jamie's face in his large callused hand.

"Son, your mother is a dangerous woman, to you anyway. Don't let her ruin ya'."

"Uh-uh," Jamie scowled, defending his mother

"Listen little man, I know you love your momma. You're not old enough to hate her."

"Uh-uh," Jamie's chin quivered.

"Just beware her. She's gonna hurt ya'."

Then he looked at Jamie for the longest time in silence. Jamie grew uncomfortable with the man and the strange seeds of thoughts that he had planted in his head. Then the man left.

He had hated that man for years afterwards, but he never saw the man again, so he kept the hate to himself. The hate was all he got to keep from the man, too. His mother found the five-dollar bill the next day and kept it. Jamie never said that it had been given to him by the man because he wanted the man to disappear—as every other man had done. Yet the memory hounded him like a lonely mutt he had paid too much attention.

He hated that memory and the man haunting it until he was thirteen when he realized the man had been right, and his heart broke. In anger, he stole a five-dollar bill from his mother's purse, but he knew that was no kind of retribution for him or atonement for her. The anger had remained and festered and grew. As angry as he was though—and as devoted as the anger was—he could never bring himself to hate the woman.

So what if she's a whore, he thought once again, speeding toward the MAJOR KEG PARTY.

Jamie pulled off the dirt road and the gate was open wide, so he drove into the pasture. He saw what had a few hours before been roaring fires were now only glowing embers, burning themselves out with small trails of smoke floating into the sky. A few people stumbled about, the beer, the liquor, and other stuff having taken their toll. He walked from one glowing heap to another, kicking dirt on the coals. The pasture looked like a battlefield that had just gone quiet, waiting for the dead to be plucked from the wounded earth and taken away for burial.

On his way back to his car, he saw RaLF's Vette with the dome light glowing inside. He knew RaLF's car because he had watched her get into it after school. It was not like he spied on her—but that was exactly what he was doing. He wasn't in love with her; Jamie didn't really even know if he liked her, but she did have something that attracted him. Perhaps it was just their recent familiarity. Regardless, he felt the attraction, and it embarrassed him. *How predictable, the poor slob falls for the rich girl*. He mocked himself.

Inside the car, he saw a resting body, feet hanging out, keeping the passenger side door from shutting, head upon the floor in a lumpy orange pool. Jamie recognized the back of RaLF's head. Immediately, he pulled her out of the waste and realized she was its source.

"Whoa," Jamie muttered, thinking she must have thrown up after passing out. A tinge of disappointment crept into his heart. He had expected more from RaLF. Taking an old handkerchief from his pocket, he held her against the car and wiped off her face. He paused several long seconds and then said her name, "RaLF." It felt odd to him. For as long as she had been tutoring him, he had never referred to her by name—or any name for that matter. But she failed to respond.

"RaLF," he repeated more freely the second time, shaking her again for a response, but her limp drunk body only squeezed out a string of gibberish.

"Up and at 'em, RaLF," Jamie lightly slapped the clean side of her face.

RaLF answered with more grunts, swaying as he held her, her head bobbing like a toy.

Aggravated, Jamie wanted to put her back into the car, back

into her vomit, stopping only from his conscious suddenly speaking up.

"Be a gentleman."

"Help her."

"You might impress her."

So he stood, balancing his drunken tutor, wondering what to do. He suddenly had a thought and softly laid her across the hood of the car. After walking to one of the beer kegs, he took a handful of wet, slushy ice that the keg had been packed in. When he went back to the car, he grabbed the collar of her sweater with one hand and raised her up, leaning her against his chest. He then pulled back her long brown hair and put the handful of ice down her back. The smell of her hair still had a hint of her shampoo, mixing with RaLF's own unique scent. Jamie closed his eyes afraid of how he felt.

She grunted.

So he rubbed the ice into her back. A quick shiver shot through her, and her eyes partly opened, quickly rolling back up into her head looking like a zombie from a midnight horror movie.

"Would you wake up?" he scolded.

"Ooooh," she moaned, "Bill?"

"No, it's me, Jamie." He wondered if Bill was one of the casualties scattered about.

Her eyes opened again, but she couldn't focus.

"Quit moving," she said.

"I'm not."

"I'm drunk," she whined, her voice weak, "Can I go back to sleep?"

"You were sleeping in vomit."

He saw that RaLF was fading, so he shook her again.

RaLF answered each shake with a grunt, smiling and laughing quietly. "What time is it?"

"It's close to 3:30."

"No it's not," she said smugly, her eyelids still fluttering between closed and open, "I'm s'posed t' be home by one."

"Well, you're late."

"Where's Shawna 'n April?"

"I don't know." He answered, unsure who they even were.

RaLF intermittently understood some of what Jamie said, understood that what he said was not good.

"Oh, I have to pee."

"Great," he thought, so he helped her off the hood of the car, but she could not keep her balance or hold herself up.

"Can you stand up by yourself?"

"I've got to pee. It hurts."

"I know. I know. Can you stand?"

"Uh-huh," she said, but when Jamie let go, she stumbled, nearly falling to the ground. Shaking his head, Jamie caught the back of her sweater.

"Do you need help?"

"I gotta' pee!" she said, dancing in his grasp.

The moon shone brightly upon them, so he helped her to the other side of the car, out of sight of any of the drunks strung out across the pasture. He turned her away from facing him, holding her by her arm pits, his fingers brushing across the side of her breasts. With his help keeping her up, she unfastened her jeans, pushed them down, and squatted.

"Thank you," she muttered as Jamie pulled her up after she

finished, fumbling with the button fly as she tried to fasten her pants back, not quite able to get the button through the hole. She grumbled, her eyes half shut, then she added, a little of her drunkenness draining away, "Could you please take me home, please?"

He almost laughed, but not because he found humor in her request; it just seemed strange that she would ask him.

"Here," she said fumbling with her keys, "take my car. My dad'd kill me if I left it here." Her words were soft as she leaned back against Jamie for support. He felt her every curve, and his arms shook with her in them.

"Am I heavy? I'm fat aren't I?" RaLF muttered as she felt him quivering.

"You're fine." Jamie rebutted and took the keys. "What about my car?"

"We can get it tomorrow. I promise."

He shifted her position and walked her back around the Corvette.

"I'm holding you to it."

RaLF looked at Jamie through squinted eyes. His face was serious, but he always seemed serious.

"Do you ever laugh?" RaLF asked.

"Sure," Jamie answered, setting her in the passenger seat, wrinkling his nose at the aroma of RaLF's earlier deposit. "I'm laughing at you, right now…" Then he watched as RaLF carelessly put her feet in it before he could warn her. He shut the door, noticing how smoothly and softly it clicked shut. He had to slam his car's doors so hard the whole car shook. Her car looked beautiful as Jamie walked slowly around it, admiring the moon and stars reflecting in the paint. Outside of the Driver's Ed car, he had never driven a car less than ten years of age, not covered with spots and blotches of rust. He slid his hand into the door handle and slowly lifted the handle. The door opened with a soft click, and he slid in behind the steering wheel. This excited him and made him nervous as hell. The car started with the first turn of the key, and he put it in gear.

"Slow," RaLF said, reclined in her leather bucket seat, her eyes closed, "don't scratch the paint.... Watta night..."

"I guess so," Jamie replied.

"I feel lousy."

"Then why the hell did you drink so much?"

"Because...it made me happy." She remained safe and distant behind the solitude of her closed eyes.

Her answer surprised Jamie, so he drove quietly for awhile, thinking; then he asked, "It made you happy?"

"Yeah, I wanted to forget."

"What?"

"I don't want to talk about it." Her self-pity hung from her like an old coat, worn but comfortable. "Do you know what it's like to be a nobody?"

This surprised Jamie even more than what she had said before, so he wondered if she was making fun of him.

"I mean, all my friends...look at Polly, Homecoming Queen. I got her a stupid dress for free and got nothing but a stupid thank you."

"What did you want?"

She thought for a moment, her thoughts desperately lost in the murky swamp of her drunken brain. "Oh, I don't know, but it's not fair. Look at Bill; he's a football hero and he's kissing Polly. I'm just... just...," her voice see-sawed in desperation. "I'm..."

"...a conceited bitch." Jamie completed her sentence, annoyed by her pitiful whining. Drunk or not, he thought it pathetic. "You have so much crap you can't even see it all. Don't tell me how bad you have it. You can't even imagine where I come from."

"You don't understand..." The alcohol saturating RaLF's brain would not allow her to hear the insult, and it bounced off leaving no mark.

Stored up from what he had left at his house, Jamie's anger grew—grew because RaLF's pity party delegated him to nothing more than an accessory in her life; because it made him even less than what he already felt.

"Ooooh, never mind," RaLF moaned, her voice fading to a whisper, and she rolled toward the door unable to concentrate long enough to know what she thought. So she closed her eyes and again took solace behind the calm darkness looming behind her eyelids.

The car remained silent as they entered the city limits. As they passed his house, he saw the truck still parked there, and the house in darkness as he expected. But he did not expect the embarrassment. RaLF could not imagine from where he came, not at all.

RaLF stirred, asking, "Where are we?"

"Nowhere," Jamie answered.

"Are we in town, yet?"

"Yes."

RaLF faded away again.

The town looked as dead as the keg party; although the night helped to hide the city's blemishes like a nocturnal makeover. He turned east, moving slowly down Grand Avenue.

"RaLF, where do you live?"

She shifted positions.

"Over there," she answered, swinging her arm around, pointing without aim or direction, never opening her eyes.

Her reply did not help him, so he pulled into a convenience store to look at a phone book. As he walked into the store, Bill Wright stood at the counter, paying for a twelve pack of beer. He looked directly at Jamie. A strange sedate but angry look defined his face.

"Are you driving that car? That's RaLF's car. Is she in there?"

"I'm taking her home," Jamie answered then asked for a phone book.

"Bullshit," Bill said vehemently.

Jamie ignored the comment as he thumbed through the pages.

"Look at me, you asswipe."

A friend of Bill's walked up behind Bill, staring at Jamie with contempt.

Jamie found the page, but he did not know RaLF's father's name, so he looked at Bill. "Could you tell me where RaLF lives?"

Bill lunged at Jamie, grabbing his sweatshirt and pushing Jamie against the store's glass front, causing the glass sheets to ripple. Jamie pushed Bill back, and losing his grip and his balance, Bill tumbled backwards into his friend's arms. "Let go!" Bill yelled at his friend who was not holding him at all.

"Hey, take it outside!" the cashier screamed as Bill went back at Jamie.

Jamie reacted with the same thoughtlessness that he had used when he called RaLF a bitch. He did not realize that he was hitting Bill until after it had happened and he saw Bill fall backwards again against a rack of chips.

"Get out of here!" the cashier bellowed.

"On my way." Jamie burst through the doors, running to the car. He slid inside, locked the door, and backed out.

As he pulled onto the street, RaLF bumped her head into the window. "What's going on?" she asked, sobering up enough to react.

"Your boyfriend," Jamie answered speeding on, turning right onto a side street.

"Huh? Bill?"

"Yeah, he's pissed off."

"Can I see him?"

Jamie slowed the car, thinking them safe, but a truck sped up behind the car to a few feet. Jamie tried not to go any faster although the car easily could; he did not want to hurt the car as RaLF had asked. But the closeness of the truck made him nervous, so he sped up to widen the gap. The truck answered, keeping close behind the car.

Ahead, the road widened to four lanes. When Jamie reached the widened road, he took the center lane. The truck sped around to the outside lane, staying parallel to the car. RaLF's mind cleared a little with the wind, and she looked out to see Bill's truck. He looked down to her and yelled, "Stop your car! I have to talk to you! I'm sorry about Polly! I love you!"

RaLF could not hear him over the rushing wind and the roaring engines, but she remember that they had fought. As the MAJOR KEG PARTY raged on, as the fires raged on, she had raged at him—the product of jealousy, self-pity, and alcohol.

"I can't hear you!" she yelled back to Bill, and then she turned to Jamie and said, "Stop the car," while still leaning out to see Bill.

"Huh?" Jamie asked, looking at RaLF.

"Stop the car!" she repeated.

As Jamie looked back at the road, something darted in front of the car. He jerked the wheel, colliding with Bill's truck. RaLF screamed. The car jerked and abruptly stopped with a loud crash. Then all went silent.

* * *

"Earl 'zat you?"

Earl stirred as the bright light swept across his face.

"Earl, if that's you, wake up?"

The light bore down on him. Earl squinted, the light blinding him, so he covered his eyes with his forearm. As he woke, his mind worked like a poorly focused film projector with the reels out of order. He smelled the chocolate that he had earlier smeared across his arm, so he licked it off, trying to remember where he was.

"I'zat you, Earl?" a voice said again from behind the bright light.

"Who are you?" Earl asked, standing up, the light following him to his feet.

"It's the police, Earl. Are you all right? It's nearly four in the morning, your parents are worried. Is there any trouble?

Police. Trouble.... The word reverberated through his head. Suddenly, he remembered he was in trouble, so he turned his trike away from the wall.

"Do you wan'us to take you home?"

"Go away," Earl said, climbing onto his trike and taking off to escape the police. When he distanced himself from the tail lights of the police car, he tried to focus, but his vision was still blurred. The headache had also returned, as if his head was between the jaws of a huge pair of pliers. "Mmmmmm," a moan squeezed from his lips.

A bright glow came up from behind him. He looked over his shoulders, his head darting from side to side, but could not see what was behind the bright pair of lights, so he peddled harder. "Trou--ble," he panted a syllable with each hard exhale. He turned, taking a small side street that ran along a deep concrete drainage ditch. The pair of lights turned with him.

"Go away," he shrieked in fear. The block was long, and ahead of him, a stop sign marked the intersection. Earl knew to stop, but he could not—not at this moment, so he peddled through it.

A horrid, piercing, screeching roar surprised Earl, as he saw four more bright lights coming at him. They began bouncing off of one another with one pair hitting the railings of a bridge, rocketing over the side railing and crashing into the drainage ditch below. The other pair bolted forward and hit the front wheel of Earl's trike, sending it spinning and Earl flying onto the pavement, scraping and rolling for several yards.

"Trou--ble," Earl said when his body came to a rest. Agony encased his body, but his fear of trou--ble pushed him to his feet and away from the accident. Behind him, Earl heard, "We'll get him later; see if anyone is still alive!" the voice fading as Earl limped deeper into the shadows of trees and houses. The blurred vision in his eyes remained and the pain in his head had increased after rolling and beating and scraping against the road. He reached up feeling something run down the side of his head. Discovering that his ear had nearly been scraped off and hung only by the lobe, he bawled, "I'm in bad trou--ble," He pushed the ear back into place. It momentarily stayed, but then slowly peeled away like wallpaper.

"Trou--ble, ooohh.....trou--ble," he huffed, limping forward, weeping, holding his mangled ear in place.

The sounds around Earl became less distinct: leaves rustling, his shoes slapping the pavement, dogs barking, his deep heavy panting, the distant wail of sirens, and he instead heard a constant swishing like the sound from a sea shell inside his head.

As a car would come into view, he would hide from it, his panic controlling his responses, and then begin again to move down the street after it passed.

In between thoughts of his trou--ble, his pain, and his weary body, he tried to contemplate what to do, but he just did not seem to be able to reason. His confusion weighed on him, and he seemed to sink underneath it, drowning in tears that would not stop, streaming through the dirt and blood miring his stained, pouting face.

So, he kept moving along the dark street, whimpering like a whipped pup.

His left arm had gone totally limp, slapping against his hip as he walked. He held his right arm, curled up to his face, gnawing on his thumb for comfort, slowing his sobs but not stopping them.

Earl's vision became increasingly blurred, but it did not seem to hinder him while he scurried through the night, passing among the shadows, going from streetlight to streetlight. He kept moving south away from the accident, and had not left the street on which it occurred.

Earl's coveralls, saturated with sweat and blood, clung to him like a second skin. His left leg became increasingly difficult to maneuver so he began to drag it. A hum and moan constantly streaming from his lips, Earl's limping body looked like an evolutionary throwback, awkwardly dancing some Neanderthal waltz.

He had made it across town, by the time a slight hint of dawn lightened the sky, but Earl did not notice it. Before him a building's outline crept into his distorted view, an image he could recognize regardless of the constant waves of confusion, tormenting his pained mind.

His church was easy for him to identify even if he could not see anything other than hazy images. It was the only cathedral in town, albeit one in miniature. So he went to it as if sanctuary awaited him there. As he dragged himself the final block, he bawled, "Hail Mary, full of grace; Hail Mary, full of grace!" the entire way. The words coming from nowhere other than his conditioned mind. When he reached the stairs leading into the building, he stopped his slow, agonizing, and crippled walk.

He grabbed a hold of the steel banister that ran up the middle of the stairs and pulled himself up. His arm shook and his good leg trembled as he raised the lame leg onto the step. He slowly progressed one step at a time, and when he reached the top, he staggered forward, the large wooden doors catching him as he almost fell.

"Hail Mary, full of grace," Earl kept repeating; the words weakening to a scratchy loud whisper. He pulled on the shiny brass door handle, and the door swung open. He toppled over onto the tiled floor of the foyer, and rested for a few seconds, unable to push himself back up, his energy spent.

At the far end of the foyer between two pair of doors leading into the sanctuary, a life-size statue of Mary, looking upwards, kneeling, her arms extended in praise of the Lord, sat in front of him.

"Hail Mary, full of grace," he said to the blurred, hazy image, not understanding the meaning behind the words.

Earl's thumb had grown wrinkled from resting in his mouth for so long, now bleeding from his gnawing. He stuck the thumb back into his mouth, still whispering his exaltation. Longing to reach the statue, he dragged himself to it, pulling with his good elbow, pushing with his good foot.

"Hail Mary, full of grace…"

Pain coursed through his body like a flooding river overflowing its banks until it erupted like a dam bursting no longer able to hold the rushing water back.

"Ooooh, Haaail Mrrry, full uv grrrrc....."

He grew weaker, and when he reached the statue he curled up at its base. He closed his eyes and his panting relaxed. A collage of memories swirled around in his mind: His parents' wrinkled faces; His father's words echoing, "Hurry back." The reverberation of his mother's singing becoming more shallow, "Awww, de do da, do da…day."

"Hail Mary, full of grace!" Earl blurted with a final expulsion.

He opened his eyes, looking up to the statue, but all he could see were dark colors, smeared and blended like a child's finger painting. He groaned, and although his eyes remained open, total darkness descended upon him. The pain, strong as it had been, ebbed, and quickly, Earl was floating, anesthetized in joy.

Chapter Ten

A Christmas Interlude

Monday, December 24

Everything else around him faded away. Motionless, breathless, Earnest stared at the red line marring his name, piercing Sunday and Monday, impaling Tuesday and Wednesday, poking Thursday and Friday, and resting its bloodied point in Saturday. His temperature rose until sweat ran from underneath the stocking cap upon his head. He slowly slipped off the stocking cap, his hair crackling with static and dancing in the air. He remained this way until a small oriental fellow bumped into him, carrying an armful of Harvey cups from the basement.

"Excuse me," he said in slow, strained English.

Earnest looked at him and then his gaze went back to the schedule. As Earnest stood, paralyzed, Helmet-head rounded the corner with his cocky jaunt. When Helmet-head saw Earnest, a small cancerous smile shaped his lips.

Earnest's strength drained away, and he meekly pointed at the red line and squeaked, "My schedule....?"

Helmet-head walked past Earnest, chewing coarsely on a piece of gum like a cow chewing its cud, glanced at the schedule and said, "I red penned ya. Ya' didn't hack it. I bent over backwards to make it work, but I gotta' beat that friggin' clown, dammit." He rolled the gum around in his open mouth. "Merry Christmas, Graves. You ain't workin' tonight. Little Chow Mein there is taking your place." Helmet-head pointed to the small oriental fellow that had just bumped into him and was now putting condiments onto a group of toasted buns. "That little yellow bastard sure can move." Then Helmet-head walked into the kitchen spouting orders like some sort of demonic fountain.

Earnest left the steaming heat of the restaurant's kitchen to return to the angry chill outside. He noticed for the first time the heavy suffocating gray of the day, the colors fading from it like some old movie, growing dull after running through the projectors of a million late late shows.

When he started his car, dusty hot air immediately blew out of the vents as the car had not yet cooled. He sat silently while the engine rumbled. A gust of wind blew past, carrying a napkin across his windshield. And then he began to back out. A car honked, so Earnest turned and saw he had almost backed into it. After it went by, he checked his rear view mirror and left the parking lot for the busy street.

With no other place to go, Earnest drove home. All of his Christmas shopping was done and wrapped in a sack in the passenger's seat: tube socks and a work shirt for his dad, some kind of deep fryer that he saw advertised on television for his mother, and the movie soundtrack to 'Grease' for his brother. As he reached their driveway, he felt too blue to tell his parents he had been red penned and replaced by a boy named after noodles, so he shot past and drove the few extra miles to the parking area below the Kaw Dam.

The dam held back the Arkansas River to create a large lake. Years ago it had flooded out thousands of acres as well as the small town, Kaw City. So, the town moved and now overlooked the great lake. Some people moved their homes, some rebuilt in the new town, leaving their old homes to the fishes, and some just moved away. But where Earnest went, he saw none of this. Below the dam, where the water was released, Earnest saw only the dam and the water the dam's gates let through.

The day's colors had faded even more, as somewhere on the other side of the cloudy sky, the sun had snuck behind the edge of the earth. He saw where a few flakes of snow had fallen upon his windshield and quickly melted, looking like falling tears. Stepping from the car, the cold was as pointed as Helmet-head's red pen, and all bundled as he was, Earnest still felt its sting.

Stepping over a rusty brown steel cable loosely draped from a row of small iron posts cemented into the ground, Earnest walked down a steep gravel incline to some large, flat, rocks inches above the river's surface along the river's bank, and then jumped to the rock the farthest into the river.

A frigid breeze blew from the north over the dam down to Earnest and carried a spray of cold water into his face. A shiver ran through his body. The overcast, gray December sky grew darker and darker, edging towards night. The water of the lake looked like diluted oil, outlined with little white ripples. Almost an hour ago—a lifetime ago—he had gone to work cocky with his employ. Now his job was gone, and so much more with it. *I can't even keep a job at a stupid fast food joint*, he moped as his ego melted and confidence escaped.

Earnest thought back to the placemat decorated with the happy Harvey crew. It had seduced him. It had told him that they needed him, and after he ran blindly into the swollen pink lips of Harvey's Fine Fried Burgers, he had been pushed away without so much as a kiss and now watched as the red light was turned back on and little Chow Mien was drawn into that den of epicurean iniquity.

Earnest squatted down on the rock, taking off a glove, and ran his fingers through the cold water as if he were stroking a lover's hair. He looked up from the water to the dark silhouette of trees lining the other side of the reservoir. Something delicately touched his hand. Looking back down, he saw a white bloated fish floating upside down, covered in a fuzzy, moldy decay, dancing around the rock as the current lead. The fish's dull, cold, dead eyes looked at him through the water. Then the fish moved on, floating along the shoreline, and before it was out of his sight, while Earnest could still see the ripples outlining it, the boy threw it a consoling kiss.

He jumped back to the shore as the fish disappeared, picked up a rock and threw it up into the sky as flakes of snow more heavily fell around him. Earnest heard the rock break the surface of the water with a small pop. There was no other sound, the night as empty as his heart.

* * *

Mary looked out of the trailer window and watched the snow fall in the glow of the street light, the ground lightly covered in white. Tiny bubbles tickled her womb. She could no longer ignore them as her body—even with her chunky build acting as a camouflage—had begun to bear witness to her condition.

Around the trailer park multi-colored lights, wreaths, and other seasonal paraphernalia decorated and illuminated most of the homes. Inside some, the silhouettes of decorated trees stood visible with blinking lights of different colors, intensities, and rhythms through windows. With the season blanketing the entire complex, Mary sensed a quiet, calm restfulness that shot quills of restlessness through her. She closed her eyes and leaned her forehead against the cold window, each exhale fogging the Christmas scenery.

"Are you ready?" John called from the living room.

She opened her eyes and stared out of the bedroom window at the distorted images outside. She wore one of John's sweatshirts, the sleeves hanging down, swallowing her hands.

"No, I'm not going."

"Mary, you said you would."

"I changed my mind. I'm not going to a stupid Christmas party at your parents."

John walked into the bedroom, clean, slicked up, clothes pressed, ready to leave. "What's your deal?" he asked.

"What's my deal?" She turned around, facing John. "Who am I? What the hell is my name?"

John looked dumbfounded, missing her point entirely.

"I'm Mary Christmas—MARY CHRISTMAS!" she answered. "My name is some perverse joke, a joke. I'm on my own now. My parents made me suffer through it for years. I don't need it anymore." she angrily insisted.

Mary caught her breath, startled by another eruption of bubbles.

John looked at her. "Are you all right? You never leave this damn trailer anymore. I'm worried."

"Enough!" She silenced him, wanting to scratch out his eyes. "I'll do what I want. Just leave."

John left the room, and Mary listened as he put on his coat.

"Bye," he surrendered from the living room.

"Good bye," she answered back, a cold harshness to her voice —not giving him any room to ask again. Then the door shut.

The television hummed in the living room, so she walked down the hall and turned it off. The silence and the calm freed her thoughts, allowing her to concentrate too hard on them, so she looked through John's tapes and found one labeled Wagner's Greatest Hits, a remnant of an intellectual renaissance John had long given up. Mary put it into the cassette deck, turned on the stereo, and began the tape. As the thunderous music shattered the silence, she stood before the speakers, listening, judging the mood. Then after several intense measures of brass and strings, she turned away.

While the music played, she checked and locked all of the doors. Her walk was determined and her demeanor resolved, and both oblivious to the music, yet it pulsed through her, pushing her.

Why did John want to tell his family about her, she wondered. Why wouldn't he let her remain a shadow? Didn't he owe her that —she had never mentioned to him that they had gotten pregnant —the reason she had gone back to the trailer—back to him. Yet he had not opened his eyes wide enough to notice.

Mary entered the bathroom and shut the door behind her, locking out everything but the music, amazed at how much a clairvoyant Indian and a little urine on a stick could change a life.

Who are you, she wondered, staring in the full-length mirror hanging on the door at eyes sad and empty. She took off the sweatshirt, and as she was about to set it on the cabinet, she moved a clothes hanger already there to the toilet seat and then put the shirt upon the cabinet. Frantic violins poured into the bathroom. Next, her jeans slid down her legs, and she put them on top of the sweatshirt. Lastly, she removed her underwear, sliding out of her bra and massaging her sore breasts. Horns, so soft that she could barely hear them, drifted into the room.

This was Mary Christmas. She stood nude before the mirror. Her hands ran over her breasts, down her round stomach, thinking her entire body was made of circles. Her skin felt soft—the color pale, speckled with moles and blemishes. The music grew to a crescendo, and a burst of bubbles danced a spiteful ballet in her womb.

Mary turned away and went to the bathtub and opened the faucet. John had left a dirty ring, so she took some cleanser from underneath the sink and scrubbed the tub. She worked slowly and meticulously, covering every inch, and then rinsing the tub of the dirty soapy water. Then she closed the drain, and the water began to rise. As the tub filled, she sat on the edge peacefully, calmly, unhurried, and looked at herself again. After the tub filled, she closed the faucet. As she was about to step into it, she paused and returned to the sink and took a bottle of alcohol and a bag of cotton balls from under it and set them beside the tub.

Lowering into the steaming water, Mary sighed. The hot water felt nice, relaxing, so she leaned back, relishing it. She splashed water on her face, rubbed her eyes, and pushed her hair back, wetting it to keep its place. Then she sniffed, and her eyes began to sting.

When she reached for the hanger that she had set on the toilet, a low, heavy, long grunt squeezed from her throat. She straightened the hook and then untwisted the top. The groan became heavier while Wagner boomed. After she straightened the hanger, she laid it across the tub and grabbed the alcohol and cotton balls, saturating a handful of the cotton with the alcohol. Then taking what was now a long piece of crooked, stiff wire, she rubbed the cotton balls up and down it like a violinist rosining a bow. Her groan squeezed out, unconscious and unending.

She dropped the wad of cotton balls to the floor with a wet splat. Mary's groan morphed into a forced chuckle, a distracted and distraught laugh. She raised herself out of the tub, sitting on the end rim, and continued to force out the half-hearted laughter as she inserted the hanger inside of her. Briefly, the metal felt cold against her. Although still laughing in deep grunts, she squinted in pain as a small barb on the hanger scratched her.

She gasped suddenly as the tip of the hanger poked inside of her, so she stopped pushing it, uncertain what the hanger was touching, uncertain how to guide it. Her breathing grew heavy and deep and frightened. "Ohgodohgodohgod...,"she said aloud and gently pushed the hanger. She moaned in pain, on the verge of bawling.

She then pulled the hanger out of her, a small string of mucus on the tip, and threw the hanger across the bathroom, clanging against the mirror on the door and leaving a spattering of droplets across the glass. "Am I crazy?" she cried. "I can't do this. I'll kill myself." Mary jumped up, grabbing a towel from the wall rod. She wanted to yank the fetus out of her body; like a parasite, it grew and grew, and she could not stop it. She could not even stop it. She looked down to see a thin trickle of blood run down her leg and hit the water, dispersing like unanswered prayers.

* * *

The two women haunted him like a stain upon the fabric of his memory. Throughout the whole month of December, as Daniel received seasonal greetings from every possible soul, the tubby, frowning visage of Mary Christmas baited him with spiteful guilt. He was pleased to be rid of her and run his paper as it should be, but as she had so completely vanished, she forced him to ponder her. Her salvation plagued him, so he prayed for her—more from annoyance than his sense of Christian obligation or duty.

And too, the image of the woman from the revival preyed upon him to pray for her. Her long blonde hair floated about Daniel's dreams and thoughts like a mist dancing upon the full moon's reflection in a lake. So he held tightly onto the memory of her and her hurried escape like a prince with a glass slipper.

He worried for both. But his concern for the mysterious blonde moved beyond merely thoughts of her eternal soul and broached realms with which he was totally unfamiliar. God had delivered her unto him, and somewhere in his message, he had failed her. Yet, this failure had mutated to an inexplicable infatuation, giving Daniel fits.

"Mary Christmas," Daniel heard while he slept, and the blank face, framed by flowing yellow hair, swelled and bubbled and reshaped to that of his former co-editor's. He raised his head from his pillow, his eyes cracking open, as the distorted vision of his father stood over him. "Merrry Christmas, son."

"Mawy?" he groaned, light streaming into his unfocused eyes, erasing the hazy phantom that his co-editor had become.

His dad patted his shoulder as he began to sit up, his father and his room becoming more clear; reality taking the place of the spooks taunting his sleep.

"Up and at em', son. Your Grandma and Grandpa are here, and we don't want to be late for the service this morning. When we get back, we'll open the presents, ho ho ho."

Daniel rubbed his eyes, clearing away the sandman's crusty remnants; then lowering his head, he saw that he was alone again. He rose from his bed, looking disarrayed and feeling very much the same and tugged his boxer shorts back up to his waist. He then wrapped himself with his bathrobe and waddled to the bathroom, running his fingers over the small patch of hair that grew upon his chest and down his bulbous stomach.

After finishing his shower, Daniel quickly dressed. Brushing at his clothes, he observed himself in the mirror but stood disappointed. Yes, the surgery had helped, but still he appeared unkempt. His clip-on tie was too wide; his white shirt too yellowed. Fashion escaped him, for the nicer the clothes, the worse they looked upon him.

He bounded down the stairs, his feet clomping upon each carpeted step, the two women still lingering on his mind like a small dog nipping at his heels. As he crossed through the living room, a banner hung over the fireplace reminded him of his ghosts; "Merry Christmas" it read, and the image with which he awoke charged to the forefront of his mind. He turned and looked at their tree. It stood tall and wide under the house's high sloping ceiling like a soldier at attention, and he wondered how Mary might be celebrating the season.

From the living room, he entered the kitchen. His parents and grandparents waited for him, drinking coffee.

"Mewwy Chwithmath, evewy one," Daniel spouted cheerfully walking through the doorway.

"Merry Christmas, Danny," his grandmother replied, leaving the table to place a kiss upon her only grandson's cheek. "Isn't it a wonderful day?" She squeezed his face, and Daniel chuckled.

He ate a bowl of cereal, wiping the dribbles of milk from his chin with his tie, while the others talked around and about him, complimenting his surgery and how handsome he looked.

As they rode to church, Daniel sat in the back seat between his grandparents. A melody came to his mind, so he began to hum it. He felt that he should know the lyrics, but they escaped him.

His grandmother bobbed her head as he hummed. "How do you know that song?" she asked.

"I don't know. I can't wemembew. It jutht popped into my head."

"I remember my papa singing that to me."

And Daniel kept humming it, wondering if she was going to say what it was because, for the life of him, he could not remember from where it came. The lyrics seemed ready to fall into his lap, but something stronger than gravity held them back. Finally, Daniel could not wait any longer, "Tho, what ith it?"

His grandfather answered, "You know, that captown ladies doo dah song."

Daniel realized that he had been humming Earl's song, so he stopped abruptly, the familiar melody scaring him; the late, great Earl scaring him.

"What did you quit for?" his grandfather asked.

"I hate that thong," Daniel snapped, and the car grew quiet. Daniel regretted his words; his tone had been rude, unexpectedly so. He looked up and saw his father's eyes bearing down upon him in the rearview mirror, and like mercury in a hot thermometer, heat rose from under his collar quickly taking in his whole head.

"I'm thowwy," he conceded, "It came out wong."

When they reached the church, Daniel's mind became entangled once again in blonde hair, reminding him once again of his failure to her as he entered the building. Prior to the woman's appearance, he would sit toward the front of the church, but now the blonde hair wrapped him like a fly in a web and pushed him where she had sat. So he took his place in the back pew while his family moved toward the front. He leaned forward, resting his forehead on the back of the pew before him. "Where did I fail?" he silently prayed as Christmas music boomed from the church's pipe organ.

And when he sat back up, he saw her. But she was no mirage, no nightmare of swirling blonde hair. Sitting beside an uncomfortable, sweating man, the woman sat on the very same pew as him.

Daniel's hands grew sweaty, and, just as in the car, his face and ears burned bright red. He looked forward, and then his head slowly turned until she entered his periphery, after which he quickly turned ahead again. As he spied her for a fourth time he saw her looking back, smiling. His mouth agape grew dry, and he realized he was panting, his giant, obese, elephantine tongue pushing its way out between his large, pouty lips like some kind of thirsty hound. *Was she really smiling?* A quiver erupted throughout his body, a horrid internal quiver that pushed him out of the pew, down the aisle, and through the doors to escape, just as she had done before.

* * *

The whole house smelled of candied yams and pie. Ian reclined across his bed, the cord of a headphone stretched taut from the stereo across the room to his head. The embers of his anger growing as he considered the seeds of his wrath. Earnest had became a shadow of his past; RaLF—a marker to his future. She had scarred him and was now more maimed than he. Ian saw it as a satisfying kind of mystical retribution. He had reasoned that in life, as in physics, for every action there was hell to pay from its equal but opposite reaction—and to have seen RaLF's reaction to her own accident would have bordered on paradise.

An old OX album boomed into his eardrums. He had never liked OX before, but he found himself more enamored, the music mirroring something in his soul, specifically a song entitled, "The United States of Anarchy." His eyes scanned the lyrics while he snarled the melody loud and off-pitch, the headphones muting all but the music.

> MOBS RULE
> KILL THE FOOLS
> DON'T WANT NO GOVERNMENT
> RAPE! KILL! WHATA' THRILL
> IT''S ALL HEAVEN SENT

His father opened the door and peered inside the room.

Ian jerked the headphones off of his head. "Why don'cha knock!?" his words angry and scolding.

"I did," his father replied, "It's time to go."

"I don't wanna' go. I don't like em'. They don't like me. And I really don't want to hear about my nose for the next four hours."

Ian's father, a tall, pear-shaped man, stood silently for several seconds. Ian stared back, watching the man think, the cogs of his mind turning, the pistons pumping, exhaust backfiring. Then he finally answered, "Fine, have a Merry Christmas by yourself," and he closed the door behind him.

Ian threw the headphones down upon the bed, OX still blaring, sounding like a swarm of insects emanating from the headphone's small speakers. He stood at his door, peering through the small crack as he held it slightly ajar. He watched his parents put on their coats; shaking his head, his father remarked, "I don't know him anymore. It's his brother all over again." And they left the house.

Ian stepped into the living room and watched through the front window as his parents climbed into their old car. The sheer fabric of the aged gold drapes muted the already dull day. Snow had fallen most of the night, and although it had stopped, the clouds remained. The gray Christmas Eve had evolved into a dreary Christmas day.

His parents drove away and he stood in rapt, brazen solitude as the dry, prickly heat rising from the floor furnace irritated his flesh. Ian went back to his room and flipped a switch on his stereo, turning on his speakers. OX's low, gravelly voice burst from the boxes like flatulence. The sound of electric guitars roared. Drums and bass rumbled in syncopated abandon. Ian's head nodded wildly with the angry rhythm, the music, maniacal and chaotic, as if an orchestrated collision of automobiles. The house grew hotter as Ian began to dance.

SEVEN DAYS OF SIN
HOW IT ALL BEGAN
NOW I'M HOOKED UP 'N PLUGGED IN
LOOKIN' FORWARD TO THE END
FRY ME, DAMN YOU!!!
I WANNA' BURN!!!

The house grew thick with music. Like a fog, it permeated the small house, and the walls shook.

SOME PIG IN BLUE FLIPS A SWITCH
AND POWER PULSES THROUGH MY VEINS
I KICK AND SPIT AND PISS AND SHIT
I WELCOME THE DARKNESS.

Ian felt free, his body writhing and whirling on fire, and the clamor of the music fed the rising flame. He took off his shirt, sweat running down his hairless chest. The guitars built walls of tumult around him, and Ian beat himself against them. He slid out of his pants like a snake does its skin, his body jerking as if he were having a seizure. Then he kicked his underwear across the room while the music roused him.

THE DARKNESS COMES
DISMEMBERED BODIES CAME BEFORE
WHAT'S IT MATTER?
WE'RE ALL WHORES
THE DARKNESS COMES......AND SO DO I!!!

The music, the pictures he conjured, his demonic dancing excited him. Sweat glistened over him, heat prickling him, his body in a jerking frenzy, red like the devil himself. Ian's whole body went stiff, quaking. The needle on the turntable lifted from the record with a loud pop. Drenched in sweat, he heaved a heavy sigh, wiping his hands down his chest. "Merry freakin' Christmas!" he howled, and the record started again. And again, as the drums began to beat, he danced.

Chapter Eleven

Dangerous Women

Monday, January 7th

If she was still beautiful, Earnest couldn't tell. RaLF moved through the hall, aloof. Her coat draped over her shoulders like a cloak, her eyes aimed at the tiled floor, she passed all without remark. Earnest watched as she approached, so unlike the beginning of the school year when she moved like a goddess, a herd of followers about her, orbiting her radiance like little satellites. Now she was alone, as if the goddess's time had passed, old and out of fashion.

He had not seen her to look at or to question, nor had any one else since the wreck, and Earnest was not so certain he was seeing her now, she had changed so. He turned away, fumbling with his locker handle as she drew near, spinning the dial over and over, curious and afraid at once. Then backing away, he accidentally bumped into her.

"Excuse me..." he said turning around, and then he saw the two eyes he had not stared into since she had hit Ian all those months ago. They looked back at him like two empty vessels, their color turned to gray.

Above her eyes, across her forehead, badly hidden behind a curtain of hair, a bright pink scar ran from the left side of her gaunt face across to the right side and down to her right temple, but Earnest barely saw it as her eyes drew his to hers. He blinked, freeing himself and looked down hoping to avoid her gaze any longer. As he looked down he noticed that when he bumped into her, her coat had fallen from her shoulders, and he saw her empty right sleeve.

When she realized what had happened to her coat, her shoulders growing cold, her eyes filled with anger. She crouched down, grabbing her coat and draped it back over her shoulders. The action so fluid and smooth, so quick, and her eyes so angry, Earnest was not even aware of what she had done until after the coat covered her again.

A million thoughts like a million comets shot across his mind: What to say? What to do? I'm sorry, he heard himself saying aloud over and over again, but when he opened his eyes, not even realizing he had closed them, she was gone, quickly escaping him, her coat bellowing around her.

His insides churned, erupting like lava from cracks in the earth's crust. He opened his locker and wanted to crawl inside of it —lock himself away from the things that could do that to his beautiful RaLF. The world seemed suddenly frightening to him, too large to control, too large to face, and as the image of RaLF's scarred and scared face and empty sleeve pulverized him, he waited to see if he would cry. His eyes burned with tears, yet something held them back.

And when the five minute warning bell rang, Earnest remembered where he was, so he shut the locker and went to his class, beginning his second semester as a senior, feeling much less enthusiastic, much smaller, than he had at the year's beginning.

* * *

For three long months, like a steep, steep hill that he clawed and clawed to climb but could not get over, Jamie's life had been difficult. Coping with the change in his mother from a hormone-driven tiger to a jittering, flittering, domestic cat confused Jamie for a while, but realizing that guilt drove the change, he expected her to devolve back to her carnal leanings at some point. For as long as his head was secured by the halo-brace—its four long graphite arms extending from a brace fastened to his shoulders and upper torso up and connecting to a brace about his forehead and bolted to his skull—his mother danced around the house, attending to her son.

"Do you need anything?" she asked.

"How do you feel?" she asked.

"Can I get you something?" she asked.

"NO! NO! NO!"Jamie answered remembering how he had wanted to bid his humiliating life farewell, yet he ended up right back more needy than before, that need sickened him.

He was uncomfortable, while trying to read the books that Mrs. Irving brought for him—and as well, reading the pity in the teacher's eyes when she came to his home.

He was uncomfortable when they tightened the bolts and his head felt as if it would pull apart.

He was uncomfortable when he went back to school, as everyone stared at him, not because of the strange brace around his head but for driving the car that killed Bill Wright—for driving the car that maimed RaLF. It did not matter that Earl had darted out of nowhere in the darkness, and he had swerved to miss him. Hell no, it didn't matter; he died anyway, and Jamie figured everyone blamed him for that, too.

Everyone, except for those who dwelled in the pit. Although they were curious as to why he had been driving her car, Jamie was one of them. They knew their rung inside that school. Whether they liked it or not did not matter, it was where they fit, so they welcomed him back into their ranks. But still that made him anxious; those who accepted him were too much like his mother. And that made him feel colder than this January morning down in the pit.

The morning had yet to become fully illuminated by the rising sun, but it did not seem to matter as the cold muted the sun's brightness anyway. The kids in the pit had separated into their own groups of sub-cliques: punk-hippies, punk-rednecks, and punk-punks, and the little groups stood around in herds, trying to get whatever warmth the others would provide, talking and blowing smoke like little refinery stacks.

Jamie stood among the hippies, the collar of his denim jacket pulled up around the thick padded neck brace that had taken the place of the halo brace, puffing on his cigarette, holding it with his pale chapped lips. He raised his shoulders, hurting his neck just so slightly, as if to break the wind for his ears. But they could not, so his ears stood out bright red, blending with his face, red as a ruby.
"This is ridiculous," Ned “the head” said, "I'm freezing. I don't need a smoke this bad." And he threw his cigarette to the pavement and walked away to the building.

"Hey Turtleneck, when you getting that thing off?" Angus,

with little Fiona wrapped inside of his heavy army jacket, asked Jamie. A new beard, thick and heavy, covered his chin.

"Don't know," Jamie answered, shaking in the cold.

"Fugly," Angus said, turning away from Jamie, "give me a smoke."

Ian looked at Angus from underneath the large hood that hid his face from the cold as well as other's stares. He pulled his hand from his coat pocket and tossed Angus a cigarette, and then took one for himself.

"Thanks, Fugly," Angus smirked, "gotta' light?"

Ian tossed him a lighter. Angus lit his cigarette in a quick, jerky motion and tossed the lighter back.

Jamie noticed the guy with the funny nose did not take his eyes off him, as if the cold had frozen him, forcing his stare, so feeling unsettled by the stare, Jamie dropped the cigarette from his mouth to leave just as the five-minute warning bell rang.

The little herds began dispersing, Angus swallowing up little Fiona in a healthy embrace, swallowing her tongue with his ugly kiss. Jamie turned away, disgusted and annoyed, and then he heard his name. He turned around, and the hooded guy with the funny nose continued to look at him.

"Your name's Fugly?" Jamie asked the hooded guy.

"No, it's Ian," he answered.

"Why'd Angus call you that?"

"You figure it out..." He took another drag from a cigarette, flung a few strands of hair from his face with the hood still hiding him. "I saw RaLF this morning."

"Yeah?" Jamie asked, stepping away.

"She looked beautiful..."

"Really?" Jamie stopped.

Ian smiled, pulling his hood back so that Jamie could see his pale pink face, and drew his finger across his forehead, tracing the line of RaLF's scar. "Beautiful," he repeated, although Jamie missed his meaning.

"Nice to meet you…" Jamie said with a wave and hurried away. After he stepped inside, he looked back at Ian, a chill shooting down his back, but the guy with the funny nose just stood in the middle of the pit, alone in the cold.

And when the final bell rang, Jamie cursed to himself, running to his locker.

* * *

She stared hypnotized at the clock, the second hand jumping from mark to mark. *Click...click...click...* The sound filled the room like a dying man's heartbeat. RaLF had forgotten how obnoxious the clock could be. *Click...click...click...* She waited for class to start, for the semester to begin, as the second hand jumped to the twelve and the first bell rang, unnerving her as the incident with Earnest had. When she dropped her coat, she had lost a protecting wall. Behind the wall, she had solitude and isolation, things she once wanted, now suffocating her.

RaLF had been out of the hospital for weeks at the time the calls and letters dwindled. Up to then she had not answered a call or any of her cards. Writing had been out of the question, anyhow. She had been right handed, so a pencil or a pen in her left hand felt awkward. When they stopped, a huge pressure upon her had been released, but as more time passed, she grew lonely and feared people had forgotten about her. Her place among the beautiful people had been more important to her than she had realized. Being popular had been a wonderful thing to take for granted, and she now feared that it had been taken from her.

Then other thoughts began to haunt her. She had never told Polly how beautiful she had been in her Homecoming gown with her crown and her flowers; RaLF had been too jealous. Now the telephone receiver was weighted too heavily with her pride, and her wall too well constructed.

RaLF completed the semester in her bedroom with her parents bringing her books and work assignments from school. Her beautiful cursive script was now big, block print in odd angles as it flowed from her pen, and when she read her old notes, tears would rain upon them, smearing her writing.

When Christmas came, she shopped by mail order.

When New Years approached, she celebrated behind her wall.

When school started again and every one else finished their first semester tests, RaLF took her tests at home.

When grades came out RaLF had her first straight-A semester. But the notion they were given in sympathy did not escape her.

She had all along told herself that she would be back at school when the second semester started, but the reality of her desire differed from her imaginings as she was a different girl now, a one-armed wonder, wandering for her place. She could not imagine playing basketball any longer. She fidgeted at being even less than she had felt the night of the wreck...the night Bill died.

RaLF's dreams lied and pretended that everything was all right. She dreamt about him, reached out to him. But her alarm would sound, and she would reach over to shut it off, and she would reach and stretch and reach, but the alarm would continue to ring, so she would stretch farther, as far as her body would allow her, and suddenly she would remember that her arm was gone. She would awaken and laugh in bitter irony that both the man she would hold and the arm with which she would hold him had both been taken from her—perished in one drunken instant that refused to be a memory, but still stood like a marking stone in her life.

Click...click...click.... The final bell rang, and RaLF pulled her wall in close about her, keeping the world distant and her fear tucked inside.

"RaLF," the teacher began the class, "it's good to have you back. You were missed."

She sat in the back of the classroom, still wearing her coat draped over her shoulders, her thick wavy hair covering her face like tattered curtains. She smiled a small forced smile, regretting the attention. Words stuck like phlegm in the back of her throat. Silence perpetrating more silence, she sat like a leashed earthquake in her desk as scattered blank faces around her turned toward her.

A scratchy thank you finally escaped her mouth.

"Welcome to World Lit.," the teacher said, her gaze falling upon each of her students. "I'm Mrs. Faulkner. We're going to have a wonderful semester exploring the written word from all four corners of the globe. You'll be happy to hear that there will be no tests, but you will..."

The crashing sound of the opening door hitting the wall interrupted Mrs. Faulkner's speech.

Ian stood in the doorway, a crooked smile beneath his crooked nose.

"Oops," he smirked, "it slipped out of my hand."

"Be careful with the door, and take a seat," the teacher scolded, angered at the interruption and Ian's tardiness.

As he entered, he saw RaLF. Their eyes met and emotions crashed like two trains colliding head-on, exciting Ian like a boy who had just gotten everything he had asked for, for Christmas, and angering RaLF like a girl whose Christmas was filled with clothes that didn't fit and toys that didn't work.

Ian took the empty seat in front of her. As he sat, he turned around grinning and whispered, "Hey, we're Twinkies now," running his finger over the pink line covering the bridge of his crooked nose, his smile large and open, baring his teeth like a jackal about to pounce upon its prey.

RaLF scooted her desk back until it hit upon the wall. She looked through her hair at Ian's impish smile, her guts twisting and swirling.

Ian inhaled deep through his nose. "Ahh, the memories..."

"Screw you," she whispered back angrily.

"You'd like to."

"Is there a problem?" Mrs. Faulkner asked the pair.

"Not with me," Ian answered defensively, raising his arms in surrender.

"Can I move?" RaLF asked, but not waiting for an answer from the teacher, she walked away from the desk, taking a seat across the room.

Mrs. Faulkner continued her introductory lecture, but RaLF did not hear her, her mind awash in anger and frustration, second-guessing being there. She sporadically looked over at Ian, who stared back at her, continuously running his finger over the scar on his nose. She hated school; nothing was the same anymore; college did not matter anymore; basketball did not matter anymore; all that mattered to her was the ringing of the bell.

Click...click...click...

She watched the clock in desperation. *Click...click...click...* And time slowed as the teacher handed out her syllabus and the class's textbooks. *Click...click...click...* RaLF's right arm ached, yet it wasn't there. *Click...click...click...* And when the bell finally did ring, she fled the classroom, ignoring the teacher's calling, running into the hall, into the masses of other students, and blindly colliding into someone again. She clutched her collar tightly about her neck, afraid to look up and see Earnest's stupid sad face again, but when she did look, she saw Polly.

"RaLF," Polly said, wrapping her arms about her. "I've been looking everywhere for you. Why didn't you ever call me?"

RaLF shook in Polly's grasp like a scared puppy, clawing at her wall with all her might, Polly's name creaking out from RaLF's mouth.

* * *

"Good lord, Graves, where do you get these ideas?" Axle Marx replied from across the table sliding a sheet of paper back to Earnest.

Earnest shrugged.

"They crack me up."

"Perhaps you're invoking the wrong muse," Anne Endo, the girl who had taken Mary's place as co-editor, interjected.

Earnest looked at Axle, "A muse?"

"Never mind, boys," Anne shook her head and began reading again.

"Hey, Danny, you want to see my cartoon?" Earnest looked at Daniel staring out of the third story window.

In the cartoon's first panel, Earnie, the protagonist, and Zeke, his sidekick, passed a sign pointing to the cafeteria. Zeke asked Earnie if he was going to have a hamburger for lunch. Earnie replied indignantly, "Of course not!" The second panel showed a stunned Zeke with a large question mark hovering above his head as Earnie went on, "The cafeteria is using German Shepards for meat." In the final panel, Zeke had a pained expression, his hand slapping his forehead, saying, "You don't mean..." And Earnest replied with sadness in his gaze, "OH YES, THE GRILLS ARE ALIVE WITH THE HOUNDS OF MUNICH!!!"

Silently Daniel turned away from the window as Earnest handed him the cartoon. He read it quickly, handed it back, and said, "Ohthithithvewyfunny."

Words crashed into words, consonants collided into vowels, pauses rendered absent and useless as the English language became a mish-mash of jumbled noises.

"Huh?" Earnest said.

Daniel's face's light pink skin turned red. He shut down the world around him, closed his eyes and directed his thoughts.

"Yeth...it...ith...vewy...funny," he said, unintentionally heaving a large breath of air at Earnest.

"So, you're gonna' use it, right?"

"Daniel," Mr. Addison said, walking through the room, motioning with his hand for the boy to wipe his face.

"Huh—oh yeah," Daniel answered, pulling up his tie to wipe his lip, a string of spittle breaking and falling to the floor as Mr. Addison left the room. He looked back to Earnest and opened his mouth to answer, but stopped and nodded his head instead. Then he walked back to the window, staring out over the vast lawn of the senior high. He grasped the window sill already forgetting what he had just read. The cartoon was funny, that he knew, but he couldn't remember why. He didn't understand why he needed to repeat the things he said, nor could he figure out why he had done so poorly on the semester tests the week before, nor could he figure out what had that blonde lady done to him Christmas morning. Since that day she had filled his thoughts even more than before. Like some angry demon she plunged her talons deep within his skull, turning his mind to mush as she stirred the gray matter into a stew.

His concentration was shot. For a second or two he could control it, but then a renegade strand would enter his thoughts, then another and another and another until a head full of blonde hair assaulted him, twisting into the fibers of his thinking, knotting and ratting and choking until it was all her. He tried to pray but his prayer closet was no longer the welcome place it once was, for it too had become overgrown with the blonde hair. And the talon stirred and stirred and stirred, and God, like everything else but her, felt far away.

* * *

As Mary drove around town, she felt as if she were becoming reacquainted, she had been holed up in that trailer for so long, only leaving to walk around the trailer park or to the convenience store down the road. So driving through Ponca City's streets, she enjoyed her feeling of déjà vu'.

For some inexplicable reason, she drove to the Deacon's church, The Holy Church of the New Covenant of Christ, a long name for a church of a few hundred members. His car set in his parking space, so she drove onto the newly paved parking lot and stopped the car. Her sisters so much older than her, she had been raised nearly alone with her parents, worshipping the old man. But the older she grew, the more difficult it became to please him. His love turned into rules; God this; Jesus that, Holy Spirit this and that. He said Christ was setting him free of the bondage of religion, and Mary watched him create his own set of shackles, so she fought him putting them on her.

Her car crept forward while she eyed the red brick church, scrutinizing its affect on her life and loathing it. She wondered if the Deacon missed her and what he would say about the life growing within, if he would rebuke her, or perhaps hold her in the Christian love he had told her about years before. At the exit of the parking lot, she stopped to look back at the mean structure another time and then pulled out onto the street.

It seemed strange to her that the Deacon would see her condition immediately, but John, the idiot, still had not figured it out. She certainly showed, but John, the idiot, just thought that she was fat and lazy.

Lazy? She had been busy learning John's game and discovering that playing house was a wretched thing. She was vegetating as his spilled seed expanded, bringing her one step closer to shoving John's head through something that would wake him from his distance and distraction. Since Christmas his mind had been elsewhere.

While the image of the Deacon's church shrank in her rear

view mirror, there was one more thing that she had to do before she could pick up John from work. When she reached the high school, the final bell had already rung and the chaos had begun. She circled the buildings slowly, looking, observing, deciphering her feelings, deciding if she missed anything. The congested traffic slowed her, but she weaved through it and completed her circle of the landmarks of her life. When she had finished, oddly unsure of how she felt, she headed to the oil refinery for John.

She barely missed a yellow light and stopped the car with an abrupt jerk at the intersection. Unconsciously, she looked over to her left to spy the driver in the car next to her. The driver's round head bobbed in a familiar fashion, and when he turned and faced her, she gulped air, seeing Daniel for the first time in months.

"Mawy! Mawy!" she heard him shout to her through her window, so she turned up the heater fan, drowning him out.

When the light turned green, she gunned the accelerator, the tires squealing, but Daniel followed after her, squeezing his car in behind her.

Mary's eyes darted from the street to the rear view mirror and back. "Leave me alone!" she hissed, turning right at the next intersection without signaling or slowing down. Her tires squealed again as they rounded the corner and Mary gained several yards as Daniel slowed and turned.

She was stopped at another red light as Daniel drove up behind her. He honked and waved madly, trying for her attention.

"Will you go away," Mary said into the rearview mirror, watching Daniel's flailing arms. She looked to the left at the oncoming traffic. She saw only one car, so she gunned the accelerator a second time, turning right, the tires squealing again.

The turn was so abrupt that Daniel could not turn behind her before the other car reached the intersection. Then he followed, watching where Mary went.

Mary laughed aloud as she and Daniel were separated by the other car, but after a block, the middle car slowed and pulled into a parking space along the street. "Crap," Mary mumbled.

Looking ahead at the traffic signal at the intersection crossing Grand, the downtown's main street, she saw the yellow glow of the signal light, so she shot through the intersection just after it turned red.

"Ha!" she yelled....

And then a siren came from behind her. She looked into the rearview mirror to see the flashing lights. Cursing, she turned the car into a parking space.

The police car parked beside her and left his car, walking to Mary's and tapping on the window.

Mary rolled the window down and looked up at the policeman.

"Where's the fire?" he asked.

"There's no fire," she answered contemptuously. "I was being followed by a lunatic. His name is Daniel. He's the editor of high school newspaper. He's crazy."

The policeman stood silently, his brow wrinkling over his sunglasses.

"May I see your license, please?"

"I swear," she said pulling her wallet from her book bag. "I was being followed. He was behind me the whole way from the high school."

"Will you take it out of your wallet, please?"

Mary shuffled through her purse, acting as if she were looking for it, and then she angrily shut her purse.

"Okay," she said with a resigned sigh, "I don't have a license. I'm living with someone and this is his car. I've dropped out of school and I haven't taken driver's ed, yet. I'm in a hurry. I'm going to pick up the guy this car belongs to. He'll drive the car. I just need some time to get my life organized. I really was being followed. The guy is a lunatic and I used to go to school with him. All he wants to do is pray and pray and pray. And all I want is to be left alone." She looked up at him, her eyes ablaze with her frustration.

Suddenly his radio blared and he answered in the walkie-talkie at his shoulder.

"You are a sad little thing. I tell you what. You go get your boyfriend or whoever it is and let him drive. But you slow down—and take care of that little one there." He pointed to her stomach with his pen. "This is a warning, now be careful." And he hurried away to his car.

She watched the policeman drive away, and then she backed into the street and headed for Conoco. She knew John would be sufficiently pissed off now. When she reached the place where he said he would be, the parking lot across the street from the main offices, he stood, shivering. So he hurried to the car and jumped in.

"Where have you been?" he asked, his face red with cold.

"Don't start on me. Daniel saw me and followed me all over town, and then I almost got a ticket."

"I'm not starting anything." He said weakly. "Isn't Daniel that Christian guy from your school?"

"Why?"

John just shrugged and then swallowed back up into himself

as Mary had seen him do many times over the last few weeks.

"Are you cold?" Mary asked, noticing John was visibly shaking.

"Oh...yeah..."

The car moved through town, the pair silent and aloof. And the longer they were in the car, Mary noticed John still shook, changing from red to pale.

"What the hell is your problem? Are you dying?"

John turned to her, passive and restrained.

"I think, I'm a Christian, and..." he swallowed, "I'm getting back with Faith..." his voice crackling like cigarette paper.

"Well, isn't that just dandy," she said shaking her head, her hair falling down in front of her eyes. "Daddy."

Chapter Twelve

Cold Nights and Cold Hearts

As he waited at the red light, Daniel watched the car take off through the intersection and the police car pursue, its lights swirling and sirens humming. He wondered if he should follow when the car behind him honked, drawing his attention. He looked up, noticing that the light had changed, so he turned left away from the police, leaving the scene behind him.

The chase confounded him, so he questioned whether it had been Mary after all. That thought suddenly embarrassed him and in turn concerned him. It was bad enough Mary haunted his dreams, but now she was sneaking into his waking hours, vying with the blonde lady for his attention.

And his thoughts returned to the sheets of blonde tapestry that covered him and controlled him. It seemed a natural progression, first Mary and now the mysterious woman, who had become like sugar in a gas tank; gumming up his life, sticking to his pistons, messing up the precision in which he worked. Yet all the while, he longed for her spark. For the first time since puberty had fallen upon him, he felt nature's carnal call.

And it was another way in which the blonde had locked him from his prayer closet—distracted with ordinary thoughts of her as he tried to pray and concentrate on his Father who art in Heaven. But when the distraction grew to include thoughts of a less respectable nature, he grew too ashamed to even try to enter the Holy of Holies, and present himself before the Throne of God.

So after arriving home, Daniel pulled down at the bottom of his coat as far as he could and carried his books before him as a kind of barricade. *Go away,* he thought, entering his house.

"Daniel is that you?" his mother called from the kitchen.

"Yeth."

"You just had a phone call not ten minutes ago." His mother walked into the room, drying her hands with a dishtowel.

"A phone call?"

"Yes, from a lady. She said her name was Faith Smith."

"I don't know any Faith Thmith."

"She said it was about church. And that Pastor Green had said it would be okay if she called."

Daniel shrugged his shoulders.

"She left a phone number for you."

"I'ww caww hew latew," he said, dragging himself up the stairs to his room. When he entered his room, he sighed, feeling tired, exhausted from the car chase and the strain put upon him by his glands. He dropped his books on his desk and fell face first on his bed.

"God, women make you cwathy," he whispered prayerfully, his head buried in his pillow. Several minutes passed, and he did not move. Finally rolling on his back, he unzipped his coat, and went to the closet to hang it up. He then went back to his desk and glanced over his textbooks. He did not feel like doing any of his assignments before spending the evening at school. He knew it would be pointless to try, his mind a million miles away, so sitting down at his desk, resting his chin in his hands, he let out another sigh and invited the blond hair back. And it came, wrapping itself about him like a virus.

He pulled open the top middle drawer of his desk, took out a pen and his journal and plopped them down on top of his desk. Opening the journal, he flipped through the pages until he came to the first blank one. Then he wrote, starting with the same Bible verse that he had used to start each entry for weeks.

Thou has ravished my heart...

The mystery woman has destroyed me; from my head to my privates, she hasn't left me alone. If I ever found out who she is, or even remembered what she looked like, I don't know what I would do. I miss my normal life. I miss God.

A knock sounded at Daniel's door.

"Wayouwa!" Daniel blurted, not wanting to be interrupted.

The door creaked open, and his mother peered in. "Slow-ly and e-nun-ci-ate," she said, speaking slowly and enunciating.

"Wath...do...you...wanth?" he repeated for her.

"Faith Smith is on the phone. She says she needs to talk to you."

Daniel growled to himself and shut his journal. Following his mother, he went back downstairs to the kitchen. His mother held the receiver toward him, her hand over the mouth piece and said, "Talk slowly, okay?"

"Yeth, mothew," he answered, embarrassed by her tone. "Hewwo?"

"Well, Mr. Davies, I had to call you. The Lord wouldn't let me rest until I did."

Mr. Davies? Daniel thought.

"The Reverend Green told me how to get a hold of you. I hope you don't mind. I know you don't know who I am, but you saved my marriage."

Marriage? Daniel grew more confused.

"I heard you speak at your church, a couple of months ago, and I realized I needed Jesus in my life."

"You wewe at the wevivaw?"

"Uh-huh, and since then, I've gotten saved and I prayed for my ex-husband's salvation. He went with me to church on Christmas day."

"Congwaduwationth, I'm happy to heaw thith."

She went to church on Christmas Day.

"I'm embarrassed to say, but you scared me that evening."

"I did?"

"Yes, oh yes... The Lord had me under so much conviction I thought you were talking directly to me. It seemed every time I looked up, you were lookin' right at me, and then...then when you gave the invitation, I just walked out. I guess you saw me. I guess the whole church did."

…walked out…

Daniel did not hear another word. *She called to thank me for saving her marriage … she walked out. It was her. She has ravished my heart... It's you. You're her, the woman suffocating me with your hair.*

And Daniel's stomach somersaulted.

"Christ can do anything is what you said, and I decided to believe you, and then I saw my ex-husband at his parent's Christmas party on Christmas Eve. It was like God had brought him there, and that night I talked to him about the Lord, and he listened to me. That was so different for him, so I knew that God had his hand in it and then he went to church with me the next day. We went to your church again, and I think we are going to join soon as a family. I thought I saw you sitting at our pew, but you didn't feel good because you jumped up. You looked like you were gonna be sick. Have you been all right?" Her words pelted him as she never stopped to breathe.

Have I been all right? Thou hast ravished my soul and you're married.... You've ruined my sleep, my days, my nights, my grade-point. And you're married... My body's become the devil's playground. Am I all right? I'm an adulterer!

"I've been okay," Daniel answered after a small pause. "Yeth, I think I wemembew you. You've got bwonde haiw, wight?"

"Yes, that's me."

That's you; that's her.

"Well, I won't keep you any longer. I just wanted to thank you for letting God work through you. God bless you. Please, say hi if you see us at church."

While you taunt me? "Okay, I wiww," he said. *I'm a fool, an idiot.*

Daniel heard the other end click. He stood silently, holding the receiver buzzing in his ear, feeling more ravished than ever. She had had her way with him, shredded him, devoured him, and she never even knew it.

"Well?" His mother stood, looking at him.

"Thee wath at the wevivaw and got thaved becauthe of my methage."

His mother glowed. "Isn't that wonderful, Hon. You led someone to the Lord."

He smiled back at her. "It'th wonderful," he replied and meant it, and then he walked back to his room—not knowing if he would rejoice or vomit.

* * *

The car, moving slowly along the street and then stopping, appeared an anomaly in this neighborhood. The faded paint, the rusted fenders, the dents, the cracked windshield, all bore evidence to the car's displacement among the giant, wood shingled, stone houses; the perfect lawns, and the perfect automobiles. But all the same, Jamie parked, staring across the barren street, down the long yard, at the house he knew to be RaLF's. Lights illuminated the grand structure RaLF called home, so different from his own.

Not exactly a voyeur, Jamie spied upon the large house. He had seen but patches of RaLF all day. The distance he kept did not allow for much more, so he had not seen her scars, and they remained the fruit of hearsay to him. He bore scars, too, four little buttons at the four corners of his head, round reminders to the brace once screwed into his skull. But somehow he did not think that would be enough for RaLF, enough to sweep the messy happenings of the past away.

Puffing on a cigarette, he watched the lighted windows, occasionally seeing a shadow behind the closed curtains. He did not know if he hoped to see RaLF; he did not know if he really had expectations beyond just being there, but all the same, he watched. An image of Ian passed though his mind—the same one that had bothered him all day—Ian's odd smile as his finger dragged across his forehead. Suddenly he saw a curtain on the second floor open and a woman's silhouette looking out into the night.

* * *

RaLF saw the familiar car across the street, partially lighted by a street lamp and partially hidden in the dark. She could see its neglected appearance even from her distance and thought that it looked out of place. *Out of place,* she thought, *like a one-armed girl on a basketball court...or in school.*

"I would like to," the counselor had said to her earlier, "You've been through so much. I will do what I can. I'll talk with Mr. Lidle to see if we can get Ian moved." She preferred God reaching down with his big heavenly hands, wrapping his holy fingers around Ian and squeezing the boy like a wrung rag.

As she walked away from the window, she thought again about the strange car. But that thought was displaced by another and then another until her mind rested upon Polly.

Seeing Polly again had felt strange. Embarrassment, glee, trepidation all showered over her, as she stood with her in the hall. RaLF's wall held strong keeping things away, but it also squeezed the things within it closer to her, so her emotions rose up, nearly suffocating her. RaLF reached out to grasp something, and Polly was standing there, for her, reaching for her with her arms open. RaLF, still frightened, held herself aloof, but Polly's eyes swelled and tears trickled forth, ruining the Homecoming Queen's mascara.

Other students walked about them as they headed to their classes, but the two girls stayed oblivious to them. RaLF did not know if she should curl up and tuck herself in Polly's care or scrape and push herself away. But Polly drew her closer, adhering to her with vehemence. "Oh, RaLF," Polly repeated in RaLF's ear.

So RaLF submitted to her friend's hug, and soon RaLF felt her fear evaporate; the wall began to crumble; her heart pounding so hard within her chest she knew that Polly must have felt it, too. Slowly the hallway emptied around them. Then the bell rang, and they still embraced, and RaLF listened as Polly wept. And she began to, too.

RaLF sat down at her vanity still thinking of Polly while her scarred reflection stared back at her. She had already learned that make-up would not help to cover the scar unless she layered it so thick that she looked both juvenile and artificial. Oh, how she loved Polly—loved her and resented her. "Dammit," RaLF said aloud, "I want to be pretty, like you, Polly, pretty like you."

When would time heal this wound? But seldom to her did time seem to improve anything—except her memories of Bill. Before the wreck, she could have listed his faults in any way one might want them. But those same faults were disappearing behind time's thick exhaust—and not only for her, but to others at school as well. Some visiting stranger might have assumed Jamie to have crucified Christ. RaLF found herself feeling much the same way. Without a memory of that night, no understanding of why she was with Jamie and not Bill, she had talked herself into hating Jamie.

She stood up from the bench, tired of looking at herself and curled up on her bed. And soon she fell asleep with the light still on.

* * *

Jamie sat up when he saw no one standing in the window any longer, wondering if he had seen RaLF, wondering if she ever thought about him. He reached over to the back seat and found a blanket. Wrapping it around himself, he waited, and waited...

*   *   *

It was very cold, and it was very dark, but Mary carried nothing but herself, her book bag, John's best coat wrapped around her, a temper that roared like an unexorcised demon, and the fetus. She had gone to him with nothing, so she left him taking nothing—except for the coat, the temper, and the fetus. She had not yet been gone five minutes when a pair of headlights came up behind her.

"Mary!" A cry came from the car as it drove up beside her, "Mary, be reasonable."

She ignored John as best as she could and continued walking until he uttered the word reasonable. "What do you know about reason, you born-again creep?"

"I didn't say I was for sure."

"You can't ride the fence and me, forever! Go away and leave me alone!"

Mary quivered, but she wasn't going to let the cold or the wind slow her or stop her.

"How was I supposed to know you were pregnant?" John yelled across the seat through the passenger's window to Mary. "You never mentioned it."

"Remember, I'm putting on a few pounds!" She turned, looking furious, her face wrinkled in disgust like a wad of discarded paper.

"Are you even sure you're pregnant?"

"I passed the test."

Her walk became swifter and more hurried, but John stayed

with her.

"Go away!" She waved him away, looking forward, following the road.

"Get in the car, Mary. It's freezing! I'll take you where ever you want to go."

"I want you to go to hell!" She snapped back quickly.

"Come on, Mary. I can't let you freeze."

Mary stopped, her anger tiring her more than the walk. She sighed with a puff of steam rising from her mouth. Then looking down she noticed a large piece of blacktop broken off of the side of the road and picked it up. "I said leave me alone!" She heaved it at the car, hitting the passenger door with a loud blunt thud. "You bastard! Go back to your wife! Just stay the hell away from me!"

"Damn you!" he yelled.

"Hallelujah, Brother John, tell it like it is!" She bellowed in the night, slapping her hands to her knees.

"Then, go ahead and freeze!" John barked back, and the car shot forward, leaving Mary in a puff of heavy gray exhaust and back in the dark.

"Yeah...well, I hope I do freeze…" she muttered, watching the taillights blur together and disappear in the distance. And she began walking again.

The silence of the night absorbed her, and the darkness wrapped around her like a shroud, walking the same path that had taken her to John's trailer all those months ago. Although the time was not much passed eight in the evening, it seemed the dead of night when only insomniacs and lunatics roamed the earth. As she walked, the oppression of loneliness enwrapped her, so much more so than she had ever felt in her life. She thought about the failed abortion, thinking that if she had been able to do it none of this would have happened, but she knew that it would not have mattered; John and Faith would have gotten back together anyway, and she would have probably ruptured her uterus and bled to death in the bathtub, making things a lot worse for her than losing John.

As the cold crept down her legs, her feet soon grew numb, feeling swollen and heavy in her shoes. To help stay partially warm, she drew her arms inside the coat and wrapped them about herself, leaving the sleeves limp and lifeless, swinging with each step.

The countryside speckled of lights. So she headed for the glow in the northwest over Ponca City. All roads it seemed led back to Ponca City, and it frustrated her to no end.

After a time, an old steel bridge passing over the Arkansas River appeared before her. As Mary crossed the midway point, she stopped and looked down. The night was so dark that nothing but blackness reflected in the water. She picked up a pebble from the bridge and dropped it over the side, but could not hear it break the water's surface. The breeze along the river blew bitterly cold, so she hurried to the other side.

Occasionally she tried running, but managed only a few quick steps before her side began to hurt, making her breathing pained and forced. What seemed hours later, she saw the glowing Red Barn sign in the distance, close enough though that she mustered up a little added effort and began a stiff-legged jog to reach it. Her body ached badly as she reached the convenience store, huffing and puffing in tired, strained agony.

Mary nearly fell through the two glass doors as she was so cold and tired and stiff. Above the refrigeration units where the beer was kept, a clock read 9:58 in bright red numbers.

"Hey, are you all right?" a lady with big hair and a big body asked from behind the register.

"Y-y-yes," Mary answered not able to control her quivering. Her feet no longer had any feeling in them at all. "I j-just nnneed-d to warmm up-p a little."

The lady looked a little closer and said, "You've been outside too long, Honey. Your lips are blue."

"I'mm f-fine," Mary replied not sure that she believed it or not and walked to an empty booth in front of the window, looking out into the small parking lot in front and the road beyond. Mary sat down and her legs instantly felt relief. She slowly crossed her legs and untied her shoes. As she slipped one off, a chime rang, as someone entered the store. Two people walked past her as she slid the shoe off. After taking her sock off, she saw that her feet looked blue, too. She touched it and the foot seemed as cold as dry ice. "Owww," she moaned. *I really did freeze; I hope that jerk's happy.*

"Mary? Mary Christmas?" someone said and Mary looked up. Earnest and Axle looked back down at her. She did not know what to do, so she did nothing but look back with a blank stare.

"Do you boys know her?" the lady at the counter asked.

"Yeah," Axle said.

"I think she needs some help."

Earnest did not like Mary, and it irked him that the lady suggested he help her. He didn't pretend to be a saint.

"You need a ride, Mary?" Axle asked her, handing her a hot chocolate that he had bought for himself. "Here."

Mary took the cup, too tired to argue, and began to drink it in small sips. "Th-thanks," she said, feeling her head pulsing, not sure when it had started. She also realized that she was dizzy, so she sat the cup down and slid down until she was flat upon the bench. "I don't feel good," she heard herself saying as Axle loomed over her, placing his hand on her forehead.

"Put her shoe on."

Earnest looked at Axle. *You put her shoe on*. But he went ahead and took the sock from her hand and slid it over her foot. Then he put the foot into the shoe, with some difficulty, and laced it up.

Mary felt herself being lifted and taken back outside.

Earnest opened the door to the back seat on the driver's side. First Axle had him putting on the girl's shoe, and now he had them putting Mary in his car because Axle's GMC Pacer was too messy. He had thought getting a soda with Axle after the evening's layout would help break more ice between them. He needed a friend since he and Ian had gone their separate ways, and Axle appreciated his sense of humor. *But the guy was just too bossy and considerate.*

After Mary was in the back seat, the two boys climbed into the front and headed for the hospital, unsure where else to take her.

Mary bounced about in the back seat much like the conversation she overheard coming from the front seat: "Where'd she come from?" “You really don't know what the pioneer man is?" "I wonder where she's been." “She looks like crap." “I told you. I don't have a clue about the pioneer man." “So did Daniel this evening. I wonder who looks worse." She heard the words, but nothing registered outside of the bouncing and the cold.

Soon she felt the car stop, heard the door open, and a rush of cold air hit her.

They pulled her out and put one of her arms over each of their shoulders. She felt like she was floating except her feet seemed unable to keep up and dragged at every other step. Through her half-open eyes she saw the door slide out from in front of her. She floated a few steps to another sliding door.

"Excuse us," she heard a familiar voice again, and then suddenly she was surrounded by a blur of people in white. Too many voices; too many sounds. She was soon resting under a pile of blankets, and she slept.

Chapter Thirteen

Spirits

Tuesday, February 12

Daniel felt a prod at his shoulder, but it barely roused him, so he quickly slipped back into sleep. Next, a violent shake took hold and continued even after he said he was getting up. Daniel rolled onto his back, and the shaking stopped. He had slept so heavily his eyes pained at opening, and after they finally were open, all he saw was a deep, translucent, blue and purple glow saturating the room, shimmering and rippling like carnival glass. He rubbed his eyes to clear them, but the room remained bathed in the thick, penetrating hues.

"Daniel," he heard within the luminous blue veil.

"Dad, I can't see you," Daniel replied, not yet fully awake.

"I'm not your daddy, silly. It's me," a child-like voice replied, coming from everywhere.

"Who are you?" Daniel asked, his mind clearing even as his vision did not. He tried to sit up but found himself in a cocoon of twisted and knotted bedding. As he wriggled to free himself, he tumbled to the floor, bumping his chin and biting his oversized tongue.

"What's going on? Who are you?!" Daniel grunted, tasting blood.

Then rolling onto his back, reeling from a slight intoxication of pain and confusion, he noticed an aberration in the glowing, almost gaseous, light above his bed. The air began to ripple and bubble, and a shape appeared to be growing from the shifting shades of light.

"I told you. It's me!" The voice repeated, more forcefully from the shape above.

Daniel stared at the object, uncertain of what he saw, so he pushed himself away, dragging the bedding that wrapped around him.

"Where are you going? Don't you want to talk to me, Daniel?" The child-like voice cried.

As Daniel crawled to the door, the bedding fell away like discarded skin.

"Daniel, why do you always ignore me?"

"Get thee behind me, Satan." the boy answered without looking back as he furiously crawled.

"I'm not the devil, silly. Turn around and look at me."

The boy awkwardly climbed to his feet and grabbed the door knob, gripping it so tightly he felt he was bruising his palms, but the knob would not turn. He jerked and pulled at the knob, but the knob remained steadfast. What little composure Daniel had to this point, fell away. With both hands still clinging to the knob, his body began to shake violently, rattling the whole door as his fear ebbed toward the surface. "Who are you, dammit!" he shrieked, turning around.

"Don't cuss at me, Daniel," the voice reprimanded, "You know better than that."

After Daniel turned from the door, his senses seemed to slow and unfocus from what he saw. The form hovering above his bed had taken human form. Daniel gasped, his legs folding beneath the burden of recognition, and he fell to the floor.

"You," Daniel croaked in disbelief. "You… You…."

"Yes." It repeated, joyfully. "Yes. Yes,"

Even as the room was thick with the blue and purple glow, the hovering body now moved in and out of the misty blue hue, revealing the rosy pink face that Daniel knew.

"You're not real." Daniel muttered from his place upon the floor, succumbing to his weary intoxication, his voice sounding of a slight but insistent vibrato.

While still floating, the thing took a sitting position, and looking down at Daniel, it extended both of its arms forward, balling its hands into fists as if clutching something. Finally it began to peddle its feet.

"Earl," Daniel moaned aloud and then whispered, "Crazy Earl," as the ghost peddled around the room, weaving in and out of the shroud of luminous colored space. Jubilantly, Earl sang his song. "De Camptown Ladies sing this song, Oh, dee doo dah dayyyyy!" He howled—the voice raining down through the blue air around the chubby heap that Daniel had become.

What is going on? Daniel asked himself.

"I'm here to see you," the ghost answered Daniel's silent thoughts, making a quick reverse peddle to brake.

"Huh?" Daniel asked dumbfounded, unable to stop his quivering.

"I said I'm here to see you. But first…I want to know why you never liked me," Earl's lower lip stuck out in an awesome pout.

The ghost's words startled Daniel. "I did...do..." he blurted defensively.

"No, no no no no. Lying's a no-no. No, no, no. I might've been brain-damaged, but I wasn't no dumb bunny."

Daniel stood bewildered in the center of the room.

"No, Daniel, you never, ever, liked me. Remember when you pushed me into the lockers, and I dropped my broom, and... and..." Earl choked on his words, "...and you never, ever, looked back at me when you walked away to... to see if I was all right." The ghost sniffed and wiped his sleeve under his nose.

A moment of Earl's sniffling passed before Daniel realized that the ghost's staring, pouting face expected a response. He sputtered, unable to think of any appeasing words.

Earl looked down to the unsettled boy, his sad face turning to a smile. He let go of his imaginary handlebars and raised his shoulders in a slight shrug. "The truth shall set you free," he said, his voice taking on a controlled almost adult quality, not sounding anything like Earl. He continued to peddle around the room, leaning back in the nonexistent seat of his nonexistent trike, once again reaching out his arms for the handlebars, tossing his head back and closing his eyes, the bill of his cap sticking straight up, pointing towards Daniel's salvation.

"Set me free," Daniel mumbled, no longer feeling the floor beneath him—awash in the rippling blue fog that filled the room and the throbbing pain in his tongue. "Yes," he finally said, almost unconscious that the word had slipped from his mouth. "Yes," he repeated, louder and more forceful. "Yes, you're right. I did not like you." Daniel felt dizzy, as if separated from himself. "You were the enemy to me."

Earl did not react but merely repeated "enemy" without expression as if he did not grasp the word's meaning.

"You reminded me how I could've been—less than I am... I was afraid of you."

"More afraid of me than anyone?" the ghost repeated, surprised.

"I was afraid somehow you would take all this away from me," Daniel said, tapping his forehead. "Every time I saw you, I pictured myself instead of you, drooling and sitting and mumbling nonsense..."

"Am I still the enemy?"

"I don't have a clue what you are..."

Earl giggled, and then in a giddy voice replied, "I'm an aaaanngel," waving his arms in the air.

"An angel?"

"Close enough."

"Am I dreaming this?"

"Does it matter?"

"But..."

"Do you love God?"

This question came at Daniel unexpectantly; its subtlety soothing him like a kick in the gonads, extricating him from his light-headed buoyancy.

"I love God," Daniel insisted, if slightly defensive in tone.

"Then why have you created an idol and forsaken your savior?"

"An idol?"

"Uh-huuh. What do you think's kept you out of your prayer closet, silly?"

"Keep Faith out of this," Daniel suddenly insisted.

"I never brought her up."

"But..." Daniel muttered, too weak to raise his voice above a whisper.

"Silly Willy, just think about it. She's even ruining your grade point average. Now, you have been blood-bought and washed white as snow, remember." Earl grabbed the top of Daniel's head and shook it, tingling where Earl touched him.

"God loves you, Daniel, and he gave you a thorn for your side, but you forgot about it."

"My thorn?" Daniel's face wrinkled in confusion. He had always thought of the Down's as his thorn.

"Uh-huh, think about it. It's so obvious."

And then Earl leaned forward into the handlebars and began to peddle faster. He hummed the doo dah song, the rhythm of the song increasing with his speed. As Daniel stood still, uncertain of his own thoughts, he noticed the blue hew began to move in concert with Earl until finally he seemed to be in the center of a silent, swirling, blue and purple tornado—the humming, the only sound he heard. Sweat began to bubble across Daniel's forehead, and the air became stuffy and thick and hot. "Earl," he moaned as darkness began to encase him. "My thorn?"

Then a distant small still voice echoed. "It's Mary, you dumb bunny," and the darkness swallowed him whole.

* * *

"I hate driving in this weather!" RaLF screamed as her new truck cut through the snow and the slush of the street. Getting used to having only one arm for the steering wheel was bad enough. But every other person on the road made it even worse. "Move it! Move it!" She growled at the car creeping along in front of her. "Either move it or lose it!" She hated how a little snow turned people into fearful mice behind their steering wheels. Seeing a chance, her hand tightly gripping the knob that had been attached to the steering wheel, she whipped around. Her truck jumped out into the next lane to pass the car, but noticing the oncoming traffic was closer that she thought, she gunned the accelerator. Her tires spun, taking her nowhere on the slick pavement. Seeing the car approach, her heart jumped into her throat and she froze. In a flash the sounds and sights of the crash filled her senses. A squealing honk burst from the approaching car, but her panic stalled her, she could only watch the lights draw closer in the morning's breaking sunlight. The car then shot past her on the shoulder, its horn blaring. Slowly regaining her senses, she crept back to the correct lane and made her way to the school in much less of a hurry, her heart thumping in her chest and her hand quivering as she gripped the wheel.

Automobiles lined up along the block, entering the parking lot in turn like a stream of ants. RaLF drove past Hershel's hut, just another ant in the procession, and began looking for a parking place. In her nervousness, she drove towards the sparsest area near the new field house at the northern most part of the campus. Snow covered the lines marking the parking spaces, so people parked their cars in disarray. RaLF found her own make-shift space and parked her truck.

She did not immediately shut off the engine, choosing to gather herself first. For an instant, the wreck flashed through her mind: a screech of tires, Jamie's voice, the impact. Her arm hurt, her right arm hurt, absent, yet it throbbed. But then, even as the pain continued, the instant was gone and her memory erased clean.

She readjusted the rear view mirror and looked in it to touch up her hair. Her bangs were now cut to cover her forehead, so she primped, spraying hairspray, keeping every hair in its place. Then she put the mirror back to reflect the image from behind her truck again.

"Dammit," she screamed hitting the dash board her agitation turning to anger, "Damn you Messereli! This is such crap!"

In the mirror she saw the same rusty and decaying car that had been quietly hounding her like a bad dream slowly pull into a space near her.

"How long do I have to put up with this crap?!"

RaLF had suffered him for as long as she could, seeing him outside of her home, following her about town, arriving at school with her. He'd already killed her boyfriend. *What else do you want from me?* And she angrily shut off the truck's engine.

She stepped out of her truck, stretching to reach the parking lot, gripping the door as she broke the surface of the snow, making sure that she would not slip, all the while her eyes looking steadily upon Jamie's car. And as she walked away from her truck, moving towards the school, traipsing through the piled snow and slushy tire tracks, her stare remained firmly locked upon Jamie's car. She could see him sitting behind the fogged-over windows, a portion of the driver's side door window wiped clear.

Within the car, she saw that Jamie never made a motion to reveal himself, and this made her revile him more, heaping anger upon anger. He, acting invisible, dared her to act, and she wanted to, but she did not know what to do, adding frustration to her anger. So lacking any immediate source of retribution, she gave him the finger and walked away through the snow and slush.

To her friends and her people, the beautiful people, Jamie had become a malignancy. She had heard the sentiments, "Someone ought to kick his ass," bantered about in conversations. And she wished someone would. Maybe then he would leave her alone; maybe then Jamie would vanish. Walking up the stairs to the second floor, her anger and frustration grew.

Along the windows, across the hall from the vice-principal's office, a group of jocks, Bill's old friends, hung out before school. It was their territory. And as she topped the stairs, she took a quick right and found herself in the midst of these boys.

"Have you seen Polly?" She asked no one in particular. Looking around, she was surprised to find Earnest Graves standing beside Axle. "I really need to see her." Polly had become her source of strength.

"I saw her with Nikki a while ago," Marc Neuhaus, a football player, another of Bill's buddies, said.

"Thanks," RaLF answered, her mind spinning. *What can I do about Jamie?*

"You okay?" Marc asked.

"Yeah, I'm just...upset." She paused, surprised as tears welled in her eyes.

"Hey, what's wrong?"

"I'm just...well...I just can't stand it anymore. He's always there, whenever I turn around. He won't leave me alone!"

"Who?"

She hesitated, "Jamie Messereli."

"What about him?" Marc's eye brows arched like a startled dog.

"He follows me everywhere. It bothers me. I don't know what he wants."

"He's following you?" Marc's face turned red.

"He even spying on my house..." Her voice trailed away as all her frustrations come together.

Marc put his hand on RaLF's right shoulder. She resisted the urge to pull away from him for some fear that he might touch her stubbed shoulder.

"All I've wanted was an excuse. We'll take care of him."

"What are you going to do?" RaLF asked, wiping her eyes dry.

"Take care of your problem.... That's all."

"Don't do anything to get into trouble, Marc. He's not worth it."

"It's worth it." Marc calmly answered.

RaLF gave Marc and the rest a consoling smile, not certain what she may have started. Her eyes rested for a second on Earnest. They made eye contact, and then she immediately broke it. "If you see Polly, will you tell her I'm looking for her?" And she walked away, not feeling any less bothered than she had before.

* * *

RaLF had looked at him, looked him right in the eyes, and Earnest wanted to believe that she had smiled, but as he could not be certain, he claimed it as such anyway. The ghost that she had been on that first day back was being reclaimed by the real RaLF. Earnest saw that her hair was different, but her face looked perfect. She was becoming RaLF again, and it made him glad.

He felt awkward finding himself along jock wall. Earnest knew that he did not belong here, but they tolerated him as Axle tolerated him. More importantly though to Earnest, Axle enjoyed his cartoon; he had told Earnest that it was one of the funniest things that he had ever read. And similar to dominoes, as Axle fell, the rest of the beautiful people became more accepting of Earnest, the geek.

"That prick is dead meat," Marc's face glowed red with anger, his hands gripped to fists.

Axle looked at Earnest, shaking his head. "You gonna' mess him up, Marc?" he said in a mocking tone and then began to laugh.

"You think it's all right if he follows RaLF around like a psychopath? Man, the lousy son of a bitch killed Bill. Don't that mean nothing to you?"

"Marc, he didn't kill Bill. Bill was drunk, and Earl rode his bike in front of Messereli. It was an accident—an accident! I don't think he should be pestering RaLF, but you can talk to him. You don't have to kick his ass."

"That hippie-jerk killed my best friend. I'll put him to the ground."

"Yeah," Thad, a short bow-legged wrestler, grunted.

"Are you all so freakin' stupid? You'll end up kicked out of school... or worse." Axle looked up and down at his friends.

Earnest leaned against the wall, trying to push himself through it, finding himself in waters much over his head. Bobbing somewhere between pacifism and cowardice, Earnest had never been in a fight in his life—except for one with a girl who lived next door when he was much younger (he didn't count it; she was tougher than him and proved it).

"Some things are damn well worth it."

"This sure as hell isn't one of them," Axle retorted.

"This Messereli guy is bullshit. What you're sayin' is bullshit."

"You guy's are screwed up." Axle remarked and walked away.

Earnest's legs shifted. He didn't know whether to go with Axle or stay.

"Well, what about you?"

Earnest realized that Marc was looking at him, "Me?"

"Yeah, you. Are you with us?"

Earnest grew tense. Moral decisions were not his forte. A flash of intense heat swept across his face, and he thought of RaLF.

Within a second, his whole life with RaLF passed through his head. A hundred different memories (both real and imagined) riding a hundred different trains on a hundred different tracks all moving in a hundred different directions going around, about, in and out of one another as if from some M. C. Escher drawing. *RaLF.*

All of his life he had harbored a strange notion, and it docked whenever he became enamored with a girl. He thought if he could not guile the girl with his looks and charm, the possibility always existed for him to become her hero—pulling her from a burning building, pulling her from a wrecked car before it exploded, pulling her from some dangerous watery depths before she drowned—and then pulling her into his sinewy arms and kissing her heartily—just like in the movies.

"Well, are you with us?"

Yes, he could be RaLF's hero.

"Kick his ass." Trying to feel noble and heroic, the words sounded ridiculous coming from his mouth.

* * *

Trouble cascaded around Ian's mind, none he was in, but something he could stir up—just like the very same *something* stirring up inside him. Since the moment that RaLF had recreated him with the smash of her fist and the slice of her ring, his life had detoured, heading him towards a dark place, as if a bone had poked into his brain and stirred his psyche. He felt like so much more than the archetypal angry young man, so much more held inside of him than anger. Sometimes he felt as if the devil led him about by his twisted nose, and he would follow like a trusting puppy right into a gas chamber.

Whatever trouble waited eluded him, but he faithfully looked for it, sniffing about like a dog hunting a bitch in heat, following hints of enticing scent scattered about everywhere, leading to her. Yearning cried out within him, and he stalked to satisfy it.

The temperature was too cold to stand around in the pit and smoke, so Ian entered the building, restlessly prowling about, a tumultuous thunder roaring inside him. Somewhere, some place, his trouble lurked, huddled and hidden, waiting for him, shrouded in such a way only he would know it. Ian sensed the bitch was near.

He wore his father's old army trench coat, and it, a couple of sizes too large, loosely hung over him. But the coat made Ian feel larger. His hands were thrust deep into the pockets; his collar pulled up over his ears; a pair of sunglasses hid his eyes. In one long low pocket inside of his coat, a fifth of vodka bumped against his knee. He liked it better than pot, the afterglow much less subtle. It was important to Ian to have a drug of choice. Everyone else did, be they hoods, heads, or the beautiful people. On top of every other reason, a drug of choice made much better drama.

The effect of the trench coat and sunglasses and even the secret bottle in his pocket, added to his manufactured persona, but Ian knew everyone created themselves after birth. His musical guru, OX, had at one time been called Algernon Cathcart, a teacher of literature in some private school in England. Now, OX was a long-haired, unruly paragon of pseudo-satanic virtue in leather and face-paint.

Ian moved through the crowds of people, picturing in his mind what he must look like to them, as if his life were a scene from a movie. The action moved in his mind though as if in slow motion. People turned to watch him; they separated, moving to the sides of the hallway. His coat wafted as he walked passed, ignoring their stares, and yet still seeing everything, knowing that in their heart of hearts, they longed to be like him: unattached and untouched, estranged and aloof, awash in ennui. His audience worshipped him, and he did not give a rat's rectum about them. Something lurked that these people could not understand. Something big had to happen, and he was determined to see that it did. He was the catalyst to their future, and they stood too ignorant to realize it. They could not smell it; they could not hear the bitch's howl.

He walked up the stairs, slowly, knowing that she lurked, waiting for him, letting the drama build, letting the audience scoot to the edge of their seats. Topping the stairs, Ian turned left and found that tension tightened inside him. His steps became quicker. The bitch barked, taunting him. She was near. He turned at the corner. The movie's action picked up—building to anxious desire. His audience blurred, and he felt that he was fighting through a forest of voyeurs.

He turned another corner. The hallway seemed strangely long —as if a new lens had been loaded onto the camera. The shapes of his audience distorted and their voices warped and bent. A low-rolling thunder reverberated across the floor. His skin tingled as electricity arced through his muscles. The scent had become bold and bitter and beautiful, and he hurried to her.

Finally reaching the end of the hall, Ian turned one more corner, nearly making his way around the building's second floor. And then the barking ceased. Halfway down the hall, jocks lined the walls. He and his kind avoided this part of the school. They were not welcome, but as he could hear the bitch's sudden low growl urging him forward, he kept walking. As he stepped across the imagined border, first noticing Earnest among them, he grew nauseated, realizing how far they had grown apart. It was not the separation that sickened him; it was the pathetic route that Earnest had taken.

The scent continued to grow stronger, so he knew that she was here, somewhere among these jerks. He kept movinging forward, walking past Earnest, never answering any possible gaze. *Where are you?* Ian questioned the bitch silently.

"Forget Axle. He's a puss."

"I don't care."

"...kick the holy crap out of Jamie...."

"He deserves it."

"...after school..."

The jock's conversation blended into one long sentence, stated by one lone speaker. Ian never turned around as the jocks spoke, nor did he ever stop or slow down as he passed them. He heard all he needed to hear; he knew all he needed to know. These were magic words, and the bitch howled, the cry long and steady like a coyote baying at the moon. A tumult rushed through him. Feeling the bottle in his coat bumping his knee, he wanted a drink. His pace quickened, and he hurried down the stairs, leaping past people who were no longer an audience, but players to what was being put into motion.

Ian made his way to a restroom and entered a toilet stall, locking the door and putting a wall between him and them. He opened his coat and pulled out the bottle. He unscrewed the plastic cap and took three quick swallows.

With the five-minute warning bell ringing, resentment whirling about him, shaking as coldness encompassed him, he took another drink from his bottle. *Here is where it all begins.* Sweat beaded his forehead. The bitch was all over him, saturating him in her potent scent.

Chapter Fourteen

Out, Out.....

The alcohol had muted any act of conscience, so Ian floated through the day without worry or concern for Jamie. The overcast, gray winter sky and the slushy dirty piles of snow made the day perfect, so when the last bell rang he hurried to his car and waited.

At first, the vodka bottle was cool in his hand, but it warmed as he held it. Taking a drink, he saw that it was nearly empty after hitting it steadily all day—never intending to become drunk, Ian just wanted to be dulled.

He turned on his tape deck and slipped in a cassette. OX's orchestrated chaos burst from the speakers, but Ian did not listen. His mind floated elsewhere, bobbing atop the vodka ocean. All he needed from the music was to fill the empty spaces of his mind like mortar in a stone wall.

While he waited, he laughed at how much he had changed—and his friend, Earnest, the lousy hypocrite, standing along the jock's most sacred hall. He took a cigarette from a pack hidden in his trench coat and lit it. The smoke rolled down his larynx, filling his lungs with hot, volatile air. He and Earnest used to gripe about people who smoked. Losers, he remembered they called them. "Guess I'm a freakin' loser, Earnie ol' boy," he muttered aloud, but inaudible under his roaring stereo, and he took another long drag from his cigarette, feeling a perverse kind of satisfaction.

When he finally saw Jamie marching towards his old car, Ian felt a slight tug of guilt. But guilt was a remnant of the past; what was to happen, had to happen. And when he saw the group of guys come behind Jamie, pulling the back of Jamie's coat over his head and dragging him to a waiting car, Ian knew that Jamie's pain would be the start of something wonderful, and sooner than later, they would pay for it.

They had turned *him* into something ugly, and they would pay for that, too.

Ian trailed safely behind the jocks' car, without a thought of Jamie. The socs, the snobs, the phonies, the jocks, the beautiful people, could never understand his kind, as the beautiful people were like a retarded, blind, deaf, and mute giant let loose in the middle of a town, meandering recklessly, squashing the little people beneath him.

And when the car left the city limits, moving until they parked near a heavily wooded pasture, Ian held his distance, watching them bundle Jamie up, his coat still over his head, and carry him from the car. Ian drove past the car to park, and stepped into the cold up the road when they were out of his sight and inside the woods. After taking a final large drink of his vodka, finishing the bottle and dropping it into the piled snow, he stepped over an old drooping barbed wire fence and darted into the woods to follow.

The snow muffled his steps, yet Ian cautiously slowed as he heard the sound of muted voices and dulled slaps through the trees. When he first saw movement ahead of him in a clearing, Ian stopped and reached for his bottle, but remembering he had finished it, he felt panic and cursed, wrapping his arms around the trunk of a tree, the bark scraping his face. Slowly the panic ebbed, hearing the slight growl of his soul reminding him of his goal. Everything turned surreal as the movie in his mind began again. He moved stealthily from tree to tree until he was nearly on top of them. Through a screen of limbs and clinging dead leaves, he saw the boys taking turns hitting and kicking the fallen body.

Ian identified them all, save for one wearing a large, puffy, green coat, his back turned towards Ian.

"Kick him again," he heard the person in the green coat say.

Him…? Here...?

Followed by someone else doing it. Jamie made no sound or any movement in response.

The guy who kicked Jamie rolled him onto his back and fell upon Jamie's stomach, looking down like a ravenous beast.

"Listen here, you piss ant. Leave RaLF alone. If you get near her again, I swear I'll destroy you! You'll wish you had died instead." Then his fist slammed into Jamie's face.

As if on cue, they all turned to leave, and the face in the puffy, green coat turned. It shocked Ian see Earnest's face, and it slightly impressed him, thinking Earnie didn't have the balls for this kind of thing. But at the same time it crushed him, and he closed his eyes, quietly bumping his forehead against the bark of the tree that hid him. *So, this is where we are now, Earnie?* And then they were gone like a pack of wolves after cleaning a carcass.

Ian stood silently behind the tree looking at Jamie curled up like a fetus. "See Jamie," Ian said, remaining hidden in the brush, "This is what those people are." Ian pushed through the brush and walked to the huddled boy in the trampled and bloodstained snow. "It's us against them."

Ian rolled him over, startled at the blood smeared across Jamie's face.

"Jamie, it's me," Ian said, "Don't worry; they're gone."

Jamie's face altered by pain and fear remained frozen, his bloodied mouth agape in a long fearful frown, his eyes disappearing behind the swelling.

"They're gone."

"I'm hurt," he whispered through his swollen bloody lips.

"Let me help you up." Ian reached down, taking Jamie's hand.

Jamie panted and grunted and moaned as he rose to his feet. He staggered and fell into Ian.

"Can you walk?"

"They kicked me in the balls." He groaned.

"What happened? I saw those guys grab you in the parking lot, so I followed you here."

"They were RaLF's friends, weren't they," Jamie grunted in more pain.

"Yeah, most of 'em," he answered, thinking that Earnest surely wasn't.

Jamie remained quiet as he tried to stand on his own.

"God, my side feels like it's on fire every time I breathe."

He tried to take a solitary step, but he crumbled and tumbled back into Ian.

Ian wrapped an arm around Jamie. "You're gonna' have to help. You're bigger than I am."

The pair tottered through the snow and brush as Jamie wheezed in pain.

"I didn't kill Bill," Jamie strained. "I didn't want RaLF to ever get hurt, you know? I mean, all I wanted..." and he began sniffing and whimpering, realizing the wreck left an empty space in his memory.

Ian had heard every word, but the facts were insignificant compared to their consequences. It did not matter if Jamie had or had not killed Bill. What mattered was that Jamie had just gotten his ass kicked, and he was assured it was a necessary thing.

"We'll get those bastards, Jamie," Ian said.

"I'm hurt."

"Yeah," Ian quietly replied.

They hobbled through the pasture, Ian straining to hold Jamie's weight.

"Can you take me home?" Jamie groaned, collapsing into Ian, forcing Ian to his knees.

Ian grunted, pushing himself back to his feet. He bent down and maneuvered his free arm behind Jamie's knees and raised him, cradling Jamie in his arms, like a groom carrying his bride across the threshold; Jamie's bloody face resting on Ian's chest wiping blood onto his trench coat. Ian's arms quivered from the weight, his face straining to a bright red and sweat running in spite of the cold, but he forced himself to hold Jamie. By the time he reached the fence his arms felt as if they were being pulled from their sockets.

Ian slowly raised one leg, balancing himself on the other, and stepped over the fence and then brought the other leg over. After he steadied, he started walking to his car, but he felt a sharp tug. Turning around, he saw that his coat was caught on a barb. Angrily he jerked it and it came loose with a sharp tear. At the car, he awkwardly opened a door and sat Jamie in the passenger seat. Jamie's eyes never opened.

Ian fell against the side of his car, his legs and arms burning from the strain and his heart pounding, panting heavily, steam rising from his mouth in clouds. He looked down at himself. Jamie's blood spotted him, and when he looked at Jamie, lying unconscious in the seat, Ian saw that Jamie looked even worse than he had noticed before.

After he got in the car and started it, Ian smiled. Jamie had played his part well. And when Ian pulled onto the road, somewhere in the distance, he heard a howl of celebration and was satisfied the pieces that the bitch had designed were falling into place.

* * *

The snow had begun to fall again, and the wind had begun to blow again, and Earnest shivered like a madman in his car. He saw the little brown stains on his coat and his bare red freezing hands. And they reminded him why he shivered so. He spit on his hand and tried to rub his hand clean, but he could not.

I didn't lay a hand on him, Earnest thought aloud, but remnants of his transgressions covered him, implicating him. Suffocating under an avalanche of regret, he wanted to go back to the morning and walk away from the angry group with Axle.

He tried to put the key into the car's ignition, buy the key danced around it from his shivers. Earnest dropped the keys into his lap and groped the frigid steering wheel as tightly as he could, but while the firm grasp stopped the quivering hands, the rest of his body quaked. He remembered every grunt Jamie made as he lay in the snow, feet and fists pulverizing him. Each smack upon Jamie's face became explosions echoing in Earnest's head, and the blood spattered like nothing he had ever seen before. No simile, no metaphor, could describe what he had helped do to Jamie.

While they drove back into town, the others acted unaffected, even pleased, and they teased Earnest about his passiveness. "Coach said bones were made to be broken," someone had uttered, and they all laughed. Earnest laughed too, but when he left them for his car, what he knew to be right and wrong burst from his conscience like an angry lion freed from a cage.

And as Earnest faced himself, anger grabbed him, trepidation lifted him from his seat, and fear slapped his face. His body trembled in the onslaught of his unsettled emotions while his guilt ravaged him.

Tap...tap...tap

Earnest looked at the window, but it was covered in condensation on the inside and snow on the outside, hiding whomever tapped against it. He felt the defiant cold invade his body like death, bringing a constant shiver. "Earnest," a muffled voice said from the other side of the window. He was so shaken by the voice that he did not dare move to lower the window and find out who it was. "Earnest," the voice repeated, "it's me, RaLF."

These shakes were for her; these damned spots were for her. His hand reluctantly moved to the window crank, and he began to turn it. The window slowly lowered with a thin layer of snow falling onto him.

Then he saw her, and his heart danced.

"Hi," she said.

In that instant, he fell in love all over again. Her pink cold face, perfectly framed by thick falling hair and a knitted stocking cap, was more beautiful than anything he had ever seen in his life, the gray cloudy sky, the falling snow, and her foggy breath softening her appearance as if behind some sheer veil. Every stupid romantic cliché he had ever seen or heard became real.

"Hi," he replied.

"Marc told me Jamie won't bother me anymore...."

He remained silent.

"I'm sorry," she continued, her voice as soft as velvet. "I...I..."

Her unsure stutter held Earnest like a hook and pulled him into her. *What?* He silently wanted to ask her but afraid to ruin this moment with words. For an instant her eyes grew blank, and then returned to the comforting stare that held Earnest.

"Thank you for wanting to help me, but..." She looked lost but then she smiled, changing the subject. "I really like your cartoon. It's very funny."

"Thank you," he answered.

Then she walked away, his gaze following her to her truck. The beating of his heart was the only thing he heard, the only thing he felt. Without thought he took the keys from his lap, slid the key into the ignition, and started his car. She had stolen away all of his fears, and then he realized what he had done was, if not right, at least just. Jamie had transgressed, not he, Earnest reassured himself. Like an angel of death, Jamie had brought destruction and despair to RaLF. So they had tried to right the wrong.

She liked his cartoon; it was funny, she said.

Damn Jamie. Damn him. Earnest felt jubilant. He felt justified.

The cartoon was funny. He was funny. She liked his cartoon.

Earnest turned on his car's defroster to clear his windshield.

Mostly, RaLF liked him again, and that made everything worthwhile. That fact made everything necessary.

* * *

Daniel sat Buddha-like against the headboard of his bed, pondering his metamorphosis. After all, he believed every word of his Bible, every living word. It breathed life into him, and he took sustenance from it. It said, "His people will have dreams and visions." And he had. It said, "The blood washes white as snow." And he definitely was.

Over and again, the dream replayed in his mind, a collage of images instead of a memory: the flying custodian, the swirling blues, the tingling touch upon his head, and Mary—Mary, the thorn. "Washed as white as snow," Earl had said, and then he had touched him.

Daniel, made white as snow.

The alarm had pulled him from his sleep this morning, his eyes never opening as he moved through the dark room, down the hall, and into his bathroom; his mind reeling with fatigue. In darkness, he brushed his teeth while his tongue throbbed; undressing, slowly, thoughtlessly, his eyes painfully peeling open; the mirror reflecting his silhouette; a soft beam of light shining across his chin and lower lip.

His arm swung behind him, reaching for the light switch. In the illumination, there was not instant recognition, as if the mirror had been replaced with a portrait of someone else. But as familiarity crept in, shock and surprise came with it. The bowl cut crop atop his head, bleached by a radiance of holy fire, had become whiter than snow, and Daniel jittered against the awesomeness of it all.

Hours later, the sheet he had wrapped around his naked body did not help to calm his constant quivering. He looked down towards his covered foot and stared at his warn copy of the Bible resting upon it, the leather cover cracked and curled; its gold leaf pages rolling up at the corners. He pulled his foot back from underneath it, and the Bible settled into the sheets.

Daniel looked at the red, glowing numbers of the clock sitting upon the nightstand: 5:27 PM. For nearly twelve hours he had sat like this, trance-like, ignoring everything around him. His parents had knocked at the door this morning, but when they tried to open it, the door moved only a few centimeters before bumping into the back of the chest of drawers he had pulled in front of it.

"Daniel, what is going on?" his father had asked, peering through the small crack of the open door.

"I'm affwicted." Daniel replied.

"What did you say, dear?" his mother asked, taking her turn at the crack in the door.

"I'm affwicted, go away!"

"What do you mean afflicted?" his father asked, "Are you all right?"

"I'm not going to thchool today. Go away."

After much pleading and posturing, unsure what else to do, they went away as Daniel had never done anything similar to this before. His mother then brought him a tray of food for breakfast; at noon his father sat a Dixie Dog cheeseburger and a jumbo order of curly-q fries beside the untouched breakfast tray.

Daniel could smell the fries, but he sat immovable like a snow-capped mountain, his thoughts restraining his desire.

"What have I done?" Daniel asked. "How many thownth do I have to have?"

Daniel, you are my child.

The voice, but less of a voice than a feeling, came quietly. With this voice, he was familiar. No flying Earl. This voice comforted him.

"Yeth, I'm youw child, tho what?" he bellowed. "I'm wetawded; I'm defowmed;...and now thith..." his voice trailed off. "I'm youw child, tho what?" Daniel's face fell into his hands just as another knock sounded at his door. He looked up at his chest of drawers.

You are my child...

"Go away!" he said angrily to the still small voice. "Weave me awone,"

"That's no way to talk to your ol' buddy," Reverend Green said from behind the door. "What's going on, Daniel. I'm not leavin' till I know what's going on."

"I wathn't tawking to you."

"Who were you talking to, then?"

Could he honestly answer this, he wondered. "God," he finally said.

"Is God in there? I've been meaning to talk to him about you." the preacher joked.

Daniel stood, his bed sheet wrapped around him, and he hobbled to the chest of drawers as both his feet prickled with sleep. He leaned against the large piece of furniture to hold himself up in spite of his aching feet.

"I..." Daniel started, uncertain of what to say. "I'm diffewent, now" he finally muttered, shaking the blood back into his sleeping left foot.

"We're all different," the preacher smirked. "It's the one thing we have in common."

"No," Daniel sharply replied, "I'm vewy diffewent... fwom mythelf." He looked up at the ceiling, his eyes burning. "I'm affwicted. Go away."

"Are you sick, Daniel?" The tone of the reverend's voice shifted to serious.

"No," Daniel stood up. His feet felt better, so he walked away from the door.

"Then what are you afflicted with?"

Mary's round, angry face popped into his mind with Earl's remark. *It's Mary, you Dumb bunny.*

"My thown!" He choked as he said it.

"Your what?"

"My thown! My thown! You know, like Pauw the apostwe had.'

"Your thorn?"

Then silence dropped between the two at the door.

Pacing, stretching his legs, Daniel wondered for what seemed several minutes about what the reverend must be thinking. He heard no sound in the hall, so he walked back to the chest of drawers at the door. Clutching to his chest the sheet draping over his shoulder, he stood on his toes, leaning over the chest, bringing himself the closest he had been to the door all day. "Wevewend Gween?" he said barely above a whisper.

The door bumped into the back of the chest again, banging Daniel's head with a sharp thud.

"Ow," he cried, rubbing his forehead.

"Open the door, Daniel," the reverend said, his voice devoid of humor. "Otherwise, I'll break it off its hinges. You know I can and you know I will."

Daniel fell back in surprise. He had never been threatened by his preacher before. And because he remembered the stories the preacher had told about his life before his salvation: turning over a VW bug and rocking it like a teeter totter with the driver still inside; stuffing a pool ball in some poor sucker's mouth, and other similar escapades, he hurried to the chest's side, sticking one hand hard against the back because he had nothing to grip. Then he pulled, grunting and straining. The heavy chest, still filled with his clothes and other junk, slowly slid along the thick carpet.

As he walked backwards, a corner of the bed sheet that he had wrapped around himself became caught underneath the chest of drawers. At first, Daniel did not notice, but as he pulled the chest farther away from the door, more and more of the sheet fed underneath the chest, finally tugging on the boy's shoulder, pulling him over. Just as the chest cleared the door and Daniel fought the sheet to free himself, Reverend Green stumbled through the door, slamming the door against the wall and sending a framed photo crashing to the floor.

Daniel lurched backwards in surprise, jumping out of the sheet in a fury of small leaps and kicks.

Landing upon his hands and knees, the reverend was struck mute, staring at the naked boy. But Daniel was not Daniel. Or, at least he did not look like Daniel, his hair, his eyebrows, his sparse chest hair, and every other hair down to his pudgy little toes bleached to a snow white. And in the time that it took all of these thoughts to run through Reverend Green's head, Daniel stood motionless like a snow covered statue.

"Daniel," his father said sharply, jarring Daniel who realized that he was just as naked. He bent over and grabbed a part of the sheet that had snaked off of him beneath the chest of drawers, pulling it apart with a loud rip, and wrapping the torn sheet around himself. His mind went blank. He didn't know what to say. So responding to the growl that he felt inside, he muttered almost childlike, "I'm hungwy."

Daniel's father grabbed something from the floor and said in a tone as if this kind of thing happened everyday, "Here's your lunch," and he handed Daniel a grease-stained Dixie Dog bag.

Daniel took it and sat down on the corner of his bed tucking the sheet between his legs. Then he began to eat the cold cheeseburger and onion rings.

"What did you...?" the reverend began, standing up. "What happened to you?"

Daniel chewed slowly. Then he answered as briefly and as honestly as he could. "I thaw an angew," he said, refraining from mentioning who the angel was, as if that bit of information would stretch the believability of his story.

The reverend let the words soak in. There were other denominations where this kind of thing would never be doubted, even expected, but he was a Baptist, and this made him nervous. He had once spoken to a priest who had witnessed a statue bleed. The guy seemed sincere, but.... But he was Baptist, and these kinds of things just didn't happen anymore.

Daniel licked at the greasy film coating the inside of his mouth as his father nervously waited in the doorway. Daniel wanted some sort of response to his physical affliction. But they gaped silently at the boy—too much for them to see him covered in white hair. After all, he had had all day to adjust to the metamorphosis.

"Son, you really need to put some clothes on." his father finally remarked while walking to the chest of drawers that now sat conspicuously in the middle of the floor.

Reverend Green sat up, resting on the heels of his feet. "When did all this stuff happen? The angel stuff...?"

"You don't bewieve me."

"It's not that, Daniel. I'm just...no, not skeptical, reluctant, maybe."

"Wha'th the diffewence?" Daniel angrily retorted.

The preacher aimed his finger at Daniel with his mouth opened, ready to speak, but nothing came out, gagged by the boy's words, so he sat down next to him.

"It'th not like I exagewate aww the time! It'th not like I make thingth up…!"

"That's precisely my problem, Danny boy. Because you're you, I can't discount what you said happened, as wild as it might sound, as much as I might even want to."

Daniel's father put a pile of clothes on Daniel's lap. "Get dressed. You'll catch a cold."

He had been so engrossed in his thoughts all day that he had never been cold until the very instant that his father mentioned it. He felt a shiver as goose bumps spotted his body.

The reverend grunted as he pulled himself back to his feet and leaned against the chest of drawers. The thing didn't shift with his weight, so the preacher pushed at it. It didn't move. His eyes scanned the piece, noticing that it was thick, solid oak. He pushed harder, and the chest stood steadfast in the middle of the room.

"Good gravy," he muttered. "You moved this by yourself?"

"Uh-huh," Daniel said standing, clutching his clothes.

"Looks like our workouts are paying off," he said, and then his face lit.

"Let's arm wrestle."

"Huh?"

"Arm wrestle," the preacher smiled.

"What? Wight now? What about thith?" Daniel squawked, running his hand through his tufts of white hair.

"If you win, I'll believe everything you say, unconditionally, unequivocally."

"What if I loothe like uthual?"

"Well, I reserve the right to question. Man, you really moved that chest... On the carpet... Son of a gun!"

"Now, Pastor..." Daniel's father said, "let's not..."

"Do you have any idea how strong your son is?"

He shrugged, not noticing that he had been put off.

"Now where can we do this?" The preacher queried, looking around the room. "Go put your clothes on, Danny."

The chest was too tall. Daniel's desk appeared too awkward, so he took the lamp off of Daniel's nightstand. It looked to be just as solid as the chest of drawers. Then he dragged it into the middle of the floor with a grunt and a giggle. Then crouching down beside it, he rolled up the sleeves of his shirt.

When Daniel entered the room wearing a baggy pair of pants and a tee shirt that read 'Conoco, Ponca City's Best Friend,' he saw Reverend Green hovering over his night stand.

"Ready?" the preacher said.

"I gueth," he mumbled, lacking any enthusiasm for this. He knew what had happened, what an awful way of proving it.

"What happened to faith?" he asked out loud, and as soon as he said it, Faith's face popped into his mind.

She's ruining your grade point.

That was why Earl had come.

"Faith?" Reverend Green remarked, "I have all the faith in the world that you'll beat me…if it happened. Now, get down here."

Daniel took his place across from the preacher. They hooked left hands for stability and grasped the other's right hand for battle.

"Start us," the preacher said to Daniel's father.

Not certain how to, Daniel's father just said, "Go…."

Both men's hands began quivering as Daniel and the preacher put on the pressure in an instant. Daniel looked up from the hands to see Reverend Green's face. The preacher seemed calm in his face, smiling at Daniel, but the boy noticed the preacher slowly turn a bright pink.

"Did I ever," the preacher croaked, "tell you about the time I shoved a pool ball in a guy's mouth?"

Push, Daniel told himself, ignoring Reverend Green's words, concentrating on his hand.

"So," the preacher grunted, "tell me about your angel."

"The woom," Daniel locked eyes upon his hand, "tuwned bwue."

The preacher began pushing harder.

Daniel pushed back; his arm had never felt so tight.

"Angew...fwew awound the woom."

As the first beads of sweat began to appear on Daniel's head, he noticed the same on the preacher's forehead.

"He towd...."

Daniel pushed and ached. It seemed as if they were at a stalemate, neither moving except for their quivering.

"Told you what?" Reverend Green asked, his voice straining.

Daniel waited to answer. He finally felt his arm move ever so slightly towards Reverend Green. Every iota of energy in his body pushed his arm.

"Told what?" the preacher repeated.

But Daniel silently let the seconds pass while Reverend Green's neck turned bright red and a vein protruding from his forehead danced. Another centimeter in Daniel's favor. A roll of sweat ran down Daniel's face and into an eye. In spite of the stinging, he kept pushing. Little by little, the preacher's hand moved backwards, unable to fight against the boy. The closer the back of Reverend Green's hand came to the table, the redder his face turned.

Keep pushing, Daniel continued to tell himself, feeling no capacity to stop.

As Reverend Green's knuckles taped the table, Daniel's mouth opened in shock. He had never come close to beating the man before, and yet this time it felt as if there were no other possibilities. With his heart pounding, Daniel began to tell of his angel, but just as the words were about to escape his mouth, his mother stepped into the room. "What in the world is going on, here?" she asked, her voice shrill with shock, seeing her son's white crop for the first time.

Reverend Green took a handkerchief from his back pocket and wiped his forehead. He stood up, panting, and smiled as broadly as his face would allow.

"Grace," he said to Daniel's mother, "your son has seen an angel."

* * *

The doodle spread across the sheet of paper like a virus, starting as a few scattered lines, sparse and unrelated, which then grew and joined to spell **HELP** in big bold letters. The word, **HELP**, encased in a cartoon word balloon (initially written as Mary's own cry) became dialog for the caricatures of John and Faith Smith she then drew. The drawings did not resemble the people they represented; nor did the pencil scratching labeled Lita Mankiller, who had rested the sharp edge of two tomahawks into John and Faith's skulls. Gushes of dark graphite blood sprayed from the couple's injuries; lines of pain splayed from their heads like a peacock's tail. A few more marks, and they were sprouting knives, spears, forks, and whatever other pointed weapons she could think of. And with the added injuries more blood spewed like a fountain.

A light tap sounded at her door. Then her mother opened it and peered inside the room. "They're here," she told Mary, a forced smile across her face. Then she drew away from the room, the door closing behind her.

Mary stabbed the caricature of John with her pencil, breaking the point and putting a small rip in her masterpiece. *They'rrrre here-ere-re-re*. Her mother's words piled on top of one another until they buried her.

"And they can go square to hell," Mary answered her absent mother in soft angry words, straightening the tear she had put in the paper and studying the drawn figure of Lita Mankiller. "I can help," Lita Mankiller told Mary again, repeating the words she had spoken to her at the hospital the same night she had walked out on John.

"I can help you," she had said, standing at the end of Mary's bed, her face hidden in darkness as light spilled from behind her, illuminating her in silhouette.

Mary had sat with her mattress raised up in the back and her blanket pulled up to her chin, covering a body that looked like the rolling hills that made up eastern Ponca City's landscape. The television across the room glowed in sharp stinging colors. The hospital had been silent for hours, and her mother had left for a cup of coffee. Mary sat bored, flipping through the channels when Lita Mankiller appeared.

"I can help you." The words were thick and heavy, and Mary looked through them to the large Indian standing like a pillar.

"What can you do?" Mary asked, her eyes suspicious, glaring as she murdered the messenger of her present state with her strangling stare.

"I can help with your problem. If it is a problem..." Lita's staccatoed voice made the statement even more strange to Mary.

"What are you talking about?"

Lita looked at the small watch that banded her wrist in silver and turquoise and backed away from the bed, moving towards the door, the light from the hallway moving across her, revealing the Indian's round, acne-scarred face.

"You know..."

And then the door shut, leaving Mary only the low electric hum of the muted television to keep her thoughts, but the sound that filled the room was by no means a match to the voice that saturated her brain: "I can help you."

The memory of the scarred face disappeared like a puff of smoke above her doodle as a harsh knock upon her door drew

Mary's attention away from her thoughts. The door to her bedroom swung open and the Deacon stood, looking less ominous than odious, his thin but fleshy face frozen in indignation. "They're here," He said to her, his voice absent its usual richness, now hollow and empty. As Mary studied him, all that she saw was the shame that he felt towards her, his prodigal daughter. He now seemed shrunken and drawn; his eyes sunken, surrounded in the dark hues of despair. Mary could not believe the effect her leaving had had upon him. He had always shown himself as untouchable and emotionless. His pain surprised her. But, so did the fact she felt untouched and emotionless. So she followed him into the living room where they waited.

John stood at Faith's side, greeting Mary, surprising her that he would look her in the eyes. Faith sat quietly upon the couch, her hands kneading one another anxiously, giving Mary a small indirect smile, reassuring her that she was doing the right thing.

This meeting seemed unnecessary to Mary. John and Faith wanted the baby. And it seemed that her parents wanted them to have the baby. What Mary wanted did not seem to matter—but then, Mary did not know herself what she wanted, her decision stalled in some intellectual purgatory.

Mary blinked and found herself in the middle of a prayer. All heads bowed but hers, she watched the prayerful bunch, listening to their humble beseeching. Except from the Deacon, he remained quiet throughout the prayer, rubbing his forehead. The longer she listened, the more the room filled with good and righteous intentions: it was asked that the baby would grow up knowing Jesus. Suddenly she wondered if the child would grow up knowing her. A hint of regret tickled her as a trio of 'amens' called back her wandering thoughts.

"So much has happened to me since I've been born again, Mr. Christmas." John said, a slight smile covering his face. "My past sins washed away..." he added as if trying to make a point to them all.

Mary looked about the room when John said this, she and the growth inside of her his past sins. But no one returned her glance. Regardless, Mary knew they thought it. Even though the binding tie that Mary had shared with John had never been drawn tight, she was amazed at how quickly John untangled it.

"I've become a new man. Faith and I have renewed our vows, privately. And we plan to publicly at our church. God has been very good to me. When I first met Mary, I was an irresponsible fool, searching for something to fulfill me, to bring me joy..."

I've put quite a few smiles on that face of yours, Mary thought.

"...but I could never find happiness. Little did I know that it was there all of the time. I'm blessed to share this with you..."

He had used the b-word. John had transgressed completely into the realm of the enemy; he was talking like Daniel. Mary snickered.

"Faith came to the Lord in October, and she prayed for me, and God must have really wanted me because here I am."

"God wants everyone," Mary's mother interjected.

Sunken into his recliner, The Deacon remained quiet, no hallelujahs, no amens. Something churned behind the Deacon's eyes, Mary could see, but she couldn't read him.

"Mr. Christmas, I've repented of the things that I've done, and I'm forgiven, but that don't make the problem right. Faith and I have prayed about this, and this is how God has led us. He wants us to raise the child, and we are ready to obey."

Like Lazarus, the Deacon rose from the chair and walked to a small desk across the room, taking from it a folded piece of paper. Then he returned to the group.

"Our lawyer drew this up. I'm not happy...."

"Deacon..." Mary's mother interrupted.

"No, I've got to say this... Mr. Smith, you have no idea the hell my wife and I went through. Knowing she was somewhere and not knowing where...and she was only a few miles away. You're an adult....I don't know about your mid-life crisis or what ever possessed you to let Mary just disappear... God might have forgiven you, but it's not that easy for me." He paused, his eyes red and swollen and moist, "You took my little girl from me, and it's all I can do not to hate you for it, regardless what the Bible says."

Mary's mother reached over, taking her husband's hand.

Mary wanted to feel something, but she did not. She remembered when she had left school she had wanted to hurt her parents. And now knowing that she did brought her neither satisfaction nor shame. She felt indifferent. As she looked at John, his manner surprised her; he didn't tuck his tail. He faced the Deacon, eye to eye and didn't blink.

"I did an incredibly irresponsible thing, sir: forsaking my wife, and being a poor influence on Mary. I just hope that someday you all will be able to forgive me."

The Deacon handed the paper to John. "This gives you all parental rights."

Faith shimmered with excitement while John, holding his somber gaze, took the paper, looked over it and signed it. He handed it to Faith who quickly signed it without reading it. Then the Deacon took the paper.

Mary looked at the strange man that the Deacon had become —the man who spoke of lawyers as if a daily occurrence, who loomed above with eyes empty and tired.

"Mary, is this what you want? It's the easiest; I don't know if it's the best. I've prayed and prayed....and I just don't know..."

Mary took the contract and felt panicked. It was her decision, but everything had been her decision: screwing John, living with John, leaving John. And now this; she signed the paper quickly, her signature unrecognizable, and her insides twisting. She rested her face in her hands, exhausted, listening as solemn words were exchanged, as the furniture squeaked and the floors creaked with moving bodies, as the door closed.

"He's enthusiastic," Mary heard her mother say.

"Baby Christian," the Deacon muttered. "Wait until he's carried his cross a while..."

"Don't you think he'll stand?"

There was more silence, and Mary raised her head, awaiting the Deacon's reply.

"God forgive me," he finally said, "I just don't care." And he slowly walked from the room, his body slouched.

Mary realized that for probably the first time in years, she and the Deacon shared a common thought—of John's future, she did not care either, but she was now in this very instant certain of one thing: John would never see that baby.

Chapter Fifteen

The Spirits of Devils
And The Hearts of Men

Friday, February 15

He looked awful; he felt awful. Earnest stood beneath the shower head, hoping the hot water would revive him and wash the dark circles from his eyes. It had been days since he could sleep though the night instead of hovering in a purgatory of restlessness—days since Jamie had lain curled in the snow—and for days that image was all Earnest could see behind closed eyes. *No rest for the wicked,* he thought. And even less for the righteous, he mumbled to himself, turning off the water.

Inventorying his miseries, he climbed out of the shower, trying to replace one memory for RaLF's fading "thank you." He dried himself, and as his stomach gurgled absent of appetite, he pulled on a faded pair of blue jeans and a red plaid flannel shirt over a t-shirt, leaving both untucked.

Earnest went to the kitchen from his room and crushed a few blocks of shredded wheat into a bowl. Then he carried the bowl to the table where his brother sat reading a book as he ate. Eddie peered over the paperback.

"You look like crap," the eighth grader said, milk dribbling down his chin.

Earnest glared at his brother but only said, "Hand me the milk," his voice gravelly with phlegm.

His brother slid the plastic container to him. Earnest poured the last few drops from the jug into his bowl, barely dampening the cereal. Cursing under his breath while shooting his brother another angry glare, he began eating the dry cereal, the stems of shredded wheat poking his gums.

Then his brother said as Earnest's spoon scraped the bottom of his bowl, "There's more milk in the refrigerator."

Earnest poured the remaining cereal from the bowl into his mouth, slowly chewing it, saying with his mouth full, "I like it this way." His head pounded. M*ore sleep would be nice*. "Get your stuff," he told his brother as he went to the sink and rinsed out his bowl.

Earnest grabbed his puffy green coat from the back of the chair and slid it on, eyeing the brown specks that spotted the coat's sleeve and wrist, and again he saw Jamie in the snow while Thad pounded him, kicked him, spattering blood on him.

An unbearable heat burned in his skull as he drove, but he had to be at school. He was expected, his act of chivalry now some kind of conspiracy of silence, so he drove unaware, almost in a somnambulant state.

"Turn in..." Eddie suddenly blurted out, snapping Earnest back into the car, realizing he had gone the five miles into town without a thought to anything around him. "The pioneer man..." Eddie prompted to circle the statue.

"Enough about the pioneer man, already! I don't have a clue what you're talking about so shut your damn mouth!" Earnest snapped.

"What's with you?" Eddie asked, confusion molding his face, "You've acted like a jerk all week."

A jerk, that puts it nicely. He ran his hand through his hair and over his throbbing head.

Eddie finally shrugged at Earnest's aloofness and began reading a book.

And while the silence continued until Earnest dropped off the eighth grader, the throbbing in his head became a pounding, and the pounding acquired a rhythm that syncopated with the radio and the mental image that returned like a continuous film loop: Thad's fist landing upon Jamie's bruised face—again and again and again. Memories blurred his vision—took his vision—so that they were all he saw, all he heard; the crunching snow, the rustling trees, the piles of cow manure melting the snow into stained slush, and Jamie in the red spotted snow, accompanied by thuds of ecstatic anger.

"No," Earnest assured himself, replacing Jamie's battered image to RaLF, looking through the car window, snow encircling her lovely red face. *RaLF said thank you...it was okay...Jamie had it coming...* But still he felt he had sold his soul for her gratitude.

Earnest rubbed his burning, tired eyes while walking the hallway to his locker, taking a long way to avoid as many people as he could—to avoid his new friends, his fellow conspirators, and make his way to the sanctuary of the journalism room.

A sudden jerk on his collar pulled him from his feet, gagging his throat. Earnest turned to see Thad, his small yellow teeth set sparsely in his mouth revealed by an evil smile.

"Howdy, pardner," Thad said, his hand gripping like a vice onto Earnest's coat, leading him into a nearby empty classroom.

RaLF's heroes huddled amongst one another in the room, whispering. Marc Neuhaus looked up and eyed Earnest and Thad as they entered.

"C'mere," Neuhaus said to them, shooting Earnest an angry glare.

Earnest went where Thad's shove directed him.

"You're the only guy here I don't know, so don't go and get all chicken shit on me. Now, I've heard that Small is looking for the guys that kicked Messereli's ass. We don't know anything about it, okay. Someone said that he dropped out of school; that's fine with me, but I heard his mom is raising a stink. I don't know about the rest of you, but I damn sure don't want any trouble with the police."

Everyone grunted in agreement but Earnest who stood silently, noticing their change of attitude. *Maybe some things aren't worth the trouble?*

"Hey, isn't that guy who found Messereli your friend?" Someone asked Earnest.

All eyes turned to Earnest and he realized he was the one being spoken to.

"Used to be..."

"What the hell was he doing out there?" Thad bellowed from off to the side, slapping a desk with the flat of his hand.

"Ain't he the guy that RaLF pounded?" Marc asked.

"Yeah," Earnest answered.

"You need to find out if he saw us."

"What if he did?"

Everyone's glare moved from Earnest to Marc.

The football player paused and then shrugged, "We'll see... As for everything else...nothing happened."

The group dissipated, leaving Earnest alone. He now realized he was no hero, and he wasn't their friend, and worse, all the absolution RaLF could give with her kind, appreciative words and her gentle, soothing voice wasn't worth shit.

* * *

The bitch scratched and snarled at Ian, whimpering for Ian's attention and prodding him to act. "It's building," she told him, "The fire's growing...feed it." Ian cupped his face with his hands, hiding all the others in the pit from his view. "Tell them stories of Armageddon..."

Armageddon, he thought, the word reverberating with its newness. OX sang about Armageddon on his new record.

Ian ran his hands down his sad face, feeling the flat bend in his misshapen nose. "What about Jamie," he blurted out to the crowd in the pit, a cloud of steam billowing from his mouth.

The bitch bayed at the name, erupting, jumping, scratching him in a flurry.

"Jamie, dammit! What about him? RaLF's friends tried to kill him."

The kids surrounding him returned his sudden madness with empty gapes.

"It's them against us. They hurt one of us...," Ian said slapping his chest as he looked around, seeing his words leaving no more effect than a feather.

"What the hell are you talking about?" Angus bellowed.

"I'm talking about Armageddon. They took out one of us; we take out ten of them." Ian grew hot with anger waiting for a response. The bitch huddled at his feet, whimpering. "Don't fail me." The silence of the others ate at him.

"Are you just going to take it?" he finally asked, his gaze upon Angus, the man who controlled the pit and whose attitude would make all the difference.

Angus took a swift drag of his cigarette, flicking the butt away, sending it flying through the air, landing near Ian's feet rolling up to the toe of Ian's boot. Ian stepped on it and slowly crushed it. Angus stood up from the bench, his arms dropping to her side. Cigarette smoke and steam rolled from his nose and mouth as he smiled at Ian.

"Fugly, yer' weird," Angus said slowly shaking his head, every cocky word shooting at Ian with precision. "Did RaLF knock yer brain loose?" He laughed and then Fiona joined him, and then others, until the bitch's baying was drowned out with their mocking.

With the laughter acting like a prod, Ian stepped towards Angus, his face awash with disdain, and asked, "Just how ignorant...?" The back of Angus's hand slapped Ian's face before he could finish his sentence, and in the next instant the giant had Ian by his throat.

"Listen you piece of crap. I don't take that from my parents, and I'm damn sure not going to take it from a little girl like you."

Ian girdled for some air as Angus raised him from the ground.

"You want a fight so bad, why don't I just shove your head up your ass and let you fight for air."

A few chuckles broke out from among the group. Angus smiled in response and dropped Ian to the ground.

"They hate you..." Ian croaked, rubbing his neck.

"They don't hate me. They don't give a damn about me." Angus laughed, patting down his coat. "Anyone got a smoke?"

Ian stared at the cold concrete beneath him, sensing that he was alone—the bitch had left as Armageddon had collapsed before it had even begun. The laughs seared him. Their lethargy burned him. And he hated them as much as he hated RaLF. A rumble began to build within him, and he felt a growl slip from his mouth and grow.

"You, pussy!" Ian screamed and charged Angus, ramming himself headfirst like a battering ram against Angus. The giant heaved and fell against the wall of the pit. Angus quickly wrapped his arms around Ian, raising him from the ground and turned Ian's world upside down.

"C'mon you son of a bitch," Angus grunted, a borrowed cigarette hanging from his lips, as he carried Ian away.

"Let me down!" Ian screamed while Angus bounced him along the sidewalk, trying to squeeze Angus's head between the calves of his legs.

"Stop it, Fugly." Angus bellowed, pounding Ian's thigh with his free hand until Ian stopped.

"Let me down!"

Finally, as the boys were hidden between two buildings, Angus asked, "So, you want down?"

"Hell, yes!!"

Ian landed headfirst upon the blacktop, cushioned only by the thin stocking cap upon his head. A sharp blunt pain shot over him.

"You jerk," Ian moaned, "Why'd you drop me."

"Because, yer irritatin' me," Angus answered, reaching down to Ian, grabbing his collar and pulling the boy's face to his own.

"Now, Fugly, I don't know what the hell you got against me...I don't even know your name...but I don't want any trouble outa' you. I don't want any trouble, period. I just wanna' graduate, get me a job, and get married. An' I don't need you screwin' that up with some kind of gang war or stupid shit like that."

A smile ran across Ian's face. "Fiona has you whipped..."

Angus slapped Ian again and shoved him against the wall, knocking the breath out of Ian. His fist shook before Ian's face. "You miserable piece of …!"

"You promised, Angus," a small voice sounded.

Ian turned away from the quivering fist to see Fiona. Slowly Angus's grip loosened as Ian tasted blood from his swollen lower lip.

"Yeah, I promised...,"Angus angrily glared as he let go of Ian.

"I'm sorry about Jamie," Fiona said to Ian, "but it's not our problem. We got our own concerns." And she patted herself on her belly.

"You're pregnant?" Ian asked as the small girl began to walk away, taking a hold of one of Angus's large fingers.

"Have an abortion," Ian muttered.

A blank stare came over Angus's face as his head turned at an angle, like a confused puppy. Finally Angus said, "I love her, stupid ass," and putting his free hand up to Ian's face, Angus pushed Ian to the ground another time.

Motionless upon the ground, Ian could hear the distant howl, reprimanding his failure. His accomplishment was nil, and RaLF would remain unrepentant and untouched. Just as the cold had began to bother him more than the pain from Angus's thrashing, a small kid rounded the corner and stood at the entrance.

"I wanna' help..." he said, sounding as if his voice was still waiting on puberty.

"With what?" Ian grumbled as he rose from the ground, wiping dirt and slush from his clothes.

"I wanna' help you get the snobs with armergeddin'."

Ian sucked on his swollen lip, not certain how to react to the boy. And then he heard the bitch's distant howl. Ian darted to the boy, grabbing his collar, lifting him from the ground, so light was the boy, and shoving him into the wall as Angus had done to him.

"Are you mocking me? Who are you?" Ian asked over the bitch's yelping.

The boy looked too small, too young, to be in high school. His chin smooth and skin clear, while his face had turned a bright pink in the cold. His wavy light blonde hair curled over his ears.

"William," the boy answered.

"William?" Ian smirked, "William, who?"

"I gotta' gun," William said drawing open his coat, revealing a pistol handle peaking out of an inner pocket.

* * *

Earnest's shame and fear carried him from the room; the boys had been right—he needed to know what Ian knew. He hurried through the crowded hallways, into the cutting cold, to see Ian carried over Angus's shoulder away from the pit. Earnest moved a couple of steps forward then stopped, indecision playing tug of war with him.

His gloved hands grabbed his head while his feet tap danced though his guilt and remorse and into fear, weighing Angus's ominousness against his own wickedness. So when Angus and Fiona returned to the pit, and no Ian in sight, Earnest darted past the pit to find him. He rounded a corner, seeing nothing but a parking lot. Slowing his pace, he searched, his eyes darting everywhere. Then he glanced down a small area between two buildings and saw Ian with some kid.

Ian noticed Earnest with a quick start, and as Earnest moved toward him, a smile spread over his lopsided face.

"So...?" Ian remarked with anticipation.

"So? You know." Earnest sputtered, trying to be cool and unmoved, but quivering inside his coat as a hot sweat swept over his face.

"I know. I saw. Shame on you, little man." Ian answered.

William's glare bounced from Earnest to Ian.

"Now what?"

"Oh, I'm not gonna' say a thing."

Earnest stood in silence, reluctant to accept this from Ian.

"But, it's not over by a long shot. Armageddon hasn't even begun." Ian continued.

"What are you talking about?"

"Cause and effect, dumb ass. Your friends, the beautiful people, think they can go through life, screwing people over and never get touched." Ian's face grew redder swinging his hand around, pointing towards the pit. "And those dumb asses will just keep letting it happen." Steam bellowed from Ian's mouth as he ranted. "Look at what RaLF did to me! Look at what you did because of her. Now you're one of 'em. Earnest, they're the freaking cause and we're the damn effect!"

"What the hell has happened to you?"

"Me!?" Ian raged. "What the hell has happened to you? I'm not the one beating up some poor slob because some tramp has me wrapped around her finger. She's laughing at you, you geek!"

"Shut up, Ian," Earnest said, angrier with each remark.

"Make me. You're a tough guy, now. I'd like to see what you can do. Oh hell, I forgot, you can't do anything without the one-armed wonder woman telling you to."

In an instant, Ian was back on the ground with Earnest atop him, hands wrapped around Ian's neck. Ian smiled as his face grew red.

"So," he croaked, "whad'aya gonna do now?"

Earnest shook, from anger and Ian's grasp of truth—there was nothing else he could do, so he loosened his grip and slowly stood back up. He raised his foot, causing Ian to jerk, but Earnest only kicked at a rock beside Ian.

"Who the hell do you think you are?" Earnest asked.

"It's not what I think," Ian answered. "I'm their judge. Yours too..."

Frustrated and impotent, Earnest walked away.

"Armageddon's coming, Earnie! Just wait and see!"

Earnest did not turn back around. He was too cold.

* * *

"Armageddon's coming!" The tone of Ian's voice and the words themselves haunted Earnest, as if Ian had made a promise, not a threat. *What in hell is Armageddon anyway?* He walked into the building with the rest of Ian's words coming back to him.

"I didn't even touch him," he muttered, reminding himself that he had been little more that a vocal spectator, but that had been enough if not worse. Being there, he had hoped to appease RaLF. And he had been successful. But as RaLF's smiling face always seemed to melt into Jamie's bloody image, his conscience would not let him be.

And still there was Armageddon.

Earnest hurried to the library to use a big dictionary. But the definition left him no more satisfied than he had been before: *The scene of the battle foretold in Revelations 16:14-16. The Final confrontation of Good and Evil.* "It's from the Bible?" he mumbled, so he looked for it among the stacks. Finding a near pristine King James Version, he opened it, the spine cracking from disuse, and flipped to the Book of Revelations.

For they are the spirits of devils, working miracles, which go forth unto the kings of the earth and of the whole world, to gather them to the battle of that great day of God Almighty.... And he gathered them together into a place called in the Hebrew tongue Armageddon.

Earnest read over it again and again, scratching his head, wondering what it meant. *When the hell did Ian start reading the Bible, anyway?* He reread it, but his eyes, burning from his lack of sleep, stuck on spirits of devils. He wondered if he was a spirit of the devil, realizing he had rationalized shades of gray out of darkness.

He shut the Bible, having no idea when was the last time he had read it. Never had his absence from church, nor the church's absence from his thoughts, his words, his actions, dissuaded him from considering himself a Christian. Most days he was fairly certain that he believed in God. Yet he never thought to wallow in it as Daniel did.

"Daniel," he said aloud. *He could explain Armageddon.* After all, people were saying that he had seen an angel.

As he left the library, the bell rang, and he quickly noticed the desolation of the hallway, but his sense of urgency overwhelmed his need to attend class, so he hurried to the journalism room.

Earnest peered into the room, and, to his surprise, saw Mary, sitting alone, writing.

"Mary?"

She glanced up and then looked back down, rubbing her forehead with the eraser of her pencil, and then she began writing again.

"Yeah?" she finally answered, realizing that Earnest wasn't going away.

"Have you seen Daniel?"

"He's in class; you know, where everyone else in this building is except you."

"Mary," Mr. Addison interrupted walking in from the next room, "don't start."

She glared at Earnest and then looked at the teacher. "Sorry," she muttered abruptly and went back to work.

"Why aren't you in class, Earnest?" the teacher asked.

"I need to talk to Daniel."

"Well, sorry, but he's in class…"

"Your dad's a preacher, right?" Earnest asked Mary, turning away from Mr. Addison.

"Something like that," she answered not looking up.

"What do you know about Armageddon?"

Mary shook her head, "It's God's final battle against Satan. You get an invitation?" Mary asked with a laugh.

Earnest hesitated and then nodded, "Yeah, kind of..."

"I bet you did." She laughed again and went back to her work.

Spirits of devils, Earnest thought as Mary laughed.

"What are you doing back?"

She shot him her familiar glare, but instead of any smart remark, she stood up from her chair, displaying her expectant glory that had been hidden beneath the table. "I'm but a wayward girl, uncertain of where to turn." She said in a southern drawl, throwing her hand upon her forehead in mock desperation.

Earnest stood silently, his mouth agape.

"Here, Earnest," Mr. Addison handed Earnest a late pass. "You get to class, now. It's bad enough to have an editor ranting about seeing some angel; I don't need you going off on the apocalypse. Now, get out'a here."

Distracted, Earnest heard only bits of what Mr. Addison said to him. He glanced down at the paper, and then darted out of the room without another word.

Mr. Addison turned back to Mary. "You sure that's the best way to handle this?" he asked, shaking his head as if to prompt her answer.

"It's not like I can hide this." she replied, her arms extended about her in such a way to showcase her condition. "Besides," she shrugged, "my life is nobody's business but my own." And she looked out of the window, feeling a kick in her womb.

* * *

The white hair poking from underneath his navy blue cap was just another reason for them to stare, yet Daniel ignored it, almost unconsciously. It was no different than the other reasons they had been staring at him since his birth. If anything, the white hair made walking through the crowded hall easier as people seemed to keep their distance, afraid of the boy who saw angels.

His life had been a billboard for God. Before the surgery, people judged him for his looks, but his actions excelled beyond the expectations of others, and he proclaimed it a miracle of God. Even after the surgery, the obnoxious lisp made him sound like an idiot, but again he showed how God had taken him further. Now, his hair pointed to his difference, the product of a secret that wouldn't stay a secret. He still did not know how word got out. He hadn't said anything, and yet within days, the titters and pointing fingers said everything.

Daniel stepped into the journalism room, and all eyes went to him. The work stopped, and silence ensued. Feeling flustered, he went to his desk and began sorting through the piles of paper, waiting for something to happen. Then a typewriter began to tap, followed by a few whispered conversations. Wanting to be ignored, he soon blended into the ambiance as just another part of the noise.

"Daniel," Earnest said hurrying to him, "I need to talk to you."

Daniel looked up from his papers, defensive in his glance.

"I need you to tell me about Armageddon."

"Huh?"

"You know, Armageddon. You're the most religious person I know. You know about God and stuff. What do you know about Armageddon? Is it the last battle of good and evil?"

Daniel shrugged. "That'th all I know."

"Nothing else? Mary told me that much."

"Mawy?"

"Yeah, this morning. She was sitting in here working on something."

Daniel's head began to erupt, as if an orchestra's brass section all blew into his ears, as if a herd of elephants were charging at him, as if an angel whispered in his ear, "Your thorn, Daniel, your thorn."

"Thee's back? Mawy'th back...to thchool? Hewe, today?"

"Oh, yeah, she's back..." someone snickered, "and then some..."

Daniel turned to see who was talking. "What?"

"She's with child." Earnest said, patting his stomach for effect.

"What?"

One of the photographers stuffed something up his shirt enlarging his belly. He began walking around the room and said, "You know, el prego." The room filled with laughter, but Daniel still didn't grasp what the others implied.

"Nice waddle," Mary said from behind them all, entering the journalism room from the adjacent classroom, "although you might want to use your arm for more support." She walked up to the photographer, took his arm and placed his hand at the small of his back. "Lean into it. You're el prego, remember?"

The photographer yanked out whatever he had up his shirt. "Sorry," he said and hurried into the dark room.

"Okay," Mary said, "take a look. Get it out of your systems. I got knocked up. It happens. Even to good little girls like me." She raised her arms and turned herself around so that all could see. Then she stopped and walked to Daniel, pushing Earnest out of her way with just her stare. “I'm surprised, Daniel. Of all the things I could say about you, being cruel wasn't one of them...”

“I wathn't...”

“I've heard you're walking on water these days, and now you're casting stones.”

“I wathn't mocking you.”

"Then what would you call it?"

Daniel looked around the room, “I…I… didn't…"

Earnest felt too distracted to do his work, hoping for a lull to milk Daniel for more information about Armageddon.

“What did you really do to your hair, anyway?” Mary sneered, running her finger along the rim of the cap on Daniel's head, her eyes set slyly upon the bumbling editor. Mary wanted to laugh at him. Him, an agent of God, was comic even in her own disbelief. "I can't imagine it sounding any more ridiculous than seeing an angel. You're pushing it with that one.”

“You think I made thith up?” Daniel asked, tearing the cap from his head, feeling his anger grow as his coif of white danced about his head in disarray. She was his thorn. There could be no doubt that she was a pain.

“I don't know what you did, Daniel. You're the one who has to live with yourself. I mean if you want to go around telling people that you're seeing angels, that's your business, not mine.”

Life would have been so much easier if he had just dyed his hair back to brown like his mother had wanted him to do. But his hair was a sign. Like the burning bush—it was a testament to all that he believed and all that he had to do. He could not dye it.

“So then, tell me about your angel.” Mary taunted him.

Daniel paused and looked around; again Mary had brought all eyes back to him. He couldn’t tell these people that his angel was their dead, mentally retarded janitor. What’s more, he couldn’t tell Mary that she was the reason that the dead janitor had come. “I can’t...” Daniel muttered, avoiding her eyes.

“Because there’s nothing to tell?” Mary queried with a smirk.

“No, ith jutht becauth I can’t.”

Mary sighed and her voice changed, carrying a tone of reposed deliberation. "Verily, verily, I say unto you, he that believeth on me, the works that I do shall he do also; and greater works than these shall he do."

"Hey, I thought your dad was the preacher?” Earnest asked.

Mary glared at Earnest, shutting him up and then turned back to Daniel.

"What’th your point?” Daniel asked, surprised by her grasp of scripture.

"Prove it.” She laughed.

"What!?” Daniel asked, wadding his cap in his grip, thinking that an arm wrestling match wouldn't appease her.

“Go out and raise the dead or something. Your Jesus said you could. Heal the sick. Yeah, that should be easy enough.” Mary began looking around the room. "Anyone know any sick people for Daniel to heal."

"Jamie Messereli, the guy who got his butt kicked after killing Bill…” someone said.

Messereli? Earnest heard, his heart nearly choking him.

"Leave Daniel alone," Anne Endo said.

"Oh, like you see angels all the time.” Mary jeered at the girl.

"You...you can't jutht teht God. If you know anything, you thould know that." Daniel said, jerking the cap back onto his head.

"I'm not testing God." Mary coyly smiled. "I'm testing you."

"Yes, heal Jamie Messereli, Daniel," Earnest said without thinking.

"No," RaLF suddenly piped in. "You can't pray for him. He killed Bill. He deserved it. Didn't he, Earnest?"

She looked at Earnest with those eyes, those pleading eyes. And her voice. Earnest knew that he was seeing an angel. *Spirit of devils,* Earnest heard again in his heart, and he couldn't think.

"Oh screw them. Go heal Jamie Messereli. I dare you," Mary taunted.

"Earnest!" RaLF called from across the room.

Daniel's eyes darted from Mary to RaLF to Earnest, his mind swirling like the blue whirlwind Earl had brought. "I jutht can't heal..." He couldn't believe this conversation was happening.

"Liar," Mary snapped coldly.

RaLF quickly moved and grabbed his arm. "Daniel, he doesn't deserve your prayers."

"You're a liar, aren't you Daniel." Mary pushed.

"No, but...but..." Daniel stuttered.

"Tell him, Earnest." RaLF continued to implore.

One thud after another, Earnest saw them land upon Jamie's face. "Thank you," RaLF had said afterwards. Those thuds became his heart beats, palpitations of joy and horror, muted by the threats of the spirits of devils.

"I can't jutht heal the thick..." Daniel protested.

"Then just pray for him, damn it!" Earnest bellowed with anger new to him. "You can at least do that for the miserable bastard, can't you!?"

And again the room grew silent.

Daniel reached up to his clip-on tie, grabbing it at its widest point, and jerked it from his collar, popping off the button holding the collar closed. "Yeth," he said, subdued, looking at his scuffed shoes as the button rolled under a table, "I can do that."

* * *

Mary shifted from one foot to another, slinging her book bag upon her shoulder. In spite of the cold, Mary's coat was opened, save for a button at the collar, revealing the extent of her condition. The doctor said she was almost six months along. The stirrings in her gut—the pokes and prods from inside and her growing discomfort—bore it out.

Her mother would be there very soon to take her back to the doctor, so she stood among the slushy sidewalks in the gray cold. "Where are you, lady?" She shivered as she cursed, looking at her watch. A little past noon, she was done for the day, still savoring the fruits of her affront on Daniel.

And then the car appeared and pulled into the U-drive—the same place John used to pick her up before. A memory flashed; she almost expected to see John staring at her from behind his steering wheel, and along with the memory came a feeling—something between satisfaction and excitement, distant and vacuous.

"You're late," Mary told her mother, pulling her foot from a puddle of dirty slush, her tennis shoe and sock soaked.

"How was your day?" her mother asked, her words spoken with deliberation and hesitancy. "If things aren't well, your father and I won't hold you to your decision. If you don't want to go to school..."

"I know. I know. If it were up to you I'd be locked away and out of view."

"Don't be absurd. Just because your father and I aren't happy with the situation doesn't mean that we're ashamed, either.

"Doesn't it?"

"Quit forcing me into a corner, Mary. I don't want to fight you. Can't we just...I don't know...enjoy the doctor visit?"

"Are you serious? Enjoy? If it were up to me, I wouldn't even go." She tossed her book bag into the back seat.

"It's important, dear. It's for the baby. It's not about you."

"Nothing here is about me, is it?"

Mary found it ironic that while she had carried it this long; her mother had developed more affection for the fetus than she had. She reached around to the back seat and took a book from her book bag and waved it at her mother. "Homework," she muttered and pretended to read until they reached the clinic.

"Do you have to go in?" Mary asked as they both climbed out of the car.

"Certainly, it's too cold out here."

Mary grunted, stuffing the paperback into a coat pocket, walking away, leaving her mother to catch up.

Thirty minutes passed between the time they signed in and Mary was called back to one of the examining rooms, happy that at least she could keep her mother out of there. The nurse took her vital signs and then handed her a gown, instructing her to change.

Begrudgingly, Mary did so and sat on the cold examining table, shifting from side to side as she waited. Finally the doctor arrived, followed by his nurse, his head, smooth and bald, glowing from reflected light. His nose was large, almost beak-like with a thick mustache underneath in need of trimming. Mary thought him too thin to be healthy. And whatever dislike she felt toward him from his appearance, was only magnified by his personality. She wanted to wipe the annoyingly constant smile from his thin face. *Let's share the misery*, she thought.

"So, how are we today?" the doctor asked.

"I couldn't tell you. I don't know you that well."

"How are you, then?"

"Dandy..."

The doctor nodded, biting his upper lip so the mustache hid his entire mouth. He put his stethoscope into his ears and checked her heart, and then the baby's. "Hmmm, sounds good. Wanna' hear it?" he asked with his closed lip smile.

"Nope," she answered.

He looked her in the face, the smile unwavering, and asked her to lean back. And after removing the stethoscope from his ears, he began rubbing her stomach, just slightly kneading it.

"Here, put your feet up in the stirrups."

Mary groaned as she heard rubber gloves stretching over the doctor's hands. And as he slipped his cold, gelled fingers inside of her, she bit her bottom lip. She shifted her hip slightly as the doctor probed, thinking she would've rather been in school.

Then the doctor pulled his hand from her and quickly pulled the gloves off with a snap. He them measured her stomach with a measuring tape. He read the measurement to the nurse and put the tape back into his pocket. "Well, everything appears to be fine. So, we'll see you again next month. Have you signed up for your childbirth class?"

"No, I don't think I'll be doing that."

"They're offered free by the clinic..."

"Nope."

The doctor nodded with his closed mouth smile. "Next month then..." and he left.

The nurse completed the paperwork, picked up the folders, looking at Mary.

"You don't seem to care about this baby very much."

Mary shrugged her shoulders. "Do you?"

The nurse scowled, and she moved to speak, but before she got out a word, Mary said, "I'm not interested. You don't know anything about me, so leave me alone."

The nurse forced a smile, a closed lip grin like the doctor's; then she left, too.

As Mary sat, she rubbed her tired eyes and then slid off of the table, slipping out of the thin cotton robe. She dressed, imagining the joy in her mother's face when she told her everything was just fine.

Chapter Sixteen

Prayers for the Sick
And Those Sick of Prayers

Daniel stepped from his house, taking a hold of the brim of his cap before the evening's cold north wind carried it off his head. In his free hand, he held his Bible with the grip of a vise, afraid of dropping it hurrying to the waiting car.

As he climbed in, the Reverend Green smiled at his white-haired adolescent protégé.

"It's chilly, isn't it?" the Reverend said.

"Yeth," Daniel answered, his mind miles away from the weather.

"Are you sure about this?" The preacher asked, backing out of Daniel's driveway.

"I don't have a choithe."

"We always have a choice, Danny."

"Doethn't the Bible tell uth to pway fow the thick?"

"Sure does."

"Well, thee, I don't have a choithe."

"It also says to pull your eye out if it causes you to sin."

"Wevewend Gween, I'm thiwius."

"I'm serious, too, Danny. Why are you really doing this?"

Daniel sighed. He wished he was doing this because of his desire to be obedient, but he knew his motivation was so much more base. "Mawy dawed me to. It'th hew way of awm wethling me."

"If you pray for this guy, and he gets better, will Mary suddenly believe in God?"

Daniel sat quietly for a few seconds, mulling over the only answer he had. "No," he finally muttered.

"What if the boy dies instead? What will she say then?"

"Huh?"

"What if you pray for him and he dies?"

"I don't think he'th that thick."

"Even worse for you if something happens to him."

"I don't know... Pwobabwy waugh at me and bwame me fow kiwwing him. But thee awweady waughs at me. Thee thinks I did thth to my own haiw..." He whipped off his cap and ran his hand over his white scalp.

"Doesn't sound good for you..." he said stopping at a red light.

Daniel closed his eyes and began a silent prayer. He knew God wanted obedience over sacrifice, but having no idea where his mission of prayer fell, he prayed for something to break the silence in his soul, but before anything came, the car had stopped, and the pastor was climbing out.

"Danny, come here. I want to show you something."

Daniel raised his head, realizing that he wasn't at Jamie's house. He climbed out into the windy cold, pulling his hat back upon his head, and saw that they were parked in the circle drive in front of Ponca City's Pioneer Woman statue. Daniel turned to Reverend Green, confused.

"What do you see when you look at this?" The pastor asked before Daniel said a word.

Daniel stared at the statue, uncertain what he meant. He shrugged and asked, "What doeth thith have to do with anything?"

"Danny, this is one of the most famous statues in the United States. E.W. Marland had it erected…" The pastor stopped and laughed, shaking his head. "He had it put up to honor the spirit of the pioneer women who helped settle the west. Now Danny, when you look at this statue, what do you see?"

Daniel scrunched his face, still confused by his pastor's sudden passion for the statue. "I don't know…."

"Ohhhh, Daniel…." Pastor Green's shoulders sunk. "Look at her…" Then his voice changed, sounding like a documentary narrator. "She walks the Oklahoma plains with her Bible in her hand. Her only protection from the blistering sun is the bonnet covering her head. She looks forward, aloof of her surroundings, paying no attention to anything but her vision of the promised land before her... and her son… who walks as proudly as she does, his right arm extended out from his side, his hand forward, clenched in a fist defiant to the odds against them. Don't you see perseverance? Defiance? Don't you see independence? Pride? Strength?" Resilience?" Then changing his voice to normal, he asked, "Do you?"

Daniel stared at the dark bronze of the statue, but the evening's darkness and shadow blinded him of the statues details, so he shrugged again. "I gueth…"

Reverend Green took his eyes from the statue and looked at Daniel. "You can see that in the statue? Really?"

"Yeth, I gueth tho…"

He shook his head, and then smiled at Daniel, "That's good, because I can't. Not anymore… I was shown something when I was about your age, and I've never seen this statue in the same way again."

"Wha awe you tawking about?"

"Walk with me, my boy. Walk with me."

The two men began to circle the statue, and the pastor stared back up to it. "Look at it, Danny."

Daniel did. As they continued, the image of the statue turned to silhouette, the moon shining brightly behind it.

"Keep your eyes on the boy's arm, Danny."

Daniel did as the pastor directed, but as they stepped around the back of the statue, the boy's fist disappeared. "I can't thee it…"

"Keep walking and keep watching," the pastor insisted.

So Daniel continued his watch, and the arm slowly began to reappear, jutting slightly from the Pioneer Woman's waist, and as he continued his walk the arm protruded further.

After several more steps, the pastor stopped Daniel. "What do you see, now, Danny?"

Daniel studied the silhouetted visage of the lady, her long flowing dress, and the boy's outstretched arm, yet the more that he stared, the boy's arm melded into an appendage protruding from her midsection. Then it dawned on Daniel what Reverend Green had been shown years ago and was showing to him.

"Thee hath…a…willie…?"

"Congratulations, Danny, the pioneer woman…is a man, and it is now all I see when I look at her. And I'm unable to unsee it."

For several long seconds, Daniel stared, and still bemused, he turned to the pastor. “Why are you thowing me thith?”

“You said that you are going to pray for that boy because your friend Mary dared you to. I would be letting you down as your pastor, and your friend, if I let you do that. Danny, prayer isn’t some divine game of truth or dare. It’s really our greatest calling as Christians, so praying for that boy on a dare will have as much effect as feeding chicken soup to a corpse.

“This statue is an honorable thing, a reverent thing, but I don’t have that perspective any more. I don’t see the pioneer women’s spirit; I just see a tacky joke. If you go into to this wrong-headed, you become that joke. God, Jesus, everything we believe in becomes a joke, especially if something goes wrong for that boy. You’ll know it. You’ll feel it and you’ll hate it. Dig deep Daniel. God is very specific about how our attitudes affect the worthiness of our prayers. This boy has been hurt; that’s why you pray for him.”

Reverent Green shoved his hands deep into his pockets and turned back to the statue, shaking his head and laughing.

Daniel took off his cap and wiped sweat from his forehead with his hand. Mary just seemed to mess up everything. The white haired boy coughed and shrugged and then conceded, "It’th the wight thing to do.... That’th why, Wevewend.”

Reaching over and lightly slapping Daniel’s cheek, Reverend Green winked at him, “Good answer…”

Daniel turned to look with the pastor. As his face blushed, a slight grin took shape across Daniel’s face, and his laughter grew, echoing Reverend Green.

* * *

Jamie woke up on the cold linoleum of the bathroom floor. His mind swam, his thoughts bobbing loosely. And when his thoughts finally held some coherence, he still did not know if he had passed out from the drunk or the pain.

"What day is it?" he said aloud, barely able to focus his eyes, his whole body aching as he rolled from side to side, unable to pull himself up from the floor. Then he laughed, thinking himself like a stranded turtle, but even laughing made him hurt. He laughed until his laughter melted to sobs, and that hurt, too.

"Oh, I hate feeling drunk," he mumbled and then screamed. "What the hell do I have left?!" And that hurt, too.

And then the pounding began.

Jamie rubbed his head trying to make it stop. And as the pounding continued, he realized it wasn't his head.

"It's unlocked!" he yelled with his strained and broken voice, clutching his side as he felt another foot kick him.

Jamie closed his eyes, but that only made things spin and hurt, so he squinted, and when the world quit spinning, his English teacher, Mrs. Irving, stood before his reclined pose at the toilet's base.

"You," he muttered, rubbing his eyes.

"Jamie," Mrs. Irving spoke calmly, "can you get up?"

"I feel like a fu...a freakin' turtle..." he grumbled as he rolled to his side again.

The teacher reached her hand down to Jamie, but he couldn't focus on it, so he waved his hand around until Mrs. Irving took hold of it. Lightning shot between his back and chest and up into his head as he rose from the floor. His teeth gritted as he held his tongue from spouting a flurry of expletives.

"Who did this to you?" Mrs. Irving asked as Jamie fell into her.

"You know better'n me. RaLF's friends...I don't know em'," he muttered, his face buried into the shoulder pad of her coat.

"You're drunk," Mrs. Irving said as she moved Jamie toward the living room.

"Yeah," he replied.

"This whole house stinks like you."

Jamie remained silent as they hobbled to the living room, and as Mrs. Irving helped him to a seat on the couch, the front door opened and Jamie's mother walked in carrying two grocery sacks.

"Miss Irvin', what are you doin' here?" the mother replied, taking the sacks to the dining area, adjacent to the living room.

"Are you aware that Jamie quit school this week?"

"He said sumthin' about it."

Mrs. Irving wanted her to say more, but when she did not, the teacher asked, "...and you approved?"

"He's growd up..." she said, taking a couple of brown paper bagged liquor bottles out of the sacks.

Placing her hand upon the drunken boy's shoulder as he settled into the couch, the teacher eyed Jamie's mother.

"He's drunk, Mrs. Messereli. When I came in, he was stuck on the bathroom floor."

"I told him not to drink, not with all those pills the doctor gave him, but I can't tell im' what to do. He's a man."

"But..."

"An' why the hell should he go anyways? Those bastards there tried to kill him. Didn't he suffer enough innat car 'reck?"

Jamie tried to listen, reclined upon the couch, but his thoughts roamed beyond the woman's words. He could not remember how many days had he been drinking, replacing one misery for another. He wanted to lie down, but moving hurt too much. So he closed his eyes again, gripping the couch's cushions to stop the spinning.

"I'm not aware of any situation at school that would have caused this, and I can assure you that it would not be tolerated...."

All the while Mrs. Irving spoke, Jamie's mother continued to take groceries from the sacks, placing them in cabinets and not giving any attention to the teacher. Her movements were slow but accompanied by a tremor. When she finished, she took a beer from the refrigerator and filled a large glass with it, adding tomato juice and a couple of drops of Worcestershire sauce, stirring the drink with a butter knife. She carried her drink with her to the dining room table heaped with crap and sat down at one of its hard wood chairs, the chair surrendering a squeak under her light weight while she grunted from the effort of her movement.

"So, teacher," Jamie's mother said, a cigarette tightly between her wrinkled lips, the flame of her lighter, quivering at its tip. Then as the cigarette lit, she inhaled, deepening the wrinkles of her lip. "What are you doin' here, anyways?" she asked, smoke billowing from her mouth and nostrils.

"Doesn't this concern you?"

"Hell yes, it concerns me. A bunch of rich punks can damn near kill my son and nothing happens concerns the shit out of me!"

"That's not what I mean..."

"See. Why should he go back to your damn school?"

"What can the school do? It didn't happen at school!"

Jamie's mother took another quick puff of her cigarette.

"Well, that's where they grabbed him. I've aksed him a million times for names, but he don't say nuthin'."

"Ian's armadillo..." Jamie mumbled, trying to explain himself, his eyes still closed and his hands clutching the couch.

What?" Mrs. Irving asked the drunken boy, unable to decipher his mumbling.

"When we kick their asssess...." His voice drifted in and out of coherence.

A knock sounded at the door.

"Come in! We're havin' a party!" Mrs. Messereli shouted from the table, a room away from the door.

Wrapped in his long army trench coat, Ian entered the house with his usual saunter but accompanied by a small kid barely reaching the height of Ian's elbows.

"Mrs. Irving...?" Ian said surprised to see her.

"You friends of Jamie's?" the teacher asked.

"I am, but William doesn't know anyone, so I brought him by to meet my buddy, Jamie."

Mrs. Irving looked at the small boy, so out of place with Ian.

"Where do you go to school?" she asked.

"I'm a senior," William replied, his voice as if unchanged since before puberty.

"See, I told you," Ian said with his crooked smile. "Nobody knows him."

Ian walked to Jamie while William stood inside the door, closing it behind him and shoving his small bare hands into his coat pockets.

"Hey, buddy boy," Ian said to Jamie.

Jamie opened his eyes, raising his head slightly from the

couch. Everything appeared blurred and indistinct, yet Jamie gave him a smile, knowing who it was.

"I'm drunk," Jamie murmured to his friend.

"Still, huh?"

Jamie broke out giggling.

"You want me to help him back to his room?" Ian asked Jamie's mother as she gulped her tomato juice and beer.

Taking a drag, she shrugged, "You done?" She asked the teacher.

"Do you know anything about who did this?" Mrs. Irving asked Ian.

"I told Principal Small all that I know," Ian answered. "You don't think I had anything to do with this, do you?"

"No..." She answered, looking down at Jamie, "I don't like watching him slip through the cracks." She patted Jamie's dirty hair, feeling as if someone had kicked her in the gut.

"C'mon, buddy boy. I've got someone I want you to meet." Ian gently pulled on Jamie's dead weight.

Jamie grimaced and moaned.

"Careful..." Mrs. Irving prompted as William hurried to take Jamie's other arm, holding it over his head as if he were lifting a barbell.

And then another knock sounded at the door.

"For criss' sake," Jamie's mother said, stubbing out her cigarette and rising from her chair. "What the hell's goin' on?" She muttered on the way to the door. And then after she opened it, she stood dumbstruck, staring at what stood before her.

"Ith thith the Metherwewi houth?" Daniel asked with a slight quiver in his voice, having taken the cap from his head.

Mrs. Messereli could not remove her stare from the white crown of hair upon the young man's head. "Huh?"

"Ith thith the Metherwiwi houth?" Daniel repeated slower, his voice still quivering.

She turned away and looked at the small frame of William, straining to help hold up her son, and then she looked back. "C'mon in and join the circus," she said, ushering him inside.

Daniel slowly stepped into the house, holding his Bible tightly against his chest. But seeing everyone looking at him, he grew nervous, picturing Mary's condescending glare. "I can come back latew." The words blurted out, and he worried that he might have to return.

"Come back for what?" the lady asked Daniel.

Daniel's eyes darted from the boys holding Jamie to Mrs. Irving. He gave the teacher a quick but uncertain smile.

"Daniel," the teacher greeted him with a nod.

"Come back for what?" Mrs. Messereli repeated.

"To pway..." he said and then added, "fow him," pointing his Bible at Jamie who had now taken an ironic pose between the two boys propping him up: one arm extended straight over Ian's shoulder's, the other arm extended the other way as William clung to it trying to keep the drunken boy aloft, while Jamie's legs were limp beneath him.

"Hey, Jamie wake up," Ian said, "angel boy wants to pray for you."

Daniel flinched at the name as Jamie's head flopped from side to side.

"Come on, everybody hold hands," Ian mocked, drawing Jamie closer to him. "I'll start. Our fat head, who farts in heaven, Howard be thy name..."

As soon as William heard "Howard be thy name," he burst with laughter, loosing his grip on Jamie, who shifted and fell to the floor, pulling Ian on top of him.

Jamie groaned, his body a fount of pain as his mother hurried to pull Ian off him.

"Howard..." William cackled, his side hurting from laughter.

"Dammit, Ian," Mrs. Irving cursed the boy's carelessness.

Daniel watched, having nothing to say. The mocking had started with such a fury the words did not quite strike Daniel. Several seconds passed before he even understood what Ian had said.

"Help me, angel boy."

Daniel looked down at Ian holding his hand up to him, and stared at the mocking face—the bent curve of the displaced nose, and he grew angry, but all he did in response was put his cap back on and pull Ian up from the floor.

A low moan escaped Jamie's mouth as he lay on his back on the floor. He began quivering, and before anyone could reach him, a geyser of vomit shot into the air and back onto his face.

"Dammit, Ian," Jamie's mother yelled, "you're cleaning this up."

William exploded with another burst of laughter.

"Listen angel boy," Ian said walking up to Daniel, "take your holy-roller crap outta here."

"Stop that." Mrs. Irving said angrily.

Ian turned toward her, seething, "Back off, this ain't school." He heard the bitch's howls in the distance. "Now listen, angel boy..." Ian began again as he turned back to Daniel, but Daniel was gone.

Daniel's body shivered with each step away from Ian. Ignoring the icy darts Ian's eyes shot at him, ignoring the echoes of Mary's ridiculing, Daniel walked to the kitchen and found a couple of dish towels on the cabinets. He soaked one with warm water; then returned to the living room and began to clean the drunken boy's face, softly repeating "God bleth thith thoul."

Daniel hadn't noticed the scabs and bruises and swelling on Ian's face, but they stood out now that he was so close, reminding him why he had come, allowing the prayer to flow easily from his tongue. After the boy's face was wiped clean, Daniel very gingerly lifted Jamie from the floor and carried the boy to what he assumed to be Jamie's room. Following them to Jamie's room, Ian watched from the doorway as Daniel placed Jamie on his bed and waited for him to leave.

But instead, Daniel continued his prayer.

The bitch yelped in Ian's ear, so he bellowed over the prayer. But Daniel continued, pulling the blanket over Jamie as he finished. Ian stopped Daniel at the door, poking his finger in the middle of Daniel's chest, but he looked past Ian, so for a few seconds, silence passed between them.

Then Ian said in a low soft voice, "Fuck you, angel boy."

Daniel pushed him away.

Ian, though, with a quick grasp of Daniel's coat, jerked the white-haired boy back to his face. Shooting Daniel his crooked grin, he said, "Armageddon draweth nigh..."

Daniel wrinkled his brow, hearing that word again.

"God bweth you," he said and walked around Ian.

"William, come here," Ian yelled from the bedroom.

Shoving his hands deep in his pocket, the small boy headed toward Jamie's room. Nearing Daniel he looked up at him, smiling.

"Howard," he squeaked, laughing again.

Daniel picked up his Bible from the floor.

"I'm sorry about that," Jamie's mother said, embarrassed by Ian, "It was nice of you to come here and all.... You know kids today..."

Daniel looked at her and shrugged. "I'm a kid..." he said, and he left the house.

* * *

Lying in her bed, Mary stared through her open blinds at the bright moon, casting light and shadow across her room.

"Everything is fine," the doctor's voice echoed in her mind, twisting, turning upon itself, stretching and folding as if pushed through some electronic synthesizer until it became the ringing of a phone—the constant ringing, and Faith's voice coming through the receiver asking if everything was fine, and her voice blending with the doctor's and the phone's ringing and the boiling ocean of time that swept beside her, roaring and crashing until she stifled her own scream by stuffing a pillow over her mouth.

She shook, her heart beating and beating until her sternum felt as if it would snap. Sweat covered her, adhering her hair to her face. She rolled onto one side and then clumsily onto the other, but nothing held back the ebb of terror in which the growth inside had wrapped her.

"Help me," Mary Christmas's voice, like the sound of a tree branch straining before it snaps from a tree, squeezed from her throat.

"I can help you," Lita Mankiller's whisper returned to her, seeping through the tumult assaulting her mind.

Sitting up, Mary hugged her pillow tightly against her chest. If there was to be any kind of salvation in Mary's life presently, it would have to come from her. So she rose from her bed and left the room, moving like a zeppelin through the darkness. In the moonlight Mary stared at the dim outline of the telephone, wrapping her fingers around the receiver. Then she let go of it. What was the number? So raising the phone from the table she slid the telephone book from underneath it. While her fingers searched the phone book, she noticed a slight quiver in her hand.

The curtains of the living room window were pulled open, and through the window she could see the grassy playground of the elementary school across the street she had attended years ago. Although her memories were faint and select, she remembered that loneliness attended there, too, before she had given up on God, before she had given up on her parents, before she had even considered giving up on herself. Mary saw lines of marching little boys and little girls, chanting, "We go straight and we don't stop," their arms wrapped around the shoulders of the people next to them, while the end person jetted his outside arms forward, hands balled into fists. She remembered marching alone because Andrew Johnson Elementary afforded her no friends. Now life afforded her too many distractions to allow her to only go straight without stopping. Then her thoughts moved on to a time she had fallen from her desk to the floor. As she had looked around her, everyone stared back and she began to cry. She remembered crying a lot back then.

Mary finally turned the rotary dial for the first digit. The phone, clicking as it sprang back to place, seemed so loud she feared that she might wake her parents. Yet, she turned the dial a second time, dialing more vehemently with each number.

"Ponca City Hospital," someone answered.

Mary paused, unsure of herself. "Emergency room, please. I need to speak to a nurse there, Lita Mankiller."

"I'm afraid we can't allow personal phone calls."

"This is not a personal call," Mary quietly growled into the phone. "I need to speak with her. It's an emergency."

Music played over the phone as Mary waited, and then the familiar voice of Lita Mankiller spoke.

"Hello."

"I don't know if you remember me...." she paused and swallowed a huge lump of uncertainty nearly gagging her, and then she continued.

* * *

As Jamie awoke, the words "God bless this soul" reverberated through his mind. Too much happened last night, faces blurring together, except for the white-haired ghost blessing him.

Looking around his room, in the dimness of the pre-dawn, he saw Ian sleeping on the floor, a blanket covering him. Someone he didn't know lay curled up upon a pile of dirty clothes with a few dirty shirts and towels pulled over him. As Jamie looked at the stranger, he wondered if he had anything to do with Ian's armadillo.

Armadillo can't be right. But his mind still bobbed along the alcohol ocean it had been swimming in for days. He laid his head back on the pillow, craving a cigarette but feeling too tired and sore to hunt one. So he closed his eyes and his mind floated away, the echo *God bless this soul* continuing into sleep.

"Jamie, wake up." He opened his eyes and found sunlight filling the room.

"What time is it?" he asked looking around, seeing Ian, whose clothes were wrinkled and hair in disarray, sticking out on one side of his head and plastered against the other side.

"It's almost noon," Ian answered.

"What day?"

"It's Saturday, dipstick."

The brightness hurt Jamie's eyes, so he rubbed them hoping to soothe them, but they continued to throb.

"It looks like a purddy day," a voice strange and unfamiliar came from across the room.

Jamie turned and saw the stranger from his dirty clothes heap standing at the window and looking out, a small boy, hooded with a dark stocking cap, while his bright blonde hair curled from underneath it. He wore an old brown, stained jacket and had a pair of Jamie's underwear stuck to his back.

Pulling himself up from his pillow, Jamie looked over at Ian. "Who's that?"

"That's our buddy, William," Ian replied.

William turned at the mention of his name and looked at Jamie. "I gotta' gun," he said, pulling open his coat, revealing the handle protruding from the jacket's inner pocket.

"Let me see..."

"No," the boy snapped back, closing his jacket and he began looking back out of the window. Then suddenly he started laughing, "Howard be thy name...."

"William's gonna' help us. He's part of our little party for the rich kids."

"Why do you always say that?" William asked, turning back from the window.

"Say what?"

"Little. Everything's little to you. Say something else for pity's sake. I'm about ready to shoot you."

Ian started laughing, "Kiss my little rear end."

"Bunghole," William muttered and looked again out of the window, enjoying the sun's warmth through the glass.

God bless this soul sifted into Jamie's mind, overpowering Ian's armadillo in his memory.

"What the heck are you talking about with all this Armageddon stuff? I don't get it," William asked.

Armageddon. Jamie realized that his drunken ears had been hearing wrong.

"Look, I'm not making this up," Ian said. He patted down his clothes; then from his back pocket he pulled out the tattered cover of a music cassette, unfolding in his hands like an accordion. Ian smiled. "This is OX's new album, Babies with Rabies."

He showed the cover to Jamie. The graphics parodied an old 1950's sci-fi B-movie poster. Several large headed pink fetuses, frothing at the mouth, hovered about a beautiful woman tearing her clothes. Pieces of the dress hung from their tiny hands. The beauty screamed in horror as the Babies with Rabies, umbilical cords still dangling from their stomachs, bared their toothless gums at her with maniacal gazes.

Jamie curled his nose. The oozing cords were a bit much.

"So...?" he asked Ian, his morning breath still strong in his dry mouth.

"Listen. These are the words to a song called Armageddon:

ALL YOU KINGS OF EARTH
THE TIME HAS COME
TO BEAR MY HATE--
TO SEE BLOOD RUN.

I BRING MY VENGENCE
FOR WHAT YOU'VE DONE
YOU'LL BEAR MY WRATH
AND SEE BLOOD RUN.

THE DEVIL'S SPIRITS
ARE FREE TO ROAM
WE'LL FEAST ON VENGEANCE
WHEN YOUR BLOOD RUNS.

Ian looked up from the lyrics, smiling.

Jamie continued the cringing that began with the picture. "I don't get it."

"Kinda' cool," William added.

"It's judgment day for the guys that beat you, Jamie."

"And I've got the honkin' gun," William added.

Jamie held his laughter every time William spoke; the words did not belong with the voice that uttered them.

"Ian, what are you getting at?" Jamie asked, with a chuckle.

Ian walked over to Jamie and held the boy's chin in his hand, guiding his eyes to look at him. "I told you when I pulled you out of the snow and carried you to my car that we would get those bastards back."

"So," Jamie prodded, "you got your idea about this from a song?"

"It's an anthem for us." Ian said and smiled his crooked smile.

"Just what are the three of us supposed to do?"

"A wonderful thing..." And his smile grew as he reclined into the pile of clothes that William had slept in the night before.

Chapter Seventeen

The Consequences of Actions, Others and Our Own

Monday, February 18th

Spiritually bloated, Daniel hurried to take his epistle to the school. The car swerved, and the tires squealed as he pulled it into the school parking lot. Hershel pointed his first two fingers at Daniel, a cigarette pinched between them, insisting that the boy slow down. But Daniel did not until he had brought the car to rest with a mighty jerk in his usual parking space.

He glanced at his watch, certain that Mary had not yet gotten to school, having beaten most of the teachers. Heaving his chest, he stepped out of his car. After taking a few steps, he stopped, ripping the blue cap from his head. With a flick of his wrist, the cap flew into the car, sliding across the vinyl seat and falling to the floor. Then he took his books from the back seat and was off to the building.

Daniel jogged to the main building, feeling his bulbous body jar and bounce with each step, and so panting and steaming in the cold morning air, he walked into the building. He didn't seem to notice the quiet as he hurried to his locker to swap out his books. Then he rushed to the journalism room to type.

After he stepped inside, leaving the lights off, he walked across the room to look out of the tinted windows. Palms pressed to the window, he flattened his face against the glass. "Pwaithe You, God," he said, his breath fogging the cold glass. But as he closed his eyes, his mind seemed to leave him, floating to other things. Without another word, he prayed, meditating on his God, feeling so full of God he thought he would burst.

When the lights flipped on, Daniel didn't notice it for several seconds. But he quickly opened his eyes when he heard the door shut.

"Where's your cap?" Mr. Addison asked, walking past Daniel, carrying an armload of papers to his desk.

Daniel ran his hand through his hair, thinking he could feel Earl's touch upon him again.

"I don't need it anymowe," he said still gazing out the window as a scrapping noise could be heard outside, three stories below. "They'we bwinging out the thtatue." He said, looking down at a papier-mâché' version of the Pioneer Woman.

"Did we get someone assigned to photograph this?" Mr. Addison asked. Then looking out the window, they saw their photographer trailing the statue as it hobbled along the sidewalk between the struggling custodians.

"You know, Mrs. Michaels's class made that twenty years ago for the Pioneer Woman Cotillion," Addison added, going back to his desk and shuffling through his papers. "They pull it out every year for the dance, so Mrs. Michaels fixes it up every year, patching up holes and touching up paint."

"Yeth, I know," Daniel said, "I wead the thtowy too." He walked away from the window and pulled some papers from his notebook. "You wanna' wead my editowial?"

Looking over at Daniel, still bending over his desk, his eyebrow arched, "Editorial? Have you acquired an opinion about something?"

Daniel handed the teacher the wrinkled pages.

"*Shooting at the Whites of His Hair,*" the teacher said, "very clever." Then he looked down at the boy's block printed script.

> For much of my life, I have been looked at as different. I have grown used to it. And even when I had plastic surgery last summer, I still found that I could not fit in. As of the last few weeks, things have grown worse so that now I am an outcast simply because I've been "touched by an angel." As if things were that simple. It seems sad we live in a world where we would rather laugh at faith than encourage it. But, I have to admit, I am as much to blame as anyone.
>
> I have never shied away from the fact that I am a Christian, but unfortunately for myself and others, neither have I ever shied away from keeping my beliefs to myself. Just recently I had to be dared into "going about my father's business."
>
> I went and prayed for the sick. Now to be honest, the dare was not to go and pray, but in fact to go and heal the sick. If God wants someone healed, He will have to do that Himself. That trick

is out of my hands. All things considered, I have never been completely healed of my own problem. It has merely been overcome, but only though God's help.

The reason I bring this up is to thank all of you who do not believe, all of you who laugh at me. I needed the kick in my backside. To be honest, I don't know if the person I prayed for was healed; God's will will be done. All I know is that I'm better for having done it.

And for every thorn in my side, every mountain that I must climb, I will persevere, knowing what is waiting for me after all is said and done.

God Bless.

"Okay," Mr. Addison rubbed his chin, "you want to print this?"

"Yeth, that ith the wethon I wwote it."

"Well, it's so...so...religious."

"Of couwth it ith. What elthe mattewth. Evewything justh fallth apawt exthept what you have gotten fwom God."

The teacher nodded his head, and set down at his desk. "What's going on with you? I have accepted a lot from you. I have overlooked a lot, but what is going here? I mean...angels?" The teacher shook his head. "Just how in the world did your hair go white? Answer me that, please."

His shyness, his shame of the gospel of Jesus Christ, snuck up upon him and wrestled Daniel down like a straw man. He realized that he no longer had a choice. "It woke me fwom my thleep...," he began slowly, "I wath afwaid and twied to weave my woom, but my doow wouldn't open."

"What woke you?"

"The angel, the thpiwit, the vithion, whatevew it wath..."

"And then?"

"Bathically, it towd me I had fowthaken God'th puwpothe for my life."

"And what exactly is that?" Mr. Addison asked sitting forward in his seat.

Just as Daniel opened his mouth, the door opened, and Mary waddled into the room. Breaking off his conversation with the teacher, Daniel held his essay towards Mary and said, "Wead thith."

Mary, looking both distracted and surprised, put her books down and took the papers from Daniel and quickly read them.

"What is this?"

"Jutht what it thayth, Mawy."

"So you prayed for that Messereli guy, big deal."

"Mawy, becauthe of you, I did thomething I nevew would have done befowe."

"So, if God didn't reach down from the sky and make this kid better, what's the point? The guy's not better." Letting go of the essay, she stepped towards Daniel, walking on the pages, and pulled Daniel's hands to her belly.

Daniel was surprised at the tight flesh.

"If you pray for me, will He heal this?" Mary asked mockingly, holding Daniel's hands firmly to her.

"Ith thomething wwong?"

"The baby is what's wrong," She laughed.

"Won't youw pawentth help you take cawe of the baby?"

Mary pushed his hands away. "You really don't get it. Physician, heal thyself!"

"Mary, are you all right?" Mr. Addison asked.

"Not yet," she answered and began to pick up her books. "You know, Daniel, you wanna pray for someone? Pray for John and Faith Smith."

Daniel's mind spun; he had tried to block her out of his mind since Earl had come. "Faith Thmith?" he asked Mary as she walked to the door, "You know hew?"

"Her husband knocked me up."

* * *

Earnest ran his french fry through a puddle of ketchup and chewed, looking at the hideous papier-mâché' Pioneer Woman statue that had been brought into the cafeteria. Over the statue hung a large paper banner inviting all to the Pioneer Woman Cotillion on Friday. Earnest had overlooked the banner until the silly statue drew his attention to it.

He took another bite of his hamburger, crunching from the heap of potato chips he had loaded it with, and saw Marc Neuhaus and his cronies sitting a couple of tables away. Beside Marc sat RaLF with her hand on his shoulder. And since that was her only hand, it made Earnest feel like garbage. "Crap," he whispered, dabbing another french fry with ketchup, thinking of everything that Ian had said about RaLF and her clever manipulations.

"Mind if I sit here?" Anne Endo asked, taking a seat across from Earnest.

Earnest gave her a smile, surprised.

From a little brown sack, Anne unpacked her lunch: a banana, a small bunch of purple grapes, and a small green bottle of water.

"Hungry?" Earnest asked her.

"No, not really," she answered, "I don't like large lunches. I feel lethargic afterwards."

Earnest could not imagine her ever eating much of anything, reminding him of a small porcelain doll.

"How come you haven't turned in a new cartoon, yet?" She asked, twisting the bottle's cap, the bottle hissing underneath her words.

"Cartoonist's block, I guess," he replied shrugging his shoulders, trying to be both clever and deceptive. The last thing he'd been thinking about was his stupid cartoon.

"Is that all?" she asked, doubting his response.

"Why?"

"Just the way you sound.... You know, without it, we still have to fill the space with something."

"Sorry...."

"I probably haven't ever said it, but I like it."

Earnest shifted in his seat, then leaned forward, closer to her. "You like it? I figured you'd think it's stupid and gross."

"That's why I like it."

She washed down a couple of grapes with water and began to peel the banana.

"Will you take me to the Cotillion?" Anne continued.

The girl's shift of topics caused Earnest to pause a few seconds. "Is your car broke down?"

"Earnest, I'm not asking for a ride. I'm asking for a date."

"Me?"

"Yes, Earnest, you. Could you think about it?"

"No…I mean yes, I'll think about it. I mean, I can take you. Sure." Earnest answered, shifting again in his seat. "It's this Friday, right? When should I get you?"

"We can talk about it later, Earnest." She slid a folded piece of paper to him across the table and placed it into his hand. Then smiling as she looked at Earnest, she packed away the remnants of her lunch into the brown bag. "This makes me happy," she said, looking at Earnest, lightly caressing his hand, and then she walked away.

Earnest watched her, admiring the shimmering jet black hair hanging to the middle of her back, swaying with each step. He cupped the paper in the palm of his hand, stalling from picking it up. Taking a deep breath and heaving a heavy sigh, he slowly unfolded it, as small pieces of the paper fell to the table where it had been torn from a spiral notebook. Her penmanship flowed, every stroke certain and bold.

Dear Earnest,

I have sensed for some time that something is hurting in your heart. I do not know from where your pain comes, but I want you to know that I care. Our spirits are stronger than anything on the outside. Feed your spirit. Choose to be joyful in spite of your pain. Our time here is too short. There is beauty in your soul. Remember, I care.

Anne E.

Earnest scratched his head, rereading the note several times, excited and confused, the letter seeming at once surreal, clairvoyant, and weird.

His enthusiasm began to ebb as in his periphery, Earnest saw his fellow conspirators take their leave, reminding him of the hurting in his heart. How could his spirit be strong if marked as a demon, fed with the blood of Jamie Messereli? He had no idea how to be joyful.

In her ignorance, Anne had extended a hand to him, Earnest reasoned. *Would she have, if she knew about any of this*, he wondered. He dabbed another french fry into the ketchup then dropped it upon the tray, having lost his appetite. He looked back up at the papier-mâché' statue and found that his humor had subsided, so he studied the statue's callow ugliness hoping he could dredge up some beauty inside of himself.

* * *

Ian ran his french fry through a puddle of ketchup upon his tray and laughed as he looked at the Pioneer Woman statue overlooking the cafeteria.

"What's so funny?" William asked, taking a bite of a burrito.

"That damned ugly statue," Ian said pointing with his french fry and then eating it.

William turned around. "Yeah. They put the same dang thing up every year for the same dang dance."

Ian watched William take another bite of his food. "Same damn dance..." he muttered and headed back to his seat. He leaned back, feeling anxious as he heard the bitch's growling somewhere in the back of his mind and nervously began to drum his finger tips upon the table top. "All you Kings of Earth, the time has come to bear my hate, to see blood run." Ian recited in a distracted whisper, "I bring my vengeance for what you've done. You'll bear my wrath and see blood run." He began to chuckle and then the laughter became stronger. "This is it..."

"This is what?" William asked, shoving another bite of burrito into his mouth.

"The Devil's Spirits are free to roam. We'll feast on vengeance when your blood runs. This is Armageddon, William."

The small boy reached into his jacket, putting his hand upon the handle of his pistol. "I'm not ready."

"Not now numb-nuts. The dance. The Pioneer Woman Cotillion. Good lord, you want us to get kicked out of school. Close your jacket, dammit."

"How come the dance?"

The bitch's growl remained in his ear. "I just…know. Think about it. Everyone will be there. This is the biggest dance all year."

"Okay...all right...so we kick the snobs' butts this Friday. Cool."

Ian quickly finished his lunch feeling suddenly jittery. "I gotta get a drink," he said to his small friend and stood up. "You comin'?"

"Naw," William said, pushing his tray out of his way.

"Later," Ian said, hurrying from the cafeteria glancing at the banner.

William pulled a rolled up comic book from inside his jacket, opened it and laid it out on the table, avoiding a spot of chili. Then from a notebook he pulled out some paper and began to draw pictures from the comic book.

He continued sketching until he noticed the cafeteria was nearly empty, so he rolled up the comic book and inserted it into a pocket in his jacket and put his papers in his notebook. Leaving his tray on the table but stuffing the unused packets of ketchup in his pockets, he looked around and saw all the ladies in white busy at work, wiping and cleaning.

As William headed out, he stopped at the statue and took a large black marker from his jacket, pulling the lid off of the marker with his mouth. He took a heavy whiff, careful not to get any ink on his nose, and for a few seconds his mind spun; then he began writing in large thick letters on the wooden base that held the statue. When he finished he hurried out, laughing at the first signs of Armageddon.

* * *

This is my day, Mary thought, standing at the curb, again waiting for her mother. When the car appeared Mary was too distracted with her thoughts of her day, to become angry. She climbed silently into the car and sat.

"I'm sorry," Mary's mother squeaked, "I just totally lost track of time."

"You know, I could just drive myself."

"We've been over this. Trust is earned. Plus, you haven't gotten your license yet."

"Whatever..." Mary mumbled.

"I've got beaucoup errands to run. I hope you don't mind."

"Like it mattered..."

Mary settled in to her seat. Her mind had already drifted off.

Soon. First, there was lunch; an hour passed. Then the dry cleaners —make a drop and pick up the Deacon's suits—fifteen minutes passed. Then the department store to kill another hour. Mary walked along as her mother dragged her through the day. *Soon*. Then to buy flowers for the dead, the dying, and the not-so-well.

"One more stop," she said to Mary, and Mary nodded, thinking soon, very soon.

The car pulled into the parking lot at the hospital.

"I want to take these flowers to Mrs. Gardner," Mary's mother said. "She's taught Sunday school for years. She's in so much pain I hope the Good Lord takes her soon."

Mary's mother pulled the keys from the ignition, dropped them in her purse, and opened the car door, but Mary didn't move.

"Are you coming?"

"I'll wait."

"I won't be gone long."

As Mary watched her mother enter the hospital, she pulled out her key ring. Sorting through them, she found a shiny new key, one she had specially made for this day. Then she slid behind the steering wheel, inserted the new key and started the car. "Physician, heal thyself," she said aloud, and remembering Lita Mankiller's directions, she left the parking lot driving south.

* * *

Ian hurt from his laughter, his ribs feeling like they would split apart. William smiled in the passenger seat as he rode, enjoying Ian's approval.

"You wrote Armageddon on the statue..." Ian erupted again.

"And a bunch of toilet stalls, across some lockers..." William said, pulling out the large marker he had used. He pulled the lid off and again took a big whiff. "Shoot fire," he muttered, shaking his head, snapping the lid back on the marker. Looking down at his hands, he saw that both of his index fingers were black with ink. "This stuff won't wash off," he said to Ian, holding his hands up to him.

Ian's laughter faded, "You better watch it. They might figure you did it."

"Naw," William said, looking out the window, "they'll never notice, never have before."

Stopping at a red light, Ian looked both ways, and then took a swig from the bottle he held between his legs. With a sigh, Ian turned up his stereo, blaring OX from his speakers. Their laughter had ebbed to silence as Ian's thoughts returned to Friday, feeling a sort of giddiness about everything. He had a date, a time, and a purpose.

As he drove into Jamie's yard, he turned and smiled at William, raising his eyebrows in excitement. "Jamie's gonna dump right in his pants." He laughed and parked the car in a spot outlined by ruts. They hurried inside, not bothering to knock.

Jamie looked up from the couch, his head propped at one end and his feet at the other. "Hey," he yawned and turned back to the television.

"Vengeance is ours," Ian smirked, hovering above Jamie, giving him a wink.

"What?" Jamie asked, rolling onto his side, avoiding Ian's glare.

"We've got a date, honey." Ian growled. "Friday, it hits the fan." Ian had imagined this so many times that he had grown near jubilant.

Jamie stretched his arms. "What?" he said, tightly squeezing his eyes closed. Then he stood up from the couch as quickly as his sore ribs would allow him. "What are you talking about?"

Watch him. Ian heard the bitch growl.

Ian grabbed Jamie's arms. "This is for you, buddy. For me. For what they've done to us."

Jamie stared at Ian, looking closely for the first time. He studied the curve of Ian's nose where it shifted to the right and flattened. He followed the pale scar that RaLF's ring had put upon Ian's face, thick across the flattened bridge and thinning as it moved toward the boy's cheek.

"I just don't get it. What are we doing? There's only three of us and I can barely move. There were at least seven or eight people that jumped me..."

"Hey, William's gotta' gun," Ian interrupted.

Jamie looked away from Ian and stared at the small senior. "Are you kidding me? Do you really think you're going to shoot someone?"

William shrugged.

Jamie looked back at Ian, "Well?"

Ian shook his head, "We're not going to shoot anyone. But it'll scare the shit out of some people. We crash that stupid Pioneer Woman dance; grab some of the guys that grabbed you.... Hell, if they think I'm fugly, they won't know what hit 'em."

"People go to prison for this kinda' shit," Jamie bellowed.

"Screw it," Ian grunted, walking away to a chair. He rocked back and forth, rubbing his head. The noise in his head—the bitch's yelping scorched his mind.

"Is this a game to you?" Jamie asked.

"Do you think it was a game to them?" Ian's voice lowered and his words became short, "Do you think it was a game to them when they planned grabbing you? Do you think it was a game when RaLF talked them into it?"

"What are you talking about?"

"I heard them talking all about kicking your ass that morning..."

"What?" Jamie's eye squinted in disbelief.

"Yeah, they planned it right outside the vice principal's office. There's your funny little game."

"You knew they were going to jump me?"

"Like I could've stopped it."

"You could've told me!"

"You knew about that," William piped in, "cool."

"Shut up, you scrawny little jerk!" Jamie snapped at William.

"It had to happen," Ian insisted, "Without it, Armageddon couldn't happen. It was out of my hands."

Without any warning, Jamie's fist flew into Ian's face, sending him stumbling backwards.

Jamie grunted as a spasm of pain shot through his chest. "How the hell could you do that to me?!"

Ian licked the blood from his upper lip. "Do you think it was easy?"

"Like this has been easy for me. You're worse than they are!" Jamie pulled at Ian's collar, raising him from the floor, shoving him into William. "Get out of here!" Jamie pushed at the pair, driving them to the door. "Get out!" He yelled over again until they were on the porch. His voice seethed through his clenched teeth.

Ian climbed to his feet as the door slammed at his face. "It's started, Jamie, with or without you...," he said, reaching inside William's jacket and grabbing the pistol. Ian charged from the porch, screaming, "I don't need you, you pussy!"

"Hey!" William yelled at Ian as he raced off.

Ian stopped at Jamie's car, aiming the gun at the windshield. He pulled the trigger, but the trigger didn't move. Ian glared at the gun and pulled the trigger again, but it remained frozen in place. "What the...?" he muttered as he kept pulling the trigger. Then studying the gun, he turned with his eyes opened wide, "This gun is a rusted up piece of shit! You've been bragging about a piece of shit broken gun?!" Ian threw the gun at William, hitting him hard in the chest.

The bitch bellowed at Ian, and the boy covered his ears. "Shut up!" he cursed angrily making his way back to the car. "Get in the car, asshole."

The small boy scurried to the car, shoving the broken gun into his pocket, and climbed in. "You don't get along well with people, do you?" he said as he shut the door.

Ian looked at William and started the car, "I don't give a shit who plays. I'm finishing this." He growled, his face so wrapped in anger William wished the gun worked. "Vengeance is fucking mine."

The car shot out of the yard and on to the road, the tires squealing.

* * *

Passing a lime green cinder block Nazarene Church and a couple of old houses with smoke wafting from their crumbling chimneys, Mary followed a long dirt road overgrown with dead, yellow weeds. She had turned off of the highway at a small shiny sheet metal building where the local Indian tribe sold cigarettes.

Mary stopped at the third house. It was not as she had imagined it. The neglect visiting the houses she had passed seemed to have made a home here. The paint adhered so sparsely in strips and flakes it seemed wrong to consider the house painted at all, appearing as if the owner decided to hell with the house, letting Mother Nature reap its slow entropic score.

"That can't be right..." Mary said aloud, staring at the weather-beaten wooden shell of the house, and put the car in reverse. Apprehension raised her foot from the brake, but as the car began to roll backwards, the huge visage of a woman appeared behind the rusting and tattered screen door. Mary strained to see the large silhouette in the dimming twilight, but the image cast was unmistakable, so Mary parked the car.

She opened the car door and stood up, struck by the strong stench of something from somewhere, a stench different from that of the refinery but no less unpleasant. Then she heard the snorts and squeals of pigs from behind the house.

"Come inside. It's cold," the Indian woman said from the house.

Mary grabbed her book bag from inside the car and flung it over her shoulder. She walked to the house, quickening her stride every step until she was inside, looking at the giant woman in silence.

"Come," the nurse said, shutting the door, its window rattling angrily, darkness now washing over the house's interior; blinds drawn over every window, and the only light in the empty room came from the small screen of a black and white television and the dim orange glow of a cigarette ash in the room's far corner.

A fat man in overalls and dirt-caked boots sat in a chair in the corner, holding the cigarette between the third and little fingers of his left hand as the other two fingers were missing. His larger features, save for his head and face which remained behind a curtain of darkness, were outlined by the television's glow. A puppy sat at the man's feet.

The musty smell of old house, pig waste, smoke, and dog filled the room, and Mary's nose began to run from the onslaught. As Mary sniffed, the puppy noticed her for the first time, barking at her in high-pitched yelps.

"Shut up, you damn dog," the man grunted, leaning forward into the flickering illumination of the television. He was a white man, Mary noticed, bald upon his scalp yet his face was covered with whiskers. The man flicked the dog, so it yelped, feet sliding as it scampered upon the wooden floor.

The bald man looked, catching Mary's gaze. He blankly returned her stare and sat back, returning to the anonymity of the shadow.

"Come on," Lita Mankiller said.

Mary felt the push of Lita's hand upon the small of her back. As she walked, feeling unbalanced, the house lost dimension and perspective as the inside grew to be larger than the outside could contain. There was no light, so she walked slowly, lead only by the gentle touch of the nurse.

"Stop," Lita whispered, placing the whole of her palm upon Mary's back.

Mary halted, hearing keys jiggle behind her. She listened as a key slid into a key hole in front of her and a bolt lock released. Then she heard a doorknob turn, and the door in front of her opened, soft light rolling out like mist. Lita's hand pushed again, so Mary moved forward.

She smelled fresh dirt as they entered the room, illuminated by several candles scattered about flickering in the darkness, casting dancing shadows upon the walls.

"Have a seat," Lita said, closing the door.

Mary sat in one of the room's two chairs at an old card table, the shifting shadows disorienting her.

"This will take awhile, so you might as well get comfortable," Lita said, walking from the door.

Mary shifted in the chair, slumping forward, resting her head in her crossed arms. She pushed the chair away from the table to let her swelling belly fall between her knees. And then she watched as Lita began to work.

The nurse turned a knob on a small tank connected to a camping stove, sitting upon a cabinet beside the door. After lighting a match she turned another knob on the burner causing a slight hiss. Then putting the match to the burner an orange streak quickly circled it.

Lita began a quiet chant, dulling Mary's mind as the dancing shadows upon the walls unsettled her senses.

The nurse took a battered stainless steel pan from a cabinet below the sink and ran water into it. From above, she grabbed a metal tin, setting the pan of water upon the flame. She broke up the dry leaves she took from the tin and sprinkled the pieces into the pan of water.

"It must simmer," Lita broke her chant but quickly began the alien verse again, taking a bowl from the upper cabinet.

As the nurse turned and walked towards Mary, she dropped something into the bowl she had taken from the sink, then sitting at the table, she began pulverizing it.

"Black root," Lita again broke her chant.

Mary did not reply, everything seeming so remote she did not feel a participant in the actions, only an observer, the large Indian a stranger, her face familiar yet mysterious, the rhythmic wet thuds of the club to the black root blurring her mind.

"You are the first white girl I've ever done this for," Lita said, her voice rough, beating the black root steadily.

"Why me?" Mary whispered, staring at the floor.

The Indian smiled with a short laugh then asked, "How do you feel?"

"All right. I'm sorry to ask this, but have you ever thought about your name in all this? Isn't it odd?"

"I guess it's just perspective," she answered, continuing to pulverize the root. "But, yes, I've thought of it…"

Mary caught a smell of fresh dirt from the root, closing her eyes as her thoughts clouded. She lost the flow of time, measuring it by Lita's slow rhythmic pounding. Awash with this alien place, she lost track as the sound, like the thick odors and the flickering lights, lulled her.

And then there was the nurse's chant, lulling her as she floated, relaxed and unassuming, until she felt herself being shaken.

"It's ready," Mary heard, realizing she had been asleep. "Undress and lie on the cot."

The room had grown very warm to Mary, yet as she

undressed, she shivered. For months she had known this as the inevitable conclusion, so she climbed onto the cot and hid under the blanket.

"Are you cold?" Lita Mankiller asked, walking toward Mary, carrying a cup and a bowl.

"No," Mary answered, quivering.

"Move the covers. They'll be in the way."

Mary pushed off the blanket, stuffing it into the space between the bed and the wall. She then sat up, crossing her legs and wrapping herself in her arms.

"Swallow this, even the leaves and stems," Lita insisted. "It is hot and will scald your mouth."

Mary took the cup and slowly brought the bitter brew to her mouth.

"Quickly," the Indian said, "It won't burn as much."

Mary gulped the drink; singeing her tongue and throat, feeling the heat deep within her, stirring her insides. The nurse took the cup, setting it on the floor. Then she sat on the bed beside Mary and put the bowl she carried in her lap.

Lita scooped a dirty paste from inside the bowl with two fingers and held them to Mary's mouth. "Eat this."

Mary slowly opened her mouth, and Lita stuck the fingers of paste into Mary's mouth. It was cold and grainy and tasted like mud.

"Swallow it and keep it down," Lita instructed as Mary gagged and wretched.

Lita forced more scoops into Mary's throat, the paste running down her chin and spurting from her mouth.

"Are you trying to poison me?" Mary coughed.

"Yes," Lita answered. "Lay back."

And Mary did, shaking and straining, holding the poison within her body.

Then Lita scooped a handful of the paste from the bowl and patted it into a poultice upon Mary's belly. What had seemed cold to taste, felt warm upon her flesh.

"Now rest," Lita said standing up, drawing a finger coated in the root paste across Mary's forehead above her thick eyebrows.

As Mary relaxed, the paste warmed her head and stomach, making her eyes grow heavy.

"No!!!" John suddenly screamed at her.

Mary tried to jump up and run, but her flesh felt knit in leaden thread, so as she tried to run, she became engulfed in gravity, unable to escape John who raced towards her in the distance as well as stood beside her.

"No!!!" he screamed over and over, spittle flying about her; the voice suddenly coming from beneath her. As she looked down, John reached up to her, up into her, both his hands grasping, reaching up inside of her, clutching the embryonic sack, and suddenly the swirling image of John became Faith's, and Faith's became that of Daniel's, and Daniel's became the Deacon's, and they all screamed, "No!!!" Their faces agonized and distorted while their arms remained deep within her womb, and her mother sobbed in the distance. Mary screamed back to them, "No!!!" reaching with her own arm, up inside herself, clawing past the others that filled her, ripping through slime and membrane, and finally grabbing a handful of wet, slimy hair, her voice shattering and breaking into a screech, pulling on the hair, pulling it free of the other's grip, pulling the ball of flesh through the slime and membrane, pulling until it slipped from between her legs, pulling it up to her face to see the red wrinkled, swollen face, the puffy eyes opening, its dark black eyes searing into Mary's...

And Mary screamed, and...

Her body jerked, and Mary grunted as someone fell across her.

"Push!" Lita bellowed.

And Mary pushed, curling up to see the fat bald man draped over her and bearing down and Lita's face between her raised knees.

"Push!" Lita ordered.

And Mary pushed, her mind caught between her dream and her present.

"Push!"

"I ammm," Mary growled, gaining her bearings as the man bore down harder, bringing more of his weight to rest upon her. Her breathing stopped—her muscles pulled taut and contracted, feeling like a tightly held fist, squeezing blood from a stone.

"Push!" Lita said, "Again!" her voice tense and strained.

So, Mary pushed, her strength balled up and channeled, the strange man weighing heavier upon her. She felt pressure build pushing against the blockage, and it built and built and she pushed and strained and grunted, and she felt as if she were tearing apart, and just before she felt herself burst, something gushed from between her legs.

Every muscle relaxed as a burst of air escaped her lungs, and the man stood up.

"Lay back," Lita said.

Mary collapsed upon the mattress, her body in an uncontrollable quiver; she felt dizzy, still aware of the man hovering over her. She panted heavily, feeling a thick sweat over her naked body. "Is it over?" she moaned and shook, pulling at the blanket tucked between the mattress and the wall and watching the man but seeing only the back of his round head. Mary felt several quick tugs from between her legs and Lita said, "Push." And Mary pushed again even more bewildered, afraid of repeating what she had just gone through. This time the man did nothing as Mary grunted and quickly felt something else ooze from her body.

Lita looked up at Mary, "Relax."

Mary fell back upon the pillow, her breathing slowing. "How long was I asleep?"

Lita looked at the man, "Bring me the hot water."

He walked over to the sink, never glancing Mary's way.

"About six hours," Lita answered. "Now, rest."

Mary closed her eyes, but the dark eyes from her dream would not leave her, giving her a shudder.

"Here, take the bucket," Lita said to the man after she had finished cleaning Mary and raised a white five gallon plastic bucket by the handle. The man took it and left the room. Lita stood and stretched, her clothes stained and spattered. She then walked around the bed, draping the blanket over Mary.

"Keep your knees up. You'll be okay." She walked to the sink, beginning the chant again.

Mary could not tell if it was the same song as before, but as she listened, the more intense other sounds became. When she heard the snort and squeal of the pigs outside, she shuddered, staring deeply into dark searing eyes that were not there.

Chapter Eighteen

Making Exits

Tuesday February, 19

Lita's chanting, as she cleaned the room, lulled Mary, but she fought sleep vehemently, prodded by a sudden need to leave.

"Here," the Indian said to Mary, handing her a large sanitary pad. "You'll bleed for a couple of days. Right now, you need to sleep. Your body is filled with poison and needs time to clean it out."

Awkwardly, Mary put the pad in her panties. Her legs quivered as she tried to slide on her underwear, so she sat up, leaving a spot of blood where she sat. Then slowly putting in one leg at a time, she brought the panties to her knees, raising herself high enough off the cot to pull them up. She fell back to the cot, exhausted.

The flickering candles about nauseated her in waves, so she fought harder to stay awake, her eyes burning from exhaustion as she kept them open.

"You okay?" Lita asked, as she finished returning everything to the cabinets.

"Yeah," Mary answered, refusing to submit to her fatigue.

"I have to go to work after I change. You rest. I'll see you after my shift." The chant drifted away as she left the room.

Mary pushed herself up again, holding her place. As she grew composed, her breathing deepened and she stood. When she finally felt steady, she pulled on her pants. After she dressed, she fell back to the cot avoiding the blood stain she had left. Her stomach churned, and for a second she chuckled in spite of her nausea, thinking she had felt this same way when she was first pregnant.

In her laughter, she found the strength to rise. Slowly, she walked to the sink and splashed water on her face. Catching her breath, Mary turned to the table and put on her coat. Then throwing her book bag over her shoulder, she heaved a heavy breath of air, ready to leave.

The door creaked, so she cautiously opened it, and she began making her way out. She could hear the sounds of the television and quietly moved towards it. As she reached the doorway of the room, she pressed herself against the wall, looking in.

The bald man turned from the television and looked at Mary.

"Lita tol' you to rest. You need to lissen to her."

Mary held her tongue and darted to the front door.

"If you did what you're told you wouldn't be fuggin' pregnant…you slut!"

Her heart pounding, Mary bolted out the door, slamming it behind her as the man ranted. Unbalanced by her need to escape and her poor footing, she stumbled and rolled down the steps to the ground. With no thought to being hurt, Mary jumped up as quickly as her weakened state allowed and ran to the car. After she climbed into the car and started it, she felt the first throbs of pain from her fall. But still, the need to leave was stronger. She backed out of the spot, and put the car into drive, speeding off with a spray of gravel and dirt.

As Mary crossed back into the city limits through the shadows of street lights, she remembered an old black and white movie about a man who had escaped from prison after being wrongly convicted of a crime. At end of the film, the man said good bye to his old girlfriend; when she asked him how he was going to live since he now had no life, he answered, backing into the shadows, "I'll steal..." That was exactly what she wanted to do, fade away into a shadow.

But something stopped her from simply disappearing. So she drove home and parked the car at the curb in front of the house. In the moonlight, she studied the house, just as she had with Lita's. But unlike Lita's, her home looked perfect; its decay inside.

She opened her book bag, taking out a single piece of paper, thinking to leave some kind of note, so sitting behind the steering wheel, she thought. Finally, she just scribbled, *its over,* on the paper. Mary set the note on the driver's seat and climbed out. Then with nothing more to say or do, she disappeared into the shadows.

* * *

As the sun broke through the shadows of night, Jamie woke. He hadn't slept well, so, still fatigued, he threw the blanket off as he heard his mother readying herself for work. Shivering in the morning cold, he pulled himself out of his bed, hurrying to the living room to warm himself over the floor furnace.

"What are you doin' up?" his mother asked sitting at the kitchen table drinking a cup of coffee and smoking a cigarette.

"Couldn't sleep." he answered, stretching in the furnace's heat, feeling his pain less. This brought a weak smile even while remembering Ian's part in it. He walked to the table, taking one of his mother's cigarettes and lighting it.

"Ian's gonna' start some trouble this week."

His mother took a drag and coughed. "Trouble?"

"Yeah, some kinda' shit with the guys who beat me up."

"How's he know who did it? I thought he didn't see nothin'?"

"He knew more than he said." Jamie took a box of cereal and poured it into a Tupperware container partially melted at the rim.

His mother stood up from the table. "Stay out of it. If he wants to do somthin', just let 'im. It'll serve those peckerwoods right. But it's his butt, not yers. You've had enough to deal with." She pulled her purse over her shoulder moving towards the door. "See you when I get home." And she left.

Walking out of the kitchen, he ate the dry cereal with his fingers and turned the television to cartoons. But all the while, his mind whirled with what his mother had said. Again, all he could surmise was that she was wrong; he couldn't stay out, already so deeply into it, a prompting to warn RaLF too strong to fight.

Reaching the bottom of his bowl, he poured the crumbs into his mouth, wishing he could hate RaLF in return, but he couldn't hate her; she was too hurt, too damaged, too much like him.

Rinsing out the bowl and putting it back in the cabinet, Jamie mulled over what Ian had said about Friday—about RaLF and her friends. And he thought about how he had laughed off the strange notion of Armageddon.

And then creeping to the forefront of his mind, like a break in a fog, he saw the angel boy standing over him saying, "God bweth this thoul." "Shit," he bellowed, looking through the ceiling for the eyes of God. "I don't want your blessing..." he cried in anger. "I only want her to like me..." His voice weakly trailed off as he moved to the bathroom to prepare for battle.

* * *

Stepping into the school building, Jamie immediately felt like a stranger. He had turned his back to it a week ago and here he was again—so many strange faces around him, and those faces he knew, seemed alien as he moved among them, looking for the one face indelible in his mind. Those mornings of tutoring were a million years ago, now. It was funny, Bill's jealousy of his time with RaLF. But Bill couldn't tell how much RaLF cared for him. Jamie could tell; he saw it in her eyes as she looked across the library at him. And he had been just as jealous of Bill.

Walking along the hallway, he glanced about to a wall of lockers, noticing the message Ian had given everyone: 'Armageddon' written out a letter per locker. But then his attention averted when he saw RaLF, her arm entwined with some guy, probably one of the son of a bitches who had grabbed him. He whipped around, putting his back to her, thinking he should go and wash himself of the whole thing. But slowly, he turned back, wanting to be stronger than his bitterness.

"RaLF..."

She turned and she and Marc stopped, answering the call with faraway eyes, but the recognition of Jamie brought fury to their glares.

"What are you doing here?" Marc moved towards Jamie, letting his grasp of RaLF fall away. He stood before Jamie, chest puffed up, his face glowing red just like Bill all those months ago.

Jamie looked past Marc's posing, ignoring his huffing, and angering Marc all the more.

"You aren't wanted here," RaLF insisted, her eyes empty of all but contempt.

"RaLF," Jamie said ignoring her words, patting a locker with a portion of William's handiwork on it, "this message was for you...."

Marc shoved Jamie into the lockers, knocking the wind out of him.

"Don't threaten her, dumbass!" Marc snarled.

Catching his breath, Jamie pushed back, putting the jock to the floor. "No, dumbass," Jamie snapped, "it's not a threat." Then looking at RaLF, he wore on, "I don't know why you blame me for Bill's dying. It wasn't my fault, but if it would make you happy, I wished it had been me instead of him."

RaLF stood silently, her face red with her anxiousness, knowing she wished it had been him, too.

Jamie shook, his eyes unblinking in their stare. "Be careful at the dance, Friday. I don't know what's happening... I just know Ian is planning something."

Marc stood up, seething, "If you don't get out of my sight..." RaLF placed her hand on Marc's arm, squeezing it.

"I'm done," Jamie said, raising his hands, "I've said more than you deserve."

"Go to hell," Neuhaus grunted.

Jamie's eyes turned from Marc to RaLF, studying her face. In spite of everything, she still had a radiance that pulled at him. "I'm already there…" he said still looking at RaLF, his chest feeling as if it was imploding.

Leaving them, he stepped outside, and as a cold foul-smelling breeze swept across his face, he realized that his mother had won. All that he had been destined to be, was coming to fruition. His future was as inevitable as dying and nothing else could be done. "Why wasn't it me..." he banged his fist against his forehead while an image of himself reposed in a pinewood coffin flashed through his mind. But there was no peace on his dead face. A sad, pitiful scowl ran down to his chin; a frown arced across his face. His hair, pulled up under his Ponca Feed and Tack cap and clothes, dirty and worn, decorated the corpse. Hovering over the deceased, his mother stroked his cold, dead frowning face. Circling the coffin, a legion of his mother's dirty redneck escapades in dirty jeans and untucked shirts, boots caked in dried mud, hats stained and malformed cocked upon their indistinct and unshaven faces. Yet in the back stood the tall stranger of his youth—the bearer of sagacious truth and infantile wealth—shaking his head, holding his hat under his arm. "She ruined ya', boy," the cowboy said, an eyebrow arched in disappointment.

Jamie opened his eyes, a tear rolling down his cheek from the wind. "I can't go back..." he said looking at the building. "But, dammit, I can't quit either. She will win…" His words were angry. His hair matted, clung to the tear trails running down his face.

As he walked away, the cold made his body ache, and each pain reminded him of the curse that he bore. And in that there seemed to be a small victory. He imagined the anger in Marc's face, and with that, a little joy came to Jamie, and his smile grew. "I'm staying, if it kills me...if they kill me.... I'm staying." So he turned back around, heading toward the door, thinking more about the resurrection of his soul than Ian's Armageddon.

* * *

A photographer walked along the journalism class tables, tossing photographs to people like playing cards, asking, "Mary gone AWOL again?"

"Watch out, she knows when you're talking about her. It's so weird how she just pops outa' nowhere when someone even breathes her name. I just hate that," a girl who sold ads said, looking at the picture that had just been handed to her. "Look at me. I'm all washed out. We can't use this..." she moaned.

"I wonder why she even came back." Axle offered, reworking a sentence for his next column.

"I guess you need to pray for her, too," the photographer said to Daniel, laughing.

"I do," he said in stark seriousness, looking up from a photograph of the writing on the school's walls.

Although no reprimand had been intended, the photographer tucked tail and looked away. Returning to the photograph, he had seen the graffiti around the building and on the papier-mâché' statue, but not until seeing the picture did he remember what Ian had said to him at Jamie's house.

"It's a song," the photographer interrupted Daniel's thoughts.

"A thong?" Daniel asked.

"Oh, yeah…" the photographer said with a smile, bobbing his head, and pulled a cassette tape case from his pocket. He put the tape into the community cassette player resting against the chalkboard with the next issue's page assignments. He pushed the play button and jammed a piece of cardboard beside it to hold the button down.

A desert wind began to blow. Then very softly a small droning began pulsing underneath the wind, and grew until it overpowered the wind with an almost classical flourish of an electrical keyboard. As the keyboard played, a slightly fuzzed electric guitar began following the keyboard in unison. Then they abruptly stopped, and there was silence for a few seconds. Then they began again with a more aggressive attack, now accompanied by a bass. After several measures they rested again and then restarted with a drum added, creating an avalanche of sound as they broke into parts.

Then Ox began shrieking the lyrics between background chants of "Armageddon," his voice's distinctive nasal sound weakened on the old tape player.

ALL YOU KINGS OF EARTH
THE TIME HAS COME
TO BEAR MY HATE
TO SEE BLOOD RUN

Earnest disliked the song. Then in the midst of the audio chaos, as the group put forth their chant of Armageddon, a memory of Ian intruded upon him. His many thoughts of Anne battling his thoughts of RaLF over the last day made room for nothing else. But then his old friend returned with the music like a specter, revealing to Earnest who the school's vandal must be, revealing the craziness in Ian's head.

Almost at that instant, both, RaLF and Daniel thought of Ian:

RaLF remembering Jamie's comments at the lockers before school; Daniel, dredging up Ian's seething words at Jamie's house: "Armageddon draweth nigh."

I BRING MY VENGEANCE
FOR WHAT YOU'VE DONE
YOU'LL BEAR MY WRATH
AND SEE BLOOD RUN

And so, while RaLF's vanity prevented her acquiescence to Jamie's warnings, and while Earnest's self-absorption prevented any action beyond self-interest, Daniel was the only one of the trio curious enough to act, the lyrics taunting him, leaving him unsure if to laugh at its hyperbole or shudder from its rage. So as the music growled from the little speaker, Daniel took his leave to give Mr. Addison Ian's name, fancying himself an anonymous source.

"Mr. Addison..." Daniel said, walking slowly.

"Hey, Daniel," Mr. Addison answered putting down a story given to him to critique. "Do you remember the woman from The Ponca City News who visits the sophomore classes?"

"Uh-huh."

"She called me last night asking me if I knew about the boy who saw angels."

Daniel's mouth went agape. "What did you thay?"

"I said I would talk with her later. If you don't want me to say anything, I won't, but, she wants to talk to you."

"Thith ith cwazy..."

"Yes, it is. I have an editor who sees angels…"

"Only one…"

"Sorry, Daniel, but you need as many people on your side talking to her as possible. That includes you."

"My thide...?"

"Sure, your side. So do you care if I talk to her?"

"I don't know..." Daniel said anxiously, thinking about *his side,* surprised there could be sides in this. "I don't undewthtand...I've nevew thaid a wowd, but evewybody knowth…" he muttered, nervously putting his hand to his forehead.

"It's amazing how fast news travels without a soul uttering a word. I won't say a word, Daniel, until you say otherwise. Now, what did you need?"

Daniel knew this to be true: news traveled like air. But, he couldn't remember why he had come to Mr. Addison, staring blankly at the teacher, reaching for an answer. Then music from the other room grabbed his attention.

"Awmageddon," he blurted. "I think I know who'th doing all the wwiting on the wawwth."

"Did an angel tell you?" the teacher asked, catching Daniel off guard. Then a smile came upon the teacher's face. "I'm kidding, sorry..."

"I'th a guy named Ian. Hith fathe ith cwooked..."

"Mr. Small will be interested in that."

"Awe you going to teww him?"

"No, you should. You can explain better than I can."

"Oh..." he said, surprised at the teacher's response, so he walked away.

"That song kicks ass…!" Daniel heard as he returned to the journalism room, unintentionally nodding his head in agreement as he picked up a picture of the vandalism and tapped it against his head. *A reporter?* Shaking the thoughts from his mind, the music continuing to blare, Daniel left the room, not so anonymous after all.

* * *

Ian slouched in the chair, hands shoved deep into his coat's pockets, drumming his fingers against the bottle hidden in its lining. Staring at the name on the door, Leo Small, Principal, Ian wondered what the man wanted.

He leaned his head back, closing his eyes, and began to drift off, when the door opened and someone called his name. He peered through his squinted eyes, and Mr. Small stood in the doorway of his office waiting.

So Ian rose from the chair and sauntered into the office.

"Have a seat," Mr. Small said.

Ian did, yawning as he situated himself.

Mr. Small sat on the corner of his desk and began drumming on it with a pencil. He was a tall man, his gut spilling over his belt.

"Are you religious?" Mr. Small asked, his drawl wrapping around each word, almost overwhelming the words themselves, as he adjusted the bolo tie at his neck and started drumming again.

"Do I believe in God or something like that?"

"Yeah, do you go to church, read the Bible, maybe see angels?"

"No, that ain't me." Ian laughed.

"Well, tell me what you know about Armageddon, then." Mr. Small said, still tapping on his desk.

Ian sat up in his seat. "I don't know anything about that stuff on the walls." The bitch suddenly howled, mocking him, so he began digging at his ear with his little finger muting her sound.

What's he not saying? The constant drumming on the desk taunted him worse than the bitch's howls. He looked up at the principal's face and saw nothing: not anger, not doubt—just an empty, absorbing stare.

"You know, Ian, the police have done a rather extensive investigation. Did you know your name was the only one that came up?"

"That's crap. I don't know anything about that stuff."

"Then, why yer name out of the twelve hunerd or so students here?"

"All I know is it's the name of a song on a new album I got. I might've asked some people about what it meant. That's all."

"You couldn't look it up yourself?"

"I said, I don't know anything," Ian asserted as William came to his mind.

Mr. Small stopped drumming the pencil and leaned back across his desk and slid open a drawer on the other side, taking out a partially chewed toothpick and studying it for a few seconds. Then placing the toothpick in his mouth, he said, "So, what you're tellin' me is that you know as much about this Armageddon stuff to fill a cockroach's ass." The toothpick bobbed from side to side in the man's mouth as he held the pencil tight in his fist, his thumb pressing hard against it.

Ian again thought about William. *If he had said something… Who else could it have been?* He then repeated, "I don't know a thing." His eyes glued to the pencil, he watched Mr. Small's hand grow taut as the pencil held its own against the principal's thumb.

"Well," Mr. Small began, as the pencil finally snapped and the eraser flew into Ian, hitting the hidden liquor bottle with a deep thud. Then, looking at the broken remains in his hand, Mr. Small threw the pencil across the room, spinning end over end and landing in his wastebasket. "That's all I wanted to hear. You can get outa' here." He shooed Ian away like a pesky bug with a wave of his hand.

Ian stood, uncertain if Small heard the thud, rubbing his crooked nose as he left the office, his insides a tumult of hysteria.

"You know he knows..." the bitch growled.

Ian's fingers moved from his nose to his forehead.

"William..." the bitch hissed in Ian's ear.

He did all that damn writing. He wouldn't tell, would he?

"The little jerk carries around a freakin', toy gun...," the bitch growled.

Ian's pace quickened, as he headed towards a rest room. Hitting the door, his fury raged, imagining his hands around William's neck. He sat inside a stall, slamming the door shut and latching it. "Dammit!" Ian barked, digging into the deep pocket of his trench coat and pulling out his bottle. He took a deep swig, the vodka fueling his anger. A cold sweat broke over his forehead, so he took another drink to warm himself, but only felt more of a chill.

The outside door opened, so Ian shifted to peek through a crack at the corner of the stall. He couldn't see anything, but a urinal flushed and the door opened again as the person left.

Ian took another swallow from the bottle. He stood up and swung open the stall door, stepping out while screwing the cap back on the bottle. And leaning against the wall, stood Mr. Small, bearing a malignant grin.

Ian froze in his steps, looking desperately at Mr. Small's smiling face.

"Gotcha'!" Small said.

The neck of the bottle slipped from Ian's hand and shattered, sending slivers of glass and vodka across the tile floor.

* * *

Small instructed Ian to wait outside of his office, but Ian figured since he was already going to be suspended, why should he wait for Small to contact his parents, so he walked out of the office and went to his car.

Ian's fury grew. *Who the hell does Small think he is*? He patted his leg, really wanting a drink, licking his lips in disappointment. He sped from the school parking lot, ignoring Hershel's gestures to slow down, and drove to William's house, feeling as if he could explode from ire alone. After an hour, the small boy skipped along the sidewalk, his face wrinkled in serious thought. As he drew closer to his house, he saw Ian's car parked at the curb and waved.

Ian rolled down the passenger window as William drew near. "Come on, we gotta' talk." Ian stared cold and sober at his little friend, so William hesitated.

"Let's go," Ian snapped, growing red with anger and cold.

So William climbed in the car.

"I heard you got suspended," William said, pushing his hair from his face.

"What do you know about it?"

"Nothin'. I just heard people talkin'.

"What the hell were you thinking when you wrote that crap all over school?"

"I thought it would be funny. You did, too. You said it was cool."

"Did you tell Small about Friday?"

"I don't know nothin 'cept what you said. It's blankin' Armageddon."

Ian back handed William across the face.

"Dammit, don't screw with me!" Ian warned.

William stuck his hand into his coat, reaching for his gun, his chin quivering.

"What are you going to do with that thing? Throw it at me?" Ian smirked at the boy's intent.

William huffed in his seat. "Nothin.' It's so rusted up." His breathing quickened to pants. "Why do you have to make fun of me? I haven't done nothin' to you 'cept try to be your friend, you bunghole."

Ian pounded his steering wheel. "Someone's messing with me!" Ian bellowed at the bitch lurking in the distance.

"Do you think Jamie told?" William grumbled.

"Just shut up." Ian growled back at William, sinking into the car seat. A torrent rushed through his head; the bitch's howls, the principal's laugh, William's whining, OX's music, each reverberating in his mind. "Why would he? When would he...?"

"I saw him at school today..."

Without knowing anything, Ian suddenly knew everything. "If that son of a bitch had regrets before..."

"You want a real gun...?" William asked with such yearning to please Ian, his heart ached.

* * *

In the dusk's fading light, Ian squinted, counting three people leaving the house in an old white pick-up truck.

"Who are they?" Ian asked.

"My aunt and uncle and my little cousin. They're going to my house." William laughed, watching the truck drive away.

They waited until the dust settled upon the dirt road, and then Ian pulled his car back onto the road and drove up to a fence surrounding the house. Before they could climb out of the car, a dachshund within the fence began barking.

"They won't bite," William said, shutting the car door.

Cautiously, Ian stepped inside the fence. A basset hound let loose one long howl then slowly waddled away while the dachshund continued yelping and nipping at Ian's feet.

Ian kicked at the dog. "I hate weenie dogs," he said, spying an old aluminum baseball bat against the fence. He grabbed it and quickly brought it up over his head. The dachshund jumped from Ian's sudden movement and ran toward the hound, yelping.

William walked past Ian. He tried the doorknob, but it was locked, so he took the bat from Ian, warning him to stay back. Then he busted out a pane of the door's glass with it, reached in and unlocked it.

The boys were quickly inside. Ian bumped into a cabinet as his eyes adjusted to the dark.

"This way," William directed, leading to his uncle's bedroom. Opening the closet door, he reached in and pulled out a shotgun like some kind of magician and handed it to Ian. Then William began reaching for something else, but he couldn't find it, so he climbed in.

"What are you doing?" Ian asked.

Then William stepped out, handing Ian a box of shells. "We gotta' take some other stuff, so they won't s'spect someone who knows the house." So the boys scurried around the house, messing it up, and filling their pockets with things that looked valuable.

As the boys hurried from the house, the dachshund again charged the pair. As a jest, Ian pointed the barrel of the shotgun at the dog and pulled the trigger. The gun exploded, sending pieces of the dog rolling off in separate directions and Ian to the ground. Ian groaned trying to catch the breath the recoil had knocked from him.

"You okay?" William rushed to him, his ears ringing from the blast.

Ian nodded and smiled, "Now, that's a real gun."

* * *

Daniel and his parents sat around the dinner table in a deep solemness that had pervaded since the janitor's visit. After blessing the food, the boy heaped mashed potatoes onto his plate, stirring in mounds of butter, saturating them with gravy and topping the pile with a heavy cascade of salt and pepper. Then he dove into his dining with such fervor he panted as he ate.

"Slow down, Daniel. You're giving me indigestion just watching you," his father said.

But Daniel's pace never slackened as the consequences of Earl's visit loomed at the forefront of his mind, requiring all of Daniel's attention.

Between the snorts and pants of Daniel's consumption, the doorbell sounded and continued to ring from the constant pressing of the button.

Daniel's mother stood up. "I'll let the pastor in," she said, relieved to leave the table.

Daniel looked up and his eyes followed her, leaving the room. "The pathtow?" he asked, licking the taste of butter from his lips.

His father shrugged.

"I love this house!" Reverend Green said presenting himself to the room, his arms outstretched. "Hey Danny boy, this train's picking up speed." He slapped his hands together and then shot out one arm, signaling the direction his metaphoric locomotive headed. "I got a call today..."

"No," Daniel protested, suddenly aware why the pastor was visiting.

"A lady from the paper asked about you, my friend."

"What?" Daniel's mother asked.

"Not you, too," Daniel groaned.

"Brother, God is raining down on you!"

"What did you thay to hew?"

"The truth..." he smiled, "as much as I know of it."

"No!" Daniel jumped out of his seat. "No!" He leaned against a countertop and saw the blue cap sitting on the cabinet, so he grabbed it, shoving it hard upon his head as if covering his hair would erase everything.

"She asked if you were real. I said as real as God, but I don't know if that convinced her. What's wrong, Danny boy? This is your chance to shine."

"I don't want to thine!" he moaned, sitting back down in his chair, the brim of the cap now pulled down tightly over his forehead, blinding him of his surroundings. "No, no, no, no.... I don't want to heaw this," he prattled on, his hands holding firmly over his ears, deafening him of the other's voices. "I'm jutht a kid," he murmured, "no thaint... It's jutht white haiw... juth an angew...."

Suddenly, Pastor Green pulled Daniel's hands from his ears. The reverend, scowling, stared at Daniel. "Be a man," he smoldered.

"I didn't athk fow thith..." Daniel pleaded.

"So what," the pastor snapped, "This is your cross to bear. Pick it up."

"I don't want to be in any thtupid newthpaper." Daniel bellowed back. "I'm tiwed of being in the middwe of thome fweak show."

The Reverend pointed his finger at Daniel. "Millions of people go to bed hoping and praying for a miracle every night but never get it, but look at you...every time you blink something incredible happens. God has touched you."

"Pastor," Daniel's mother interjected as Reverend Green caught his breath, "hasn't he done enough for now?"

"This isn't about what Daniel's done. It's about what Christ's done. He didn't say it was finished till he was dead on the cross."

"I'm tiwed of talking about my thtupid haiw..."

"This isn't just talking," the reverend resolved, his arms flailing wildly. "You're bringing a real God to people. He doesn't always work in mysterious ways...sometimes they're bizarre, sometimes strange...and sometimes...he doesn't work at all.... But the thing is...the thing is...we glorify him in it all."

"Fiwst, Mithtew Addithon, now you."

"What does Mr. Addison have to do with this?" Daniel's father asked.

"Oh...the thame lady talked to Mithtaw Addithon. And thee

wantth to talk to me. Miththaw Addithon thaid if I don't talk to her, thee'll make me out to be a wunitic."

"My goodness..." his mother frowned.

Then in a soft whisper, leaning onto the dinner table, resting his chin in his hands, Daniel muttered, "I thaid I would."

The pastor glowed with a kind of victory. He placed his hand upon the boy's bleached crown and said, "God is pleased."

Daniel sighed, “I hope tho.”

Chapter Nineteen

The Brightness of Shadow
The Darkness of Light

Friday, February 22

"Be my son."

Daniel's eyes popped open, the faint whisper immediately waking him, as he feared a second appearance from the holy messenger. Swinging his arms, kicking his legs, he tried to throw his blanket away, but in his confusion he again fell to the floor with a loud thud.

Quickly he looked around, his eyes darting all about, searching for some inkling of the angel, but all he saw was the faint hint of light creeping around the window blinds. With a heavy sigh, he melted to the floor, wrapping his blanket around him.

He searched for the words that had roused him from sleep. "Be my son," echoed in his mind, and he thought, *I am your son*, imagining that he submitted to his God in every possible way.

Walking in faith, Daniel found, was like constantly walking off a cliff's edge yet expecting the ground to rise for the next step. And as he occasionally had times of doubt, the doubt acted like a safetyline tied around his neck. If his will was free, he found the consequences of exercising it quite costly.

Prostrating himself, his face pressed into the floor with fistfuls of carpet, "If I am not youw thon, what am I then? Who hath twied to pweathe you more than me?" A tear welled up and slid down his cheek as his chest tightened. "Why do I alwayth fail you?"

Then again the same still small voice sounded ever so silently in his head, "Today, be my son."

Sitting up and arching his back, Daniel looked up past his ceiling into heaven, tears spotting his t-shirt. "I am youw thon..." he groaned, his arms outstretched from the sides, almost heaving his chest. "I am youw thon," he repeated, his voice cracking in an anguished cry. "Today and awwayth..."

Remembering the interview, his face grew flushed. The edge of the precipice lay beneath his feet. And while his mind raced with thoughts of the interview—his fears of being mocked—of being the reason for some to mock God; to be His son, Daniel knew the only move he could make was forward.

An unexpected knock sounded at the door.

"Daniel," his mother said stepping into the room. "Are you awake?"

"Yeth," he said opening his eyes and peering at her from over the bed.

"Why are you on the floor?"

"I wath pwaying."

"Oh..."she said and paused, "Faith Smith is on the phone. She said it was an emergency."

"Thith eawly?" he asked and wrapped his blanket around

himself like a robe. Yet even with the interruptions, his thought had not been distracted, and his soul still stood at the edge. "I am youw thon," played over and over again in his head as he left his room.

"Hewwo." Daniel saw it was almost six in the morning.

Faith's voice quivered, "She killed my baby..."

"What?" Daniel asked, rubbing his eyes to wake himself, thinking he had heard wrong.

"Mary killed my baby. She did it...she did it..." her voice turned to sobs, "it was my baby..."

"She kiwwed it? What do you mean?"

"On Tuesday... she stole her momma's car and when she brought it back, she left a note that said it was over."

"What wath ovew?"

"My baby was over, Daniel. She didn't want me to have it. She was blinded with jealousy because John came back to me, so she killed it."

"How do you know that?"

"Daniel, don't be so blind. Mary is an angry, evil girl. What else could it mean?"

"Maybe thee lotht the baby thomehow...?"

"You're talking like a child. Her own daddy thinks so. Please don't argue with me. All I've done is cried for two days straight."

"I'm thowwy..." he replied, bewildered by the call. "If you need anything..."

"I need you, Daniel..."

In an instant Daniel's world stopped. Distant thoughts of Earl vanished. His own sonship to the creator blurred. And the tapestry of her flowing blonde hair curled around him, drawing him from the precipice of his faith.

"Me?" he asked, feeling shamefully carnal.

"Tomorrow evening...no, I mean tonight. It's Friday, right?"

"Today?"

"Yes, of course today," she snapped and then quickly quieted her tone. "Oh, I'm sorry. I'm just so tired. We're having a memorial service for the baby..."

"Memoriaw thervithe?"

"Yeah, John and me and Mr. and Mrs. Christmas. I wondered if you might give a little eulogy."

"Me?"

"You're a good man. God sent an angel to you. You're like a saint..."

"No.... You don't undewthtand. I'm not a thaint..." He wanted to explain to her the angel reprimanded him because of her, not because he was faithful.

"You're a good man, Daniel. Would you speak over my dead baby?"

Daniel fell mute. If he was a good man, he was lost to explain how. "I'ww thee..." he muttered, staring down at his feet.

"Please, Daniel," Faith pleaded.

Daniel moved the phone away from his ear and looked up. "Ith thith what you mean? Wiww thith make me youw thon?"

"Do you mind if Wevewend Gween comes?" He asked Faith.

"It's private, but he can come It's at Deacon Christmas's church at seven. This is the first time I've felt happy since Tuesday, Daniel. Her voice softened, "I don't think I'll ever be able to forgive her."

"You have to," he answered, rubbing his eyes, not thinking about his words.

"I don't know how."

"You'ww find a way..."

"I'm sorry I got you out of bed. I had to talk to you." She paused, then adding, "You really are a good man."

"Yeah," Daniel's voice not hiding the irony he felt in his heart.

He held the phone to his ear. From the other end he heard a faint sigh, then Faith's phone hung up. "Bye," he repeated, quietly placing the receiver in its cradle, feeling the ground beneath him crumbling away before he could take his faithful step over the edge.

* * *

Jamie ached in the cold, so as he stepped out of his car, he stretched and twisted, trying to wring the pain from his body. In the distance, he saw William pull a can of spray paint from his coat and shake it; then in one swift motion, William hit the can against the palm of his hand, popping off the lid in an arc high above his head.

"Hey!" Jamie yelled, taking off in a pained limp, as William began painting a large A on the tan brick wall of the school. Strangely, a couple of students walked past as William painted, but they moved on as the boy sprayed the letters R and M.

Weaving through cars, trying to reach the vandal, Jamie lost sight of William, so when he finally approached the wall, all that remained was the incomplete attempt. A drip of paint slowly oozed down the bricks while the spray can rolled across the asphalt, bumping into the building; the two students staring, unaware why he screamed at them.

"Didn't you see him?" Jamie panted, looking all about for William.

One shrugged, while the other grunted, "We didn't do that."

Jamie walked to the can, kicking it. "Dammit," he muttered, the spray can spinning across the pavement and rolling under a car.

Frustrated, he walked to the pit. He took a cigarette from inside his jacket and lit it, angrily puffing on it, pinched between his lips. Across the way he noticed Ned "the head," so he walked to him and sat down.

"Long time, no see," Ned said.

"Do you know a scrawny little punk named William?"

"Huh?"

"About this tall…" He held his hand about four feet from the ground.

"That runt's shorter than Fiona. You sure he goes here?"

"Yeah, I'm sure."

"Hell, I thought I knew everybody."

Jamie stood up. "Guess not..." he said, flicking his cigarette to the ground. "All week I've seen him, but before I catch him, he disappears. Like chasing a ghost...." He walked off, climbing the steps out of the pit and headed into the building.

A fresh coat of paint covered a group of lockers, but still the faint shadow of the word could be seen bleeding through.

At lunch, Jamie kept his vigil, studying the tables for the little vandal. As he picked at his food, across the lunch room he saw him rise from a table near the ugly statue already marred. Without a thought, Jamie darted up without his tray and headed towards the door, but before he took two steps, a lunch room monitor sent him back for it.

Quickly he grabbed his tray and disposed of it. Hurrying to leave, he looked in every direction but again saw no sign of William.

Frustrated, Jamie darted out the exit and there stood William, his back to the door as he wrote on a pipe railing to some steps.

"You!" Jamie stormed.

William turned, curling his nose at the sight of Jamie. "Ian's doing this for you."

"I'm not part of this," Jamie snapped, grabbing William by his coat.

"Let go of me, you, turd," William said, swinging his fist, trying to knock Jamie's hand away. "Armageddon's started, so just shut up. If you want to be some kind of hero...just try. You're too late. Screw you...you...you puke-face." His high whiny voice made the words more threatening by their absurdity.

Jamie's grip loosened, and in a blink, William was gone, his mocking laughter trailing behind.

* * *

Daniel did not hurry to the journalism room after school, as usual, instead he lumbered from the classroom to his locker. Feeling hollow, he poured his books into it, indifferent if he had homework, then gently closed the locker door. Stares from other students were less frequent now, although not entirely absent, so he blocked their derision from his mind. Far worse though was what waited at home.

As he drove, Daniel altered his route, pulling in to the Deacon's church, where the memorial service would be. He parked his car near the front entry and walked inside where an old man vacuumed the foyer, his movements slow and shaky.

"Howdy. Can I hep ya' wi' sump'in?" the old man asked turning off the vacuum, his voice soft and airy and weak.

Daniel silently shook his head, "I'm jutht going in thewe fow awhiwe..." pointing to the sanctuary. "I'm thuppothed to thpeak at a memowial thewvithe, tonight."
"Alrighty, didn't know sump'in was goin' on tonight," the old man coughed, "I'll be right out here if you need me." And he turned the vacuum back on.

Daniel watched the stooped old man, and for a second, Earl stood in the old man's place, dust mop in hand. Turning away, Daniel took a deep breath, and walked into the sanctuary. Daniel had never been in this church, but he felt at home; the relics of Protestant ritual filled the place.

The pulpit stood as a centerpiece before the congregation, an ornamental cross carved into its front. A communion table sat before the pulpit, and like the pulpit, adorned with carvings and a scripture: *God so loved the world that He gave His only begotten son*.

His eyes moved past those, past a candelabra loaded with candles, past several banners along the walls proclaiming different names of Jehovah to a glowing stained-glass image of Christ crucified, between burgundy curtains far behind the pulpit.

The sanctuary was dark, save the light shining through the stained glass, bringing it life. Across the sanctuary, Daniel extended his hand to the window, "Oh, dear Jethuth," he said aloud, taking a step towards the glowing picture. He walked up the steps to the platform, past the podium, squeezing himself between the chairs that filled the choir's risers to finally stand before the baptistery, recessed into the back wall below the stained-glass picture of the crucifixion.

Between choir chairs, leaning against the wooden ledge of the baptistery, Daniel stared into the stained-glass image. *It's beautiful*.

The artist had erased the ugliness of the crucifixion and had given the savior a regal face, perfect hair and beard all gleam and sheen, and light smooth skin without wrinkle or spot. But most striking was the Savior's almost feminine eyelashes, long and dark, curling up from his closed contemplative eyelids. The beauty of the action transposed upon the body of the actor.

Again Daniel stretched his hand to the window, as if Christ would pull himself from the cross to take it. In his longing to be closer, he climbed upon the wooden ledge of the baptistery. It shifted under his weight, unbalancing Daniel, but before he fell, he caught himself on the frame of the opening to the baptistery. Remaining motionless, he found his balance while his eyes glued to the spout that filled the pool. Then, his balance secure, the rippling water reflecting the dancing colors of the stain glass Savior, he carefully climbed down.

"Oh, God, take thith cup fwom me..." he whispered, searching the face of Jesus, confused and disturbed by the cross he himself carried. Daniel looked at the crown of thorns upon Jesus's head and the trickles of blood running down his forehead and felt a prickling pain across his own forehead. Then his eyes moved down to the wounded chest of the Savior where the soldier had pierced his side with a spear, and Daniel's own side began to ache, so he probed at the soreness. Then he studied the hands staked to the cross, opening and closing his own hands to stifle their throbbing, and like an ocean, he was swept away by the sacrifice made for him. The image, the essence of everything Daniel lived for. "All thith fow me..." His bloodless stigmata sent his heart reeling. "Teach me to be youw thon," he pleaded. "Tell me, what to do," he moaned, haunted by the looming interview. Daniel cupped and wetted his hand with the water in the baptistery, then gently dabbed his face as if it were anointing oil.

With a sudden sense of urgency, but without looking back to the stained-glass picture, Daniel left the sanctuary rubbing water from his eyes and drove home. The reverend's car was parked at the curb behind another car with a 'press' sign on the dashboard. He walked into his house and saw his parents and the pastor sitting, talking to the reporter. A tablet poised in her hand and a tape recorder on the coffee table. They all turned as he walked into the room. He quickly took off his coat and threw it and his book bag into a chair in the corner. Then sitting down on the couch beside the Reverend, he looked at the lady, "Letth get thtarted."

"Hello, Daniel, I'm Julie Barnes," the lady smiled, holding out her hand. Daniel shook it; she had a firm handshake. "Good to see you again. I remember you from Mr. Addison's class." Her eyes affixed to his white crest.

"Daniel," the reporter began and looked into the boy's eyes as she spoke. "Your pastor, your parents, even your teacher have told me you are reluctant to talk to me. Put away your worry. All I want is your story. I'm a reporter, not a judge. Okay?"

For a few seconds, Daniel remained motionless, his already-squinted eyes closed even more, and then he nodded slowly to her.

"Your mother said you were born with Down's syndrome. You don't look like it. Or act like it."

"I had thurgury. To make me wook mowe nowmaw."

"And you've really excelled for someone with your handicap."

"I'm not handicapped. God heawed me. Exthept fow my lithp..."

"And your hair," she added. "Or did you change that?"

"Of couthe not. It wath Eawl." Daniel immediately realized his slip, never intending to reveal that the angel was anything other than a run-of-the-mill angel.

"Earl?" Reverend Green asked.

"No, I thaid angew." Daniel interjected, trying to cover his mistake.

"So an angel, not Earl, changed the color of your hair..." She interjected.

"Thatth wight."

"Okay," Her smile was nice, Daniel thought, even pretty.

"Tell me everything that you can about that night."

Daniel shifted in his seat and looked down at the tape recorder, watching the spindles go round.

"It wath only a few weekth ago...but it theemth longer..." he looked up at the reporter, "ath if itth alwayth been thith way...." He had played over the events so many times in his mind that it seemed odd to put it into words, so he struggled on how to begin.

"Your pastor said that you were asleep..." Ms. Barnes prompted Daniel.

"Yeth, thatth wight...I was thleeping.... I don't wemember if it wath a voithe that woke me or something elthe. My woom wath bwue...like a bwue fog...and in the middle of evewything wath thith...thith thing...like a baww or thomething...and then it came."

"What did it look like?" she leaned forward, her elbows on her knees.

Vividly, Daniel could see Earl hovering above his bed, singing and peddling around the room.

"Like an angel...I gueth." he answered, picturing Earl's cap and coveralls.

"Did it have wings and a halo? I've never seen an angel."

Daniel closed his eyes and put his head in his hands. "Thith ithn't wight," he said softly to himself. *Be my son.* He looked back up.

"Hath God evew thpoken to you?" he asked the reporter, searching her face.

"I don't know..." She shrugged slightly.

"Do you evew pway?"

"On occasion."

Daniel leaned back in the couch. "You thee, God doethn't talk with thundew... mothtly he jutht talkth with a whithper. If you don't pay attenthion--you'll mith him. I wath mithing him… tho he found a way to get my attenthion."

"God sent an angel to get your attention?"

"Yeth, He wanted my attention...tho, he thent thomebody I knew." He gulped, never having alluded to this before.

"What are you talking about, Daniel?" The Reverend asked surprised.

"Daniel?" his mother began.

The reporter looked at the astonished faces in the room. "You knew the angel? Had it come before?"

"No, no, no..." Daniel shook his head, "I knew him when he wath alive."

There was sudden silence and then everyone asked at once who it was.

Daniel held his head down. "It wath thomeone I did not tweat wight—

Thomeone leth blethed than me."

"Well," the reporter said, "that would get someone's attention. Who was it?"

"I won't thay."

"Okay, he woke you up, and everything in your room was blue. Then what?"

"It thcared me. I feww out of my bed and bit my tongue." Daniel stuck out his oversized tongue, showing the faint pink outline across it.

"That must've hurt..."

"I wath tho thcawed, I didn't notithe. I twied to leave, but the door wath locked. And when I thaw him, he towd me I wath lothing my way—that God gave me thingth to do, and I wathn't doing them."

"What weren't you doing?"

"Thtuff...again, I won't thay."

"Are you doing the stuff now?"

"Ath I can."

"How does your hair fit into this?"

"Befowe the angew left, he thaid that Chwitht'th blood wathed me white ath thnow. He gwabbed the top of my head. I fewt a tingew all ovew and then he vanithed. Aftew that aww my haiw wath white."

The reporter looked to the others. "How did you react to all of this?"

Daniel's father looked over at his wife. "I'm still reacting. This is the first time I've heard some of this." Daniel leaned forward on his knees and looked down at his feet.

"You've got to understand, Miss Barnes," Daniel's mother said patting her hand on her husband's knee, "Daniel has never been one to make up stories...so as strange as the story sounded…we had to listen."

The pastor laughed, squeezing the boy's bicep, "Daniel has his ways of convincing us."

"So what are you doing, now, Daniel?"

"Whatever God wanth me to do. I jutht keep lithtening fow the whithper."

"You're quite a preacher."

His mother smiled proudly. "Tonight, he's going to be speaking at a service..."

"I'd like to see that," the reporter said.

Daniel looked over at his mother, "No, it'th pwivate..."

"It would be great for the story."

"I don't think it would be wight..."

Daniel's mother said, "Some acquaintances of ours lost a baby, so they asked Daniel to speak because he helped them find the Lord."

Daniel stood, "No, it'th pwivate." He shook his head. "Any mowe quethtionth?"

"Thank you so much for your time, Daniel, Mr. and Mrs. Davies... Pastor…. This has been interesting. I will be in touch."

"Very happy to," the reverend answered. "I'll walk out with you."

Daniel looked at the reporter, then at the pastor. "I've got to pway...." he muttered quietly, and he hurried up the stairs to his room where he fell to his knees waiting for the whisper.

* * *

Earnest's eyes fixed upon the cross hanging from Anne's neck, resting between her small breasts, the chain lost in the fuzziness of her white sweater, giving the cross an effervescence.

"Your pizza'll be right out." The waitress said, setting their drinks on the table.

"Thanks," Earnest smiled, looking at Anne as she sipped her water.

"Were you embarrassed that I asked you to the dance?"

"Naw," he shrugged.

"Well, I wasn't sure. You haven't said much to me since I asked you."

Earnest gulped his drink, worried he had already screwed up. "I'm sorry. I didn't mean anything.... I didn't want to be pushy."

Earnest's left leg shook nervously, bouncing on the ball of his foot.

"Why would I?" she shook her head. "I asked you."

Earnest remembered her sweet, strange little note about the pain in his heart, and immediately heard the thuds to Jamie's face, the kicks to Jamie's gut, and Jamie's pained grunts. Then he heard RaLF's absolving thank you. He looked away from Anne, running his hand down his left thigh, pressing on his knee to stop the bouncing.

"So," he looked up. "Did you see my cartoon? I think I put a crack in my cartoonist's block."

"No, I haven't. Did you show it to Daniel?"

"I put it on your desk."

"Don't tell me about it. I want to be surprised."

"It's not one of my best."

"You always say that," she laughed.

"Yeah, but I mean it this time."

Then taking another drink, Earnest was suddenly struck by how pretty Anne looked, gazing at her olive complexion and the slight fragility of her small hands, puzzling over why he hadn't noticed before.

"That note you gave me…" he said, watching a drip of condensation slide down the side of his glass. "It was kind." His voice quieted to an empty whisper, "but..."

"Excuse me?" Anne asked, not hearing what he had said.

He reached for a sugar packet and tapped it against the table, the cross again catching his eyes. "In your note..." he squirmed slightly, "when you said I had a hurting in my heart, what did you mean?"

She took another sip of her water, smiling, trying to catch Earnest's eyes. "Something deep down is bothering you."

Earnest noticed that she was moving her head oddly from side to side, so he looked at her face. When she returned his gaze, he had to look away.

"That's the first time you've looked me in the eyes all evening."

"I can't…" he answered, sitting up, staring at his glass.

"Why?"

"Because I'm afraid you'll know everything." His throat squeezed tight with his unexpected honesty.

He turned silent as the waitress put the pizza on the table between them, sliding to face her but looking past her to the traffic outside the window.

As the waitress walked away, Earnest lifted out a piece for Anne, feeling her intent stare as he placed it on the plate she held out to him.

"Thank you," she said and put the plate down, not diverting her eyes away from Earnest, and then asked softly but directly, "What is there for me to know?"

He placed a piece of pizza on his own plate, but before he could take a bite, his arms fell to his side. He looked at Anne, locking his eyes on hers, their color so deep and rich they resembled glistening dark brown drops of caramel on sparkling white glass.

"You wrote about my aching heart," he leaned forward, "but it's more than that. My guts are all twisted; and my stomach feels inside out.... You feel sorry for me even though you don't know why. But if you knew everything, you wouldn't like me." He laughed, staring at a light above an adjacent booth. "I'm amazed I could have a hurting heart because at times...I don't even think I have one." His eyes burned, as if he had just shattered the windows to his soul.

She slid from her side of the booth and moved next to Earnest, her hip touching his, her hand upon his forearm. "Earnest, I don't feel sorry for you. If there's something wrong and I can help, I will. I like you, really. You make me laugh. But feeling sorry for you never entered into anything."

"You know the guy who was in the car wreck with RaLF, Jamie Messereli...?"

"I know who you mean."

"A couple weeks ago, RaLF went up to some guys and told them that he was bothering her...so they took him out after school and beat the living shit right out of him."

Anne's hand moved down his arm to his wrist. His first instinct was to pull away—thinking he didn't deserve her affection, if that was what it was it—but her touch froze him.

"I was one of them. I didn't lay a hand on him, but I didn't just watch; I egged it on. And worse, I was pleased. When we got back, I went to my car, disgusted at myself. For a while, I honestly regretted it. But before I went home, I heard a tap on my window and rolled it down. RaLF was there, and she said thank you to me." Earnest took a drink of his Coke and sighed. "Anne, when she said that, every regret I had disappeared, and in a split second, I was proud, and my only regret was that I hadn't done more. But now, I just hate myself..." He looked down with a pained ironic grin, "My God, Anne, am I evil or what?"

"If you were evil…" she squeezed his arm as she spoke, "you wouldn't be telling me, now."

His leg began bouncing again. "Everyone blames him, like it's his fault Bill died. Forget Bill was drunk...." He glanced to see Anne studying him. "You know what's really funny? Those guys won't even talk to me now."

"Does it bother you?"

"It pisses me off. I feel like I sold my soul to them, and they threw it away."

"They value you, Earnest, as much as they valued Jamie Messereli. That's all."

Anne's words held Earnest in silence. He arrogantly had thought himself better than Jamie, and now, he shamefully realized he still felt that way.

"If you don't want to go to the dance, I understand. We can forget about this..." he shrugged his shoulders.

"Earnest, I'm disappointed, but I asked you to take me, and that is still what I want. Now if you don't mind…." She took a bite from the pizza on Earnest's plate.

He smiled back at her and fell into the depth of her eyes.

* * *

Jamie rolled off the couch, holding his place in the book he had been trying to read. He stretched to ease some of his aches, but they wouldn't leave him, clinging to him like a leach. He turned on the TV for the noise, hoping for a distraction to ward off Ian's evil spirits. But they flourished in his mind so that the drone of the flickering images never made an impression.

He sat down but bounced back up and walked to the kitchen and opened the refrigerator door. Without thinking he reached in and grabbed a beer, but before he opened it, he stopped himself and angrily tossed it back inside.

"All I want is a Coke," he huffed at the sparse refrigerator, slamming the door, the few things inside rattling. Sticking his hand in his pockets, all he had to pull out were his keys and lint. So he went to the bathroom and took an old tampon box from under the sink. His mother said no burglar would look there. And he pocketed some of her mad money.

Grabbing his coat, he left the house, the windows alit and the TV glowing. The frigid night air gnawed as Jamie climbed into his car, pulling up his collar and blowing into his hands. The first time the key turned, the engine growled with disapproval, but eventually surrendering, sputtered to life.

As he drove to the Quik-Trip, William's shrill voice taunted him. However, Jamie couldn't believe that Ian planned this Armageddon thing for him—altruistic retribution seemed an odd notion from Ian.

Jamie shoved a tape into the 8-track player, OX blurting out his heavy metal preaching. With a quick jerk, Jamie yanked out the tape and tossed it out of the window, the music reminding him of Ian. "I did my part," Jamie insisted, steam curling from his mouth.

"I warned RaLF." The windshield fogged over so he tried to wipe it clear, but his view only blurred.

Telling RaLF wasn't enough, his wrenching guts told him. *Just what the hell could Ian and William do, anyway?* Blurred by drunken clouds of memory, he remembered William's gun. "That's just more of Ian's BS," he laughed. But over his laughter came a nagging thought that doing nothing was what Ian had done to him. Ian had known those bastards had his number. And Ian did nothing.

"William, you scrawny piece of crap..." Jamie barked, quickly changing lanes, "show me Armageddon."

As the heater blew hot air into the car, beads of sweat sparkled his forehead, so by the time he pulled into the parking lot of the Hutchins Memorial Auditorium, sweat and uncertainty at what he could do drenched him. After parking the car he ran, huffing and puffing with every ache and pain in his body, hearing the heavy thumping pulsing through the walls.

People filled the foyer, so as Jamie tried to weave between them, they pushed him back, the music deafening all to any other sound.

Behind the ticket table, three pairs of doors opened to the dance. Jamie could see the whirling lights as a mirror ball rotated above the dancers, shooting rays of light across the room.

To Jamie's left, he noticed the first of the three pairs of entrance doors shutting. "Excuse me," he grunted, unable to get through.

"Get back, you jerk," someone yelled.

"Why is this door closed?" another voice faded into the music.

"I need by..." He cursed the obstacles around him, as the middle pair of doors closed. He looked at the third pair, and then fell into the ticket table shoved from behind.

"Watch it!" a girl selling tickets snapped.

"There's a couple of lunatics in there. One of 'em's named, Ian. He has a crooked face...with a scar…." he drew his finger over his nose and cheek. "Has he bought a ticket?"

"Like I know...."

"Here, I need to get in." he slapped his money on the table, glancing at the last pair of open doors.

"Are these supposed to be locked?" another voice asked in the chaos.

While the last pair began to shut, Jamie moved towards them.

"I need to stamp your hand!"

"Hold those doors..." Jamie yelled, close to the shutting doors.

"I can't get in," someone tugged at one of the other doors.

Just as the third pair had nearly closed, Jamie saw William's smiling face in the crack, waving.

"Open that door...!" Jamie screamed to the people nearest it, desperately pointing his finger at the door as it latched.

They looked at him with the same disdainful looks they always gave him.

"Get out of my way..." He fought through them, grabbing a hold of the door handle. Yanking it, the door barely gave, a chain rattling, holding the doors tight.

"Dammit!" Jamie pounded the door, screaming over the disco beats filling the building. "Ian, you son of a bitch, you bastard...open this..." He beat the door until his fists went numb with pain, so he began kicking it.

A chaperone yelled for him to stop, but he kept wailing at the door, hearing nothing over his screams and the music.

Arms wrapped around him, pulling at him. Quickly he began fighting the grip instead of the locked door.

"No, don't....!" Too much like the woods—and he began to kick and flail. More arms pulled him to the cold tiled floor, and he curled up, "Don't.... Please don't..." His yells turned to weak yelps.

He opened his eyes, and he saw the trees and the snow, and the fists coming down upon him, the feet barreling into him, heard the names, the taunts and the threats filling the air. He was there, and he lay quietly to take his beating.

"Jamie...." A different voice shattered the noise, rousing him with a harsh shake. Mrs. Irving stood in the middle of the woods with him. She shook him, and the woods began to fade into people. "Jamie," she said, "your nose is bleeding." She rolled him to his back, holding his head back while his eyes danced around the faces staring down at him.

Then the music behind the locked doors stopped with the sound of a needle scratching across the grooves of a record.

"Jamie, what do you know about this?" Mrs. Irving asked, giving a tissue to the fallen boy.

"It's not my fault..." he answered. Then he waited, fearing the next sound he might hear.

* * *

The spider hung from a single strand of silken web as Mary lay on the cot watching it swing like a pendulum above her, propping her head on her coat and book bag, eating the communion crackers she had taken from the church's kitchen. Since taking up residence in the Deacon's church's basement, her diet had mostly consisted of those crackers and a generic, white-label grape juice.

The unexpected creaking of the floor above distracted her. The heavy steps, she recognized as the Deacon, while the second set of steps, light but sharp as high heels coming down upon the wooden floor, was her mother.

Mary leaned up upon her elbows. "It's Friday..." she muttered to the creaking ceiling as particles of dust fell into her eyes from above. Irritated and tearing, she set up, batting her eyes to clear them.

Isn't it Friday? She covered her face from another avalanche of debris. "Dammit." She cursed through gritted teeth, patting dust from her dirty, matted hair. She stood from the cot, running her hand down her wrinkled and disarrayed clothes as if those few strokes would refresh them. Then yanking a string dangling beneath the light, she darkened the room, curling up in her cot and pulling her musty blanket over her head.

She closed her eyes hoping to sleep, but her mind wandered to her parents. Slowly she brought the blanket down from her face and peered into the darkness, playing her imagination like a movie. She watched her mother read the note she left in their car. The note too subtle, she handed the note to the Deacon. He read it aloud, at first not grasping it either, but as he reread it, revelation came and his face turned crimson.

"What does it mean?" her mother asked, confused.

Furious, nearly impudent towards his wife's naiveté, "Just what it says," he growled back, calling John and Faith to declare there would be no baby—just that quickly and coldly. Everyone but him cried. He on the other hand held his stoic pose, almost disdainful of the other's tears.

Mary rolled onto her back, shielding her eyes of more dust as the feet squeaking and shuffling above her grew in number, as her imaginings became as concrete as fact. Then the organ suddenly rumbled with a flourish of her mother's fancy finger work through the walls of the church. This unexpected intrusion rustled Mary from the cot, jumping to tug the string again and bathe the basement with dim light.

"Let uth pway," though distant and muffled, a familiar voice floated through as the organ's clamor died.

"Daniel," Mary said, catching her breath.

The heater kicked on and drowned out the boy's prayer.

The organ boomed again over the heater's rumbling—so loud Mary felt it. *I run and run, but I get nowhere....* She ran a hand through her mussed hair, catching a tangle with a finger. *And there's always Daniel to see me fall.* In the dim light of the basement, she moved through the maze of junk and headed to the door—the mystery of the angel boy's appearance too intriguing to ignore.

From the storage room, she made her way through the kitchen, past a dining area. Just within her periphery a mouse darted, causing her to jump. "Damn rats!" she snapped, so she hurried up the stairs into the church.

The small congregation joining the organ in a hymn sounded weak and subdued as she drew closer. "That's what happens when you have church on Fridays," she mused. Then the song ended, and the organ's rumbling faded to Daniel's reflections.

"I'm at a loth how to begin, ow what I thould thay. Loothing thomeone you know and love ith awfuw. But to loothe thomeone you love but nevew met..."

Daniel's words drifted to Mary, faint but decipherable. She stepped from the stairwell and into a hallway, running along the sanctuary. Across from her was a door, so she peeked into the sanctuary through the diamond shaped window at the top. Daniel stood towards the front of the platform at the mammoth ornate wooden pulpit, gauche in the mean surroundings. Candles burned in candelabras at his sides.

Her parents sat in the front pews with John and Faith Smith. Faith was red faced, eyes swollen with a tissue at her nose. John held anguish in his eyes, his face contorted like a sad clown. The Deacon looked just as she had imagined he did reading her note, staunch and controlled with never a wisp of emotion. It made her smile. Lastly, in the back of the sanctuary, sat a man she did not know.

As she continued to look around, she noticed something peculiar setting on the large communion table in front of the pulpit where Daniel stood. It was some kind of a picture, an odd, unrecognizable black and white blur placed in a fancy golden frame, a large spray of flowers spread out before it. She stared at the image, drawn to the bizarre thing, squinting and straining to decipher what she saw.

Then it struck her. *Loothe thomeone you love but never met....* The framed picture was her ultrasound.

Mary stepped backwards away from the door. *This is crazy.*

"Excuse me," a lady said walking up to Mary, "Is Daniel Davies speaking here?"

"What?" Mary asked, looking up, surprised to see anyone.

"I'm doing a story for the Ponca City News about Daniel." She spoke softly. "Do you know him? He says that he saw an angel."

Mary looked up at the lady, "I know he did."

"You know he saw an angel?"

"No, I know he said it." She answered, looking back through the window.

"In thpite of ouw mithewy, we mutht wemembew that God can uthe anything fow hith good and fow ouw good." Daniel's words rained down upon Mary like hail.

"What about my good?" Mary asked looking at him. "What about my stinking good..." she repeated louder. Then she turned to the reporter. "He's in there."

The reporter nodded, "I recognize his voice."

"Let uth wejoithe. Ouw loth ith Heaven'th gain."

"It's my gain, you dumbass," Mary remarked.

"Do you know what this is about?" The reporter asked, peaking around Mary.

"Uh huh," Mary nodded her head.

"And you've got to fowgive Mawy..."

"Did he say Mary? Who's Mary?"

Mary turned toward the reporter. "I am."

"...not jutht with youw mouth, but in youw heawt. And you've got to pway fow hew like you've nevew pwayed befowe."

With no thought of consequence, with no thought at all, Mary pushed open the door, hissing, her teeth clenched and a finger aimed at Daniel, "Don't you dare pray for me, Daniel. Don't you dare!"

Startled, Faith let out a wail, so John's arms shot around her. Mary's mother hurried toward her, while the Deacon held his place.

"I don't need your prayers..." Mary snarled at Daniel. "I don't want your prayers." Mary turned and looked at the others in the sanctuary. "Leave me and my godless soul alone." Her eyes fell upon her mother's; never had she read this much pain in the woman's eyes. It baffled her, so she turned to Daniel again.

"What are you doing here?" John bawled. "You…you shouldn't be here!"

Standing mute, Daniel's Bible slipped from his hands and fell to the table in front of the pulpit, knocking the framed ultrasound picture to the floor. The impact distracted Daniel, his eyes darting from Mary, to the frame, to Reverend Green in the back, and then to the reporter unexpectedly scribbling onto her tablet behind Mary.

"No," Daniel insisted. *She's not supposed to be here*. The reporter seemed oblivious to his shout.

Faith yelped. The anguish she wore like a mask turned to horror as the picture crashed to the floor. She moved to reach it. "My baby...!" she moaned and jerked away as John pulled at her shoulders.

"You wanna' know why I'm here?" A smirk crossed Mary's face. "For the goddamned irony of it."

"Mary," her mother said, her voice sinking in disappointment.

"Don't take the Lord's name in vain in my church." The Deacon corrected, oddly calm.

"Do you have any idea how stupid all this is?" Mary threw her hands up in disbelief. "A funeral for a fetus...?"

"You…!" John shook, reason seeping from him. So he sat to calm himself, burying his face in his hands, mouthing a silent prayer.

"I'm a what?" Mary taunted John, recognizing the same mad look he had the night he had attacked her, the night she had met Lita. "Am I the devil?" Then moving towards Daniel, she asked, smiling, "What do you say I am?" Her hands wriggled at the sides of her head like horns.

"You'we my thown." he said to her, her eyes searing his soul—

his whole body ablaze, his voice pointed, his hands trembling, seeing before him in the rumpled disheveled girl, the handiwork of God—the very reason the angel came.

"You are the devil..." Faith cried, forgetting all calls for forgiveness. "Haven't you done enough to ruin my life?"

"As if screwing John was the best decision of my life..."
John stood back up, his nostrils flaring. With one fist clenched, he pointed to his wife and said "Stop it!" Then he looked at Mary, "That's enough!"

"It's over. Right, Mary? Isn't that what your note said? …You killed my baby, right Mary?" Faith taunted Mary, her voice straining. Then she walked to her, shoving her hand into Mary's soft stomach. Even though Faith had expected this, even though Faith's head told her that it was true, Faith's heart had not accepted it. The softness she felt brought reality to her like an avalanche. Her jaw quaked with her breaking heart, "You killed it!"

"I didn't kill anything!" Mary insisted, pushing Faith's hand away.

Daniel watched from the pulpit thinking this was the kind of tension Mary must love. Then again he saw the reporter watching and writing as the craziness unfolded.

"Why, Mary? Why'd you do it?" John walked toward her, drooping in sadness.

"Because it was your baby…" The words came without hesitation.

Instantly John's hand clinched to a fist as he marched toward Mary. So focused, he did not realize he stepped upon the damaged picture of the ultrasound, the sound of shattering glass shrieking throughout the sanctuary.

As Faith saw John's foot descend upon the picture, she answered the glass's shriek with her own cry, breaking free of her frozen pose with a swift sprint and falling upon the picture, the shards of the frame's broken glass stabbing through her blouse. John never noticed Faith, pulling back to hit Mary, his action bathed in such rage no thought precipitated. And nearly as quickly, Daniel grabbed John's wrist.

"No...."

John held his stance and glared at Mary.

Mary held her place, never taking her eyes from John. "Go ahead," she said, not taunting or a teasing, but because she thought it inevitable. "Go ahead.... You've hit me before."

His hand numb and his heart hollow, if not for Daniel's tight grip on his wrist, John would have fallen to the floor in a heap. "I'm… shit..." he muttered, heaving, remembering the night he had pushed her. *Why?* He could not recall. And then, crashing on him with the weight of a lifetime of sin, it came to him; he had been angry because she would not have sex. *Oh, God, forgive me…*he ached.

Then her mother walked to Mary. "Did you know that Mrs. Gardner died Tuesday? As you drove away to do God knows what, she passed away in front of me. She never even knew I was there. She used every ounce of strength she had to breathe. Her life left her in a slow exhale, everything that she had ever known, gone." She grabbed Mary's face in her hand. "Don't you understand how precious life is...?"

Mary jerked her chin out of her mother's hand. "I'm not going to be a surrogate for them. Let them work out their own penance."

Faith pulled herself from the broken picture and turned to Mary, "Just because you hate me, you didn't have to kill the baby!"

"Hate you? I don't even know you… Don't be so vain." Mary shot back, shaking her head at the cries of blame. Then she noticed the Deacon, still quiet. "Well, Daddy, are ya' gonna' take your shot?"

The Deacon shifted in the pew, leaning forward on his elbows. "Is the only thing you want from me, ridicule? What would it matter to you, anyway, Mary? Anything I said would be a waste of time. You disregard me. You disregard anything that anyone says."

Then the church grew silent. John wiped his eyes and walked to Mary. "This is my fault. The damage that I've done to you…. Forgive m…"

"No!" Faith bellowed. "It is all her fault!"

"Faith, that's enough." John snapped back.

"I don't care if she burns in hell! She's a murderer! She needs to ask us for forgiveness!" Her face glistened in sadness and tears, her words lost in whimpers.

Mary's mother walked to Faith, putting her hand on her shoulder. "Don't say that. You don't mean it." She reached out to help Faith from the floor. But Faith determined to hold the ultrasound to her chest, broken glass and all. She looked at Mrs. Christmas, "Your daughter killed my baby." Then looking back down at the picture, small smears of blood from her chest staining the image, her tears became rolling sobs.

"Murderer..." Faith whispered.

Mary glared, confused by Faith, said, "It's not my fault you don't have kids."

Those words were the seeds of madness. Faith charged at Mary, bellowing her hurtful cry.

"Get away from me!" Mary screamed over Faith's incoherent

bellowing and darted towards Daniel to escape the charging woman. But she did not move fast enough to avoid Faith, twisting and stretching to grab a hold of Mary. Like dominoes, they crashed to the floor, Mary's momentum sending her into Daniel, and Daniel falling to the floor with a thud, unbalancing one of the candelabras filled with burning candles beside the pulpit.

Slowly, the candelabra tottered until gravity tripped it, and it fell into a banner that read 'Jehovah-Shalom" leaning against the wall.

"Murderer...!" Faith screamed again at the girl as she pulled Mary closer to her.

Scurrying to his feet, Daniel's eyes darted around the room. He turned to watch a flame quickly consume one of the Jehovah-titled banners and move to another.

Mary clawed at the floor like a cat, but she could only slip and slide across it, unable to get a hold, as Faith's grip held tightly.

The Deacon stood panicked, not seeing Mary and Faith, distracted by the growing wall of fire. "My church," he croaked as the flames climbed up the wooden wall.

Daniel lunged at Faith, grabbing her arm. "Let hew go," Daniel grunted as ash and smoke from the burning banners floated about them.

"Let go of me, freak!" She barked.

Daniel grimaced at the words, squeezing harder. Faith, eyes mad in the thickening smoke-filled air, swung her fist, catching Daniel under his left eye, sending him backwards onto the candelabra. The base stabbed his back, hurting him—but not as badly as her words.

Flames danced among the banners, scorching the walls and catching the carpet and choir chairs lining the wall. Reverend

Green jumped to the platform shooting at the flames with a fire extinguisher. Smoke and steam bellowed, filling the sanctuary with a loud angry hiss. Unexpectedly, the spray shrank to a dribble, leaving the pastor impotent to the flames. "Dammit," he said, throwing the worthless extinguisher to the floor. Smoke filled the sanctuary. Faith tugged Mary on one side; John pulled at her from the other, and feeling his hands on her shoulder made her fight more vehemently. But pulling away from him pushed her nearer Faith's clawing.

"I'm trying to help…" John shouted to no avail as smoke swirled around his face, blackening his features.

"I'm a murderer," she coughed, reeling with the familiarity of his down cast glance upon her. "So what?"

A pair of hands came around her neck from behind. "My baby..." Faith screeched, her voice hoarse and raw from the smoke, pulling Mary back to the floor.

Mary gagged and choked, her face glowing red, her gnawed, blunted fingertips digging under Faith's fingers.

Reverend Green stepped over the empty extinguisher to Mary's mother and the Deacon, frozen as the flames engulfed the sanctuary. "Go!" the pastor ordered through the bellowing smoke. The Deacon remained motionless, so Pastor Green grabbed the man and shook him, "Deacon, get your wife out of here!" pushing them towards the door.

"Mary?!" Mrs. Christmas pleaded.

"I'll get her! You get out!"

The pain in Daniel's back and face took his breath, already strained in the thickening smoke, but he pulled himself up, finding himself in the center of the fire and the raining ash. Through the smoke, he saw the blurry silhouette of Mary and Faith and John in their strange ballet. But then a loud pop echoed over the flames, over the cries of the others, over the throbbing of his pain. He looked and saw the stained glass crucifixion surrounded in flames, a crack now webbing through the savior's face, disfiguring him.

"I am youw thon," he shouted, the sounds around him a muffled rumble.

Another pop sounded and Daniel watched another crack shooting from the stained glass nail piercing the savior's hand.

"Daniel, time to leave!" the Reverend Green yelled behind him.

The cracks in the savior's face held Daniel, speaking of his place among the children of God, reminding him of his thorn, and Daniel knew he couldn't leave.

"You go! I'm in Hith handth!" Daniel yelled back, pushing him away. And there Daniel stood amidst the flames, looking to the pained, bowed head of Christ. "You thee!" he coughed loudly at the picture. "I am youw thon...!"

Smoke and sweat burned his eyes, but through the pain, he saw his thorn fall between John and Faith behind the thick veil of swirling smoke. And then he saw the final banner, engulfed in flames, fall from its place and like a blanket wrap around the trio upon the floor.

"You're gonna' freakin' kill us!" Mary shrieked in a mad frenzy as the flame's heat and ash burned at her face, kicking and pushing, sensing that Faith really did mean for her to burn, whether it was in hell or not.

Daniel watched the banner fall, seeing the object of his prayers encased in fire. A thrust from his heart sent his bulbous body charging through the bellowing smoke and flames engulfing the walls. When he reached them, both hands shot into the flames, grasping the burning banner of Jehovah, yanking it from around them. And when he saw the ball of fire he held in his hand, he took off for the baptistery.

Daniel huffed and groaned in pain with each clomp of his feet, the burning of his hands spurring on his pace to the holy water. Charging up the platform, he looked to his stained-glass savior, holding out his hands, the fiery ball an offering. The fire seared his hands as he pushed through the first row of chairs. A folding chair in the next row shifted under Daniel's heavy weight, and stepping upon the wooden ledge, it broke beneath him.

For an eternity, Daniel fell, the baptistery's faucet spout filling his vision. The banner's flames hissing as it hit the water. Closer and closer the spout drew to him until crashing into his skull with a hard sharp thud.

"Let her go!" Reverend Green yelled at Faith, drowned by the roar of the fire as he painfully lumbered towards the three, his eyes burning. "Stop!" He pulled on Mary, breaking both John and Faith's hold.

Now free of Mary, John reached for Faith who acquiesced to the smoke and the flames and him. "Why?" She bawled, streams of wet soot smearing her face. "Why did you kill my baby?"

"I didn't kill anyone," Mary sputtered as the Reverend Green pulled her away. "I was saving myself…." Then, she snapped at him, "I don't nee ..."

"I don't need your crap," he coughed and grabbed Mary's collar, shoving her away from John and Faith towards the doorway, the girl fighting every push.

Crashing through the doors, the frigid February air slapped the reverend. He began quivering immediately.

Mary broke away in his distraction, "Why can't you fucking Christians leave me alone!" she screamed, stumbling down the steps, sirens blaring in the distance.

"Oh, Mary!" her mother ran to the girl, reaching to hold her. "Are you all right?"

"Don't touch me." Mary growled, pushing her away with her glare.

"Oh, baby," her mother implored then suddenly asking, "Where's your father?" She looked at Reverend Green, panic stricken, "Where's the Deacon?"

Panting, the pastor turned toward the church, flames dancing behind the stained glass of the brick building, the glass blackening from the smoke inside. The Deacon stood before it, his arms upraised as John pushed Faith out the front doors.

"Burn!" Mary screamed at the building. "Burn, damn you..." she yelled angrily and fell to the ground in a silent, quivering heap. Her throat knotted. She fought against it, but a tear fell from her eye. She began to sob, overwhelmed by her complete sense of disintegration. Her arm reached out, but in her empty grasp, her eyes opened and she saw that she was alone. So in her sobbing, she wrapped her arms around herself.

The flashing lights and blaring sirens of fire trucks brought even more people from their homes, and the church was soon surrounded.

Every muscle in his body taut, the Reverend Green huffed and growled. He looked at the church and back at Mary and then scanned the strangers in the lawn. "Stupid...stupid..." he kept repeating in his anger, pacing, desperately wanting to hit something.

"Pastor," the reporter said, moving towards him, "this was different..."

"This was a joke..." he answered angrily, then realizing who she was he asked, "What are you doing here?"

"Where's Daniel? I'd love to hear what he thinks about this."

Looking around, he realized he had overlooked him; remembering the boy pulling the flaming banner from Mary.

"Oh sweet Jesus..." he muttered, charging the church's doors.

* * *

Mawy, I'm sowwy... so sowwy... Although his head pounded, he was mostly unconscious, swirling in a familiar translucent blue. *Mawy… wath a ..wath a wittle wamb....* In spite of the water lapping at his ears he heard Earl's hushed distant 'doo dahs'. *Eawl?* They drew closer, blending with the screeching of his burning lungs, starved for air. Listening closely for the angel's return, he heard popping, as if his neurons were bursting like kernels of corn. The blue began to darken. *Eaw…?* He could not remember, and the name devolved into an utterance of sound bearing no more meaning than a grunt. *Eeeeeaaawwlll,* he grunted as pretty lights flashed and popped in his mind. *Pwi lites....pwi lites...,* his thoughts swam.

Chapter Twenty

Armageddon

Ian drove around the Hutchins Memorial Auditorium, puffing on a cigarette, his forehead wrinkled. William brooded in the passenger's seat, imagining the things going through Ian's head as OX spewed final judgment from the speakers.

William turned down the music. "Whose blood's gonna flow, exactly?" He chewed on his bottom lip.

Ian flicked the cigarette out his window, looking poised and posed, as if some character other than himself. He felt the bitch's growls turning to a purr, appeased. "I dunno, maybe yours... maybe mine.... definitely theirs." He laughed, "Getting scared?"

"Naw," William shook his head, taking out a pocketknife and opening it. He turned out one of his coat pockets and ripped out the hem. Then he filled the lining of his coat with several lengths of small chain link piled on the floorboard.

After loading his coat, William reached for a padlock from the floorboard, unwrapped and unlocked it and began filling the other side of his coat. As William reached for the second lock, Ian parked the car behind the auditorium along a wall of pine trees, their scent wafting through the window. Coughing, Ian stepped out of the car and lit another cigarette—still outside himself, looking down and watching his own actions being carried out. He leaned against his car, and closing his eyes, in a flash the evening unfolded before him: colored lights flashing, bats swinging, guns firing. He rubbed his eyes, and with the car door slamming, Ian was pulled back to watch William come around, his coat bulging from the hardware he carried. Taking the cigarette from his mouth, Ian began whistling, moving the front seat forward. First, he took the stolen bat and put it inside the lining of his trench coat. Next he pulled the shotgun from the back and loaded it with four shells from his coat pocket.

"What are ya' gonna do with that?" William asked.

"Make some noise..." Ian chuckled, putting the shotgun inside the lining opposite the bat, positioning them to be as unobtrusive and inconspicuous as possible. Now unable to lean back into the car he looked to William, "Hand me the bottle in the back."

William gave him the bottle. "Does it bother you that sissy-boy's not gonna' help? Makes me madder'n who-dunnit..."

Ian took a gulp and heaved a sigh from the warmth in his gut. "To hell with him." Ian's voice cracked so he cleared his throat. "Look at me; look at my face. I'm a freak because of RaLF...."

"Aww, it ain't that bad," William muttered.

Ian took another drink, not listening to William.

"Hell, I never needed Jamie. I never needed anyone.... I was trying to find an excuse when I had one all the freakin' time."

William listened, kicking a rock from the drive into the dead grass.

Ian took another drink, "This is great!" he shouted. His muse pleased; the bitch's howls of delight in his ear. His heart pounding, he walked toward a trailer parked at the loading dock of the auditorium with the name airbrushed onto the side in colorful balloon letters: "Doc Rock's Mobile Music Machine."

"Let's go raise some hell!" He yelled not looking back, putting the vodka in a side pocket, pulling down a flap to cover it.

William readjusted the collar of his coat as the weight of what he carried pulled it down, rubbing his neck. He hurried to follow Ian, but it was difficult to do so and not rattle. He finally fell in step behind Ian as they entered a dimly lit back hallway through a back door that had been left unlocked.

Ian turned to William and smiled. "See, it is meant to be."

The music reverberated throughout the building; the beating of the drums amplified what he felt in his chest. Ian went to a set of doors that went into the auditorium, but they were locked as were all the other doors at the back of the auditorium. A door suddenly opened, and a couple of sophomore girls hurried through, one crying.

Although impeded by their loads both Ian and William rushed to enter the dance and closed the door behind them, walking in behind Doc Rock's sound booth, the music a thunder of repetitive beats. A kaleidoscope of colored lights illuminated the darkness as the mirror ball shot beams of light across the floor and about the auditorium seats rising from the floor nearly to the ceiling.

The assault on Ian's senses increased his inebriation so he closed his eyes. The howling in his soul told him that the bitch was pleased. His breathing deepened into a heavy pant. He glanced over, seeing William pulling out the chain.

"Not now. Let's look around." He smiled his crooked smile, his face twisting until almost a snarl, so William refilled his pockets, and followed Ian among the sea of bobbing bodies.

As William wove through the maze of dancers and watched Ian hover about in his euphoric daze, sweat ran down his face. Wearing his coat, he found the air thick and stuffy at belly level and glancing about he saw very little but bellies at his height. But then he saw above the heads of the dancers, sitting on scaffolding above the doorway they had sneaked through, the papier-mâché' statue of the Pioneer Woman watching over the dance. Straining within the flashing lights and darkness, he saw the faint remnants of his writing across the base.

"Ian," William said, scurrying behind, grabbing a hold of the army trench coat.

With an abrupt jerk, Ian turned and yanked his coat from William's grip.

"The statue..." William said meekly apologetic, pointing to it.

"So?" Ian snapped back and returned to searching for the group that had jumped Jamie. It never occurred to Ian not to look for them since Jamie's desertion. They were more than just bullies. They were the beautiful people, mutilating anyone who did not conform. His heart raged as he began to find each among the dancing hordes.

He grew anxious thinking about the final three names, so his eyes began darting around more desperately, hunting the faces of Earnest, Marc, and most importantly RaLF. Nothing was possible, without her nothing was necessary.

"Have you seen RaLF?" he growled at William who only shook his head, wondering how Ian expected him to see anything. Frantically Ian turned back and in one final sweep he saw all three: RaLF and Marc, dancing in the periphery of the crowd and the multi-colored lights, and Earnest, walking into the auditorium with a girl. Ian was pleased, languishing the notion of Earnest's humiliation in front of her.

"Go," Ian ordered, turning back again to William, "chain the doors." And the bitch howled again.

On Ian's word, William took off, the chains rattling hardly muffled by the lining of his coat. So small and anonymous, William wove through the dancers to the rear doors. He quietly wrapped a length of chain through the handles of the paired doors and put a lock through the links, so the doors couldn't be pulled from the other side.

Once he finished both sets of doors, he hurried to the front thinking he did not have a lot of time before some dummy would be pounding on the door, so he raced through the crowd while they motioned the letters of YMCA.

There were three pairs of doors at the front, so leaning against a wall, he pulled out three lengths of chain and hung them around his neck. Anonymity was his blessing, so in silence he closed the first set of doors, locked them with some chain.

With the second pair of doors he began to feel anxious. He wiped his forehead with his sleeve, almost breathless, seeing the crowd outside. He thought he saw Jamie in the foyer too, but he kept moving, and as the doors closed, he took the second chain from his neck and quickly secured the second pair of doors. The chain on the first pair of doors began to shake from someone pulling on it.

Taking the last piece of chain from around his neck, William moved to the last pair of doors. The music segued to a Bee Gee's song that William kind of liked, but he wouldn't admit it to Ian. Ian's rantings about disco, "songs about dancing to songs about dancing," were ugly enough that William didn't want the ridiculing. *As if that OX Armageddon crap Ian listened to was music.*

His hands clenched to a fist with the chain wrapped around it, gripping so tightly that the chain made link shaped impressions in his hand. When he reached the door, the light streaming in from the foyer hurt his eyes, so he blinked and looked around.

Everywhere people were talking, absorbed in their own worlds, so stepping into the light, he let the chain unravel from his grip. While the chain dangled, he pushed up the door jam from one door and slowly closed it and quickly went to do the same to the other door. Just before it closed, he saw Jamie, who looked back so surprised that William laughed, waving to him as the doors latched. Quickly, he threaded the chain through the handles and closed the lock through the links. The door jerked, but the chain held. William smiled, hearing Jamie scream at the door, pounding on it like a madman. As people turned, hearing the yelling and pounding from the other side, they also noticed the chains as William faded into the crowd and onto Armageddon.

* * *

After sending William to lock the doors, Ian walked back towards Doc Rock's booth and took a seat. In the darkness, behind flashing colored lights, he drank from his bottle, laughing at Mr. Small somewhere in the crowd, hoping that the old man had seen him because he was ready for him, now. Ian scanned the crowd, still waiting on William, so he pulled the bat out from inside his coat and patted it against the palm of his hand. Closing his eyes, he leaned his head back and stroked the bat. When he tried to imagine what he was about to do, he drew a blank. The bareness of his imagination though made it easier for the bitch to push him forward and fill his thoughts.

When the Bee Gees started singing, he shouted, "Turn that crap off!" Gripping the bat tightly in one hand, he gulped more vodka from the bottle in the other, his head falling back against the seat. His growing intoxication brought strength to his swimming mind. With eyes shut, the music floated unimpeded into his ears. The falsetto of the Brothers Gibb obscured the words in Ian's mind, only deciphering the word 'tragedy,' which brought a chuckle. Then with a nudge, Ian's eyes popped open.

"We're locked in," William said, clicking a lock onto a length of chain.

Ian rose from his seat. "Let Armageddon begin…" Holding the bat to his side, he walked behind Doc Rock, and took a stance. The bat streaked through the air, crashing down upon the DJ's head, sending him to the floor in a heap. Across the soundboard a girl stared at Ian in disbelief. He smiled back reaching for the turntable.

The flashing lights turned solid, illuminating the entire auditorium, as Ian dragged the needle across the record's grooves, bringing the auditorium to silence.

"Hi," Ian leaned into the microphone, the lights blinking in synch with his words. "I need your attention, please." His voice sounded subdued. In the reflected rays of light of the mirror ball, crowds of dancers gathered, struck dumb at the abrupt stop of the music. Realizing that he didn't yet have their attention, Ian pulled the shotgun from his coat, cocked it, pointed it into the air and pulled the trigger. The barrel flashed in the dark room and with the loud blast, every light sparked in a blinding flash.

Pieces of papier-mâché', chicken wire and ceiling tile showered Ian as the room filled with screams and panic. Shaking debris from his hair, he saw the Pioneer Woman's son's arm had been rendered a stub. He leaned back into the microphone, "You might as well quit trying to leave. You're all mine, so give me your attention!"

"What the hell…?" Mr. Small moved with his vice-principal towards Ian, rays of light floating over them. The stare of a shotgun barrel stopped Mr. Small where he walked, so he motioned his assistant to back away.

Then looking past the gun, into Ian's crooked smile, he insisted, "Nobody has to get hurt."

Ian sneered, "Nobody has to die, but somebody has to get hurt…"

"I'll be damned if you're gonna' touch one person here..."

Ian cocked the gun again; a shell fell to the floor, and pointed it at Mr. Small. "Damned is right, asshole. I brought hell to you." Ian smiled. "You wanna' know about Armageddon...? This is it, you fat fucker!"

The shotgun fired. Mr. Small fell to the floor, grabbing what was left of his foot, shredded by buckshot, blood pooling around him. Some students screamed. Ian rubbed his forehead, the vodka's throbbing made more piercing from the students' cries of panic and Mr. Small's cries of pain.

"Small... no one can stop this... not even me… even if I wanted to...."

Ian heard the bitch howl in delight.

The vice principal ran to Mr. Small.

"Get back!" Ian pointed the gun at him.

As he stopped, the vice principal felt a prod through his pants, looking over his shoulder, seeing a kid poking a pistol into his butt.

"He's hurt."

"He's just the first." Ian conceded.

William's big grin erased his solemnity. "You heard him...you mother effer," he squealed. This was the best day of his life, the day he became visible. "On the floor, or I'll shoot your bunghole."

The vice-principal moved to the floor, glaring at William. Taking out several feet of chain, William wrapped it around the vice-principal's feet and hands and locked it, leaving him fettered like a piece of livestock. "Ian," the vice-principal yelled, "You're getting yourself in a lot of trouble over one suspension."

"You asswipe, you think this is about me being suspended?" Ian barked into the microphone. "This is Armageddon!"

The vice-principal rolled onto his side. "Let the kids and Mr. Small out. He's hurt. I'll stay."

Ian laughed. "Poor slob, No one's going anywhere. William, shut him up!"

William looked down, walking around him. Then he slid off the vice-principal's shoes and socks and crouched down before him. "Put a sock in it," he snickered, stuffing the man's socks in his mouth, laughing.

"Anyone else a hero?" Ian spoke as he climbed on the sound booth, clutching the shotgun in one hand and the bat and the microphone in the other. "Nobody else has to get hurt. Well, nobody but the people on my list..." He looked over the crowd, the mirror ball still turning and reflecting light across the captives. "Somebody turn on the damn lights."

A flurry of kids moved to a wall where several switches had been blocked off. With the room illuminated, he could see the fear more easily. His eyes swept over the crowd, and he felt so strong. "Everyone!" He shouted, "On your bellies!" Quickly everyone in the auditorium obeyed but a scattering of boys and teachers. He shook his head, feigning disappointment, and sat the bat and microphone down. Then putting the shotgun to his shoulder, he fired, splintering the auditorium's floor near Mr. Small's head. The principal howled from pain, splinters and stray buckshot striking him. The bitch howled in ecstasy.

"Listen, assholes! No heroes. Just do as I say, and Armageddon will pass. Leo over here is bleeding pretty badly and if we don't get this over with…it's on you. I really don't want to shoot him again. On your bellies!" And the few stragglers dropped.

"Thank you. Now let's get started. Marc Neuhaus, come on down. You're the next contestant for The Price is Your Head!" He bellowed, but looking around, he saw no one moving towards him. Ian held the microphone and scowled, insisting, "Marc, you've caused enough pain around here. Have the balls to face your own. Bring RaLF. I've gotta surprise for her, too." He looked over to William and winked, "Having fun?" Ian loaded two more shells into the shotgun.

The small boy stood to the side, swinging his bit of chain, his rusted gun tucked into his pants. He smiled at Ian then looked back at the crowd, so frightened by the notion of death they submitted like children, so frightened his gun didn't have to work.

Slowly, Marc rose from the floor, standing next to RaLF who remained prostrate, frozen yet quaking in her place, Jamie's warning mocking her. She had disregarded him and now found herself staring down the devil. Her whole body shook, looking at Ian's crooked grin. *Is this about me hitting him? Doesn't he see he had it coming?* Uncertain if she should be afraid, if Ian would actually use the gun on her; she wasn't even sure this was real.

"We haven't got all night, RaLF. Get'cher ass up! I got places to go… people to hurt, you know, like you hurt Jamie."

Her eyes narrowed. *This is about Jamie?*

"He killed Bill!" she shouted, rising to her knees.

Marc grabbed her shoulder whispering, "Shhh, don't piss him off."

Instinctively, RaLF pulled away, self-conscious of her stubbed arm being touched. "He's crazy!" She exploded, looking to those around spread out upon the floor. "Ian's crazy!" She pleaded, but the frightened faces looking back unsettled her, and she realized no one would be helping her here.

The shotgun exploded, bringing more debris to the floor. Ian, standing on the sound booth, hissed at RaLF through gritted teeth, "I'm a freaking lunatic! Get your asses up here! Lonnie Crothers, Thad Bishop, Cooter Olivetti, you, too!"

Marc turned to RaLF, "Stay here." And he moved toward Ian. Anger burned his face. Soon, the other boys stood near Marc, worry covering each of them.

Ian admired his catch, smiling. Then he looked to RaLF, holding her distance, and shook his head. "You can't hide. You're part of this."

Suddenly thrust forward, she stumbled. RaLF turned, and William stood behind her. "Move!" His face wrinkled in an odd scowl. If RaLF hadn't been so frightened, she would have laughed at him. But his bizarre appearance made her more anxious, so she reluctantly moved forward to stand before her judge.

"Such beautiful people…" Ian's head shook, his voice lilting, an insincere smile upon his face. The gun slung over his shoulder, the bat hanging from the hand with the microphone, his expression grew ugly and angry. "All you losers," he screamed at the crowd, "you see these assholes? You know who they are? They're the reason you're miserable." Venom spewed from his voice. "They're the sons a'bitches picked first to play their stupid games on the playground when you were little…and they're the people who did the picking!" Suddenly, he wanted a drink, but he didn't dare put down the gun. "They're the beautiful people who call you names and insult you because you don't look right or you don't dress right…." Scattered around the room, small bursts of hand claps sounded, surprising Ian, so feeling more justified, he jumped to the floor.

"Whatd'ya think of our reunion, RaLF?" Then he leaned into her, sniffing her hair. "Some things don't change, do they?"

"Go to hell!" She spit.

"I've gone to a lot of trouble here; I don't think you appreciate what I've done…" Ian paused, scratching his chin. "Wait a minute. We're missing someone." Then swinging around to face the crowd he said, "Not exactly a beautiful person, but…Earnest Graves, come on down! You get to play, too!"

Anne grabbed Earnest's arm at the first shot. And Earnest held her tightly as they fell to the ground. But she felt him shaking as Ian began calling names. And when Ian finally called Earnest's, she watched the color drain from his face.

"Don't go, Earnest," she warned.

Without looking at her, he resolved, "I've got to go. I earned it." Then he stood and moved away. Anne's eyes followed him as he took his place among the chosen.

"Earnie, old buddy," Ian gushed into the microphone like a talk show host. "You didn't think I could forget you, did'ja?"

Earnest shuddered at the crooked grin running across Ian's face. He turned to look at the others, but not one returned his look. Even here this confederacy ostracized him, and he felt more sad and angry than scared.

"Can you tell us why I've called you all here today?" Ian stuck the microphone in Earnest's face.

Earnest glared at Ian who appeared so happy and pleased, and then Earnest remembered Anne's words about his hurting heart. "Jamie..." he muttered into the microphone.

"I can't hear you!" Ian screamed back like an army sergeant.

"Jamie Messereli, damn it!" Earnest snapped back.

"Jamie Messereli?" Ian's face filled with melodrama, "What does he have to do with anything? After all, he killed Bill Wright. Right RaLF?"

"We," Earnest said, glancing at RaLF, "except for RaLF, grabbed him after school and took him out in the country and... beat him up..."

Again, feigning surprise and indignation, "Oh.. .my... god...," he moaned. "You hear that, people? These five big guys beat up poor defenseless Jamie Messereli. He had just gotten better, too.... after killing Bill. Isn't that right, RaLF?" Ian quickly faced RaLF. She turned, refusing to look at his crooked face.

The few people who had applauded Ian's rant booed.

Ian looked back at the crowd. "I can tell by your pained

expressions, you guys don't give a rat's ass about Jamie Messereli. Honestly, I don't give a rat's ass about Jamie Messereli. I'm just sick of these bastards playing god."

"Amen," William yelled from the side, swinging his chain in wide circles.

"Thank you, Brother William," Ian yelled back.

Someone yelled, "Whoo Hoo!"

"And thank you…" Ian responded, gratified. "RaLF," turning his attention back to her. "Isn't Earnest a geek? I mean, what kind of a name is Earnest? A freakin' geek name…"

Earnest's heart twisted as Ian prodded RaLF. He looked at her to see her looking back.

"No," RaLF answered.

"Sure he is. That's why you broke up with him in third grade. It was third grade, wasn't it Earnest?" He glanced at his old friend and then looked back at RaLF. "You've hardly said a word to him since then. Look at him, the poor jerk. How in the hell did he get mixed up with you clowns, anyway?"

"I don't know," she grunted back.

"Yes, you do…" he said with a coy smile. "You knew the geek has been in love with you his whole pathetic life."

"Shut up, Ian!" Earnest yelled.

"Whatever," Ian jeered with a laugh, "I've got the gun! Hell, I've got the girl! And you ain't got shit." Then he turned back to RaLF. "You knew, didn't you?"

RaLF continued looking at Earnest, "Yes," she answered softly.

She knew?

"He even has a little shrine to you..." Ian continued, embarrassing his old friend.

"Stop it!" Earnest fumed.

"He still has a note you wrote him in third grade, and some stupid refrigerator magnet he bought from your campfire group."

"Shut up, Ian!" Earnest bellowed, his face crimson.

In one swift sudden motion, Ian swung the shotgun around, pointed it at Earnest and yelled, "Bang!"

The suddenness of Ian's movement, the burst of Ian's yell frightened him so badly that Earnest pissed himself. His chest about to burst, Earnest could hear the high-pitched cackling of William calling for Ian to see Earnest's wet pants.

"Oops," Ian snorted, holding out the shotgun for William to take.

Slowly William walked towards Ian, taking the shotgun. It felt heavy in his hands. Purposely, he avoided the trigger and cuddled the gun to his chest.

Ian then set the microphone down and walked a few steps away. Still holding onto the bat, he pulled out his vodka bottle. He unscrewed the cap, held the bottle towards Mr. Small. "Bottoms up," Ian toasted and took a drink. The alcohol's warmth soothed him. He listened for the bitch's approval but noticed the howls changing to laughter. He sipped again and laughed with her, screwing the cap back on the bottle, feeling his mind bobbing along the vodka current.

Ian shook his head, walking towards Marc. He swung the bat to his shoulder and spoke into the microphone. "You like being Bill's sloppy second? I mean, isn't RaLF your date tonight, Marc?"

But Marc stood silent, motionless.

"Did you know I loved her, too, back when she was a whole woman? But then, she did this to me..." He pointed to his face, "See this scar..." He brought his face close to Marc's. "The doctor removed a diamond that had come out of her ring. I still have it. Hell, Earnie, I guess I have my own shrine to RaLF." He backed away from Marc. "You help kick Jamie's ass?"

Marc held his silence.

"Such a man, Marc, but our audience wasn't there to see you kick him when he was curled up like a baby in the snow. Disgraceful, kicking a man when he's down."

The bat unexpectedly cut through the air, crashing into Marc's face, and he toppled to the floor.

RaLF screamed, covering her mouth with her hand followed by shrieks from other students along with a few calls of approval.

"Shit!" Lonnie, one of the others called up, cried.

Marc's hands covered his face as he writhed on the floor, yelling and moaning, blood oozing between his fingers. RaLF moved towards him.

"Don't you move, RaLF. He's on his own." Ian warned and walked past Marc's kicking legs, picking the microphone back up and climbing back on the sound booth. Then putting the bat to his mouth, he kissed it. "This is Armageddon, Marc. How does it feel to be one of the beautiful people, now? Appears to hurt like hell." He laughed. "Damn, I love this!"

He shook his head at the other boys. "Hey, Lonnie," he said stepping over one of the turntables, "do you hate disco as much as I do?"

Lonnie slowly nodded, agreeing with Ian.

"Man, I hate disco," Ian shook his head and brought the bat down upon the Bee Gees record he had scratched, breaking it into pieces.

At the sound of the crash, RaLF screamed.

"Oh shut up..." Ian charged. "This is all your fault. So just shut the hell up, princess!" Breathing hard, he leaned on the bat like a cane, wiping his forehead as the heat of his alcoholic haze rose. "Are you hot, Lonnie?"

"Uh-huh," Lonnie looked up at Ian.

"You play golf, Lonnie?"

"Uh-uh."

Ian pulled the bat up to his shoulder like a golf club, then swinging it down, connected with Lonnie's face.

"Fore!" Ian howled, Lonnie already on the floor.

He turned to RaLF, her face red and swollen from crying. "Your friends are dropping like flies." He jumped back down to the floor in front of her. "Isn't it exciting, wondering when it's going to be your turn?" Then looking past her he said, "Thad, aren't you a wrestler?"

"Kiss my ass," Thad snarled.

"It came in pretty handy when you grabbed Jamie, didn't it."

Thad stood motionless.

"I wrestled once...." Ian continued, walking towards him, "stupidest damn thing I've ever done.... You know what, Thad? I hate you freakin' troglodytes." And he pulled the bat up to his shoulder.

Thad flinched.

"Oh, no," Ian shook his finger at him. "Take it like a man. You earned it."

"I'm not gonna' stand here and let you hit me..."

"Then don't stand..." Ian swung the bat into Thad's knee. Thad staggered, grabbing his leg, swearing, and before he could dodge it, the bat pounded his cheekbone, sending him to the floor.

"Okay, Cooter, you miserable piece of shit," Ian turned, shoving the bat into the boy's chest, "What the hell kind of name is Cooter anyway? Your parents hillbillies?"

Cooter kept silent, too scared to reply, shaking, unable, unwilling to take his eyes from Ian.

"Don't you arrogant bastards do enough around here without tearing us apart? Five against one—poor guy never stood a chance."

Cooter stood dumbfounded by the question. "She said he was bothering her. We was just trying to help. He killed Bill..."

"And that's a bad thing? Bill was the biggest asshole in the whole freakin' school. If anyone deserved a miserable death, it was him."

Tears streamed down RaLF's face. "No…" she muttered.

Cooter remained silent, as Ian stared at him. Something about the silence struck Ian as odd, so he said to Cooter, "You're not very smart, are you?"

Cooter looked down, embarrassed, and with that misplaced stare, Ian sent Cooter to the floor with another thud.

"William, give me the gun," Ian's smile returned to his face as he took the gun, and then spread his arms, laughing. The gun in one hand, the bat in the other, Ian had never felt such power. "They're celebrating in Hell tonight!" He screamed while his eyes swept over the crowd, the bitch's approval all over him.

This is beautiful. He tucked the bat under his arm and reached for his bottle. "This is worth celebrating." He unscrewed the cap and began gulping, working his way to the bottom of the bottle. When he pulled it away, he looked over to Mr. Small, who had begun dragging himself away, a bloody trail behind him. Ian kept his smile throwing the empty bottle and hitting the principal in his back. "Be still," he said; then turning his attention back to Earnest, pointed the bat at him. "Your turn."

His wet pants clinging to his legs, Earnest's eyes moved up from the bat to Ian. He didn't want a turn. But he couldn't fight the notion that he deserved it. Regardless, his feet seemed bolted to the ground.

"Take it." Ian insisted, holding the bat's narrow end for Earnest to grasp.

Earnest stood silently.

"Take the damn bat, Earnest."

His stomach knotting, a chill moving up his legs, Earnest closed his eyes. *Just do it. Get it over with...*

"William," Ian's glare turned to a scowl, "go over to Earnest's geisha girl, and if he hasn't taken the bat when I reach ten, blow her knee caps off. Hell, Earnie, between her and RaLF, you'd still have at least one whole woman."

William looked at Ian, bewildered at his slurring words. The gun wasn't anything more than rusty junk. What was he supposed to do with it? Ian's stare grew more emphatic, drawing William over to her with a turn of his head. He placed the barrel against Anne's leg. She felt it quivering against her leg, so she looked at William and his hands shook.

"One," Ian began, and quickly, Earnest grabbed the bat.

"My turn for what?" Earnest's voice cracked.

"It's the present you've always wanted. RaLF's yours."

"What?"

"Come on, Earnie. RaLF... plus bat... Do I have to spell it out?"

"I can't do that."

"Two…," Ian counted without any hesitation.

Earnest looked over at Anne, shaking her head at him. His heart pounded, while his hands grew sweaty.

"Stop counting! I have the bat, Ian." Earnest barked at Ian.

"Earnest, please..." RaLF pleaded, sobbing, her face glistening with snot and tears. And Earnest's eyes began to moisten, too. "Do you really think I'd hurt you?" he said to her in a voice so soft that no one heard him but her.

"My game, my rules, Earnie…" Ian continued. "Don't make me hurt your girlfriend. RaLF didn't care what happened to Jamie." He turned and looked at her, and then he looked back at Earnest. "She doesn't give a damn what happens to you. So… three!"

Earnest shook nervously in Ian's stare, "I didn't care either!" he ragged, his voice cracking as he stared at RaLF's whimpering face, the scar across her forehead more pronounced as she cried.

"Four...."

"I'm so sorry..." Earnest said to RaLF, his voice weakening as he weighed one girl against another, the bat so heavy he felt that he couldn't hold it.

RaLF's eyes glistened with her tears, and she bit her lower lip.

"Five….!" Ian screamed. "For crissake, do it!"

Silently William stared down the sight, into the denim of Anne's pants. His eyes burned with nervous sweat.

"No, I can't!" Earnest yelled, lowering his arms.

"Just do it, damn it…" Ian ranted, running up to Earnest, screaming and spitting.

A boy walked nervously toward them.

Red with fury, Ian turned to the boy growling "What?!"

“The police handed this through a crack in the door.” The boy slid a radio across the floor a few feet from Ian and backed away.

Ian stomped over and picked it up. He looked at it, seeing a button on the side stickered with tape reading *PRESS HERE*. He pressed it, barking, “What do you want?”

“Are you the person in charge?”

“I’ve got the radio. What do you want?”

“I’m Officer Hatch with the Ponca City Police Department, and I want everyone safely out of there. What will it take to happen?”

Ian found his thinking buoyant and distant. And after several seconds of troubled concentration, he responded, “You got nothing!” Then he threw the radio to the floor, breaking it into pieces.

Ian turned back to Earnest, grabbing his collar. "It's no different than Jamie!"

RaLF’s heart jumped at Jamie's name, as she realized he had tried to help her and she had blown off his warning like dust.

"I never hit Jamie...” Earnest answered, his voice, along with his arms, growing weaker. "I only watched."

Ian nudged Earnest away, shaking his head. "You’re pathetic.” He hissed, pounding Earnest’s mouth with the butt of the shotgun. Earnest fell to his knees, heaving for air, the bat dropping from his hands as he held his throbbing lips.

Ian turned and stepped closer to RaLF, placing the warm barrel of the shotgun against her face while lightly tracing the scar across her forehead with his fingers. "Did it hurt?” He whispered to her, his voice soft and venomous. “I hope it hurt."

RaLF listened to his taunting but looked away, reviling Ian's touch as his finger slid across her glistening forehead.

He scrutinized her face.

"You're not as pretty as I thought..." he muttered, almost as an afterthought.

"Stop it!" she screamed, hitting Ian's hand away.

Ian caught her wrist, twisting it backwards, pulling her by her arm. "Are you watching, Earnie? See how easy this is."

Earnest slumped to the ground, his face to the floor. The taste of blood strong in his mouth, he rubbed his tongue over loose teeth. "Damn," he thought looking at the blood in his hands. He looked at Ian but didn't see anyone he recognized anymore. His hands found the bat and curled around it.

Over to the side, the four boys stirred very slightly, slipping out an occasional moan or cry, like Jamie curled in blood splattered snow.

Earnest imagined himself tackling Ian, while William shot him, leaving him to die in RaLF's arms, then thinking how ridiculous to have those thoughts. In his heart of hearts, Earnest recognized his cowardice, the occasional whiff of urine, the wet pants chaffing his thigh, branded him a coward. It had played out that way with Jamie, as it was playing out now, watching again—too afraid to muster an action.

Ian tugged RaLF back to the sound board and the other boys. Scooping the microphone up from the floor, he stopped and looked out over the sea of dancers and sneered, "They walk on you, they screw you over..." Looking down at Marc, whose face had swelled and discolored, he asked "You okay?" Marc grunted.

"It's hell to be ugly!" Ian laughed. Then looking up, he growled at the girl, "RaLF!"

"You're the devil!" she screamed, quickly jerking herself from Ian's grip, moving away from Ian along side of the sound booth, slapping at the air with her hand as if she could just shoo him away.

"Oh, no, I'm God!" Ian laughed, moving toward her.

"You're crazy," RaLF shrieked

"Like I give a damn, what you think!" Ian swung the butt of the shotgun, catching RaLF in the face, sending her flying upon her back, and Ian stumbling as the alcohol worked with more furor.

He looked down upon RaLF, surprised as had never intended to hit her. He had worshiped her, too. But looking at her, blood trickling from her nose, her glazed, surprised eyes, motionless in her shock, Ian sighed unexpectedly satisfied.

The thud, as the gun butt hit RaLF, hit Earnest as sharply. "No more..." he muttered, his heart pounding like timpani, and found his hands curling more tightly around the bat while tears streamed down his face. Slowly, he rose to his feet.

Ian laughed while the effects of the alcohol overwhelmed the touch of his rage, and the floor began to rock beneath him. He reached out to support himself, his mind shifting with the floor, but the sound booth seemed to move away from him. He looked for William, but he too was distant, as if Ian were looking at him through the wrong end of a telescope.

A growl escaped his lips, and he heard the bitch in duet, so close to his ears it tickled him, so he put his hands to his ears to quiet her. "Yes!" he bellowed, wanting her to know that he heard her. "Yes!" he heard her answer. Suddenly a shifting shadow moved toward him. "Yes!" he screamed, and he raced toward his god.

When they collided the bitch went mad, sending Ian to the floor beside RaLF. Suddenly he realized his demon lover wasn't there at all; it was Earnest, shrieking madly, blood covering his lips and teeth, holding the bat at Ian's throat. In his madness, he pulled the shotgun from Ian's grip by the barrel and threw it away. It slid across the wooden floor, but came to a stop in front of William.

Atop of Ian, holding him to the floor, from the corner of Earnest's eye, he saw William and realized his mistake. As Ian pushed against him, Earnest jumped up hoping to beat William to the shotgun, and lunged in that direction.

William?" Ian coughed, only seeing the dark ocean of faces looking towards him, rolling like waves across the floor. The bitch's growls grew louder with the twisting and turning, sending him into a fit of coughs.

"William?" he called again, his voice nearly absent. "RaLF!?" He battled his coat trying to stand, hunting for the bottle he had emptied several minutes before. Slowly he stepped away from the sound booth, moving like a blind man, his arms flailing, his lungs straining, coughing and gagging, hunting for something else upon which to lean.

Earnest moved too slowly. William stood, gun in hand, grimacing as if he were caged, swinging the gun around, erratically pointing at nothing and at everything. But most peculiarly, he was growling. And when Earnest looked at him, William's eyes reflected something that Earnest had never seen before.

The world spinning, Ian tried to keep up with it as it moved. "RaLF," he said straining, his tone almost pleading, forgetting he had knocked her to the ground. But as he circled the sound booth, she escaped his view.

Doc Rock slowly awoke from the battering Ian gave him. "Help me," he moaned. Unbalanced by the pain in his head, he reached forward for support, pulling himself from the floor, accidentally turning the remaining turntable on so that the cued record began to play, a drum and bass joined a group of anxious violins.

The lights and the disco floor flashed to the music, sending Ian's drunken, raging mind reeling, tripping over his own feet, landing upon the floor and hitting the back of his head against the floor.

Tear this disco down, the music commanded. And the bitch's curses pulled him from the floor. Underneath the rumble of the bass, he heard the blurring of words, and he turned to see a parade of Doc Rocks charging toward him. "William," he shrieked once more. William turned to see the disc jockey moving towards Ian, and the gun seemed to fire itself, sending him to the floor from its recoil as the disc jockey's body whirled in a slow motion pirouette, a red mist blurring him as he fell to the floor. William let loose a crazed, incoherent cry, seeing people moving about, and pointing the gun at them. Some screamed and some charged the chained doors as he picked himself from the floor, still growling and pointing.

Earnest backed away from William, noticing after the rush for the door, Anne now stood alone. His face ached, his head throbbed to the pounding of his heart. When their eyes met, Anne pointed at RaLF then moved toward her. Earnest watched as Anne's eyes darted back to William, each step drawing them closer to RaLF. William ignored them, heading towards the sound board, madly, aimlessly swinging the barrel of the shotgun around.

Ian continued to stare at the fallen disc jockey's body, expecting it to do something, unaware of the faint taste of the man's blood on his lips. Neither the chaos of the crowd nor the loud thumping of the music pierced Ian's ear. He was only conscious of the bitch's growling and the agonized look upon Doc

Rock's lifeless face. He crouched beside the dead man's body, his eyes locked on the gaze of its face, the bloody speckles reminding him of Jamie. His hands slowly grazed the man's face, smearing the spots across the ashen face.

He looked up, his view rippling like heat rising from hot asphalt and heard William bellow, "You want out?!!" Then William threw a small pair of chain cutters and keys into the panicked crowd. Again Ian turned back to the dead man.

"I did that?" William asked, as the warm touch of steel pressed below Ian's ear at his jaw line. "I did that." He repeated, but as a declaration.

Ian held his silence feeling the bitch's growls turn to mocking laughter.

"Are you happy? We spilled blood...like you said." William questioned in his high-pitched voice as he looked down upon the bloody mess.

Ian didn't hear. The bitch's laughter filled his ears.

"Armageddon's over. Did you win?" William's voice quivered, the gun barrel shaking against Ian's jaw line.

One of the three pairs of doors opened and a wave of panicked students poured out. William closed his eyes. "Oh my goodness," his voice croaking and quivering, and he pulled the trigger, the recoil throwing William back while the gunshot sent Ian spinning.

Ian wanted to scream from pain, but he could not. He reached to his face, and his hand became drenched in warm blood. Submitting to his shock, his eyes focused upon the stubbed arm of the papier-mâché' statue above him. He gurgled as he breathed, his mind swimming, and his eyes slowly closed.

William looked at Ian and the bright red meat making up the lower half of his face. He cocked the shotgun.

Falling to his knees, William propped himself with the shotgun, his fingers gripping the hot barrel. Closing his eyes, he listened to the music fade into the clicking of the needle as it reached the end of the record. He butted the barrel against his forehead, stretching his hand to the trigger, but unable to reach it. So he pulled out the large marker he had used all week to announce Armageddon. Stretching, he jammed the marker against the trigger, and with a final thrust…the gun sounded with an empty click.

"Set the gun down...!"

William looked at the officers surrounding him, their guns drawn. He opened his hands, letting the shotgun fall away, and stood up, his arms to the sky. Looking over, a large crimson bubble popped in the mess of Ian's face.

Chapter Twenty-One

Aftermath

Friday, March 1st

Earnest Graves rubbed his tired eyes as he drove silently to school, again running his tongue over the braces straightening the teeth that Ian had put into disarray the week before. His thoughts rallied around his first day back at school in a post-Armageddon world. He looked into the review mirror, and reexamined his face. His eyes were framed in dark circles and puffy from insomnia; however, the bruising and swelling of his lips were fading.

He found it ironic that he wanted to go to school. No one pushed Earnest to return…except for Earnest. He needed to be there, tired of carrying the weight of Ian's Armageddon alone. He needed to see Anne's face to make sure she was really fine. He needed to see RaLF. And surprisingly, he needed to see Jamie Messereli—not having a clue to what to do when he did. But he knew he needed to, to bring sleep again.

After karma's execution of balance at Ian's hands, Earnest still didn't find he felt better. The guilt that had wrapped him like a shroud after Jamie's beating harassed him just as before. Maybe if Jamie had been the one who had hit him, he'd feel better. But Ian only brought retribution with his wrath, not any sense of justice, so karma kept him stirring, restless in his shame.

Earnest drummed the steering wheel as he drew closer to town, trying to squelch the jitters running over him. "So...," he said as a distraction, turning to his brother, Eddie, who sat unusually quiet staring back at him.

"Did you want something?" Earnest asked, his voice uncertain, somewhat surprised with himself not being irritated by his brother's staring.

"It don't look so bad... your face and all." Eddie readjusted in his seat, unable to find a comfortable position. "Mom said to leave you alone, but I wanna ask you something."

"Sure, she's just a worry-wart."

"How's it feel to be a hero?"

Earnest didn't trust the word. He had heard it before from others, from his mother, from Anne, from the Ponca City News. But there were no heroics in him that night, only fear and desperation sweltering in urine. So he felt a fraud. "Eddie, listen to me, it's a crock. Friday night, I was more scared and mad than sensible. If I was a hero, nobody would've been hurt. And neither would've Jamie."

"Well, people are sayin' it at school. Your old teachers are sayin' how proud they are of you. Even if you were scared, I think it took balls, what you did."

Earnest glanced at the rearview mirror, not seeing a hero stare back, just a guilt-ridden piece of human debris. During his days at home, between doctor and dentist visits, his thoughts swirled about Ian and Armageddon, never seeing his actions through a prism of bravery. He had only acted from the sheer fear of what Ian might do next. And as each '*next*' drew closer to him, instinct reigned.

"Thanks..." Earnest gave Eddie a hollow smile, unsure how to explain how poorly the label fit and just how badly he wished someone had been able to stop Ian a long time before the first shotgun blast.

When Earnest joined the parade entering the high school parking lot, he noticed that his body was still alight with jitters, his fingers drumming, his left foot bouncing, his heart knocking against his ribcage. As he passed Hershel, the parking guard gave him thumbs up. Earnest smiled and thumbed him back.

He drove to the farthest end of the parking lot. As soon as he shut off the ignition, he felt uncertain about what he was to do. He stepped out of his car, finding the chill welcoming. His first step, he took without a thought, but as he drew closer to the school, each step became more burdensome. His nose tickled, so he pulled his handkerchief from his back pocket and blew into it.

"Earnest!" a voice cried.

He turned to see a pair of pretty blondes, those to whom Ian had referred as the beautiful people. Earnest sneezed into the handkerchief and said hello.

"Thank you for what you did, Friday. That guy was a madman," one said.

"Yeah," Earnest agreed with a patronizing nod, "he has problems."

"You're lucky he didn't kill you," the other girl said. "Did he do that to you?" she asked, her eyes looking to his lips.

"Yeah,"

Then the first girl kissed his cheek. "You're awesome," she said and added walking away, "My boyfriend was such a wuss."

Earnest softly touched the cheek where she had kissed. Stunned by the first conversation in three years of high school with either of them, he kept walking, surprised they had even known his name. As he moved along the sidewalk overlooking the smoking pit, a few people pointed at him.

"Hey, buddy!" Angus brayed from the pit, a cigarette hanging from his mouth and Fiona hanging on his side. "You put it to Fugly!" He laughed.

Earnest smiled and waved, another patronizing gesture, and walked inside.

Earnest remembered his counselor wanted to talk. But he wasn't ready for the emotional regurgitation. He wanted to see Anne, expecting she could help more than anyone. Up the stairs to the third floor, swimming through the "atta' boy's," the "way to go's," and the pointing fingers, he hurried to the journalism room. Remembering his brother's question, he thought, these people don't get it.

Stepping into the room, his eyes zeroed in on Anne, bent over, looking at unfinished layout pages. They had spoken every evening on the phone; her soft voice and soothing words were a salve to his soul, making his inadequacies all the more obvious to himself.

"Earnie!" Axle shouted, looking up from his writing.

When Anne heard Earnest's name, she looked up. At first she hesitated, but when she saw the need in Earnest's tired and worn countenance, Anne went to him.

"It's good to see you," she said.

"You have no idea..." The dark jewels of her eyes warming him, he wrapped his arms around her, smiling so wide his lips hurt.

She lightly patted his back as the others encircled them.

"How are you, Earnest?" Mr. Addison walked in from next door. "People have been asking about you all week."

Anne started to back away, but Earnest held her. He didn't understand, but he needed her there. So, she stayed at his side.

"My mouth is sore. I had to get braces. I heard the others will all be okay."

"Over time..." Mr. Addison nodded.

"Is RaLF back?"

"Not yet. Poor girl's had a helluva' year, first, the wreck and now this..." Mr. Addison looked about the room, "You guys need to take care of her."

"What about Jamie Messereli?"

Mr. Addison shrugged his shoulders. "Don't know anything about him." The teacher rubbed his forehead, "Friday was a bad day, all around. Anne, I talked to Daniel's mother yesterday. He won't be back. It doesn't look good for Daniel, not at all..." Mr. Addison's eyes reddened and began to tear.

"Daniel?" Earnest asked, confused. "What's up with him?"

Anne looked at Earnest sadly, "He was at Mary's father's church for some kind of ceremony. There was a fire, and somehow he fell in the baptistery. He was nearly drowned by the time he was found."

Earnest fought a snicker. That sounded too weird, Daniel, the angel boy, nearly drowning in a *church* baptistery—and at Mary's father's church. But the solemn look on Anne's face made him feel like a jerk.

"What's going on with him?" One of the other students asked.

Mr. Addison's voice cracked, "I don't really know..." He headed to his desk, but stopped before leaving the room and turned around. "Earnest, I'm glad you're back. You look exhausted, so take care of yourself. I have no idea what pushed you to do it, but you kept things from being worse. Thanks for taking care of Anne. I need her around here." Then he gave a frustrated chuckle. "I can't believe this…" His words trailed off into silence as he walked away, and the five minute warning bell sounded.

The students gathered their books and left except Anne who stayed with Earnest.

"How are you doing?" she asked.

"It's better than being at home. Ian haunts me there. When I'm about to fall asleep, I see him, and he keeps me awake. I know he's not dead, but it's still like his ghost is there."

"Is this any better?" She asked then smiled, "Ghosts can hide here, too."

Earnest laughed. But as he looked around the room, he realized she was right. This was the same room where Ian harassed RaLF about how wonderful she smelled. He had been here when Ian gathered him for the lunch the day RaLF smacked Ian and scarred his nose.

"Can I eat lunch with you?" Earnest changed the topic.

"If you would like to."

"Nothing would be better."

The pair walked out, Earnest finding remnants of Ian with nearly every step.

* * *

As the clock broke its silence, Mary remained reposed, curled upon her side, staring at the red glowing numbers, blinking and changing as the minutes passed, and yet she remained unmoved, waiting on the knock, hoping for the knock—the shave and a haircut knock. But there was only the buzzing to raise her, so she rolled out of bed, turned off the buzzing, and in the silence, listened, hearing only her own breathing, so in her isolation, she prepared for the day.

After showering, after dressing, she reluctantly went to breakfast. Drawing closer to the kitchen, she heard her parents, so she stopped to listen. The things they were saying didn't matter to her. But there was a quality in their voices as they conversed she wanted to hear. She didn't know if it was new or if she had only just noticed it, but they shared a bonding, and as much as she ranted about gross sentimentality, she found solace in the tone even as she felt more separated from them. In the weeks she had lived with John, she had fought any opportunity to build a relationship. It was habit with her. So, she stood mutually torn and mended.

When she finally walked into the dining room, her parents made no notice of her entrance, nearly finishing breakfast while Mary's food cooled upon the plate. She melted to her place and ate, their silence louder to her than any comment or reprimand they used to give her. That they now didn't seem to care if she ate without blessing—that they now acquiesced to her faithlessness—seemed even more harsh.

Before, the conflict between her and her parents propelled her; her rebellion fueled her, but since the church fire, they offered nothing to resist. They talked, just as they had before, but as if she wasn't there, about the builders at the church, the faithfulness of the congregation, about everything but her.

"I'll be home after school," Mary said, interrupting them.

"That's fine. We won't be here. We're playing golf with Rex and Evelyn this afternoon. We'll also be having dinner with them at The Blue Moon." The Deacon handed her a twenty dollar bill, releasing the responsibility of dinner to her, "You're on your own, tonight."

...and every other night. Mary took the money while rising from the table. Her parents had become everything that she ever wanted: mute providers. In the last few days, the Deacon had even bought her a car and forced her to take the driving test. They provided her every need without a word. But it was done with such an antiseptic touch that Mary didn't enjoy it, and found herself resenting their inaction as much as she had their previous actions.

"Just tell me you hate me." Mary slowly spoke to the pair, her voice hoarse while the words rolled out. "I'm a baby killer. You're justified, aren't you? So say it."

Her parents talking stopped, and they stared at her. Then the Deacon slowly shook his head. "Isn't that like you—looking for the easy way. It would be easier for you if we called you a baby killer, if we hated you, wouldn't it? Well, we don't hate you."

The Deacon stood up, patting his perfect suit. "You can take care of yourself. So I'm just here to provide. You have food. You have a car. You'll have your college education. But, I'm tired of your mocking and your condescension. I wish we got along. I wish we could like one another, but I reckon that isn't to be.... You won't let it. And I'll be hanged if I'm willing to make the effort anymore. It took burning down my church, but you've worn me down." He adjusted his tie and left with his plate. His words came curtly, so matter of fact, that Mary felt the chill linger long after her parents cleared the table, as she stood alone, gripped in the blessings of answered prayer.

* * *

Jamie massaged the back of his neck, hoping to rub away the awful stiffness he woke with every morning, as he moved containers around in the refrigerator, looking for milk. Not finding any, he grabbed a can of Coke instead. Walking back to the counter, he opened the can and poured it over his cereal, the fizz of the soda blending with the cereal's snaps, crackles, and pops.

He carried the bowl into the living room, reclining on the couch.

"Are you coming home after school?" his mother asked, walking into the room.

"I'm working." Jamie answered, his mouth full of cereal.

"Then, are you coming home?"

Jamie shrugged. "Don't know."

"I ain't gone out since I don't know when because of that bastard's stunt. No trouble, tonight." She leaned over, kissing Jamie's forehead, leaving a lip-shaped smear below the hairline.

He looked at her, annoyed with her kiss, wondering what she would drag in that evening and held up the bowl, "Thanks for breakfast," he mocked. Then he rubbed his forehead, wiping away the remnants of her maternal affections.

She walked to the door and stepped out, insisting, "No trouble." The door rattling shut behind her.

Jamie ate his cereal and grew more bothered with his mother's warnings. She wouldn't approve of his real intentions, but he was not concerned. Jamie ate his cereal and thought of RaLF. She wouldn't approve either, yet disregarding her was not as easily done; the best he could do was to pretend it wasn't there. Before meeting RaLF, he had been invisible because she didn't know he existed. Since the accident, she didn't see him because she didn't want him to exist. Now, when their paths crossed, her evasive looks made him long to grab her, shake her, tell her she would never be rid of him; he was a tattoo upon her soul, and nothing could change that. Now, after Ian's craziness, he wondered if she hated him even more—if that was even possible.

* * *

The sound of conversation stopped when Mary entered the journalism room. This was nothing new; however, it now felt different. Her classmates were no longer intimidated by her, just annoyed. So, she quietly took a chair at one of the middle tables. Soon the bell rang to start class, and she sat silently. Sporadically, a person would glance at her, but they would turn away before their eyes met.

Except for Anne, who looked directly at Mary, holding her eyes and smiling back, which gave Mary a bit of a start. Then Anne walked to her and took a seat.

"Things are crazy here. How are you?"

Mary looked at her. "All right, I guess."

"...and the baby?"

She answered abruptly, "I lost it," feeling a kick to her gut, so she started chewing her fingernails. Mary had lulled the pregnancy question over and over in her mind. She had made such a production of telling everyone in the class, and now her flamboyance was biting her back.

"I'm sorry, Mary."

Mary immediately suspected Anne, but then Anne leaned forward and hugged her. Mary's eyes darted uncomfortably around the room as the others stared back.

When Anne let go of her, she whispered, "God never gives you more than you can handle. If there's anything I can do, let me know," standing up to return to her work.

"Can I do something? Write something?" Mary wanted to be busy, distracted, but realizing she was getting dangerously close to begging, she stopped.

Anne stood silently for several seconds. "Since Daniel's not going to be coming back to school. Would you mind writing something to honor him?"

"No. That wouldn't be right."

"I'm sorry, I wasn't thinking. You could write about how people are spending their spring breaks, instead."

Mary thought about Friday night, about how angel boy had pulled that fiery banner away from her. For only an instant, a myriad of Daniels raced through her mind. And she thought about what her parents had said about Daniel's injuries and his damages, and how these separate notions of Daniel compared to one another. He told her he prayed for her, and she wondered what he was praying for—why had he prayed for her at all. His talking to God drove her crazy, all his damned praising and blessing to a god that put him in a hospital bed in such a wretched state. She looked up, staring through the ceiling into eternity, hating God's inconsistency and coldness.

"Wait. I'll do the write up on Daniel." Mary reconsidered, In spite of him, in spite of herself, she would do it. Besides, he deserved better than what anyone else could do.

"Thanks." Anne smiled, patting Mary's shoulder. "Can you finish by next week?"

Don't ask me, tell me. She nodded at Anne, amazed that Anne got anything done as accommodating as she was. Then she pulled paper and a pencil from her book bag and began her notes.

Things I know about Daniel:
Religious,
Irritating
Worked hard his whole life
Prayed for me
Saw an angel?
Hair turned white (freaky)
Good typist
Had plastic surgery to hide down's syndrome (who would've guessed it).
Wore clip on tie
Clothes looked a mess.
WEAK!!! Gave in too easily

Mary paused, tapping the table with her pencil. She thought about the student profiles published before and the trivial garbage they usually contained. What's your favorite color? What's your zodiac sign? Who's your favorite music group… movie… song…

book… food… blah blah blah…? Mary didn't know any of that, except what was more than likely his favorite book. Her pencil continued to tap the table as she strained for something beyond the surface, writing the last thing she knew for certain:

Vegetable

* * *

Jamie slid his lunch tray to the table and sat across from Ned "the head".

"Hey," he said.

"Hey," Ned "the head" answered back. "How's it goin'?"

"Like crap. Everyone thinks I had something to do with Ian's Armageddon. They won't let me go to vo-tech, so I have to stay in the office for half the day. Hell, I was at the police department answering questions all day, Saturday."

"What ya' tell'em?"

"That I didn't have anything to do with it. I tried to stop him."

"That was some crazy shit."

Jamie smeared a french fry through a pool of ketchup. "I didn't know he was going to do anything like that."

As he took a bite, some students began cheering; then applause began to crescendo throughout the cafeteria. He looked around and several people were on their feet, clapping. He turned towards Ned who only shrugged. Since Jamie couldn't see anything, he stood with the others. And there he saw Earnest standing at the entrance to the cafeteria. Jamie dropped to his seat, staring at a lunch he no longer had an appetite for.

* * *

The applause sounded for a couple of seconds before Earnest realized it was for him. He stood motionless, uncertain what he should do. He turned to Anne, who appeared less taken aback than he. Slowly, a smile came to his face, not a sincere smile, but one given to appease. He nodded his head at the standing mass and waved to them, uncomfortable with their greeting. He told himself they were clapping, not for him but, because none of them were the ones chosen for punishment. Then, as his hand lowered and the students' applause ceased, Jamie Messereli came walking toward him, passing to the exit, his eyes focused angrily at Earnest.

Earnest turned to Anne. "I've got to talk to him." But his feet felt immovable.

"That's Jamie Messereli?" Anne asked.

Earnest nodded.

"Go, otherwise, Ian will haunt you with that, too."

Earnest darted from the cafeteria, seeing Jamie halfway to the next building.

"Jamie!" Earnest yelled to get his attention.

He turned to answer the voice, and upon seeing Earnest, the anger returned to his face. He stopped, holding an unlit cigarette between his lips. When Earnest approached him, Jamie held his silence, waiting to hear what Earnest thought to say.

"Hi," Earnest huffed, catching his breath from his sudden sprint.

Jamie remained silent, taking the cigarette from his mouth.

With a deep breath to calm both his breathing and his heart, he blurted, "I was there...when you were beaten up."

"I know." Jamie shifted on his feet, holding his icy stare.

"I need to say this..." Earnest's voice grew calmer as he caught his breath. "I made a mistake. It was wrong."

Jamie nodded. "I know that, too."

"I'm sorry for what I did."

"Yeah? What would that be exactly? Throwing me in the car? Busting me in the face? Kicking me in the chest? My back? Kicking me in the balls? Tell me. What are you sorry for?"

"Jamie, I didn't lay a hand on you that day."

"Oh, yeah, I remember you. You were the one telling them to stop." Jamie slowly shook his head, rolling his eyes. "Kiss my ass. If you didn't do anything, what are you sorry for?" He turned to walk away.

"What I did was worse."

Jamie turned to Earnest again.

"I justified it. I wanted to believe RaLF… that it was the right thing to do. We were wrong. You didn't deserve it…any of it…"

Jamie shook his head and looked to the ground, "You're right. I didn't deserve it. But now you're a hero. You stopped the bad guy. And I'm still the guy that's blamed for everything. It doesn't matter what happened to me."

"I don't know why everything spun out of control… I'm not a hero. I'm as far away from that as you can get. I deserved what Ian did to me…even more. I'm sorry. And that isn't enough."

Jamie's shoulders drooped. A few loose strands of hair fell into his face, so he pushed it from his face. His eyes did not let up on their coldness at Earnest. "What did Ian do to you?"

"He busted up my mouth with the butt of his shotgun."

Jamie paused and said, "We've got something in common…"

He turned away from Earnest and walked to the smoking pit for a cigarette. As he sat on a bench, he lit it thinking, *I didn't deserve it*, wishing RaLF could see that, too.

* * *

RaLF drew him like a rat to a trap. He, like his mother, had been stuck within the four walls of their small house for too long, and, like her, had abstained from his vice for such a time it gnawed like a hunger. Never fighting the desire but relinquishing himself to it, Jamie guided the car across town to her curb.

Lighting a cigarette, he leaned back. RaLF's house sat down the road from where he parked, but he could still see her illuminated window. Slowly the car's windows fogged, and he began to quiver. He took a deep drag from his cigarette, as he pulled a blanket from the backseat and wrapped it around himself, waiting for the dancing silhouette of his own soul's tattoo.

The passenger door opening roused him awake. He had dozed off, his thoughts swirling about RaLF and Earnest and Ian. Sitting up, he shook his head trying to clear his mind. He wiped his eyes to see RaLF sliding in. She sat silently, looking straight ahead. He held no anger toward her, so he sat silently beside her, his eyes moving over her. She reached for the cigarettes and the lighter on the dashboard, took one from the pack with her mouth and lit it, taking a deep drag and exhaling out the side of her mouth. A cough escaped her mouth.

"I didn't know you smoked." Jamie said, surprised.

"I don't. It makes you stink."

He saw her hand tremble as she held the cigarette.

"Are you cold?" he asked, offering her the blanket.

"Yes," she replied, but as Jamie placed it about her shoulders, she didn't know if it was a chill a blanket could take away.

"Are you all right?" Jamie asked, starting his car and aiming the vents at RaLF.

"I don't know what the hell that means anymore," she said, her voice uncertain. "If you mean from last week…I got off easy. Just some bruising…inside and out…. If you mean something else…? I don't know." Then she awkwardly turned to face Jamie. "I want to know about the night Bill died."

Jamie pushed his hair from his face, looking past her, into the fog of the window behind her. "I don't remember much," he started, and cleared his throat to stall the story. "It was late when I got to the keg party, so it was pretty much over. When I saw your car, the light was on inside and you were face down in your own puke. I pulled you out of the car. You woke up and begged me to take you home in your car cause your dad would kill you if anything happened to it.

"I stopped at the Quick Trip to find your address in a phonebook because you were too drunk to tell me. Bill was there buying beer. He was so pissed off when he realized I was with you that he tried to start a fight. I drove off but they followed, and the rest I only know what I've heard. Earl pulled out in front of me. I swerved to miss him and hit Bill's truck…" Jamie shifted uncomfortably in his seat. "I should have let him drive you. But,…I wanted to be with you…"

RaLF took another puff, her thoughts so self involved she missed his final words. "I think about that day and I wonder if I could've done something different. What if I hadn't had that next beer? It's like dominoes, you know. You make one stupid decision and then something happens and then something else…" She adjusted the blanket to cover herself better. "Why did you warn me about the dance?"

"I had to… It was like you sprinkled me with your magic RaLF dust. I was under your spell so I had to."

"You're so full of it." She laughed, slapping his arm.

Jamie chuckled, but he knew it was true. He was under her spell whether she believed it or not. Then his face took a slight grin. "You had to pee before we left the keg party. You were too drunk, so I had to help you take your pants off."

RaLF covered her face with her hand. "No way."

"Yes, seriously. I held you up while you took the longest piss in history."

'That's so humiliating." She shook her head.

"It should be. Drinking's bad for you, too."

Her smile weakened, "You can't imagine…"

"Wanna' bet?" His words softened as his face turned to sadness, studying the floorboard of the car. "Why do you hate me?" Looking at her would be too much.

"I don't hate you, Jamie. Not anymore… Ian took it away from me. Bill could be an asshole at times, and if he hadn't been one that night, this would've been a better year for both of us."

"There's a good moral for ya': Don't be an asshole."

RaLF lightly slapped his forearm again. "I'm serious." She had a slight laugh in her voice, although she meant her words.

"I'm sorry." He relented, letting his smile fade.

"Don't be. You're right. Too many assholes, doing asshole things."

"RaLF, you getting hurt is the last thing in the world I would ever want. When we were in the hospital, and I couldn't see you, I thought you were too torn up, and it about killed me. When I realized you just didn't want to see me, I was relieved because I figured you were better."

The pair sat quietly, letting the minutes pass. Jamie noticed RaLF was no longer shaking. "Now, you tell me something."

She waited for his question, crushing the butt of her cigarette.

"Why did you sic your new boyfriend on me?"

"Marc's not my boyfriend. He's just been a shoulder. But, I wanted you to hurt like I did. As far as I was concerned, it was your fault, and every time I turned around, I saw you and not Bill. It felt like you were mocking me."

"I never meant to hurt you."

"I wish I could say that."

RaLF stared at Jamie for several long seconds. "Tonight, when I saw you out here, I wasn't mad anymore. It was like Déjà vu, but with a chance to do something right. I was happy to see this beat up piece of crap."

Jamie laughed then asked, "Are you going back next week?"

"I don't know. I thought this would be the best year of my life, but it has been nothing but shit."

"For me, every year is shit. This has just been a high year on my shit meter. But I can't quit, cause then I lose and Ian wins."

RaLF laughed, "And what do you win if you stick it out?"

"It doesn't matter. I'm just sick and tired of people like Bill telling me I can't finish, that I can't even run the race. I don't mean to be rude, but that's how I feel." When he realized that RaLF didn't take offense, Jamie reached over and gave her a light punch on her arm. "You can wade through three more months of this crap. Things can't get any worse."

"Don't kid yourself."

"Well, I'm not quitting."

Jamie began to feel their conversation wane, but he wasn't ready to end it. "How are your friends, the ones that Ian worked over?"

"They're getting better. I've been afraid to see them. Marc's mother blames me. I feel pretty lousy, but I don't think I could ever be miserable enough for her. You understand that, don't you?" RaLF unwrapped the blanket from her shoulders and handed it to Jamie. "Thank you." She opened the car door and stepped out. "I wish we did this, months ago. I hope you can forgive me."

"Don't worry about me."

She gave him a smile that didn't hide her sadness. "You don't need to come around here anymore. If you want to talk, knock on the door, okay?" She shut the car door, and began walking towards her house.

Jamie quickly rolled down his window and called to her.

She turned back around.

"So, did Earnest Graves really stop Ian like they said?"

"What body I have left is still in one piece. He's my hero." She waved, and turned back to her house. When she went inside, he waited a few minutes, but the curtain to RaLF's room remained unmoved. Jamie put the car into gear. It sputtered and jerked forward, away from RaLF's house.

* * *

With each kiss, Earnest felt the cutting of his still tender lips by his orthodontia and tasted blood. With the rush of blood came the echo of Ian's taunting and the blow to his face. So as he felt the press of Anne's lips, behind the veil of his curtained eyes, the shadows of Armageddon loomed.

His hand quivered while his fingers moved along the soft curve of Anne's cheek. He tried to draw himself back to the present using Anne as his anchor. As her scent, clean and sweet, wafting potently from her hair and perfumed neck, pulled at him, his weaker parts remained Ian's eternal victim. With his eyes closed, his thoughts ran rampant, racing across a myriad of vanished possibilities allowing none of it to have happened—and it was ridiculous to consider.

Lightly, Anne caressed the hand that Earnest held upon her waist. Earnest let Anne slowly guide his hand up the weave of her sweater, his hand moving past her stomach. His jaw grew painfully taut as they continued their kiss, Anne nudging the hand upward, finally, delicately placing Earnest's hand upon her small breast.

His breathing shortened as the pounding of his heart pushed the very breath from his lungs, his hand frozen, cupped upon her breast. Earnest, pulled between Ian's hold upon him and the hold he had upon Anne, felt naively uncertain. So, with his heart racing and his breath hissing, a rapturous fury encased him. Defying Ian, he grabbed the back of Anne's head with his free hand, and drew her into him as if he could not get her close enough. While the wire work in his mouth ground into his lips, while bolts of pain shot through his jaw, as his teeth clenched in his impassioned confusion, his hand frantically kneaded Anne's breast, wadding the cup of her shallow bra and her blouse.

"Stop," she bristled, pushing Earnest away, as she rubbed her chest and lips.

Earnest sunk into the couch, his hands curling into fists, reeling from the collision of his passions, those warm for Anne against others cold for his maimed friend.

"What's wrong, Earnest?" Anne snapped, pushing away the strands of her hair hanging down like a veil, covering her face.

Earnest's hands began to shake, as he silently held them out to the girl as a kind of conciliatory gesture to her. "I'm sorry," he mumbled, trying to thaw the coldness incarcerating his heart.

Quickly, Anne grabbed his shoulders. "Sorry for what, Earnest? Tell me what you're sorry for."

"Hurting you, I guess.... I don't know..."

"Then how can you be sorry?"

"I don't know.... I'm sorry for so many things..." He answered again, avoiding her piercing eyes. "I feel so screwed up...." He hit himself angrily upon the forehead. "Ian is choking the life out of me. He won't get out of my head."

"Earnest, you're choking the life from yourself." The irony of her word's harshness against the softness of her voice slapped Earnest. Anne stood, taking hold of Earnest's collar. Her dark eyes shot through him; then ever so slightly she squinted, focusing her stare. She said in a voice as gentle as a summer breeze, "You've been declared a hero, but you won't save yourself.... Ian broke your teeth, and you're letting him rip apart your soul. I'm here for you, but until you face your demons, I can't save you from yourself."

"How do I do that, Anne? I don't know what to do."

"I don't know either, Earnest. I just know you'll never laugh again until Ian's ghosts are away."

He looked at her and could not believe that someone could be so concerned for him, and he blurted, "I think I love you, Anne."

Anne's eyes grew wide, and she placed her finger on his mouth to silence him. "In five months, I'm going away to college. You don't have any idea what you're going to be doing.... Neither of us needs to think about love." She stood up from the couch and pulled on Earnest's hand until he was on his feet. "Thank you for the evening, Earnest. And I promise, I will do whatever I can to help you shoo away Ian's ghost." She handed him his green coat, and led him to the door. "I'll see you later, Earnest." And she gently placed a kissed upon his cheek.

Embarrassed at her ushering, an unexpected desperation came upon him as Anne opened the door. As he was about to speak, she put her finger again to his mouth.

"Shhh." She said softly, afraid of what he might say. "Go, face your demons."

So Earnest stepped into the cold, and the door shut behind him. Immediately his breath turned to steam illuminated by the half-moon, hiding behind scant thin clouds, as he stood motionless upon the porch. Never had he felt more directionless, more aimless. *Demons?* As he walked to his car, an overwhelming pain twisted his hollow chest, tearing him—ravaging his shredded soul. Angrily, he pounded his fists upon the frost-speckled Ford, gritting his teeth so intently he thought his jaw would fly apart. Earnest was a hero too weak to cry, collapsing onto the car under the weight of his own confusion.

The cold glass of the windows stung his palms as he pushed himself back up. He caught his own reflection in the window, his mouth and chin obscured by the brightness of the moon's reflection. He stared into his own lonely eyes; burning with dry tears, the reflected eyes looking callously back, becoming the remnants of Ian's tattered face.

"Damn you," Earnest croaked through his braces, blocking the rippling image with his hand. He slowly walked around the car, Ian's mocking eyes filling his mind, pushing out every other thought. A compulsion moved Earnest to see his anti-Christ. It was there where he could exorcise the demon he had welcomed—that Ian had blessed.

* * *

Mary stood in the hallway, stifling the urge to wretch from the smell of the hospital. She tried taking a deep breath, but the antiseptic odor only made her nausea worsen. So fanning herself with her hand, the slight breeze cooled her and muted her discomfort. Her composure regained, she slowly pushed open the door.

A woman sat at the foot of the bed, leaning forward, staring so deeply at the soul resting in the room she didn't hear the sweep of the door across the floor. Mary stood silently for a few seconds examining the woman.

"Excuse me. Is this Daniel Davies's room?"

The woman turned to Mary, but it took a second to register with her that she had been spoken to. "Oh, yes. I'm sorry. My mind was a million miles away."

"Are you Daniel's mother?"

"Yes. What can I do for you, sweetie?" her voice weary, she stood, the weight of exhaustion upon her, brushing the unkempt hair from her face.

"I worked with Daniel on the school newspaper…"

"Come in." A smile came upon her face, "Daniel said you guys kept him on his toes."

Mary stepped into the room.

"Thank you for coming. He'd appreciate it." She stuck out her hand to Mary. Reluctantly, Mary shook it. Then her gaze left Mary and returned to Daniel. She pat Mary's shoulder, then ran her hand down Mary's upper arm.

As badly as she fought it, she turned to Daniel. The roundness Mary remembered was gone; he was gaunt and pasty in his complexion. His eyes were closed, while his face melted to his chin causing his lips to turn down into an exaggerated frown, glistening with spittle. Tempted to wipe his face as she had seen Daniel do with his tie, Mary held her place. Looking down she noticed both his hands wrapped in gauze.

"I need some water…" she blurted, turning to the sink. Not seeing any cups, she ran water into her hand and drank from it. For extra measure, she splashed her face.

"Are you okay, hon?"

"I don't like hospitals." She fanned herself another time.

"I can think of hundreds of places I'd rather be, too."

Mary nodded, "What happened to his hands?"

"He burned them in the fire."

The fire had grown from nowhere. Faith and John and flames surrounded her, kicking and screaming. She was pulled out of the fire; rather the fire was pulled from her. For a brief, short second, from her periphery, Daniel ran from her, his arms flaming in the smoke….

"How is he?" Emptiness filled her chest.

"We don't know. He's in and out. Every now and then he'll mutter something. Sometimes, he sings. I don't know where that comes from. He doesn't like to sing because of his lisp. The doctors tell us his brain was damaged from oxygen deprivation, but he'll have some memories that come back. They tell us he'll never be normal again. But he's never been normal. He's my miracle boy."

"He's definitely unique..." While they worked together, he had only given Mary aggravation, but looking at the person in the bed, she didn't see Daniel and had nothing but pity for the poor soul who was there. She walked closer to the bed, Daniel resting as still as a corpse. "I'm writing a story about Daniel for The Poncan. Would it be possible to ask you some questions sometime?"

Daniel slightly stirred as Mary spoke, so his mother reached to stroke his face.

"I could talk about him for hours, but I don't think he would want me to. He doesn't like to talk about himself. An article would embarrass him, especially now."

"Grace, here's your tea," Reverend Green and Daniel's father walked into the room. "Oh," The pastor grew still, seeing Mary.

Daniel's mother took the steaming cup. "Is something wrong?"

"I wasn't expecting Mary."

"Mary? Are you Mary Christmas?"

She shifted uncomfortably.

"Hmmmmmaaaa." Daniel groaned and wiggled, his eyes remaining shut.

His cry took all attention from Mary. Daniel's mother took a damp cloth from the bedside table and wiped his face.

"Mmmmaaaawww." Daniel continued, his eyelids fluttering.

"What are you saying honey?" his mother asked, trying to pull him closer to her.

Daniel moaned again, "Mmmmaaaawww, MMaawy."

Daniel's mother looked at the girl. "He said your name."

Mary looked at her and then at Daniel.

"Come here." Daniel's mother pulled Mary to Daniel. "Say something to him."

Mary looked at everyone in the room, and their expressions insisted the same. So she turned to Daniel and whispered, "Hi."

"Louder, so he can hear you. And touch him. Let him know you're here." Her words were insistent to Mary. When Mary hesitated, Daniel's mother grabbed her by the wrist and placed her hand on Daniel's shoulder.

"How are you, Daniel?" Mary said, more loudly than before.

Daniel's eyes continued fluttering, while his legs slowly moved beneath his sheet.

"MMMMyyyythrrrrr."

Mary looked up. "I think he said mother."

"Don't stop." Daniel's mother insisted.

"Daniel, I don't know what you're saying."

"MMaawwy….mmyyy…..thrrrrn."

"Oh, oh, oh…." Mary backed away, bumping into a rolling tray behind her, remembering what Daniel whispered to her before all hell broke loose at the church.

"What did he say, Mary?" Daniel's mother begged.

Mary ached at the memory. "He said I'm his thorn."

"What?"

"The night of the fire. He told me I was his thorn."

"Myyythrrrrnnn…"

An avalanche of revelation and grief fell about her as she backed toward the door, her eyes never leaving Daniel. "No," she moaned over and again until she reached the door and stopped. Mary looked at Daniel's mother, woefully. "This is my fault. He burned his hands saving me. He's here because of me.

I'm....I'm sorry. I...I never should have..." Then she darted from the room.

Holding her hand to the wall of the hospital's maze work of hallways, Mary steadied herself looking for the elevator. Blame had always been something passed on, a burden for others to carry. Her load had been anger and condescension, tolerating others to exasperation. Now all exasperation pointed to her. At the elevator, Mary reached for the call button as she heard someone say her name.

She pressed hard against the button as if the more pressure put to it, the sooner the elevator would come.

"Wait, Mary!" Reverend Green rushed to her.

The elevator doors parted. Mary looked inside the empty compartment but let her finger fall from the button to her side. As the doors shut, Mary snapped, "I'm waiting." Again, her first instinct was to fight. But turning around, the Reverend's reassuring glance blunted her.

"Mary, you'll crush yourself carrying the blame for Daniel's accident."

"You're not going to say that God's will be done, that this was God's will for Daniel, are you?"

"Heaven's no. That would be heartless, shallow thinking. To the depths of my soul, I know God had a plan for Daniel and this wasn't it. "

"Why did God let this happen? This is why I can't stand him."

"I have to accept bad things happen even if it rips my heart out."

"That's an acceptable answer? Bad things happen? The Deacon's a preacher and he doesn't love God like Daniel does. But, Daniel is the one suffering."

"I've never known anyone who wanted to please God as badly or who felt as miserable when he failed as Daniel. It isn't right, is it?" As the pastor looked at Mary, his eyes glistened with his sadness.

"No, it isn't."

"Come back to Daniel's room."

"I can't..."

"Why not?"

"I just can't. It wouldn't be right."

"It wouldn't be right if you didn't. They need you to. Tonight was the first time Daniel responded to things going on around him. He knew you were there. Believe it or not, Mary, you brought them some hope."

"Not after what I've done. I put him in here."

"I can't make you come back. But if what you said is true about his hands… he went back for you, and it cost him a lot more than you have to lose." The reverend backed away from Mary to return to Daniel's room.

Mary's eyes followed the pastor, her heart pushing her where her head did not want to go.

* * *

Ian's hospital stay had become a collage of pinpricks and probes upon a background of misery. Constantly fighting the restraints holding his arms to the bed's sides, he had only managed to weaken himself—but doctors kept pumping things into him to keep him sleepy, peaceful, and alive just as resolutely as he fought his pitiful state.

The punch line of an old joke kept coming to mind as he lay static and hazy: a man and a woman who had longed for children were finally blessed after years of trying; sadly, when the bundle of joy was born, it was only a head. On his twenty-first birthday, his father welcomed his son into manhood by tucking his son under his arm and taking him to a tavern, to toast him. When they arrived, the old man ordered a round for everyone. After the father toasted his son's future, a pretty young barmaid kindly poured the drink into the young man's mouth. Suddenly, his face turned a bright red, his flesh percolating as smoke shot from his ears. A huge explosion rocked the tavern, filling the air with dust and smoke. After the air cleared, standing upon the bar was the young man, like Adonis, his body whole, tanned and tone, naked as a newborn. As everyone stood in amazement, the doors flew open and dozens of SWAT officers in full regalia lined the walls aiming their rifles at the naked young man. Slowly, an officer walked to him and said, "Boy, yer' under arrest for indecent exposure." The boy, sighed, and said…

I should've stopped when I was a head, sifted through Ian's brain, a mocking mantra to his semi-decapitated state.

Should've stopped when I was a head. He couldn't even laugh, worse, he couldn't remember the sound of his laugh…or his own voice; after eighteen years with them, they had vaporized along with his jaw line from William's spiteful blast.

Thoughts of his own funeral wrestled him from sleep, amidst the echo of his own eulogy, when the door slowly opened. He shut his eyes, feigning sleep. A light tap of footsteps slowly approached his bed. Since he no longer had a mouth, he waited for the nurse to place the thermometer into his ear or take hold of his wrist for a pulse or wrap his arm for blood pressure; he waited for her to check the multitude of tubes running in or out of his body, but his waiting went unanswered as the visitor's hushed breathing counted out the seconds of the person's uncertain intentions.

"Holy shit," a familiar voice whispered.

Ian opened his eyes but an indiscernible crack, and beyond the mesh of lashes, through the room's dark shadows, he saw the puffy green coat. "Earnest," he imagined himself saying, a jaw moving, a tongue curling around each consonant and every vowel.

Earnest didn't breathe, seeing Ian in the bed. His hair dirty and matted while the pale translucent flesh of his unwrapped face clung so tightly to his skull it appeared there was no skin at all. Below his eyes, gauze completed Ian's face, allowing an opening for Ian's upper lip, protruding like a canopy for the wad of bandages and tubes below it.

"Shit," Earnest repeated, gagged by his senses. The flames of his hatred fanned and fueled by his surprise and revulsion.

Then the demon's eyes opened, the only part of his face untouched, and Ian peered over the gauze's edge, staring resolutely, unwavering, unblinking, into Earnest. But while Earnest stared back, he could see even the eye's scars and felt his own eyes moisten as he shook, freezing in his anger and hate.

Although surprised, Ian felt indifferent to Earnest's appearance; his mind unable to conjure any other reaction. He turned on the light behind him with the remote attached to his bed. And with the room illuminated he held his eyes locked upon the eyes of his old friend.

Earnest slowly shook his head, a tear running down his check. "Look what you've done to yourself..." Breaking the stare, Earnest looked away. “You are so incredibly messed up...”

Earnest picked up a paper tablet and pen from the bedside table and tossed them on Ian’s lap. "Why?" he asked, unbuckling the strap around Ian's right hand. "Why, dammit? What the hell did you hope to prove?” He hissed between locked teeth.

Before picking up the pen, Ian stretched his fingers and waved his hand, relishing freedom. "Why?” He heard Earnest ask, but instead he scribbled "HOW YA DOIN OL BUDDY" in big sloppy block letters

Earnest read the remark and looked back. One of Ian's eyebrows arched higher than the other as he smirked behind his bandages.

"Cut the bullshit. Why did you do this?"

Ian thought for several seconds, and then jotted, Y NOT?

Earnest stepped away, huffing with anger. He looked out of the window between the slats of the blinds and watched the traffic below. "This didn’t have anything to do with Jamie, did it?” Earnest turned back around, “RaLF embarrassed you that much?"

Ian stared coldly at Earnest as he wrote again. When he finished, he showed the cold words to Earnest, keeping his stare hard upon Earnest while his old friend froze reading them.

ASK YOURSELF Y U HELPED BEAT JAMIE. U R JUST LIKE ME.

Earnest shook his head. “Don’t go there. We are not alike.” But as the words were coming from his mouth, Earnest feared that Ian was right. He was like him. So Earnest shook his head harder, as if he could shake the demon away. “No, no, no! Ian I will not be like you. No!” And he stared into Ian’s cold eyes refusing to avert his gaze.

Ian looked away and scribbled more.

JUDGE NOT LEST YOU B JUDGED!

"You talk about the snobs being beautiful people, and how thoughtless they are. Well, what the hell are you? You're worse than Bill or RaLF or any of them ever were. Who the hell do you think you are?"

I AM HATE

The words echoed in Ian's mind. Unexpectedly a familiar growl sounded. Not since Armageddon had he heard from her.

Earnest didn't understand Ian's comment. He reread it again, but it made no more sense to him the third time than the first time. "That's it?"

Ian turned the light off, only the partial moon and the streetlights illuminating the room, and pushed the tablet and the pen from his lap onto the floor.

Earnest felt lost. He could say nothing, do nothing, that would be worse than what had already happened to Ian, so he backed away, thinking about Anne—and the time wasted entertaining Ian's demons.

The bitch's howls grew louder in Ian's mind until he ached from the volume. He held his stare upon Earnest as the boy backed away; then he remembered one more thing.

Earnest stood at the door, awkwardly uncertain of his next move, so saying nothing he studied the room and the equipment keeping Ian alive. *I am hate.* He turned to step into the hallway, but was called by a strange clucking noise. He turned to see that Ian was somehow making the guttural sound, waving him back. So, Earnest walked back to the bed, picking the tablet and pencil up from the floor.

Ian wrote quickly, strangely feeling an impossible smile come across his face, and handed the tablet back to Earnest.

TELL RALF I SAID HELLO

Earnest tossed the tablet back onto Ian. "After all this...you're still an ass." He left not looking back a second time.

*   *   *

Ian rubbed his forehead, throbbing with the bitch's howl. *Why are you back now?* Opening his eyes, he realized his hand was free. So fumbling with the other restraint, he released his other hand and stretched his arms. With one long graceful sweep, he yanked the IV from his arm, clucking in his throat, and then pulled out the other tubes intruding upon his body. Every tug burned like hell, pulling him deeper into another level of agony.

The bandages and his gown grew damp with blood, yet he lowered the side rail and moved his feet off the side of the bed. His legs wobbled as he tried to stand, so he used the IV stand to support himself as he walked to the bathroom. Since the door had no lock, he jammed it shut, placing the IV stand between the clothes hook and the narrow room's wall. He shook badly, so he sat on the toilet to catch his breath, wheezing through his nostrils.

Exhausted, the headache continued pounding and his body throbbed and burned where he'd pulled out the tubes. Sliding off of the toilet, he curled up on the shower floor, the tile cold against his bare ass. The bitch's howl now silent, she again left him alone to deal with what she had started. Shivering, he pulled the shower curtain from its rings and wrapped it around himself. Gently he leaned back, wishing his gown covered better, and he looked up at the ceiling, making a slight growl of his own in the back of his throat. Then closing his tired eyes, he ran his fingers over the damp bandages, exploring the strange shape of his face, the crook of his nose, his lonesome jetting upper bridge of teeth, and the steep slope down to his neck. His chest heaved as a moan burst from his throat. *Damn you!* He cursed himself with his indiscernible wail, banging his head hard against the tiled shower wall. He screamed his guttural Neanderthal scream—howling from the depths of his being, pounding his head harder and harder against the shower wall, the room echoing with the apocalypse of his soul.

* * *

Earnest stepped into the night's cold, pulling his handkerchief from his back pocket and wiping his nose. To his right, someone sobbing huddled on a bench, so he looked away. For a second, he wondered if her story had as crappy of a resolution as his; the loose ends still scattered and detached.

The whimpering girl could not be avoided because of the landscaping and shrubbery, so Earnest attempted to ignore her, but as he drew closer, he recognized Mary. The notion came if he walked quickly, he could appear to overlook her, if she saw him. But after his third step beyond her, he stalled. *U R JUST LIKE ME*. So fighting his Earnest tendencies, he turned around.

"Mary," he whispered, trying not to startle her but dull her inevitable wrath.

She looked up, red faced from crying and the cold, and was startled all the same.

"What are you doing here?" she snapped, aggravated at seeing Earnest of all people.

"I was leaving and saw you here. I was visiting…" He rethought his answer, not wanting to associate himself with the local madman any more than he already was. "I know someone here."

"I know. Daniel's here."

Earnest had forgotten about Daniel in the midst things. "Did you visit him?"

"Anne asked me to write a story about him." She wiped her eyes with the sleeves of her coat.

"I heard you crying and wondered if you were okay."

"Yes!" she barked back. "I'm fine. That's why I'm sitting out here in the cold crying. I'm cleansing my spirit."

"I've had better days…" he answered, trying not to take offense at her but failing. "Why do you make it so damn hard to be nice to you?" He pulled a pair of gloves out of his coat pockets. "I don't know what's colder, the weather or you…" So, in spite, he sat down next to her.

Just as she was about to snap at him again, she sighed, too blue to fight, and muttered, "Sorry, I just feel like shit…"

"It can't be easy being pregnant."

Mary shook her head. "I'm not pregnant, anymore."

"Oh, sorry…" he said, and cut any other comment, uncertain how to follow Mary. So he leaned forward, elbows on his knees.

"Yeah," she sighed and turned to Earnest. "Daniel drove me crazy, but it kills me to see him like this. You know how hard it was to understand him whenever he spoke. Now everything's a jumble."

Earnest nodded, "Sometimes, I needed an interpreter."

Mary chuckled. "But, somehow I always understood his hallelujah talk. He drove me crazy."

"Did he really almost drown in a baptism pool at church? That's the weirdest thing I've ever heard." Earnest blew his nose again, and then asked, "What's wrong with him."

"Everything," She answered, heavy in despair, "His mind's gone. He's not Daniel anymore. He's not anyone anymore…" She grew quiet and wiped her eyes again, sniffing.

"Oh shit," he whispered, feeling his own sense of shame at how he treated Daniel at times.

"Do you believe in prayer?"

"What do you mean?"

"Just that. There is no reason for Daniel to have gotten where he was. I mean if it was work alone that brought him to being normal, wouldn't every kid with Down's syndrome be worked to death until they were normal? Is it really possible he was prayed to normal?"

"That's a question for your dad."

"When I see the Deacon, I don't see God. Actually, I don't know what I see. It's different every day. But it's definitely not God. With Daniel, on the other hand, I see something good." Her eyes began to tear. "Even when I ridiculed him, I still thought he was a good person. I feel sorry for him."

Earnest wiped his nose again, "I know what you mean, but I didn't come to see Daniel, tonight. It was Ian Warner..."

Mary nodded, "There's a real crazy man."

"I have never in my life seen someone as messed up as Ian. But I don't feel sorry for him. I thought if I talked to him, he could explain his damn Armageddon to me; make it make sense to me. But, he can't talk with half of his face blown away. He just writes crazy stuff on a tablet. Hell, the more he said, the more I think he had it coming."

"You know what it says about you if crazy people start making sense…."

"It's just people have been calling me a hero all week, but I don't feel like one."

"What do you feel like?"

Earnest quietly laughed and said, "I feel like you… like crap. Thanks for asking."

Earnest leaned back in the bench, and the pair sat quietly for several minutes. "So, did the cleansing cry thing help?" Earnest asked, still looking straight ahead.

"Not a bit."

After a few minutes passed he slapped his hands together and stood up from the bench and said, "Well, I don't feel like crying, anyway. I need to find a laugh, and I know just the trick." He took a hold of her arm and brought her to her feet. "And you're coming with me." Then he pulled her along, walking towards his car.

"What are you doing?" She snapped.

"Mary, trust me. I'm a hero, remember? Actually, I'm feeling a little better already."

Earnest unlocked the passenger car door and held it open for Mary. She reluctantly climbed in, a scowl on her face. Earnest ran around to the other side of the car. After he sat down, he quickly started it and began backing out of the parking space.

"Well?" Mary asked again. Seeing Earnest's sudden lightness began lifting her spirits and a slight smile moved to her face.

Earnest pulled his car into traffic and headed south. "It's something my brother showed me… Now, Mary, I don't suppose you've ever seen the Pioneer Man…"

Ponca City News.
Monday, May 26, 1980

The Class of 1980 Graduates: Ceremony Undampened by Storm

By Louis Applebaum

The threat of thunderstorms and tornado warnings did not stop the graduation ceremonies for the class of 1980 although, they had to be moved inside of the recently reopened Hutchins Memorial Auditorium because of forecasted rain. Even though the limited seating allowed each of the 418 graduates only four guests, the pomp and circumstance of the event was as grand as ever.

Principal Leo Small opened the ceremony and received a standing ovation having recovered from the Armageddon attack in February. The invocation was given by Deacon Joseph Christmas, whose daughter, Mary, was one of the graduates. Valedictorian Anne Endo, who will attend the University of Missouri to study journalism, addressed her classmates, encouraging each of them to learn from the tragedy that had occurred in the same building as the graduation ceremony and be more accepting of others. Local business man and state senator, Albert Honneycut, served as the keynote speaker for the ceremony.

The emotional high point of the evening came as the diplomas were to be distributed. Daniel Davies received the first diploma of the evening. Davies sustained brain injuries in an accident in February, resulting in him being unable to complete the year. However, he had completed enough credits to graduate. The students cheered him as he crossed the stage unaided. He lightened the heaviness of the moment when he approached the microphone and began singing,

The Camptown Ladies. Each of the boys who were injured in the February Armageddon incident also received rousing applause as they crossed the stage. The rain held off until the end of the ceremony when a loud clap of thunder sounded and a heavy downpour followed. The good feelings of the evening held as most of the graduates and their families waited for the storm to pass.

The Hutchins Memorial had been closed in order to make repairs for damages that had occurred when Ian Warner brutally assaulted several classmates during the Pioneer Woman Cotillion on February 22. Warner himself was seriously injured when his accomplice, William Dawes, shot him. Warner was later found dead in his hospital room after barricading himself in the restroom.

Acknowledgements

This book owes a debt of gratitude to several people who over time have read and offered comments. Thank you to each and every one of you. I am also grateful to my family for giving me the time to write and rewrite this tome a multitude of times.

Ponca City is a real town; however the Ponca City in this book has only existed in my mind. Several liberties were taken with the geography and landmarks.

Many thanks to the One from whom all blessing flow.

Dad, you were definitely one of the good guys.

Shelby Guinn is a teacher in Las Vegas, Nevada. He can be reached at shelbytheshelf.guinn@gmail.com. Entropy is his first novel.

Made in the USA
Charleston, SC
17 August 2012